The First Child

ISBN: 978-0-9975516-9-3 (Paperback)

Any references to historical events, real people, or real places are used fictitiously. Names, characters, and places are products of the author's imagination.

Book design by Jessica Bussert.

Printed by Kindle Direct Publishing, in the United States of America.

First printing edition 2019.

First Child Publishing
PO Box 1842
Nashville, IN 47448

The First Child

Sharon Bussert

This is dedicated to the one I love...

1991

Maria closed the car door and turned toward the bench. Her reflection, caught in the car window, startled her and for a moment she stared as if seeing a stranger who seemed vaguely familiar. She reached up and ran her hand through her hair. It felt strange having it so short and she knew the color was ridiculous. She stared at her reflection, frowning. She had cut her hair and bleached it just yesterday so no one would recognize her. Now she slipped on a pair of dark glasses and crossed the sidewalk to the bench. In her hand she held a copy of The Burlington Free Press which she nervously rolled then unfurled to roll it again. She had meant to read it, or at least pretend to, but nerves made reading impossible. She glanced at her watch. Any minute now.

Shivering in the cold she laid her unread paper beside her and sat back to study the school. It was a small building, long and low and made of bricks, with a row of windows that ran the full length. Even with everything covered in snow she could tell that the grounds would be well cared for. The sidewalks were neatly cleaned, the snow covered bushes trimmed. A nice school, she thought. Children of the elite. Probably rich. But what's that mean? Rich doesn't mean he's been happy. It doesn't mean he's adjusted. She heard the bell ring and looked up expectantly. Children began to come out of the school, slowly at first, then in a flood. They called out to friends, ran to parents. She watched until the flow had slowed to a trickle, then turned to the man who sat beside her, wanting an explanation. Before she could ask he spoke, "There he is, in the middle, denim jacket, green backpack."

She spotted the boy, walking between two friends. From this distance she could see only that he was shorter than his companions, sandy-haired and handsome. As he came closer she studied his face, looking for her eyes, her mouth, any features that would show he was hers, but he was still far away and at this distance she couldn't tell. She startled slightly as he broke away from his friends and began to run directly toward her. He's recognized me, she thought. Even after all these years and with this awful hair. He's running right to me!

She was just ready to get up, hug him and welcome him back into her life when the man beside her gently laid his hand on her arm, reminding her that she must act rationally. Of course he isn't running to me. Ridiculous to think he could know who I am. He was a baby. Still, she wanted to call his name, tell him who she was. She gripped the hand of her companion and bit her lip, reminding herself that she mustn't.

The boy crossed the street, passing not ten feet from where she sat. She squeezed her companion's hand to keep herself from reaching out to him, pressed her lips together to avoid calling his name aloud. He ran to a tall, blond woman and smiled up at her. As Maria watched the woman smoothed his hair, then kissed his cheek. She wanted to scream out. *You have no right. He's mine. I am the one who should fix his hair, kiss his cheeks, pick him up at school.* As she watched, the boy slipped his hand into the woman's and they walked away.

Maria slumped forward on the bench, covering her face with her hands. Her shoulders shook with her sobs and the man beside her leaned forward. Laying his hand on her shoulder he said softly, "We should go. You don't want to attract attention here until you've made a decision."

Blindly she stood up and allowed him to take her arm and lead her to the car. As he opened the door she looked back, but the boy and the woman had gone, and the sidewalk was empty.

PART ONE
1987

CHAPTER

ONE

Chavo's eyes darted about, searching for the right person. The crowd rushed along, jostling him, but he wasn't afraid. He spent most of his time on the busy sidewalks and in the subway stations and he was well accustomed to life on the streets of Madrid. Moving swiftly he ducked beneath the arms and handbags of taller people, blending well with the crowd, attracting no attention. He was eight years old but small for his age, and anyone noticing him would have guessed he was younger. Today he wore a pair of torn jeans and a stained white T-shirt. His shoes were black leather. They had been nice at one time but now the left one had a hole on the bottom and the entire sole threatened to come loose. He had left his jacket behind because the day was warm. Spring had arrived and a smile played on Chavo's lips. Spring and summer would bring the tourists and their money. Tourists meant no more being hungry. He felt no hesitation about what he was going to do. His earliest memories were of going out with his dad, watching while he pick pocketed the tourists, and it never occurred to him that stealing might be wrong.

He thought back to the past summer, remembering long, happy days with his dad. From the start it was clear that he wasn't to tell his Mom. 'She won't like it,' dad had said, 'but there's no work. Somehow we've got to eat.' And dad would be so pleased, Chavo thought. I've gotten so good and I'd be such a help to him. He wished, not for the first time, that he had an address and could write to his dad.

He'd been gone for two months and Chavo was beginning to think he wasn't coming back, even though he was too young to pick up on the talk around his neighborhood. There the old widows, living alone and struggling to survive, would sit and gossip after he ran past. They talked about how his dad, Octavio, had taught Chavo to pick pockets hoping the family would somehow survive after he abandoned them. At eight years old Chavo still believed his mother's story that his dad was in the North, looking for work, but he was beginning to doubt that his dad would send for them. He missed his father and consoled himself with memories of how he had smiled when Chavo had lifted a wallet or a watch. By the end of last summer Chavo had been really good at spotting rich tourists.

Just after Christmas his dad had started taking him out of school, taking him on the subways again. 'I don't want you to lose your touch,' he'd said. 'Just be careful. Remember that. Your Mom needs your help. You got to eat, she's got to eat, and now the baby. You have to be careful. I'm counting on you to help out.' He never referred to little Anita as anything but 'the baby,' as if she had no name. Chavo was too young to notice that too but the old widows noticed and sadly shook their heads. Sitting together in the afternoons they would say. 'He won't be here long. He doesn't want to think of her as his child.' They'd been proven right. One day when Chavo woke up Octavio was gone and his Mom said he'd gone north to look for work. The children believed it but the widows had seen it all before; the fear in the face of a young wife, the restlessness of a man tied down by a family. They shook their heads thinking it was even worse this time, with the baby so little, and the Mama sick. But no one was in any position to help out, so they looked the other way when Chavo came home with a pocket full of money and a tale about the work he'd found for the day.

Now Chavo quickened his steps. Up ahead was the woman he'd been looking for. Everything about her screamed rich American. That's what his dad taught him to look out for. She was taller than a Spanish woman, fairer skinned, and most noticeably, she carried her purse swung over one shoulder, oblivious to the jostling crowd as she gaped at the sites. She approached the Metro stop and started down the stairs. Falling into step beside her he waited until the crowd was packed tightly, pushing forward to the ticket window. Quickly he slid open the zipper and reached inside. The pesetas were right on top, not even in a wallet. He stuffed them into his pocket, ducked under the turnstile and hopped on the train that was ready to pull out. Retreating to a corner, he pulled the bills from his pocket and counted. His heart leapt as he saw a 5000-peseta bill mixed among the smaller ones, and he smiled. Supper, milk for Anita, and candy. He didn't worry about the American girl. She was rich, and would eat well even without her 5000 pesetas.

Chavo ran through the narrow streets of Atocha, proudly carrying his bag of groceries. He had gotten their favorites--eggs, chorizo, potatoes and bread, plus some oranges for Mama and Anita, milk, and a chocolate bar for himself which he had already eaten. His mouth watered in anticipation of the tortilla his mother would make for dinner. Rounding a corner he stopped suddenly, realizing he'd forgotten to buy an onion. Briefly he considered returning to the store but the weight of the groceries and the ache in his legs made him decide against it. Shrugging his shoulders he continued on his way. He could stop and ask Señora Oreja for an onion.

Turning onto an even narrower street he looked up at his building and smiled. His mother sat at the third floor window watching for him. "Mama," Chavo yelled as he approached the building, "Look, look what I've got." She smiled at him but did not move from her seat. He opened the door and began his climb up the stairs. The stairway was dark, lit from above by a single, dim bulb that did not penetrate all the way to street level. Paper littered the area. Chavo knew his building wasn't as nice as many in Madrid. Here they had no portero to keep the stairs clean or to change the bulb when it burned out. He remembered once he had gone with his mother to visit someone. They had gone to a fancy building with an elevator and a portero. When they left he had asked his Mama if she would like to live in a place like that. She had just shaken her head at his foolish talk and told him to hurry so they didn't miss the bus.

Reaching the second floor he paused briefly outside the Oreja's door. He hesitated, shifting from one foot to the other as he tried to decide the best course of action. Mama did not like him asking the neighbors for things. She was always saying he wasn't to be begging like a tinker. But it's not really begging, he told himself. I've got money. I can buy a new onion tomorrow. That decided, he shifted the groceries to his other arm and knocked on the door.

He heard noise inside and then the door was opened by 11-year-old Maria. She was a thin, small girl, dressed in a pair of stirrup pants and an oversized blouse. Seeing Chavo she wrinkled her nose in disgust.

"Quién es? Who is it?" Her mother called from the back of the apartment.

"It's only Chavo. Probably come to ask you for something to eat." She looked at Chavo disdainfully.

Chavo bristled and held out his bag of groceries. "We have something to eat."

"Then what do you want?" Maria demanded.

"I need to talk to your Mama," he retorted and then added, "Please".

Maria led him through the apartment. It was neat and clean with freshly painted walls. He could smell the Oreja's supper cooking. Three-year-old Luis played happily on the scrubbed tile floor. Through the balcony door he could see 8-year-old Julia taking down the laundry that had been drying. Señora Oreja smiled at him as he entered the kitchen. Unlike her daughter she was always polite to Chavo. "Hola niñito," She greeted him as he came into the room. "What can I do for you?" She was a pretty woman, about the same age as his own Mama, but she looked much younger. Her dark hair was swept onto the top of her head in a stylish bun and she wore a bright dress and pretty white sandals with a narrow heel.

Chavo hesitated, wishing Maria would leave the room, but when she didn't he began, "I was bringing Mama some eggs and potatoes so she could make a tortilla, but I forgot the onion." It was a statement of fact, and not a request, but the meaning was clear.

"See," Maria yelled in glee. "I knew he would ask you for something to eat. He always does. No wonder they call you Chavo!"

"Maria," her mother spoke sharply. "Go and help your sister with the clothes." Maria glared at Chavo, but obediently left the room.

"Now," said Señora Oreja, "You need an onion."

"Please," Chavo replied. "I've got some money. I'd be glad to get you one tomorrow and bring it back. It's just that I forgot about the onion until I was almost here, and I ..."

"Never mind all that," she said. Turning to the cabinet she picked up a large onion. "Take it and don't worry about replacing it. Do you have any milk for the baby?" Chavo nodded. "Good boy. Go on up to your Mama then. She'll be wondering where you are."

"Gracias." Chavo smiled and ran back into the hallway. He hurried up the remaining flight of stairs and banged open the door.

"Quiet, you'll wake the baby," his mother admonished him." Where'd you get the food? Tell me you didn't steal it."

"No, Mama. I had money. I was working today. I bought it from Señora Lopez. You can ask her." He said it only because he knew his mother wouldn't. She never went out any more, not since Anita was born. Señora Lopez would certainly mention the 5000 peseta bill if she had the chance. Already she had cuffed him on the side of the head, and told him to keep his stolen money out of her store. But he had smiled and told her he worked for it, and she had invited him back in. She didn't think for a minute that he had earned the money, but she hoped her 8-year-old, working beside her in the store, would believe it. Chavo knew Señora Lopez couldn't afford to turn away business. She had six kids and her husband was always at the bar playing cards and drinking.

Cristina smiled at Chavo. She didn't believe that her son really worked but she was grateful for the food and usually too tired to worry about where it came from. Anita would wake up any minute and need something to eat. As she took the food into the kitchen Chavo crossed the room and sat on the sofa. It sagged low with his weight. Looking around the room Chavo remembered Maria's comment '*No wonder you got the name Chavo.*' The apartment was shabby and crowded. Chavo slept on the couch while his mom and Anita shared the single bedroom down the hall. The kitchen was old, with years of grease coating the walls. His real name was Octavio, same as his dad. Chavo was a nickname the kids had given him. He hadn't thought much about it at the time but now it hurt. Chavo meant money and everyone called him that as a joke, except his mom. She called him by his given name.

Looking up he watched his Mama making the supper. In sharp contrast to Mrs. Oreja, her hair hung lanky about her shoulders. She wore an old black dress, which was fraying around the hem and the sleeves. Her once bright pink sandals had faded to pale and were covered with dust. But most of all her face was tired and she looked old. She stood at the counter slicing the potatoes. The only decoration in the room was a row of photographs which sat on a shelf above the stove. They were all dead people except his dad and Chavo knew his mom put the pictures there when she was specially praying for someone. His grandma was there, wearing an old black dress, standing in front of a small house in the country. It was the house where his Mama grew up. His grandpa was there too, wearing a suit and looking very serious. There was a picture of a little boy, Mama's brother who had died when he was five. Next to him was a picture of Octavio. He was a handsome man. Thick black hair curled over his head, and dark eyes sparkled, contrasting with his olive colored skin, even in the photograph. His smile revealed even, white teeth.

Chavo wasn't sure whose fault it was that his dad had gone. He weighed the disappearance in his mind. Dad was always happy to see him, so surely he wasn't the cause. Maybe it was Anita, he decided. She seemed too little to cause problems, but ever since she was born Mama had been sick and then Dad went away, so it must be her.

"Octavio," his mother called from the kitchen, "Go get Anita and come for supper. Wash your hands." Chavo hopped up and ran down the hall, his melancholy disappearing in anticipation of the tortilla cooking on the stove.

CHAPTER

TWO

D aniel left his office and strolled across the campus, head up, letting the wind blow full in his face. All his life he had loved the winter, the cold and the snow. Today the breeze was brisk and the ground covered lightly with snow. Students hurried past, heads bowed against the wind, books tucked under their arms, or huge backpacks slung over one shoulder.

"Hey Professor Bayley. Cold enough for you?" Looking over his shoulder Daniel saw one of his students jogging down the pathway, backpack thumping on his shoulder. He started to reply, then waved as the boy hurried past, anxious to get out of the cold.

He smiled, remembering how he had ended up at Columbia. He had come to graduate school planning to leave New York City as soon as he finished, but he had liked it so much he just stayed. It had been a good decision. He had met Katherine the very next year when she was enrolled in his U.S. History class. He had noticed her as soon as she entered the room but ignored the attraction because he couldn't date a student. She had really started the relationship. Three weeks before graduation she had come to the office on the pretense of clarifying an assignment. Katherine, who'd never needed clarification on anything. Then the truth. She'd sat on the edge of the desk and said 'You know, I graduate in three weeks. Former students aren't off limits for dating'. Then she left. The next day she walked into class like nothing happened and three weeks later as she handed in the final she said 'Meet me at BJ's tonight.' It wouldn't have even occurred to her that I might not show up, he thought.

Nearing the bus stop he saw his bus waiting and broke into a run. The driver waved, indicating he wouldn't leave, so he slowed to a quick walk. Boarding the bus he showed his pass. "Thanks for waiting."

"Too cold to leave you out there 'til the next one."

The bus was nearly empty. It was too early for rush hour. Every semester since Andy was born Daniel had arranged his schedule to be finished early in the day. He would get the bus across the river, pick up his car and his son, and then meet Katherine back at the transfer station at a later time. Sometimes she just caught a cab to the apartment if she was too late. He was glad that today she would be off early enough to meet him.

Katherine sat at her desk working frantically. Every few minutes she glanced up at the clock and the passing minutes fueled her stress. Mentally she ran through the rest of her day. Meeting to go to, finish this design, supposed to meet Daniel early today. I'll never make it and he'll be furious. Lately he's forever on me about working late, complaining about how I'm harming Andy. He doesn't understand what it's like. All I want is a chance to make it in this business. Teaching isn't like advertising. I slow down for one minute and I'm not the agency's hottest up and coming star and my chances for a promotion are down the tubes.

She picked up the phone and punched in Daniel's cell phone number. "Daniel," she said, not giving him a chance to say hello, "listen, things are really crazy here today. I'm going to have to stay late."

Daniel frowned. "Katherine," he said, "tonight was going to be family night. Come on, Andy's got to see you occasionally to remember you exist."

She put her head in her hands, eyes rolling upward, and stifled a sigh. "There's nothing I can do. Give me an hour. Take him to supper or something then meet me at the transfer. He'll be awake."

"He needs more than to just be awake. He needs time with you. When ever I show up alone he wants to know where you are."

Katherine pursed her lips tightly, holding back her comments for a moment. Eventually she replied, "Oh, he does not. He's practically a baby still. He doesn't have any concept of time. He can't possibly notice if you get there an hour before me. Take him somewhere fun and he'll never notice. I gotta run. The big wig called me to a meeting." She hung up without giving him a chance to respond. As she walked through the building she wondered if she was right.   Andy is getting bigger, she admitted, and he might notice that I'm not around.   Sometimes she hated being a mom and competing with all the single women and the men.   It was too much responsibility.

Reaching the meeting room she tapped on the door, then entered.   Bill was already seated at the table.   Looking up he nodded toward a chair.   "We're just waiting on Keith."   Nodding in return she took a seat and opened her portfolio.   She glanced at the work she had done, confident that everything was in order.   She figured the meeting was a formality to insure that Bill had everything ready.   She looked up at him, thinking how lucky he was.   Tomorrow he would be on a plane to Paris to direct the photo shoot.   Too bad I passed that one up, she thought.   That was for you, Daniel.   Bill doesn't work half as hard as I do, so of course he was happy to step into my ad campaign.   He'll never do anything this good by himself.   She sat back, regretting that she had ever suggested Bill take the overseas work.

She looked up as the door opened.   Keith came in and sat down.   Katherine studied him briefly.   He was middle-aged and graying, but still good-looking.   Sharp dresser.   Always expensive suits.   She looked at him expectantly, anxious to get the meeting started.   He was all business, never wasting any time on small talk.   He was looking at Bill, and surprised her when he asked, "Well Bill, what are we here for?"

Bill cleared his throat and began.   "As you both know, I'm scheduled to leave for Paris tomorrow night."   He spoke stiffly, as if reciting a prepared speech.   "You may not know that my wife is pregnant with our third child.   Yesterday she saw the doctor due to a complication and he's confined her to bed rest for at least a couple of weeks."   He paused, looking at the two of them and taking a deep breath.   "Unfortunately, there's no way I can go to Paris."   He stopped and looked at Keith, waiting.

Keith was frowning, shaking his head.   "Bill, you know we're counting on you for this.   You've been our contact.   They're expecting you.   Isn't there anyone else who can stay with your wife for a couple of days?   This isn't a long assignment."

Bill shook his head.   "I'm really sorry to let you down but I have to be available.   Her mother's staying during the day but she can't stay round the clock, and the other kids are worried.   They need me."

Katherine sat, watching the two of them carefully.   She recognized in Bill the same devotion to family that Daniel displayed and knew there was no way he was going.   Nothing would make him change his mind. She smiled, then bit her lip to hide it in case the others looked at her. This could be her chance to seal the promotion.

Keith leaned forward in his chair, speaking earnestly. "We need you! Don't you know what this account is worth to our firm?"

Bill nodded his head, looking slightly defeated. "I know, I know, but I can't go. Not with Janie sick. If anything happens to the baby I've got to be here."

Keith sat back and studied Bill. Slowly he shook his head. "Listen, I'm saying this as a friend, not a supervisor. OK?" Bill nodded. "If you don't go there is no way in hell you'll be considered for that promotion. No way in hell. And as your supervisor I'm saying you better pray O'Neal is willing to go because if we have to postpone we may well lose the account."

Katherine had sat silently throughout the exchange. Leaning forward she now said, "I'll go."

Keith looked at her in surprise. "I thought you made it clear early in the game you weren't interested."

Feigning surprise Katherine shook her head. "Not at all. I'm very interested. I just wanted to give Bill a fair chance. I get my share of the out of town work."

"Can you keep on schedule? You've got a kid to think about too, don't you?"

Katherine smiled. "That's not a problem," she said, shaking her head slightly. "My husband is used to caring for him and his schedule is very flexible."

Keith smacked his hands onto the tabletop. "That's settled then. You designed the thing. You're better prepared than O'Neal to take over. Get your schedule cleared and you're on it." He glanced at his watch. "Now let's get out of here. It's quitting time."

Katherine returned to her office feeling elated. Paris. She hadn't been to Paris in years! Not since before Andy was born. She opened her calendar and began dictating a message to her secretary. "Katy, Unexpected change of plans, I'm going to Paris to direct the shoot. I need to get some things rescheduled. Let's see, tomorrow I had a lunch with Mr. Boniger. See if you can set that for next week instead. On Wednesday Ms. Schmidt of the Schmidt Agency is coming in at 9:00. See if Keith can meet her instead, and if not get her rescheduled. Then I've got," she paused. "Oh shit! Oops, sorry." She reached over and turned off the machine, still staring at her calendar. Andy's birthday. Damn, she thought. I can't reschedule a birthday. He'll be four on Friday, and I won't be back until Saturday. Daniel is going to hit the roof! I'll never hear the end of it .

She sat for a minute, frowning at this unexpected problem, pondering her options, but there didn't seem to be any. I'll tell him it can't be helped, she decided. We'll move the party to Saturday. Turning the machine back on she continued dictating her schedule changes. Then, glancing at her watch she grabbed her briefcase and hurried out. The meeting had hardly taken any time and she could meet Daniel earlier than planned. She waved for a cab, not wanting to wait on the bus.

As soon as she reached the transfer station she headed for the payphones and punched in Daniel's cell phone number. "Hey Honey, it's me. I got done earlier than I expected, so we can do the family thing after all. I'm at the station now."

Daniel didn't answer at first, then said, "Can you get a cab? We can't come right now."

"Why not?" She was instantly irritated, but tried to sound cheerful.

"I just got to the park with Andy. We haven't been here 5 minutes."

"So? Just put him back in the car and come get me."

Daniel shook his head, disbelieving. "That's not fair to him. We just got here. He won't understand why we're leaving right away. I told him we'd stay an hour."

Unable to keep the irritation from her voice Katherine snapped, "So? He doesn't know what an hour is. Tell him you're coming to get me. That'll make him happy."

"No it won't. Just get a cab." Daniel's voice was tense. He hated arguing with Katherine in front of Andy.

Katherine recognized she was getting nowhere. She turned whiny, pleading a little. "But I want to do the family thingy. I want to be with you all."

"Then get a cab to the park," he replied shortly.

"Let me talk to Andy!" Her voice was once again impatient. She could hear Daniel calling to Andy, then prompting him to talk.

"Hi Mommy!" As usual Andy sounded cheerful.

Katherine smiled, willing the irritation out of her voice. "Hi sweetie! Guess what? Mommy's at the station waiting for you all to pick her up!"

Andy nodded his head, not answering.

"Do you want to come pick Mommy up?" she asked.

"No!" he shouted into the phone.

"You don't want to pick Mommy up?" She sounded puzzled.

"I want to play!"

"But what about Mommy? I want to play too. Can't you and Daddy come pick me up?"

"We are. We're staying at the park one hour, no longer, then we need to pick up Mommy." He sounded like a miniature Daniel, obviously repeating what Daniel had told him earlier.

"Let me talk to Daddy," she said, no longer caring about speaking sweetly. She waited while the phone was passed back. "Well, I guess the park wins," she said. "I'll see if I can get a cab." She hung up without saying goodbye.

In the cab she decided she wouldn't tell Daniel about the trip or the birthday until morning. Then she would mention it casually and avoid a long discussion. Daniel would have to get to class no matter what he thought about her going. She stepped out into the cold wishing they could do family things indoors, but Daniel and Andy both loved the cold. She stood on the curb, looking for the two of them. They were on the far side of the park, Andy in the swings, Daniel pushing him. Wrapping her coat about her she began trudging across the frozen ground. As she got closer Andy spotted her and began shrieking at the top of his voice. "Mommy!" He kicked his feet wildly and took one hand off the chain to point in her direction. Daniel stopped the swing and lifted Andy down. He hurtled toward her like a rocket. "Mommy!" He ran directly into her, full force, and wrapped his arms around her leg.

She smiled down at him, feeling guilty that she would miss his birthday. Worse than that, had completely forgotten his birthday until she saw it written in her calendar. She stooped down to hug him and talk but he turned and ran back to Daniel and the swings. She followed along, greeting Daniel with a kiss. "It's freezing out here! I don't know how you two can stand it."

"We're a couple of polar bears, aren't we buddy." Daniel lifted Andy back into the swing.

"Polar bears," Andy echoed.

Katherine asked about Daniel's classes and students but avoided talking about her day. She shifted from foot to foot, hating the cold. The wind seemed to go right through her coat, and her skirt and dress shoes offered little protection.

"What do you say we get out of here, take Andy to Antonio's for dinner?" she asked.   The upscale Italian restaurant was near their apartment and one of her favorites.

"No," Andy shouted.

"He doesn't like Antonio's.   Too much sitting still and being quiet." Daniel spoke softly, wary of another argument.

"Of course he likes it. He loves spaghetti."

"Spaghetti," Andy echoed.

"You want spaghetti?" Katherine asked.

"No! McDonalds!"

Katherine made a face. "I'd rather have spaghetti."

Daniel laughed. "Me too but we better save that for a night we have a sitter. He's full of energy today."

She nodded. "What do you say we go though. I'm turning to ice."

Daniel wrapped his arms around her protectively. "My poor señorita. It's all that sun when you were little. Can't take the cold now." Katherine had grown up in Spain, and it was a frequent joke between the two of them that she needed the sun to blossom. Daniel scooped Andy off the swing and tucked him under his arm. "Come on buddy. Let's go play at McDonalds." Wrapping his free arm around Katherine they headed for the car.

Driving home Daniel asked, "Can you get him to bed tonight? I've got a stack of papers to grade before class tomorrow." Katherine wanted nothing more than to sink into a chair and put her feet up but she agreed. By the time she bathed Andy and tucked him into bed Katherine was exhausted. She sank gratefully into a recliner in the living room and picked up a copy of Vogue that lay by the chair. She flipped through it, not reading, but studying the ads, comparing her own work to what was in print. Daniel sat on the couch, papers strewn around him, reading and making notes for his students. When he put the papers down an hour later Katherine was sound asleep in the recliner. Putting the papers back in his briefcase he went over and woke her.

"Come on sleepy. You need to get to bed. Andy pretty well wore you out, didn't he?" Gently he took her hand and helped her to her feet. He frowned and pulled her hand closer, looking at her ring. "Looks like you've got a prong loose. I'd better take that in to the jeweler before you lose the stone." Her wedding ring was a gold band, set with three small diamonds. He slipped it off her finger and placed it in his briefcase. "I'll have them look at it tomorrow."

CHAPTER
THREE

Even before Katherine was fully awake she was aware of a feeling of dread. She rubbed her eyes, trying to focus her thoughts. There was something unpleasant she had to do. The birthday, she remembered. I have to tell Daniel about the birthday and the trip. Glancing at Daniel she saw he was still sleeping. Quietly, trying not to wake him, she crept across the floor and into the bathroom. She would tell him after her shower. She was just finishing when he entered the bathroom.

"Daniel," she spoke loudly, over the sound of the running water. "I need to talk to you about work."

"Yeah, what is it?" She talked to him about work nearly every morning, telling him her schedule, what time to expect her, what might cause a delay. She shut off the shower. "Just let it run. I'm getting right in," he said. She turned it back on and stepped out, wrapping herself in a large towel.

"Something unexpected has come up."

Daniel stepped into the shower and began shampooing his hair without answering.

"You know Bill? The guy who's supposed to be doing the Paris shoot this week?" Daniel didn't answer, so she went on. "Well, his wife is really sick. He's totally refusing to go and he's supposed to leave tonight."

"Yeah, so what? You need to stay late to give someone else the information?"

19

"It's worse than that. I need to go. There's no one else who knows the information and I can't possibly convey it all to someone in one day. We've considered all the other options."

"Today? You need to leave today?" he asked. Then shouting, "No, Katherine." He opened the shower door and stared at her. "You can't do this. You can't just keep running your life like you're single, pack up and go whenever you want."

She dropped the towel to the floor and wrapped herself in her robe. Turning to the mirror she began combing her wet hair. "It's not a want. They're demanding it. I've got to go."

Daniel continued to lean out of the shower, ignoring the water dripping onto the floor. "No, you don't!" he said angrily. "If Bill can say no, so can you. You don't have to do whatever they say. Not when it interferes with your family."

Katherine turned away from the mirror. "Bill is never going to get anywhere in that company. He's lucky to even have a job."

"That is not the point. The point is you have a family and your son needs you. You can't just pack up and disappear at a moment's notice."

She turned back toward the mirror, ignoring the comment. "You're getting water all over the floor. Finish your shower then we'll talk." She turned and left the room.

Daniel finished quickly, furious with Katherine. Obviously she had known yesterday and could have mentioned it earlier so there was time to discuss it. He climbed out of the shower, grabbed a towel and walked, still dripping wet, into the bedroom.

Katherine sat at her dressing table, applying her make-up. She was already dressed for work, wearing a tailored business suit with a frilly blouse. She didn't look up as he entered the room. "Katherine! You know we agreed you wouldn't take any more last minute trips. In fact, we agreed when Andy was born you would stop traveling altogether."

Katherine continued applying her makeup calmly. She would hold her temper no matter what, having already decided that she was going. Daniel will just have to accept it, she thought. It's not like he didn't know what I was like when he married me. I've always been driven to succeed. He knows I want that promotion. He knows what it takes to get it.

"Katherine. Aren't you even going to answer me!"

Slowly she applied her lipstick, blotted it, and then turned toward her husband. Daniel had turned away from her and stood looking out the window at the view of the Manhattan skyline. It was still dark out, and the lights of the city reflected off the Hudson River which flowed past their building. Normally the view gave Katherine pleasure, but now she hardly noticed it, her every thought focused on work and the upcoming trip. She knew that she would go on the trip and yet, for the first time, she felt a bit uncertain. She really did want to be a good mother, and lately Andy had been asking her about her absence from the family. He was starting to notice the late nights and Saturdays, and she had seriously considered cutting back. But the firm had virtually assured her a partnership if she could land this account, and she had worked hard for it. She knew that stepping in at the last minute was a huge help to the firm. They would almost have to show their appreciation with the partnership. Of course I've got to go, she thought, but after I get the partnership I'll cut back some. Andy's too young to remember things that happen now, she reassured herself. Still, she was aware of a nagging irritation. She was too devoted to the firm. She would miss her son's fourth birthday. But he's only going to be four, she reminded herself. Surely he can't know what a birthday is about, and I can always make it up to him. When I'm a partner I'll have more freedom, more time and money. I do all this for Andy anyway. I just want him to have the best schools and the trendiest clothes and toys. Everything is so competitive these days. I don't want him to suffer for lack of money.

She glanced at her watch. They were both going to be late. Slowly she walked toward Daniel. "Listen," she said, "it's not that I want to go away. But there's no other choice. Really. Bill is canceling at the last minute. I told you I'm the only other person who knows this account, and we're talking about a million-dollar account. It could take months to reschedule the models and the shoots. It would cost the firm a fortune. Probably cost us the account. Somebody's got to be on that plane tonight, and it's me. You know I've been talking about cutting back, and I haven't taken a European assignment since Andy was born! And I promise you I won't take another after this, no matter what. I'll tell them I can't do it. Andy's getting bigger. I don't want him to grow up with the memory of a mother who was always gone. I'm going to cut back. I promise."

I mean that, she reminded herself. I love Andy. I just don't find the role of Mommy particularly satisfying. Daniel is better at nurturing, and I'm doing what's best for the family. By working hard at my career Daniel is free to spend time with Andy. If I didn't work so hard he'd be pressured to earn more. Andy had been a difficult baby, and after her 6 weeks maternity leave Katherine had happily handed him over to the daycare center without a twinge of guilt. Now that he was almost four she found him to be less trouble and more interesting, but she still preferred to work late and arrive home to find her son bathed, fed, and ready for bed. She reassured herself that it was quality time that mattered most. It was true she had agreed to stop traveling when their son was born, but she hadn't known then how much she would miss the freedom. She loved her husband, but relished those trips when she was on her own again, living under a generous expense account, doing the work she enjoyed the most.

Daniel turned away from the window. She could tell he was still very angry. "What about L.A., Chicago, and all the rest," he asked? "Andy misses you then too. You're gone every month! Are you going to cut back there too, or will it be just a couple of days, honey, I have to, honey, I couldn't get out of it, honey?"

She recognized the truth in what he was saying. She did travel a lot. In fact, even though she hadn't taken any overseas assignments since Andy was born, she averaged a couple of trips a month, and had ever since Andy was six months old. "I promise. I'll cut back on all of it. After this trip, after this account, they're going to make me a partner. You know that's what I've been working for. Then I can cut back. The other partners do it. They hand the running to the assistants. They never go on overnights unless it's for fun." She swallowed her guilt at the half-truth, knowing that as a partner she would have more freedom, but would still be expected to travel. "Daniel, you know how important this partnership is to me. Please try to understand."

Daniel had known from the time she first mentioned Bill's wife being sick that she was going. Nothing he said would convince her to stay. In his mind he had already worked out the plans for Andy's birthday, what he would tell him, when they would celebrate, but anger drove his comments. "What about Andy's birthday? You're going to miss his 4th birthday? How can you make that up to him!" he asked.

She bristled at Daniel's attack and struck back, trying to defend herself. "He's three for Christ sake! We'll celebrate when I get back. He doesn't know when his birthday is." She shook her head not sure if she was right or wrong.

"He knows his birthday is Friday. He's been talking about it for a week! Of course he knows when his birthday is," Daniel said. It occurred to him that Katherine might really believe what she said, really believe it didn't matter. He shook his head. This was not the time, with both of them already late for the day, to have that argument. He had a class to get to, and she couldn't discuss anything reasonably when she was late for work.

"Look," Katherine said, taking charge. "This is what we'll do. I'll come home early tonight, and I'll pick up Andy. I should be able to get him by 4:30, and we can all spend some time together. Tonight I leave, but it's a late flight and he'll be ready for bed when I go. I'll be finished on Friday night. I'll catch an early flight on Saturday, and be back here Saturday afternoon. We'll have a birthday party on Saturday night. He won't know the difference."

"No," Daniel said. "He will know the difference, but it's the best we can do." He was anxious to end the fight, knowing that if Andy heard their angry voices he would be upset. Katherine would never back down, and he decided to drop it. If she was determined to go he didn't want their last day together filled with anger and fighting. Reaching out his arms he enfolded her in a hug. "Alright," he said. "Go to Paris and get your account, and have a little fun while you're there. We'll have the birthday Saturday. Just promise me you'll be careful."

Glancing at the clock on the wall Katherine realized she was already late. Anxious to get away she brushed off his fears. "Don't worry. I'm a big girl. I can take care of myself. Anyway, I know Paris like the back of my hand, and I'll be back before you know it."

Katherine's day flew past as she made last minute arrangements of what she would need for the trip. In hindsight it seemed to her to be a good idea she was going. Bill supposedly had 'everything ready,' but she kept finding gaps in his work and things she needed to arrange. She glanced impatiently at her watch. Prepared or not, there was some information that only Bill could give her, and he'd been out of his office all afternoon. She buzzed her secretary. "Katy, has Bill called me back?"

"No ma'am. I don't believe he's back yet."

Katherine glanced at her watch again. Three o'clock. If she didn't leave by four she'd never make it home on time. She picked up the phone and buzzed Bill's extension. His assistant picked up.

"Mary, is he still not back?" she asked by way of introduction.

"No, Katherine, he isn't. I don't know what the holdup is. He had a meeting with O'Neal. I could try to buzz them."

"No, don't bother. I'll just pop over and see them." She grabbed her folder of information for the Paris job and went down the hall to O'Neal's office. His assistant tried to stop her, but Katherine waved her away. "I've got to talk to them both about the Paris job. You know that's important."

The girl wavered. She was new and didn't really understand company procedures. Knowing that the Paris job was important, she stepped aside and let Katherine pass.

Katherine knocked, and without waiting for an answer pushed open the office door. The two men looked up, startled. "What's this?" O'Neal asked. "Amy let you in here?"

"Don't blame her. I told her I belonged." She walked quickly to the edge of the desk, eliminating any possibility she had just poked her head in.

"Well what's the meaning? Barging in and interrupting us like this."

Katherine hesitated. O'Neal was higher up than her, and would have some say in her promotion. She wondered if she had made a mistake, and decided prudence was the best approach. "I'm sorry sir. I know I shouldn't intrude. It's just that I had some very important things to go over with Bill regarding the Paris job, and I leave tonight. It's getting late, and I was hoping you might have some input also." That should gain me some brownie points, she thought. Acting like I care what this jerk thinks. She smiled charmingly.

He frowned at her over the top of his glasses. "I don't know why you thought it was appropriate to interrupt our meeting. Your questions will have to wait. We'll be finished up within an hour."

She glanced at her watch. "I'm really sorry sir. Unfortunately I have another appointment at 4:30, and won't be available. I need to leave by 4:00 to be there on time. That's why I interrupted. It won't take but a few minutes." She thought, irreverently, that he was an exceptionally ugly man. While his body was trim, his face looked swollen with fat and huge jowls hung on each side of his chin. His salt and pepper hair was eternally in disarray, and the half-frame glasses he wore when working looked ridiculous.

O'Neal shook his head. "Sorry, but we're in the middle of something just as important. Push back the 4:30, and we'll try to finish a little quicker."

She'd heard O'Neal was a controlling man, and realized they had entered a power struggle. He had the power to make her wait, but he would be in big trouble if his bosses knew he was withholding the information she needed. "No way I can push it later than 5:00," she said, groaning to herself. Daniel would be furious. "I really can't make it any later. I guess I can try to get some of the questions answered by phone after I arrive." And, she added to herself, I'll make sure everyone knows who created the need for lengthy international phone calls.

O'Neal frowned as if he could read her mind. Looking at Bill he asked "Can you do this later? Apparently not everyone is a team player today." He looked pointedly at Katherine.

Bill nodded. He was anxious to redeem himself after backing out of the Paris job. "No problem sir. I can stay late tonight."

"Give me five minutes to move the other appointment, and I'll be back." She turned and went to her own office to make her call in private.

Katherine grabbed the phone and punched in Daniel's number. Before he could even speak she cut in, "Daniel, I need you to get Andy from daycare. If you do it I can be home by 6:00. I'll get a cab from the station. We have to go over some last minute things."

"Kath! I thought we were going to spend some time together, all three of us, tonight."

"We are," she assured him. "I'll be home at 6:00. I promise. We'll get dinner and we'll play with Andy. I promise I won't be late."

"Andy will be exhausted by the time we get dinner made and finish eating. Can't you make it a little earlier?" he pleaded.

"I'll see what I can do. I'll try to get there by 5:30. You won't be home before then." And I'll never make it before 6:00, she admitted to herself. "Thanks hon. I gotta run." She hung up without giving him the chance to say goodbye. Sighing, Daniel gathered his things and headed for the door. It wasn't that he minded picking up Andy, just that once again Katherine was putting the office first. He went out into the cool afternoon air. The day was noticeably milder than yesterday. Spring would arrive soon. Katherine anxiously awaited spring each year, but he and Andy were happy in any season. Differences in background he supposed. Katherine had moved to New York when she was fifteen. He had spent his life upstate, and his vacations in the mountains of Vermont with his grandparents. Andy it seemed would be like him, loving the snow and the brisk air as much as the summer.

The traffic was light, and the bus reached the Jersey Transfer Station quickly. Daniel unlocked his car door, his gaze taking in Andy's booster seat and the books and toys that littered the back seat. Katherine complained constantly about the mess, but it was one area he refused to budge on. He had insisted that if Andy had to go out to daycare everyday, the trip to and from the day care would be enjoyable. He had assumed that when Andy was born Katherine would quit her job and stay home. In his experience that was what mothers did. He was shocked when he brought up the subject to Katherine and she had laughed as if he were joking. Now, four years after that discussion, he had adjusted to the reality of who Katherine was. She would never fit his idea of what a mother should be. She valued the money and the power of her job too much. When Andy was six months old and she had taken a 5-day assignment in L.A., Daniel had accepted that he would be the primary parent. Since then he had handled the day care, the meal preparation, the bathing and dressing. Katherine arrived home after Andy's bedtime at least a couple of nights a week. Until recently Andy had seemed oblivious of his mother's schedule. Recently though he had changed. At bedtime he would cry if she wasn't home, insisting he wanted her to read to him, and shunning Daniel until she arrived. It had started after a week long trip a couple of months ago. Andy had taken her absence hard, having trouble at the daycare, crying a lot at home, and generally being difficult. In spite of Katherine's shortcomings as a parent Andy clearly loved both of them and like all three-year-olds one day he preferred Daddy, the next Mommy. Daniel hoped this trip would be a time he preferred Daddy. Even though it was a short trip, he didn't want to see Andy suffer.

Pulling into the daycare parking lot he regarded the facility where Andy spent so much of his day. The building was bright and cheerful. The playground, empty now, was safe and a three-year-old's dream. Inside, the walls were filled with the artwork of busy children. Daniel stood in the door, watching, waiting for Andy to notice him. He was busy with a fire truck, his sandy hair falling into his eyes as he crawled along wailing like a siren at the top of his lungs. Suddenly he caught sight of Daniel. Immediately he abandoned the truck and ran screaming in Daniel's direction. "Daddy, Daddy, Daddy," he shouted over and over. With full force he slammed into Daniel's legs and hung on.

"Hey there, buddy," Daniel said, ruffling Andy's hair. "Have a good day?" Andy nodded, knocking his head against Daniel's leg repeatedly. The day care provider came up carrying Andy's coat. Daniel didn't know her. He hated that his son was cared for by people he didn't know. He knew the facility was good, and they screened their people well, but the turnover was high. Every few months a new face. Every day four providers who might be the one Andy ran to. Daniel listened carefully as the woman related the mundane details of Andy's day; lunch, nap, behavior. He thanked her then told Andy to put on his coat.

Instead Andy began to jump up and down. "Where's Mommy? Where's Mommy?" he chanted over and over, not stopping to hear the answer. Daniel took Andy's coat from the teacher, and began putting it on his jumping son.

"Andy! Stand still," Daniel ordered, then instantly regretted his impatience. He hadn't seen his son for hours, and was irritated in minutes. Your son is more important than dinner, he reminded himself. Still, the dinner would be overdone. He had put a roast in the oven this morning and set the oven to start baking later in the day. He had figured Katherine would meet him and they would be home by 5:00. The roast would be overdone, and they liked it rare. But that's not Andy's fault, he reminded himself. Kneeling down he hugged his son. "Come on buddy. Let's go home."

As soon as they entered the apartment Daniel set Andy on the floor. "Wait here," he told him. "I have to get the oven turned off." Immediately Andy began running in circles around the living room, arms out, playing airplane. As Daniel pulled the roast from the oven he heard the door open.

"Mommy," Andy yelled excitedly. "Look, Mommy." Daniel heard a beep and the electronic voice of the answering machine. "You have deleted three messages."

"Andy," Daniel yelled running from the kitchen. "Don't do that!" He pulled his son from the table. "How in the hell did he learn that?" he asked Katherine. Without waiting for an answer he turned to Andy holding him firmly by the right arm. "Never touch that again!" he ordered his son. "Those messages are important. Mommy and Daddy need those."

"Oh Daniel," Katherine cut in, "it's not that big a deal." She was laughing, and Andy pulled away and ran to her. "It's just a couple of messages. They'll call back if it's important." Andy threw his arms around Katherine's legs and hid his face. She reached down and stroked his hair.

"How did he even know it was up there?" Daniel asked.

When Katherine didn't answer Andy tentatively peeked at Daniel, then proudly announced, "Mommy showed me, and I 'membered it too. Didn't I, Mommy?"

"You sure did," she replied, smiling at her son. Then, looking sheepishly at Daniel she added, "I let him delete the messages yesterday after I played them. I didn't think he'd remember."

"Never mind. They'll call back if it's important. Come on. Let's eat dinner. It's overcooked and getting cold."

Dinner was a wild affair. Andy hadn't had time to calm down from the daycare, and he always spent the first hour or so talking in a shout--the way you had to talk to be heard over the noise of the other kids. Daniel and Katherine gave up trying to hold a conversation, and gave their attention over to their son. He sat playing with his food. Several peas had rolled off the plate, and he pushed them about the table with his fork.

"Andy, eat some of the peas," Daniel encouraged.

"Tell Mommy what you did today," Katherine interrupted.

"I fell off the swing," Andy shouted. "I hurt my arm. Want to see?" He twisted around trying to pull his sleeve up over the elbow. Accomplishing this task he showed off the elbow with no sign of injury.

"Oh my!" Katherine feigned interest in the non-existent wound. "Show me where it got hurt."

"Right here. See. See that. I fell on the ground. My arm got hit on the ground," he shouted, pointing to his smooth skin. "Can you get me a Band-Aid? I need a Band-Aid."

"No Andy," Daniel said. "You don't need a Band-Aid. Your arm isn't even hurt."

"I want one," Andy whined. "It hurts. I need a Band-Aid."

"Mommy will get you a Band-Aid," Katherine said, getting up from the table. "Band-Aids always make it feel better. Do you want Snoopy or dinosaurs?"

"Snoopy, Snoopy, Snoopy." Andy shouted, happy again.

After dinner they gathered in the living room, sitting on the floor, surrounded by toys. Katherine tried to concentrate on her son, but her mind was on the clock and her still-to-be-packed luggage. After half an hour she got up. "I've really got to get packed," she said. Daniel bit his lip, not commenting. He didn't want their last hours together to be filled with fighting and tension. Over enthusiastically he tried to engage Andy in play again, but Andy trailed after Katherine, following her into the bedroom.

As she began to fill her suitcase Andy began to pout. "Where are you going, Mommy?" he asked, tears brimming in his eyes. "I want to go with you."

"No, no, honey," Katherine soothed. "Mommy's going on a business trip. Little boys don't go on business trips."

"Well, why can't Daddy go," he whined. "I want you to stay here."

"Daddy can't go because he works for a different business. This is Mommy's business trip." Crossing the floor she glanced at her watch and realized she had to leave soon. She picked up her son. "Listen sweetie, Mommy doesn't want to go away, but I have to. I'll only be gone a few days, and when I come back I'll bring you a surprise!"

Suddenly brightening Andy shouted "What? What surprise?"

"It's a surprise," she reminded him. "I can't tell you or you won't be surprised." Quickly she set him down and grabbed the suitcases. "I've got to go now. Daddy will take good care of you, and I'll see you soon." Kissing him on the cheek she turned to Daniel. "Bye Honey," she said quickly. "Thanks for understanding. I'll make it up to you both." With a perfunctory kiss she opened the door and was gone.

CHAPTER

FOUR

On the airplane Katherine settled happily into her seat. The firm had booked first class so she could stretch out and work on the way, but she didn't need the extra time. With her usual efficiency the campaign was ready to roll. She stretched her legs and opened her carry-on bag. After removing a magazine and a novel, she fastened her seat belt. The hostess stopped by to check on her.

"Care for a drink before we take off?"

She asked for an orange juice, and settled comfortably into her seat. As the plane lifted off her spirits soared. No matter how long she lived in New York Katherine was really European at heart. She closed her eyes and thought back, remembering her childhood.

I was always so happy there. It wasn't until I started school that I realized I was different. That first day, the other girls keeping away from me and calling me 'la Americana' and laughing at my name. It wasn't until then that I realized how different we were. I ran straight home and asked Mama what it meant, and she told me not to worry about it, so I waited for Papa and I asked him. He took me by the hand and sat me on the couch, my legs sticking straight out in front of me. 'Niña,' he said to me, 'I am an American. It means I was born in another country, one called America. I came to Spain to work. That was before you were born, before I knew your Mama. My government sent me here to work on the military base. I am the American. You're Spanish.'

'But why do they make fun of me?' I asked him.

'Some of the Spanish people don't like the Americans being here, and they aren't used to it. The base has only been here a few years, and most of the men don't

30

have children. But there's nothing wrong with being an American, being an American is something I'm proud of. When you're bigger you can visit America and see for yourself. You get to choose something most people have no say in, you can choose to be an American or a Spaniard.'

'Why do they laugh at my name?' I asked him.

'It's different,' he told me. 'Your name is American. I named you after my grandmother.' Then he gave me a picture of her to keep in my room.

I could have hated being different, but Papa taught me to be proud of it. Eventually Papa found me a different school, one where more daughters of the military went. The first day there I sat next to Maria, and we became friends. My best friend until I left Spain ten years later.

She drifted off to sleep remembering Spain. When she woke up the plane was already beginning its descent into Paris. All thoughts of childhood were gone as she planned ahead. She pulled her date book from her carry-on reviewing the next few days. A meeting in two hours to present the main shoot ideas and meet the model, then some afternoon shots in the studio and around town, and evening shots around the city. Tomorrow we fly to the south for the beach and the country shots, then back to Paris tomorrow night. Friday we select the proofs and we're done. Katherine felt no stress at her tight schedule. The pace exhilarated her. The stewardess came by with hot washcloths, and she gratefully took one, dabbing at her eyes to help wake herself up.

Daniel pulled into the daycare parking lot. A group of 5-year-olds occupied the playground, the girls gathered into little groups with their dolls and games, the boys showing off their daring as they swung from bars, leapt from slides and occasionally singled out a girl to chase. Entering the facility he saw that the artwork had changed. Today bright finger paintings hung outside the doors. He scanned the pictures, looking for Andy's. Not seeing it he went on, opening the door to relative calm. He had arrived at snack time. Fifteen three-year-olds sat around a long, low table. Each had a banana and a half glass of milk. One teacher was busy wiping up someone's spilt milk while a second tried to console the child wailing in the background. Heading over to his son, Daniel leaned down and ruffled his hair. "Hey Buddy. Have a good day?" Andy nodded, his mouth full of banana. "You finish up and I'll get your stuff."

Leaving Andy he walked over to the cupboard where each child had a section. He got Andy's coat, and picked up the papers that were stored there. Glancing through them he saw it was all Andy's artwork; a macaroni and paper creation, cartoon characters scribbled on in bright colors, the numbers 1 through 10 with pictures of animals. Gathering the things, Daniel returned to the table.

Andy was finished with the banana, and gripped his milk cup in both hands. "Hannah spilled her milk," he announced loudly, looking at the little girl who had been crying. "She only used one hand and she spilled it." Andy was smug, clearly believing that he was beyond accidentally spilling milk.

"Finished?" Daniel asked. "Come on. Let's get your coat on." Andy got up obediently and stood still. He seemed strangely subdued. Sending Andy on an errand to check his now empty cupboard, Daniel grabbed the opportunity to talk to the teacher. "Everything go okay today? He seems quiet."

"Actually," she replied "he's been a little out of sorts today. He cried several times, and he hit one of the kids while she was saying good-bye to her mom. It's not like him."

Daniel nodded. "His mom left last night for a business trip. I think he's probably missing her.

As if on queue Andy ran up and interrupted. "Daddy," he began, his fist hitting Daniel's leg repeatedly, "is Mommy coming home tonight?"

Daniel caught the pounding hand and held it still. "No, honey. Not tonight," he replied.

"Tomorrow?" Andy squinted up at him, blinded by the overhead lights.

Daniel shook his head. "Not tomorrow either, but soon. She'll be home around your birthday."

"That's a long time," he protested.

"Not really that long. It'll pass before you know it. Now come on. I'll take you to McDonald's on the way home."

Daniel sat in the restaurant for a long time, letting the playland slides and happy meal distract his son, hoping to bring him home tired. After an hour Andy ran over and laid his head on Daniel's leg. "Tired?" Daniel asked.

Andy nodded, his head rubbing Daniel's leg.

"Let's go home," Daniel said. He gathered up the trash, giving in to Andy's pleading to keep the happy meal bag, now stained with grease.

By the time Andy was bathed and in bed Daniel was exhausted. He sat on the couch flipping channels endlessly, uninterested in any of the programs on the TV. He had wanted to call Katherine, but it was too late given the time difference. By 10:30 he was nodding off on the couch, and went to bed.

The next morning Andy seemed more himself. He was full of energy, unable to sit still for breakfast. He spooned his cereal into his mouth, squirming in his chair and spilling a generous amount onto his pajamas. When he had finished, Daniel lifted him off the chair and sent him down the hall to get dressed. The phone rang and Andy ran and grabbed it. "Hello," he shouted. After a pause he yelled, "Mommy!" Then he stood quietly, holding the phone, and nodding or shaking his head in response to Katherine's questions.

"You have to talk so Mommy can hear you," Daniel prompted. He knelt on the floor beside Andy, and could hear Katherine's questions as she tried to make conversation with her three-year-old. "Say yes," Daniel urged in response to Katherine's question 'Did you have breakfast?'

Andy nodded, then said, "Yes."

"Tell her what you had," Daniel encouraged. "Tell her you had Froot Loops."

"I had Froot Loops," Andy said obediently. After another minute of prompted conversation he handed the phone to Daniel and ran into his room. Daniel could hear him in the background shouting, "Mommy got me a present. Mommy got me a present," over and over again.

Despite what she had told Daniel about giving up traveling, Katherine was thoroughly enjoying the Paris job. Her ad campaign was good, and she knew it. So did everyone she worked with. They deferred to her, allowing her to direct the shots and set the schedules. As an added bonus, the model was a pleasure to work with, exactly the type of person Katherine had in mind when she designed the photo shoot. She was friendly as well as beautiful, and she fit believably into each of the scenarios Katherine had designed.

Katherine planned to show the model dining in one of Paris' most elegant restaurants, wearing a tiny black sheath dress, gazing up at a sexy man; on the beach in a tiny red bikini, running through the waves; shots in jeans and a plaid shirt, sitting on a fence outside an elegant country home. The ads were for a new perfume, and she wanted to show a perfume that went with an active woman, that fit into every aspect of a modern woman's life. Katherine knew it was a great campaign, and everything was falling into place. She thrilled at the pace of her days, free from the stresses of meeting Daniel's expectations and Andy's demands.

At dawn they had boarded a charted plane and flown to Southern France where she had spent the whole day directing shots, first at the beach, then in the town and the countryside nearby. On the flight back to Paris, the whole group was laughing and joking, exhilarated by the day's work, eagerly anticipating receiving the proofs back from the lab. As they neared Paris Katherine gazed out the window, seeing the Eiffel Tower and the Paris skyline lit up. She smiled, thrilled to be involved in the whole campaign. When someone suggested they all get dinner together she had quickly agreed, happy to be free from the demands of her husband and son.

Thursday evening Daniel again took Andy to McDonald's for supper. He felt guilty that Andy was living on French fries, but thought Andy needed the change of routine. He was clearly missing Katherine, and asked several times if she would be home that night. A fast food dinner and a playland seemed small concessions to avoid the hours at home with Andy waiting for her to arrive.

Daniel planned to cut short the Playland and get home a little earlier to straighten up the apartment so it would be neat when Katherine returned. Tomorrow, Andy's birthday, he would find something special for the two of them. Whether Katherine believed it or not, Andy knew it was his birthday, and expected something to mark the occasion. Saturday night they would have a little party with Daniel's parents coming down, and three friends from the daycare helping to celebrate. Katherine would be exhausted by then, but she managed well on little sleep. In fact, she almost seemed to thrive on it.

Handing his son a sucker Daniel said, "Come on Andy. We've got to get home. I have to clean up before Mommy comes home and thinks we didn't take care of things while she was gone. Are you going to help me?" Andy nodded agreeably as they headed to the car.

At home Daniel surveyed the apartment. Andy's room was a mess, the bathroom was littered with dirty clothes and towels, and the sink was piled with dishes. Putting Andy in his room Daniel left him with instructions to "put the clothes in this basket and the toys in the toy box", and left without much hope it would be done. He quickly washed the breakfast dishes and ran the vacuum, poking his head into Andy's room periodically to check his progress. Nothing was getting done, and Daniel accepted that Andy's room would remain a mess.

He went into the bathroom to clean up. When he finished Andy wasn't in his room. "Andy," he called "Where are you?"

"I'm writing Mommy a letter," Andy replied. Daniel found Andy in the living room with the contents of Katherine's desk strewn all over the floor.

"Andy!" he shouted angrily. "What are you doing! That's Mommy's desk and you don't get into other people's things without permission."

Andy's lower lip trembled, and he replied, "Well, I wanted to write Mommy a letter and she has all the paper for letters." Andy had indeed found the stationary, and had filled several sheets with random scribbles. He looked up at Daniel, his eyes filling with tears. "Will you send Mommy my letter?" he asked, his voice trembling.

Kneeling beside his son Daniel explained, "Mommy is coming home on Saturday. We don't have time to send the letter all the way to Paris. I'll keep it here for her until she gets home, and she can have it then." Andy nodded in agreement, but remained teary eyed. Picking Andy up Daniel returned to Andy's room. As he undressed him and got him ready for bed he tried to bring back the former good mood by talking about the fun birthday plans he had made.

"Do you know what tomorrow is?" he asked. Andy nodded. "Tell me. What is it?"

Andy wiped his hand across his eyes, rubbing at the tears. "My birthday," he said eventually.

"Aren't you excited?" Daniel asked.

Andy didn't reply until Daniel finished pulling his pajamas over his head. Then he asked, "Is Mommy going to be here?"

Daniel kissed Andy's cheek and sat him on the bed. "Mommy will be here for your party on Saturday. Tomorrow you and me are going to Kid's Palace for our very own birthday celebration. Then you go to sleep, and when you wake up we'll do something fun, and then it will be time for us to go get Mommy!"

Andy smiled. "Then she'll see my letter. Right?"

"Yep."

Andy smiled broadly. "And we'll have a birthday party with pizza and ice cream. Right?"

Daniel nodded. "Yep."

"And she won't ever ever ever go away no more. Right?"

"Well, I hope so." Daniel replied, without conviction.

After Andy was tucked into bed and his favorite book finished, Daniel returned to the living room and began cleaning up the mess. In addition to using several pieces of Katherine's best stationary, Andy had wrinkled several more. Setting those aside Daniel returned the others to the drawer. He picked up a pile of bills that had been knocked to the floor and began stacking them neatly. He paused as he came across a letter from Sally, Katherine's old roommate. Over the years Sally had become a good friend of Daniel's too, and Katherine always shared her letters with Daniel. Looking at the postmark he saw that it was recently sent. Katherine probably hadn't had time to show it to him yet. Sitting in a nearby chair he began to read the news from their old friend.

Sally was a travel photographer, and she usually wrote about places she had been, jobs she had worked on. But this letter was different. Now she went on and on about how hard it was to find a decent man to date. She described one bad date after another, and wrote about how much she wished she had a child. Daniel stopped reading, realizing that this more intimate letter had probably been intended for his wife alone, but then continued, feeling intrigued at this secret look at women friends.

> ...I hope your letter was just a momentary unhappiness, mailed off before your mood lifted. Seriously Katherine, do you realize how lucky you are to have Daniel and Andy? I'm telling you, it's lonely out here on your own. Everyone has moments of doubt, times when they wonder if they are doing the right thing. Everyone wakes up one day, having a bad day, and wonders 'What if...,' But think about all you have. A husband and a son who adore you, a great job. Any doubts you have about your life would exist no matter what you were doing. Married people spend their lives wondering what it would all be like if they hadn't married, hadn't had children, had more children, etc. But I'm telling you, single people spend their life wondering if the guy they decided not to marry was the right one. Wondering if there will ever be another chance, wondering if Mr. Right will show up 5 years too late to have children.

> Don't forget to count your blessings, even if you had a fight with Daniel, even if Andy is too energetic and you're tired. Women all over the world would envy you and want your life. Don't forget to appreciate what you have.

I'm off to Mexico in two days, but I'll be in New York in July. Let's get together. It's been too long. Give my love to Daniel and Andy.
Love, Sally

Daniel sat back in his chair, wondering what Katherine had written to provoke such a response. Clearly she was questioning her happiness and her life. Had she written it after an argument? Was she really unhappy with her life? Daniel knew Katherine was moody, prone to doubting herself despite her professional success, but was an argument with him enough to introduce serious doubt about their marriage? Was a rough day with Andy enough to make her wish she wasn't a mother?

Daniel shook his head, suddenly feeling he didn't really know his wife. He considered calling Sally to find out what the original letter had said, but decided against it, not wanting to look like a snoop. Instead he searched through the desk, wondering if there were other letters he hadn't seen. There was nothing, just that one. Maybe it was a momentary unhappiness, with a letter sent off before she could reconsider, he thought. Still, Daniel felt doubt. What if Katherine was unhappy? Would she ever consider leaving him? She had been really angry before this trip, but had sounded happy to talk to him on the phone. He got up, looked at the rest of the mess Andy had created and decided to leave it for morning.

CHAPTER

FIVE

Friday morning Katherine woke up early. She hoped to get the final pictures selected early in the day, and have the afternoon to shop. One of her joys of visiting Paris was to return home with a couple of outfits all her friends would envy, and it had been years since she'd been to Paris to shop. She had the afternoon planned out, a quick stop in Galerias Lafayette and then visit some of the little boutiques in the neighborhood. Then back to her hotel to pack, and after that she'd treat herself to a nice dinner out and get to bed early. In the morning she'd just grab a coffee and get a taxi to the airport. She knew she'd be exhausted by the time the party started, but being there was all that mattered. She smiled thinking about her busy day. It was the kind of day she liked best, never a moment to rest, always busy, always important.

She dressed quickly, selecting a plain black dress, close fitting, above the knee, stylish enough that she'd look like she belonged in a boutique. She pulled three pair of shoes from her suitcase, studied them, then slipped on her black flats. She glanced at her reflection in the mirror, turning one way and then the other. Dissatisfied, she pulled off the flats and slipped on her heels, then rushed out of the hotel and ducked into a nearby café for a cup of coffee and a croissant. After breakfast she hurried over to the office to select the final pictures and finish the job. With luck she would be finished by noon, giving herself several hours to shop.

Andre, the executive in charge of the Paris office, sat at his desk, head resting in his hands. Katherine paused before opening the door, studying the man she had been working with for the past few days. Andre was middle aged and chauvinistic, a hard man to work with. His hair was graying at the temples and he wore a mustache which drooped down at the edges. Taking a deep breath Katherine pushed open the door and entered the room.

Andre looked up at her, his face a picture of tragedy. "Katherine, oh Katherine, we have a disaster," he said.

She mentally added melodramatic to his list of unattractive traits. She had already solved half a dozen 'tragedies' in the short time she'd been here. "What's the problem now," she asked curtly.

"The photography lab. They've ruined half our film. We hardly have anything left." Once again he cupped his head in his hands, shaking it slowly back and forth.

She frowned, momentarily stunned, and then with her customary efficiency recovered. "I'm sure we've got lots of good shots even if the lab ruined some of the film. We've shot hundreds of frames."

He shook his head mournfully. "No, it's really bad. They've ruined most of the beach shots, all of the city shots, and some from the studio. All we have left are the countryside plus a few from the beach and the studio."

Katherine frowned, sensing a real problem. The ad campaign simply wouldn't work without all the components. This wasn't a one-time ad; it was a campaign, requiring all the parts to run properly. She glanced at her watch then spoke quickly. "Let me see what we've got." Looking through the pictures she saw that for once Andre wasn't being melodramatic. There really were an inadequate number of pictures.

Putting down the folder she addressed Andre, prepared to take charge and to fix the problem. "All right, get the model and the photographer on the phone. Have them meet us downtown to repeat the shots in an hour. See if you can get Marguerite from Beaux Cheveux. She's good at creating the looks I want and she's fast."

Andre continued to look at her mournfully, still shaking his head. "It's not so simple. The model..."

She interrupted him, angry that her plans had changed so abruptly. "I never said it was simple. I said get it done!" she shouted.

Her anger fueled his, and he shouted back at her, "The model flew to Italy this morning for a weekend shoot! We can't get her here in an hour."

Katherine didn't reply, her mind working furiously on a solution. She now had less than 24 hours until her plane took off. If she missed that flight she'd miss Andy's already-moved birthday. She ran through possible solutions, crossing them off as she went. Bring back the model. No, no time. Get a different model. Maybe, but probably not possible on such short notice. Anyone new would have to look convincingly like the original to avoid re-doing all the pictures, and they had to have someone experienced in order to accomplish the staggering amount of work in just one day. Definitely not possible to find anyone. Reschedule the shoot in a couple of weeks and come back to Paris. Daniel would be furious, the company would balk at the expense, and the campaign would have to be delayed, but it seemed the most likely option. Pulling up a chair across from Andre's she presented it.

He shook his head again. "It won't fit the clients deadline. I've already left a message for your home office, asking that you stay until Tuesday. The photographer and the model are available Monday. If we work hard we can redo the city shots in one day. We'll do final selection on Tuesday, and you fly out Tuesday night. I think we can manage with what's survived from the beach and the studio.

Now it was Katherine's turn to shake her head. "I can't stay 'til Tuesday. I've got commitments at home."

"I've worked with your office before. They'll reschedule your other appointments. It won't be a problem."

She shook her head again, frowning. "It's not business, it's personal. My son's birthday. I promised I'd be back on Saturday for the party."

Andre looked at her for a long time. "You see why mothers shouldn't work. They worry about birthdays. I have five children," he said proudly, "and I don't even know when their birthdays are."

They argued for the next hour, with Katherine realizing that she was losing ground. Andre had no sympathy for her predicament, and he had the home office on his side. The argument ended when Andre stood up abruptly. "I have other things I must do besides sit here arguing with you. There is nothing else we can do. I understand you planned to go home tomorrow, but the job will not be finished. The model will be here on Monday to finish. What I want to know is will you be here or do I need to call your office and ask them to send someone else."

Katherine slumped in her chair, groaning to herself. There was really no question. She had to stay. It would cost a fortune to send someone else over, and they wouldn't be able to accomplish the work as quickly as she would. Demanding to go home would cost her the partnership, and she had worked too hard for that. She glared at Andre. "I'll be here," she hissed and stormed out of the room.

Wearily she walked from the main office on the Champs-Elysee to her hotel a few blocks away. Normally she loved Paris, but now, trapped by her job and facing an angry husband, she despised it. I shouldn't even have to be here, she thought. They're professionals. They should be able to repeat those shots perfectly. Even as she thought it she knew it was unacceptable. Her firm was getting paid a fortune to direct the campaign, and that included directing the shots. She surprised even herself with her longing to be home. A year ago she would have reveled at an extended stay in Paris, but now she worried. Daniel had told her Andy missed her a lot, and she hated to think of him suffering. Besides, she was weary of fighting with Daniel. The last year had been filled with arguments about her work, and now she wanted it to end. She loved the power of a business meeting, loved giving her presentation, loved meeting the world-class models, but she missed Andy's chatter. Missed seeing his sturdy little legs running to greet her. Missed sitting with Daniel at the end of the day, talking about the ordinary things of day-to-day life. She felt herself slipping into melancholy.

Entering the hotel room she sat on the bed and looked around. The hotel was nice, but not lavish. Her window looked out over a small courtyard. By the window was a wooden desk and chair, stained very dark. Across the room stood an armoire. The double bed and a nightstand were the only other furniture in the room. The bathroom was small but nicely done in tile. The shower was modern, American style with sliding glass doors and plenty of water pressure. Katherine remembered the first time she had traveled to Paris on the firm's expense account. She had been prepared to make due with a small hotel room and shared bath, the same way she had traveled when on her own as a student. Her secretary had booked the room for her, raving about the wonderful price. She had taken a taxi from the airport and arrived at a charming little place called the Hotel Saint Honore. She had liked it so much that she had made it her own place, always staying there when she traveled to Paris. Now, after several years away, it was nice to be back. It was on a small side street just off the Rue de Grenelle. In addition to being convenient to most of their Paris accounts, it was also within walking distance of the Eiffel Tower and numerous boutiques. From her previous stays she felt like she knew the neighborhood, and had discovered certain cafes and restaurants she enjoyed visiting. Normally when she returned here she felt she had come to her "home" in Paris. Today there was no joy in the room.

She lay back on the bed, putting off the call and the confrontation she was sure it would cause. What can I tell him, she asked herself? He's going to be furious no matter what I say. I'll have to convince him that it's necessary. She closed her eyes still wondering what to say.

When she awoke she lay still for a minute, trying to recall what she was doing laying in bed in the middle of the day, then she remembered the call. She sat up, smiling, suddenly inspired by how to tell Daniel. She would say she could lose her job. That would convince him. He'd be upset, but he'd tell her to stay. Her job was too important for family finances.

She reached out and picked up the phone. Punching in the country code and phone number she sat listening to the ringing. Her own voice answered her. "Hi, you have reached Katherine and Daniel's house. We're not able to come to the phone right now but leave us..." She hung up on herself, realizing that Daniel must have already left for work. She looked at her watch, trying to calculate the time difference. Daniel would be in transit.

Her joy and relief of earlier was gone, and she sat on the bed, feeling unhappy. Her day was ruined, and her planned shopping trip no longer held any appeal. Today Andy was four and she was missing it. Tomorrow his party would be held without her. Unexpectedly her eyes filled with tears. She stared blankly at the wall, not knowing what to do. Daniel said she was being moody when she acted this way. All she knew was that sometimes she got just what she wanted and still felt miserable. She couldn't discuss it with Daniel. He didn't understand. She would try to tell him that she loved her job but felt something was missing, and right away he started talking about how she should spend more time with Andy and that would make her happy. When she tried it she just felt frustrated.

Picking up the phone she dialed the number for Sally, her old roommate. The machine picked up. "Hey Sally, it's Katherine. I'm in Paris on business. I know it's a lot to ask, but can you give me a call. I really need someone to talk to, and I don't want it to be Daniel right now." She left the number and hung up.

She continued staring at the wall, and then, impulsively she made a decision. She would tell Daniel she could fly home tomorrow, as planned, then get a flight back on Sunday night. It would be expensive, and she'd have to pay for the extra ticket, but it would show Daniel she cared. Even as she dialed the phone to check on flights she half hoped Daniel suggested she just stay in Paris. As long as he wasn't mad she would enjoy the weekend, and if she bought the ticket she could forget about shopping. As soon as she had the information she needed she reached for the phone once more and dialed Daniel's office. "Daniel," she exclaimed as he picked up, "It's me. It's Katherine. I need to talk to you about something."

He was happy to hear her voice, but immediately wary. Katherine was forever coming up with changed plans, and they weren't for the better. "What's up?" he asked.

"It's the advertising shoot. Some of the pictures were ruined and have to be redone. They're asking me to stay..."

"Katherine!" he interrupted, his fists clenched in anger, "I can't believe you are calling me to..."

"Wait," she pleaded. "You don't even know why I'm calling you. I wanted to tell you they asked me to stay until Tuesday, demanded it really, but I've thought of another plan. I could come home tomorrow as planned, and fly back on Sunday night. I don't want to miss Andy's birthday. I want to be there."

Daniel resisted the urge to point out she had already missed Andy's birthday, and remained silent. Over the years he had adjusted to Katherine's impulsive nature, and her mood swings that went with it. Still, he couldn't believe this was the same Katherine who had barely had time to say good-bye. "Are you serious?" he asked. "You'd be exhausted."

"I could do it though. I just hate the thought of being here for the weekend. Of course I'd have to cover the costs."

"Yeah, and what will the firm say if they find out?" he asked.

She grimaced at the thought of it. "I'm sure they wouldn't approve, but if I don't incur any costs to them what can they say? The weekend's mine. As long as I'm back here on Monday morning they can't say much."

"Have you checked the costs?" Daniel was the one who kept track of the finances and knew they were already living beyond their means.

"I did check. It's pretty expensive. I could get one for about $1500. But I'd be willing to do it if we decide that's the best thing. I won't even shop while I'm here, except I've already bought a couple of things for Andy. I could fly out tomorrow as planned and get there in time for the party Saturday night. There's a seat available Sunday afternoon to come back."

Daniel bit his lip. Twenty-four hours for $1500. A lot of money. "Are you sure you want to do all that traveling?" he asked. "That's a lot of flying for 24 hours at home."

She didn't answer immediately.

"Katherine, are you all right?" he asked. "Tell me what it is. I can tell something's wrong. Are you depressed?" Katherine's moods, or depressions, or whatever they were scared him sometimes.

She ignored the question about depression. "It's not that I want to spend my weekend on an airplane, but I want you to know you all are important to me. I know you already planned the birthday party and all, and I don't want you to have to move it again."

He could hear the melancholy in her voice and decided to be cautious. Pressure would just sink her further into depression. "Well, it's just family and a couple of friends coming," he said. "I could call them and tell them it's postponed. It's not such a big deal."

She ran her tongue over her lips, wetting them. Daniel was leaning toward having her stay, not wanting to spend the ridiculous amount for the flight. "What about Andy?" she asked.

"I'm taking him to Kid's Palace this afternoon. I told him we'd have a party on Saturday, but I was vague. I can keep him entertained a few more days if I have to."

Katherine felt relieved. If Daniel wasn't angry she'd prefer to stay put. She could have quite an enjoyable weekend here alone. "Well," she said, "tell me what you want me to do. You're the money one."

"Why don't we just move the party to next Saturday," he replied. "Andy'll be upset you're not coming back right away, but he really hasn't figured out when to expect you. Anyway, our own little party tonight should keep his mind off you not being home. I can't wait to see you, but it really does seem foolish to take the time and money for such a short trip."

Almost immediately Katherine felt better. Daniel wasn't angry, and the weekend stretched before her, just waiting to be filled. It reminded her of her student days, having a whole weekend free with no one to think about but herself, free to do whatever she wanted. She decided to go out and visit a couple of boutiques and then stop at a little bistro she liked. She hadn't been there for years. At the boutiques she tried on various outfits, reminding herself that anything less than $1500.00 meant she was actually saving money. Daniel wouldn't see it that way, but it made sense to her. She bought two, paying for one with her credit card, the second with cash. "I can't have my husband knowing what I paid for these," she joked as the salesclerk wrapped the outfits. The woman laughed and nodded knowingly.

Pleased with her purchases she walked to the bistro and without reading the menu ordered the Plat du Jour for a late lunch. Her mood had improved and she didn't much care what she ate. She loved French food, and it came with a nice house wine. The bistro was small and dark, very relaxing. A bar stretched along one wall, bottles of wine and liquor stored in racks on the shelf behind it.

Katherine sat at a tiny table by the front window, looking out at the quiet street. The strain of fighting with Andre and anticipating a big fight with Daniel had left her tired in spite of the recent shopping fun, and she wanted to shake off the feeling. Sitting back she breathed deeply. Through the door she could see a newsstand, and decided something to read with dinner was just what she needed to relax. She went out and stood, browsing the magazines, hoping to find something that would interest her. *L'Etranger.* The magazine caught her attention, and she picked it up. Beneath the title it read "For English speakers living in France." Without bothering to look at the contents she paid for the magazine and reentered the restaurant. As soon as she sat down the waiter brought her food. "Bon Appetit," he said politely.

"Merci." She looked at the food, hungry and eager to see what she had ordered. On the plate were thin slices of beef covered in a mushroom sauce. Next to the beef were several potatoes cut to bite size and broiled to golden brown with spices clinging to the edges. A medley of fresh vegetables, lightly steamed, completed the meal. A half carafe of red wine had been brought to accompany it all.

She cut up the tender beef, then opened her magazine. Slowly she perused the table of contents, only half paying attention. *How to look French chic; Must try escargot; Weekend getaway-don't leave the city.* She paused, cutting a bite of meat and chewing it thoughtfully. Maybe I'll be a tourist this weekend, she thought. I could visit the Louve, see Notre Dame, make an evening visit to the Eiffel Tower. It's been years since I've visited Paris. She smiled in anticipation, planning her days.

The door to the bistro opened and two French women came in talking loudly. One walked a small white poodle with a pink bow in his hair. Her hair was blond and sleeked back, and she wore a bright green mini dress covered with a large black jacket. The other had an Italian look about her. Long dark hair gleamed on her shoulders. She wore a black pantsuit, obviously made of some outrageously expensive fabric. Katherine eyed the suit enviously, thinking how much nicer it would look on her. The woman wearing it was too thin, no hips.

The pair sat at the table beside Katherine. She continued looking at her magazine but listened to their conversation. The blond was loudly bemoaning the upcoming weekend. She was upset that her husband's children were coming up from Nice to visit him and the husband had to be gone all day Saturday, and expected her to entertain his little darlings. As if that wasn't bad enough it was supposed to rain all weekend. At that news Katherine's spirits fell again. She didn't want to run through Paris in the rain all weekend. Neither did she want to sit in the hotel room and feel sorry for herself. She sighed, and with effort returned to browsing the contents of the magazine.

French vs. English--Where should the kids go to school?; Paris Metro-- Learn it and love it! Seeing nothing that interested her she began idly flipping through the pages, her eyes drawn to the ads. *French language school.* Boring. Too much text. For people who are living here it might work, she thought. They have a captive audience. She flipped through the articles looking for advertisements that might inspire her. A full-page ad showing a beautiful sunset leapt out at her. Attention getting. That's the sort of picture that makes you want to be there, she thought. She studied the page more closely. Spain. She should have known it right away. She smiled, almost feeling the warmth of the sun on her skin. There was a place she hadn't been in years. She felt an odd longing, almost a homesickness, for her old neighborhood of Moncloa.

She sat back, remembering long sunny days with her mother, going out to do the shopping. *Together, Mama holding my hand tightly, we would walk down the stairs from our second floor apartment. Mama always ignored the portero, but I would smile at him as we hurried past. On the ground floor of the building was a bar, but you didn't have to pass through it to go outside. We would turn right, passing by the outdoor patio of the restaurant next door. Just beyond the restaurant was a tiny grocery. Mama would pass it by, continuing on another half block, and turning down a side street. There, all in a row, stood three shops. First was the butcher. In we would go, and Mama would select some chorizo, a cut of beef, or some chicken. Then we moved on to the fruit stand. Here, Mama would buy plums and pears and lots of beautiful fresh oranges. Next she would select some fresh onions and garlic which she used in nearly everything. Finally we would go to the third store. Here Mama would get a couple loaves of long, crusty bread.* The very thought of it made her mouth water.

When we left the bread store to start for home, I carried the bread while Mama carried everything else. At the little grocery we would stop in for eggs, butter and milk. When we needed flour or sugar Papa went to get it so Mama didn't have to carry the heavy bags. At the apartment the portero would be sitting at his desk, and Mama would sail past, arms loaded with packages, while I hung back and smiled up at him. Sometimes he slipped me a sweet before Mama called for me to hurry up and I ran up the stairs.

As soon as the groceries were put away Mama would slice off some of the bread, spread it with butter, and we would eat it together, dunking the hard crusts into the huge mugs of coffee we drank. Mine with plenty of milk and sugar, Mama's strong and black.

She smiled at the memory. Those had been simple, happy times. Her biggest worry was whether her mother would discover the sweet and take it away, her biggest joy standing on the balcony to wave to her Papa as he got off the bus and walked toward the apartment. By the time she had reached the age where teenage girls fight with their mothers, her mother was dead, and her Papa so saddened that she had never had the heart to fight with him. She had simply taken over the running of the house, and without any fuss or anyone even noticing had become an adult.

A wave of sadness swept over her. Sadness for her mother, whom she felt she had never really known. Sadness for her father who had died a couple of years ago, and a strange homesickness for a place she hadn't lived for 16 years. I really should go back she told herself. It's probably changed so much I wouldn't even recognize it. She wondered if Daniel would enjoy a visit and how Andy would handle the language difference, and realized immediately that it wouldn't work. Daniel would fret and worry over the change in Andy's sleep schedule and meal times, forcing them to be just another American family on vacation. Katherine would want to relive the feeling of being Spanish, of eating dinner at 10:00 PM and then going out for a night of dancing that wouldn't end until sun-up. She smiled, remembering sleeping the morning away and three-hour lunch breaks. A trip like that would have to be taken alone. She looked at the photograph again, a plan forming in her head. She could go this weekend, leave tonight and be in by mid-morning. Stay for the weekend, and come back to Paris on Sunday night, arriving in time for the Monday meeting. A new energy flowed through her, and she quickly finished her meal. Leaving her money on the table she ran out into the street. The rain had started, and she snapped open her umbrella, enjoying the knowledge that she probably wouldn't need it in sunny Spain.

At the hotel she quickly packed her carry-on suitcase and threw on more comfortable clothes. She grabbed up the phone and dialed Daniel's number. His voice mail picked up. "Hi, you have reached the voice mailbox for Daniel Bayley. Today is Friday and I'll be out of the office the rest of the day. If you need to speak to someone immediately press zero for the operator. Otherwise leave me a message..." She hung up and dialed the home number. Her own voice greeted her for the second time that day. She waited through the message, and then spoke. "Daniel, it's me. I've just come up with a great plan. Since I'm stuck here I'm going to get the train to Madrid, visit some of my childhood haunts, and I'll check in on Aunt Rosa. I know she won't know who I am, but I'd still like to see her before she dies. I'll catch the Sunday train back to Paris, and be home Tuesday evening. I'll call you from Madrid. Give Andy my love. You too. Bye."

She glanced around the room. It was a mess, but she didn't want to waste time straightening it up. No one would ever see it. She picked up her carry-on and hurried out. In typical big city fashion, the rain had caused a shortage of taxis. Debating for a minute she ducked out into the rain, running the two blocks to the nearest subway stop. She entered the underground tunnel wet but exhilarated. The mad dash through the rain to catch a subway to the rail station brought back fond memories of her childhood, running along holding Mama's hand, as her mother called to her, "Hurry up. We'll miss the train." And later, when she was a student, she had spent a year back in Spain, studying at the University of Segovia, using all her free time to wander Europe, running from one train to the next, enjoying the sites in between. Now she felt oddly free. It was a feeling she hadn't experienced in years, not with Andy and Daniel depending on her.

Chuckling to herself she thought maybe she could relive that time a little. What a wonderful, carefree time, the year before she had met Daniel, when she still believed the whole world could be whatever she wanted it to be. She would check into a little pensión somewhere, share a bathroom with the other guests, and eat in little cafes. Avoid the big tourist hotels and restaurants all together. After all, she told herself, Papa told me I was Spanish, and he was right. In my heart I still am. I won't have a phone number for Daniel if I'm not in a big hotel, but it doesn't matter. I'll call him from the Telefonico, and he can call me when I'm back in Paris. She would relive a bit of her youth she decided. No fancy hotel, no fancy restaurants. It would be fun to get a little freedom from the pressures of life.

The subway pulled into the Gare d' Austerlitz, and Katherine hopped out. Glancing quickly at the posted schedules she saw that the next train for Spain left in an hour. She was early. Checking her purse she found plenty of francs for her ticket. She'd need more on Monday, but she could avoid cashing the traveler's checks here, at dismal train station rates. She went to the ticket window and bought her ticket, carefully recording the amount in a notebook she kept in her purse so she didn't mix up her personal expenses with business. She bought a copy of Complice, a popular Spanish magazine, and a couple of candy bars for snacking, then went over to the track to wait. It occurred to her that she should buy some pesetas so she could get the subway and a meal in Madrid without needing to change money. She glanced at her watch and decided she had time to visit a bank nearby. Taking her suitcase she crossed the street. The bank was security laden, with a locked door that was opened by a remote buzzer, then a second locked door. Inside, security cameras scanned the room and a guard stood by. Several people were waiting in the line, and just as Katherine joined it a gentleman, dressed in a business suit stepped up behind her. Glancing at her suitcase and the American passport she held in her hand he asked in English, "Leaving Paris?"

She turned toward the speaker and saw a handsome man, not too tall, with dark hair and olive skin. He was wearing an expensive Italian business suit. He had a small scar on his right cheek, but it didn't detract from his good looks, just eliminated the perfection of a model. She nodded. "Just for the weekend. You too?"

He nodded. "Going home."

Before she could answer two windows opened up simultaneously. Katherine approached her window and signed a traveler's check, forgetting she had intended to buy pesetas. It wasn't until the money was counted out and she had put it away that she remembered and asked that it be converted.

The bank clerk frowned. "It would have been easier to do in one transaction," he said angrily.

"I'm sorry. I just wasn't paying attention."

The businessman glanced her way again. "Going to Spain?" he asked.

"Yeah, just for the weekend."

He smiled. "I'm from Barcelona, but on my way to Madrid. Have you visited Spain before?"

"Actually, I was born there. I haven't been back for quite awhile though."

Switching from English to Spanish he said, "It's a much nicer place to spend the weekend than Paris. The people won't be so rude." He raised his eyebrows and glanced at the bank clerk. They both burst into laughter at the inside joke, then left for the train station, still talking.

CHAPTER

SIX

The train pulled in 15 minutes before its scheduled departure time. Katherine said good-bye to Ricardo, her new friend and entered a coach car. Ricardo was traveling by sleeper, but Katherine had been unable to get a ticket, and she was resigned to sitting up all night. She found a compartment in the second-class car occupied only by a young French woman and her daughter. She guessed the little girl to be about four. She was a cute child with long, dark hair, and a fussy white dress with too much lace. The child sat primly on the seat, eating a croissant her mother provided for her a bite at a time.

"Bon Soir," Katherine said to the mother and daughter. Both answered politely, but the mother immediately opened the book she had in her lap, an indication she wasn't interested in conversation. Katherine didn't mind. She had always hated traveling next to someone who insists on being her best friend for the trip. She settled back and opened her magazine, but instead of reading she watched the little girl, and wondered what it would be like to have a daughter, someone she could dress in fancy clothes. Andy absolutely refused to dress up, but a daughter would be different, she would naturally identify with her mother.

She stared out the window wondering if she should consider having another child. Daniel was all for it. She was less certain, and she was the one who would have to go through pregnancy and childbirth again. She didn't relish the thought. Andy had been a difficult birth. Hours of hard labor had finally ended in an emergency cesarean. Still, to have a daughter in addition to her son would be something to think about. Maybe she would discuss it with Daniel.

Eventually the little girl fell asleep, leaning on her mother's shoulder. The woman got up and stretched her out on the seat, smoothing the dress and retrieving a sweater to be used as a pillow. She sat down on the same side as Katherine, giving her daughter as much room as possible. Katherine felt a surge of annoyance. It would be an uncomfortable night with two adults sharing one side of the coach while the child took the other side. Still, she told herself, the child should be comfortable if possible. She tried to relax and recapture the feeling of freedom she had experienced earlier. It certainly wasn't the first night she had sat up on a train, and really wasn't a big deal. Taking a sweater from her own suitcase she bunched it into a wad and tucked it into the corner. She leaned back and closed her eyes, the rhythmic swaying of the train lulling her to sleep.

Katherine woke up as the train slowed down. The conductor walked the aisles calling for everyone to get off the train and go through customs. The mother and daughter had gone, apparently getting off at some station in the middle of the night. Katherine groaned to herself. She had forgotten that Spain required a change of trains at the border. It was a throw back to Franco's time as ruler. Damn man, she thought. Always worrying about foreigners coming into the country. He had built the tracks a different size than other European trains, guaranteeing that the crossing would be difficult.

Wearily she gathered her things and joined the line of people waiting to go through customs and board the Spanish train. All around her were a mix of people. Spaniards returning home after travel to other parts of Europe, French heading to Spain to enjoy the sunny beaches, Africans crossing Spain on their way home to visit friends or family. She waited her turn, observing the custom's agents. A single glance at a passport seemed to determine whether luggage would be inspected or not. Americans, Spaniards and French were waved through with a minimum of questions. Africans were mostly required to join another line where their bags would be inspected. She wondered briefly what they were searching for. Drugs most likely. Two large dogs sat behind the customs table, agents holding their leashes, just waiting to be called into duty.

Reaching the front of the line Katherine handed over her passport. "American," the agent said in English. "Why you are coming to Spain. Vacation?"

"Yes," she answered.

"How long you will stay?"

"Three days," she replied.

He nodded, stamped the passport and handed it back. "Spain is too big to visit in 3 days," he said in a derisive tone.

Without answering Katherine took the passport and picked up her suitcase. She boarded the waiting train, found a seat in an empty compartment, and was asleep within minutes.

When she woke again it was daylight, and she was alone in the compartment. She was surprised she had slept so soundly and felt so well rested. Looking out the window she tried to determine how near Madrid they were. The conductor poked his head through the doorway.

"Billette, por favor." She handed over her ticket. He punched it and handed it back. "Madrid, dos horas." He muttered.

"Gracias".

She could hear him at the next compartment "Billette, por favor."

She turned and gazed out at the landscape. The area approaching Madrid was barren, brown land punctuated by desert plants. While it did not hold the beauty of the coasts, or the lush green of Galicia, it was beautiful to Katherine. She remembered riding through the countryside with her mother on the bus to go see her grandmother. *Funny how families just peter out, she thought. Mama always talked about all the relatives, her cousins, her aunts and uncles, and then for me there was only Aunt Rosa and Grandma. And Grandpa, but I can't remember him, because I was only three when he died. Six children, and only three lived to adulthood. Mama, Uncle Manolo, and Aunt Rosa had lived. The others died, the oldest fighting in the civil war, and the two youngest, within a week of each other, of some unknown illness. The last time I saw Grandma, she was all alone. Manolo had gone to France so he could work and send money, and he had never come back. Mama had died, and Rosa was living in the home, never able to visit. Grandma regretted ever letting Rosa go to the home. 'I should have kept her with me where I'd know she was happy,' she had said. And when I suggested she visit Rosa, what did she say? 'An old woman like me, going into the city. I've never been there, and I won't go now.' Grandma never even went to school, and Mama only went to sixth grade, and here I am, no relatives, but a college graduate, traveling the world. Funny how life turns out.*

I should go see Aunt Rosa this weekend, Katherine told herself. Make sure she's happy and being cared for properly. She frowned, a sudden wave of guilt washing over her. She had ignored her aunt for years, only sending occasional pictures, and she was Rosa's only family. Manolo didn't keep in touch. Rosa was an embarrassment to him. Rosa, born mentally retarded, had lived with her parents until after Katherine's mother and father married. They were the ones who had brought Rosa to Madrid and placed her in a home, planning for the future when her parents would die, and Rosa would be alone. It's funny, Katherine thought, how she, the handicapped child, lived to old age while her brothers and sisters had all died young. Except maybe Manolo, she reminded herself. She had never met Manolo.

She stared out the window, wondering what it would have been like if she had stayed in Madrid. Spain hadn't turned out bad, but when they left no one knew what was coming. After the initial shock of her mother dying, Katherine had taken over the household duties as expected of her, but she was never content with the arrangement. Even at fifteen she was ambitious, and her ambition had been frowned upon in conservative Spain. Her teachers had encouraged her to think of marriage and children, keeping a house, making life pleasant for a husband. She had wanted to work, and not just in any job, but one with power and prestige. Such ambitions were unacceptable in a girl, though not to her father. He had always told her she could do what she wanted. When she asked him about the discrepancy, he had explained she might have to leave Spain to accomplish her goals. She had proclaimed with all the fervor of youth that she would never leave him, but when he explained that since her mother had died he lived in Spain only for her, Katherine had quickly conceived a plan to move to New York. She had visited New York three times to see her grandparents and loved it, so ten months after her mother's death they had packed up and gone to America.

Though it had been a culture shock at first, Katherine had taken to New York and finally been able to show her ambition and intelligence. She'd only been back to Spain twice since then. The first time at age 20, to study for a year and the second time for her grandmother's funeral when she was 23. On that second visit she had assured herself that Aunt Rosa was well cared for, and really didn't understand who Katherine was. The old woman had been happy to see her, and had eagerly pointed out the photos she had of Katherine sitting on her bedside table, but she had been equally happy to see the nurses. Katherine assured herself there was no reason to visit, but she continued to send an occasional photo or gift.

Looking out the window she saw the first buildings of the city in the distance. The farthest out were big blocky apartments where many of the poor lived. Row after row of government built buildings, unlandscaped, basic and ugly. Further in the buildings were wonderful old structures with modern ones mixed in. The train pulled into the bustling Atocha station. Excited now, Katherine gathered her suitcase and hurried out.

She stopped by a map, studying the Metro stations, trying to orient herself. She spotted the Puerta del Sol and smiled. It was the hub of the city, and not far from where she had grown up. The perfect place to stay. She descended the stairs, paid her fare, and ran to board the waiting train. She was naturally cautious of the subways in New York, but had never been afraid of any European subway. The car was filled with mothers taking their children into the city, businessmen returning from appointments, tourists talking in a variety of languages as they tried to negotiate the foreign city. The car was crowded, and she ended up standing, hanging onto a pole near the doors.

At the third stop a young, ragged couple boarded the train, carrying a limp child. Speaking in a loud monotone the father addressed the occupants of the subway car. The Spanish people ignored him, obviously used to such occurrences. The tourists stared with interest or fear, not understanding the rapid speech. Katherine only felt saddened. Though she had not witnessed it first hand until now, friends had told her horror stories of the street people drugging their babies and begging for money to treat the "sick" child.

"Hello, my name is Pedro and my child is very sick. I do not have money to buy the medicine and cannot find work. Please help me." Finishing the speech the father wandered the subway car holding a little cardboard box with a few coins in it. He passed the Spanish people quickly, receiving a few pesetas, but clearly not expecting much. Reaching a group of Americans he stood before them, handing over a crudely lettered sign saying the same speech in English, French and German. The tourists read it and dug into their pockets. Each one dropped something into the box. When he approached Katherine she looked away, and he passed, mistaking her for a Spaniard.

Leaving the train at Puerta del Sol Katherine hurried toward the escalators. The first flight was out of order, and people trudged up the steps. Music reverberated through the subway tunnels, and on each level she passed a group of musicians who played or sang, a hat or container set before them for donations. As she came up the steps into the blinding sunlight the crowd momentarily overwhelmed her. This was a different Puerta del Sol than she had grown up with. Hundreds of people rushed past, pushing their way up or down the subway entrance.

Leaning against a building an old man, apparently crippled, sold lottery tickets. He wore them clipped onto his shirt for easy display, and his sole sales pitch was a loud monotone shout of "Para hoy." Young women, stylishly dressed, rushed past old women clothed in black from head to toe. Near the lottery man a young woman sat, two limp children in her lap, and the obligatory box of coins on the street before her. Walking a block further Katherine's way was blocked by an old woman, aggressively begging. The street was littered with advertisements handed out forcefully by young men. Most people simply took them and dropped them on the street, not bothering to read them or look for a trash can.

Spotting a sidewalk café, Katherine ducked through the crowd and seated herself at a table. A waiter came up, and she ordered coffee and churros. With a nod he headed inside for her order. When he returned she asked if there was a pensión in the area.

"Turista?" he asked, looking surprised.

"Sí," she replied. It pleased her that she was not immediately spotted as a tourist, but was assumed to be a Madrileña.

With a broad wave of his hand he indicated the buildings across the street. "All of them," he said. "Some are nice, some not so nice. I don't know who has a good place. Just ask to see the room before you pay."

Finishing her coffee, Katherine picked up her bag and crossed the street. She wandered a bit, enjoying her freedom; the slightly familiar yet different feel the city had after all these years. She stopped in front of a run down building. Clearly it had once been grand, but that had been years ago. Still, something about it attracted her. She furrowed her brow, wondering what seemed so familiar, then smiled and nodded to herself. She gazed up to the third floor. Maria's building. Of course Maria wasn't there any more, but this was a building where she had spent many happy hours.

Maria had been her best friend up until the time she had left Spain. The two girls had played together daily, and Maria's nanny had always said they could have been sisters they were so alike. Katherine remembered her mother walking with her, holding her hand, and delivering her safely into the care of Maria's nanny. Maria's parents were almost never home, and her nanny hadn't allowed many guests, but Katherine had always been welcome. The home had been beautifully decorated. Oriental carpets over polished hard wood floors; heavy, dark furniture; hand-made lace curtains. Maria and Katherine had spent hours playing dolls on the floor. And hours more gazing out the windows at the activity in the streets. Maria hadn't been allowed out except for very special occasions. Her father had worked in some sort of government job, and her parents had given the nanny strict instructions to keep her inside, away from the dangers of the streets. Despite their closeness, they had lost touch when Katherine moved away. There had been letters at first, and when Katherine returned to Spain to study there were excited plans to get together, but the meeting had been a disappointment. Maria, at twenty, was unmarried and pregnant, tragically unsure how to handle her situation. Katherine was excitedly planning a career, and unable to relate to Maria's dilemma. Though they had tried to connect, they had found little to talk about, and gradually their letters had become just a signature on a card each Christmas. Katherine realized that Maria had never even answered her inquiry about the baby. I suppose she had it adopted, Katherine thought. Spain in the 1970's was no place to be a single mother.

Katherine approached the front door of the apartment building, walking up several steps. Three different pensions advertised on the outside of the building. Not sure which one, if any, occupied Maria's former apartment, Katherine decided to wait until the locked outer door was opened by someone else, and then duck inside. Standing on the steps she was filled with a longing to see Maria again. They had never spoken after their last meeting, but surely, she thought, years of friendship could provide an hour of conversation over coffee. While she waited for the door to be opened she dug her address book out and checked for Maria's address. It should be simple enough to find her phone number, she told herself.

The outer door opened and she stepped inside and climbed the stairs to Maria's former apartment, happy to find that it was now a pension. An old woman opened the door, and Katherine looked about eagerly. She was disappointed to find that the apartment was shabby and worn, nothing like it had been. Clearly the old woman was poor, and she catered to student travelers looking for cheap rooms. It's depressing, she thought. Too depressing for me. Politely she declined the room the old woman offered, and seeing her disappointment felt obligated to explain that she had often played in the apartment as a child, and that she wanted to remember it as it had been. She'd stay somewhere more inviting, she told herself. All her hard work had earned her a little luxury.

As she stepped back onto the street she heard someone call her name. Ricardo, the man she had met the day before in the Paris bank, was waving to her. She smiled and walked down the steps toward him thinking that maybe they could have lunch together.

SEVEN

Maria stood by the answering machine, surprised to find her hand shaking uncontrollably. How had Katherine found her, she wondered. She had never expected to hear from her after all these years. She sat down, willing herself to stop shaking, remembering Katherine and the fun they had had together. How she would love to meet and reminisce about the past. But Katherine was risky, the only person still living who knew about the baby and who might bring her fragile world crashing down.

She crossed the room and poured herself a sherry. Taking a sip she sighed, and allowed herself the rare luxury of thinking about her youth and all that she had hidden from her husband. She had never told him about her rebellious period: the year she had spent living with Alejandro, or the little boy she had given birth to, then placed for adoption. Now she allowed herself the luxury of remembering. For one brief year she had almost broken free from her parent's strict control. She smiled, remembering how it had all begun, and the role Katherine had played in her decisions.

I was just out of school, not quite nineteen, and Papa had arranged for me to marry that rich playboy, the son of his business friend. At first I was excited. Marriage and a family seemed the logical next step for a woman my age. But then I wrote to Katherine and asked her to come for the wedding. And she called me, the only time we had spoken in person since she left. 'Are you crazy?' she shouted at me. 'Married, at eighteen? What about getting an education and having a life? Don't throw your life away on some man you don't even love.' She seemed so alive and full of plans, and I realized she was right. Planning the wedding was fun, but I didn't really know the man I was going to marry.

Maria pushed her hair back and sipped her sherry again. *It was so hard to go against Papa's will. I'd never done it before. I guess in trying to break free I really overdid the rebellion. Demanding that he allow me to attend university wasn't a bad thing but moving out to live with Alejandro was a bit much. He represented everything Papa was against, and I don't suppose I really loved him, just loved that he shocked people so much.*

She sat back and allowed Alejandro's image to fill her mind. *Carefree and outspoken, he had worn his hair long, and always had a marijuana cigarette or two in his pocket. Though he spoke out against the government my father represented, at the time that only added to his charm. When I discovered I was pregnant I wasn't even worried. In the crowd I was running with it was no big dea, and I just figured we'd get married.*

The night I planned to tell Alejandro I was pregnant he interrupted me and explained in detail things about his life I didn't want to know. He wasn't just against the government he'd said. He was actively fighting for separation from Spain. I had always known Alejandro was a Basque, but I hadn't wanted to admit that his politics were so strong. Every question had lead to another answer I didn't want to hear. Yes, he participated in bombings against the government. Yes, he had probably killed people, though he couldn't say for sure. By the end of the evening he had scared me, and I never told him I was pregnant. Instead I gathered my things, slipped away, and went to a home for unwed mothers. After the birth I had no choice but to returned home, and beg forgiveness. They never knew about the son I placed for adoption or what Alejandro had said to turn me away from him.

They had taken her back, her mother gratefully and her father angrily. He had declared that no man of any means would ever marry her, and had forced her to live in almost total seclusion. Though her needs were provided for, any dreams of education and freedom were gone.

When her parents were killed in an auto accident, Maria had been left alone. When Jose, a friend of her father's had proposed marriage, it had seemed a lifeline to Maria, and she had married him quickly, ignoring the fact that he was older than her father. He had proven to be just as controlling also. His friends had little in common with his young wife, and he discouraged Maria from developing friendships of her own. Jose's death last year had left an emptiness in Maria's life, but not really sorrow, for their relationship had never been based on love.

She forced herself to think of Jose's will, the sole reason she was afraid to see Katherine. In his final act of control over her he had left her an income, enough to live comfortably forever, with the stipulation that she never date, remarry or have children. Thus she lived in her solitary world, rich but lonely. Jose's friends had no desire to contact her, and after so many years she no longer knew how to make friends. Had never known how to make friends really. Katherine had been her only childhood friend, unless she included the old woman who had lived upstairs from her family. They had shared cookies and milk whenever Maria snuck away from her nanny, but she hadn't been a real friend, just a nice old lady.

Maria shrugged off her sadness, reminding herself that she was wealthy and able to do whatever she wanted with her time. She had never worked, and while Jose's will didn't offer an allowance generous enough to pay for servants, she was able to travel and never lacked anything other than company.

Maria looked at the mantle clock. Katherine had said she would call back. The question now was should they arrange to meet. Surely there could be no real danger, she thought. It wasn't as if Jose's lawyers had spies after her. No one would ever know about the baby. Maria was superstitious, and gradually she decided that they were meant to meet. Otherwise Katherine's call would have missed her. She sat back, sipping the last of her sherry. She would arrange to meet Katherine. They could meet in Puerta del Sol, near her old apartment. The familiar environment would provide something to talk about if the conversation became forced.

Katherine wandered happily down the street, deep in conversation with Ricardo, her new found friend. She was pleased with the way her day had turned out. Ricardo was proving to be an attentive and entertaining companion. Her second call to Maria had been answered, and the two women had arranged to meet after lunch. Katherine made a mental note that she still needed to call Daniel and find a place to stay, but decided she would put it off a little longer. Ricardo had asked her to lunch, and she was looking forward to continuing their visit.

In Sol the crowds were overwhelming, and Maria saw that some sort of demonstration was taking place. Anxious to escape the crush she ducked into a nearby café and ordered a coffee. As she drank it she made a plan. She wasn't due to meet Katherine for a couple of hours.

She would walk over by her old apartment and find a place to get lunch. She slipped out the door and walked quickly away from the square.

A few minutes of walking put her out of the worst of the crowds, and she stopped in a small restaurant and ordered the plate lunch. Just up the street she could see the building where she had grown up, and as she ate she reminisced about her childhood and her friendship with Katherine. When she had finished lunch she left, walking in the direction of the building. Overwhelmed with memories she approached the front door and pressed the buzzer. When the door unlocked she stepped inside and gazed at the building. It had been luxurious when she lived there. Now it was faded and rundown. The old elevator, a great luxury in her childhood, was still there. Maria shook her head. It was nothing more than a cage on pulleys really. Probably terribly unsafe. Still, she opened the door and stepped inside. She remembered riding up with her mother, asking if she could push the button for their floor, and Mama always let her, though Papa had usually pushed it himself before she got the nerve to speak to him. Now she shut the door and pushed the button. Slowly the elevator groaned upward, giving Maria time to study the building through the open walls. The marble steps were cracked and dirty, a far cry from the polished steps of her day, and the walls needed a coat of paint. By the time she reached her destination the automatic lights had shut off, and the building was gloomy.

She pressed the buzzer on her old apartment, not sure what she intended to say when someone answered. Eventually an old woman opened the door and greeted her. Maria didn't answer immediately. She was gazing past the woman, looking at the small hall table that she was sure had belonged to her parents.

"Are you looking for a room?" the woman asked.

Maria was jerked back to reality. "No, well, yes. I'd like to see the rooms."

Alicia stepped aside and let Maria enter. She pulled a wad of keys from her pocket and crossed the hallway. "This room is very nice," she said. She tried one key and then another, and eventually the door opened. Maria walked into the room that had been her nanny's. Though her nanny had had the smallest room in the apartment, it had still been nicely decorated. Now she was greeted by worn carpeting and mismatched fixtures. Involuntarily Maria stepped backward. The room was a reminder of the sort of places she had lived with Alejandro. Never before and never since had she stayed in such a dingy place.

The old woman turned to Maria. "It has a lovely view of the street," she said, crossing the room and opening the blinds. "The bathroom is just down the hall."

Maria shook her head, overwhelmed by the confusion of seeing her childhood home reduced to such poor condition. Would anyone actually pay money to sleep there, she wondered. Sharing a bathroom with strangers, and trying to rest on the narrow, sagging bed? "Sorry," Maria began, "I'm not interested, I..." Seeing the woman's look of disappointment she felt obligated to explain. "I lived here as a child," she said. "This was my nanny's room, and I'm not really looking for anywhere to stay. I don't even know why I came here. I was just passing by, and I wanted to see my old home. I'm sorry to waste your time."

"No, no," the old woman cried. "It's okay. You want to see the rest of the rooms? I don't mind."

Maria shook her head, unable to bear the thought of seeing her beautiful room or the formerly elegant living room decorated so poorly. "No, thank you. I really have to get going. I'm supposed to meet a friend." Quickly she turned and left, letting herself out the front door and taking the stairs to the ground floor. I shouldn't have come here, she told herself. I'd rather remember it like it was.

She wandered slowly back toward Sol. She was a little early to meet Katherine, but she would find somewhere to sit down and wait.

Katherine and Ricardo entered the Plaza del Sol, and Katherine saw that some sort of demonstration was taking place. A dozen members of the Guardia Civil stood in the plaza. Katherine looked at the gathering with curiosity, but following Ricardo's lead kept to the outside, away from the commotion. On the far side of the plaza Katherine saw a lone woman standing in front of the shop where she and Maria had agreed to meet, looking around curiously. She kissed Ricardo lightly on each cheek, said good-bye, tucking the slip of paper with his phone number into her pocket. As she started across the plaza she wondered what Maria would be like after so many years.

CHAPTER
EIGHT

Daniel sat back and watched his son. Their party for two had been a success, but he was tired and wanted to go home. Andy knew it was his birthday and was using the knowledge to his full advantage, ignoring most of Daniel's directions unless they were repeated again and again. When Andy looked his way he motioned to his son, but Andy took off in the other direction. By the time Daniel reached the play area Andy was inside a small tunnel, laughing hysterically. "You have to get me!" he shouted.

Daniel leaned down peering into the tunnel. "Andy, come out. We have to go home."

"No!" Andy shouted, then laughed again.

"Andy, I want you to come out now!" Daniel crouched at the end of the tunnel reaching his hand out toward his son.

"No! You have to get me." Andy was on his hands and knees, just out of reach.

Daniel felt irritated. "I can't come in there. It's too small. Now come out!" he said angrily. Andy laughed and crawled further from the entrance, enjoying the game.

"Andy! You're making me very mad. Come out here now! Anyway, I need to talk to you about Mommy." He had not yet told Andy that Katherine would not be home as planned, or that the party had been rescheduled.

Suddenly serious, Andy scrambled out of the tunnel. "Mommy's home?" he asked excitedly. "Is Mommy home now?"

Taking his son's hand so further escape was impossible Daniel replied "No, not yet. Mommy had to change her plans. She's coming home in a few days.

Andy twisted, trying to free his hand. "When? Is she coming home now?"

"Not now, Tuesday." Daniel held tightly, refusing to release his son.

"What's Tuesday? Is it tomorrow?"

Daniel stopped and knelt down by his son, still holding his hand firmly. "Tomorrow is Saturday, then Sunday, then Monday. After that she's coming."

Andy's face crumpled in fury and sorrow. "You said she was coming when I went to bed!" he shouted. "I want Mommy to come home now!"

Daniel pulled Andy closer to him and spoke softly, "I know. I did say she was coming home when you went to bed. But it's going to be Tuesday, when you go to bed."

Andy stopped, confused by this line of thinking, then changed the subject. "I don't want to go to bed. I'm not tired."

Choosing not to answer Daniel shepherded Andy to the car. He considered stopping off at McDonalds since it had gotten so late, but decided his stomach couldn't handle any more fast food, and so he drove home, ignoring Andy's non-stop stream of chatter. As soon as they entered the apartment, Andy began to run around in circles. Daniel tried in vain to settle him down or interest him in a toy, but Andy continued at full speed and full volume. Scooping Andy into his arms Daniel carried him to his room. "You play in here while I get dinner started," he directed his son. He waited until Andy was engrossed in playing with a large truck, and then quietly left the room.

In the kitchen he sat at the table for a minute, worn out by the week he had just completed. Without getting up he opened the fridge and surveyed the contents. Half a pizza, a pack of carrots, a stalk of celery, onions, some beef he had set out to defrost, and now didn't feel like cooking. He was distracted and moody tonight, aware that he still had to call everyone and explain Katherine's change of plans and reschedule the party.

Sighing he got to his feet and removed the beef from the shelf. It wouldn't keep another day, so he'd better cook it. He opened the pantry and spotted the wok, wedged into the back corner, buried under a pile of miscellaneous items. "Damn pantry," he muttered aloud. "Always a mess. Why can't we live somewhere with a little more space?" Even as he said it he recognized that his exhaustion was the cause of discontent. The apartment they had was great, bigger than anything they had looked at in Manhattan. Leaning over a box that was sitting in the middle of the pantry floor he began moving things. Styrofoam cups, paper plates, a box of Dixie cups in bright colors. One by one he moved them into a new pile, freeing the wok. As he reached into the pantry one last time he heard the answering machine in the living room beep and the electronic voice, "You have deleted two messages."

"Andy! No!" Daniel yelled. He scrambled to get out of the pantry. The wok bumped against the cups and plates he had piled beside it, knocking them to the floor. He emerged from the doorway to see Andy climbing down from the table, smiling. He stormed into the living room, grabbed Andy firmly by the arms, and marched him back to his bedroom. "Stay in there until I have dinner ready!" he ordered.

Looking up at him Andy's eyes filled with tears. "I just wanted to show Mommy I 'member how to do that."

Still angry Daniel replied, "Well Mommy isn't here, and I told you not to touch that machine any more. Now don't leave this room!" Andy sank into a heap on the floor and began sobbing. Daniel glared at him, unable at the moment to feel any sympathy, then slammed Andy's door loudly, making his point. He returned to the kitchen and glanced at the pantry, now even more disastrous than it had been. Going to the refrigerator he removed onions, a green pepper, and several carrots. He pulled some potatoes from the storage bin, washed it all, and began chopping. After five minutes of steady chopping his frustration began to ease, and he could feel compassion for his son, who after all just missed his mother. Quietly he went down the hallway to check on Andy.

Andy sat in his room, quiet now, looking at a book Katherine liked to read him. Hearing Daniel he looked up, his face grubby and streaked with tears. For a moment they stared at each other. Andy's lower lip quivered slightly. "Hey Buddy," Daniel said, "Come here." He held out his arms and Andy ran to him, burying his head in Daniel's neck. "Sorry I got mad," Daniel said, "but you really do have to leave that machine alone."

"Mommy wouldn't get mad," Andy reminded him. "Mommy would laugh."

Looking at his son seriously he instructed, "Even if Mommy would laugh, if Daddy tells you to leave something alone, you don't touch. Understand?"

Andy nodded solemnly. "Sorry, Daddy."

"Alright. Now why don't you come in the kitchen with me and you can help make dinner."

Saturday morning Andy slept late. Daniel was thankful for the quiet moment. Taking his morning coffee into the sitting room he calculated the time difference. 1:30 PM in Paris now. He could call Katherine while Andy was sleeping. He dialed the number and asked to be put through to her room. A moment later the clerk came back on. "I'm sorry sir. There's no answer."

"Could you tell her I called?"

"Of course sir," and the efficient clerk took his name and number, promising to deliver the message.

Daniel sipped his coffee, imagining Katherine doing the same while relaxing in a Parisian café. He missed her, and felt lonely for adult conversation this morning. He called his brother, who wasn't in, and left a message just saying hi. Mentally he reviewed a list of Andy's friends wondering if anyone would be up for a trip to the Brooklyn Children's Museum, so both he and Andy could talk to someone their own age. Before he could make any calls he heard Andy's bed creaking. A moment later the apartment shook as Andy literally jumped out of bed. He came tearing down the hall and dove onto the couch beside Daniel, kicking him in the process. He had a huge grin on his face. Laying on the couch he bounced up and down, his head hitting Daniel's leg.

Daniel watched him, unsmiling. "Hey buddy," he said, "I was thinking maybe we'd go over to the Children's Museum today. See if Kelly or Justin can come along. How's that sound?"

"No," Andy shouted.

"No? Why not? You like the museum."

"Mommy," Andy replied, reverting to baby talking. "Airport. Mommy."

"Mommy's not coming to the airport today. She's coming later."

"You said today!" Andy shouted, upset over the confusion.

"I did say today, but then I told you Mommy had to change her plans. Remember?"

"I want Mommy!"

"She'll be here soon, but not today." Daniel reached over and pulled his son into his arms, hoping to give some comfort.

"Tomorrow?" Andy asked hopefully.

"No, not tomorrow either."

"When?"

"Tell you what," Daniel replied, "You come and eat some breakfast, and later, after the museum, we'll call Mommy up and talk to her."

In reply Andy slid off the couch and bounced into the kitchen. "I'm a bunny. See? See me being a bunny?"

While Andy ate Daniel made calls, trying to round up some company for himself. Eventually he reached Andrew's mom who agreed that a trip to the museum sounded like fun. She had been a last resort because Daniel found her tiresome, but Andy really enjoyed her 3 children, so if nothing else the kids would help entertain one another. He asked about her husband coming along, and grimaced to hear he worked Saturdays, so there would only be her to talk with. Never mind, he told himself, I'm doing it for Andy anyway. He hurried Andy through breakfast so there would be time to run a few errands before going.

As soon as they returned home Andy ran to the phone. "Call Mommy now," he demanded.

"Ok. Just let me get her number."

"You don't know Mommy's phone number?" Andy looked alarmed.

"I have it written down. I just don't remember it."

Andy scowled at Daniel. "Even I know my phone number," he said. "Everybody should know your phone number. That's what my teacher says."

"It's just the hotel she's at. Her phone number is here, the same as ours."

Andy just stared, looking confused. Retrieving the number, Daniel dialed the hotel. Once again the desk clerk told him no one was answering. "I left a message earlier. Has it been picked up?"

"One moment." There was a pause, then the clerk returned. "No sir, that message hasn't been picked up yet."

"Well, I dread seeing that Visa bill," Daniel joked. "I'll try back later."

"Why didn't I talk to Mommy?" Andy shouted as soon as Daniel hung up.

"Mommy wasn't there. She must be out shopping or site seeing."

"You don't even know Mommy's phone number," Andy accused. "You can't find her. You don't even know where she is." Angrily Andy ran out of the room and down the hall to his own bedroom. Daniel debated whether he should follow, or let him calm down on his own. He could hear the angry stomp of feet, but no sobs, so he left Andy alone.

He tried to call two more times later in the day, the last time when it was 1:00 AM in Paris. The surly night clerk didn't speak English, so Daniel tried his high school French, but wasn't sure the clerk understood. Eventually he gave up. Katherine would call tomorrow. She had probably stayed out late and wanted to call back when she was sure Andy would be awake. She was always forgetting about the time difference. If she remembered she would realize that Andy was still awake. He hoped she remembered the difference when she woke up. He didn't want a call at 3:00 AM.

The next morning after breakfast Daniel put in Andy's favorite video, a sing-along that his parents had bought last Christmas, then quietly went to his room and tried to call again. The surly desk clerk was still on duty. Speaking carefully Daniel asked for Katherine's room. After a brief pause the clerk came back on the line, and a flood of French greeted Daniel.

"Parlez vous Anglais?" Daniel asked helplessly. "I don't understand." Everything the clerk said was incomprehensible. He tried for five minutes, then hung up, frustrated. He tried again later in the day, reaching another clerk, but getting the same stream of French, and understanding none of it. Finally he resolved to wait until Katherine called. Though vaguely worried, he reassured himself it was just Katherine being thoughtless. He could imagine the conversation when she did call.

Him: "Where have you been. I've been calling and calling."

Her: "Oh yeah, I got your message. I was going to call back but then I got caught up in shopping, and next thing I knew it was too late."

Him: "Too late there is just right here."

Her: "Oh hell. I forgot about the time difference. What time is it there now? Am I calling in the middle of the night?"

And on and on. It wouldn't occur to her to apologize for the anxiety she caused him, nor for the difficulties Andy had dealing with her absence. She would go on and on about the things she had bought, and he would worry about the bills, and she would assure him that everything was much cheaper than buying the same items in New York, and he would think, but not say, that much cheaper than New York still didn't mean they could afford it. He would be relieved to hear from her, and not mention his anger at her long silence, not wanting to fight long distance.

He puttered around the apartment, not wanting to leave in case she called. Andy was restless, but didn't ask for her. To keep him quiet Daniel fed one video after another into the VCR, and Andy sat glued in front of the TV. By dinnertime Katherine still hadn't called, and Andy hadn't asked about her. Daniel fixed Andy a peanut butter sandwich then sent him to his room to play. He decided to try Katherine one more time. Automatically he glanced into Andy's room as he passed by. Andy stood by the bed, an action figure in his left hand, and a bear in his right. He was holding a conversation between the two, bouncing the "talking" one up and down while the listener was held still.

"I know where your Mommy is," the action figure said.

"No you don't," answered the bear.

"Uh huh. She's dead. She went to Paris and she dieded."

"She did not," the bear yelled. "We just don't know her phone number."

"She don't have a phone number. Her phone number is the same as ours," the action figure taunted.

"You're stupid. I don't like you." The bear kicked the action figure, and Andy threw the figure across the room. Daniel pushed the door open wider and stepped into the room. He sat on the bed and pulled Andy onto his lap.

"Hey buddy, are you worried about Mommy being gone?"

"No." Andy kept his face turned down, not looking at Daniel.

Daniel gently took Andy's head and turned it toward him. "You seem a little worried to me."

"No I'm not." Andy shook his head furiously and turned away again.

"Tomorrow we'll call Mommy at a different phone number. We can call her at work. I know that number."

Quickly Andy turned to face Daniel. "What is it?"

"What? The number?"

Andy nodded. Daniel made one up, knowing Andy wouldn't remember, but might feel reassured. "We'll call her tomorrow. Okay?"

Andy nodded again, his head resting against Daniel's chest. "You tired?"

Another nod. "Let's get you to bed." He changed Andy into pajamas, and started to read a story, but Andy was asleep before the first page was done. Quietly he crept out of the room, relieved that Andy was asleep, and angry at Katherine for her silence.

The phone woke Daniel. Groggily he groped for it, glancing at the clock. 3:08. She had forgotten the time difference.

"Hello."

"Where the hell is your wife," a voice on the other end screamed at him.

"What? Who is this?"

"Joseph Strauss. From the Strauss-Brach Agency. Do you know where your wife is?" The man was roaring at the top of his voice.

"Paris." Daniel said. "You know she's in Paris. You all sent her there." He pushed the covers away, fighting sleepiness, trying to clear his head.

"Hell she's in Paris. She's not in any part of Paris she belongs in. She had a fight with our Paris representative about having to redo a shoot today, insisted she needed to be home for the weekend, and disappeared. The hotel says she's still staying there, but they can't actually tell me when they saw her. She didn't show up for the shoot this morning."

Daniel sat up, fully awake now. "She's not there?" His voice was frantic and he shivered with cold. "When did they see her? I haven't talked to her for days."

"What. You don't talk to your wife? Haven't you heard of long distance?"

Daniel was mad. Katherine had always said this guy was a jerk. He willed himself to stop shaking and to think calmly. "There's no need to be rude. I'm obviously very concerned."

"No need to be rude! I've got a million dollar account and no one there to direct the shoot, and you tell me not to be rude. Your wife is supposed to be there. If we lose this account it's her fault."

"Hey," Daniel shouted into the phone to get his attention. "I've lost a wife. That's more important than an account."

"What do you mean you've lost a wife? Don't you know where your wife is?"

"No! I've been telling you I haven't heard from her. I tried to reach her all weekend, but she was never in. She didn't return my calls."

Mr. Strauss was finally quiet. "What's your name, son?" he asked.

"Daniel."

"Daniel, are you telling me that you don't know where your wife is? She didn't pull this because she was upset about being kept there over the weekend?"

"That's right. I talked to her on Friday. She said she needed to stay. That was the last time I talked to her. She was going to do some shopping in Paris over the weekend."

"Well, we can't find her. I'm sorry to tell you this way, sorry I hollered at you, but we can't find her. I figured she had just come back home, angry about the whole mess."

Daniel shook his head. "Katherine wouldn't do that. She's not like that."

"No? Well I've never met her myself. No way I would know. All I know is she was plenty mad on Friday."

"Not by the time I talked to her. She was unhappy. She had to miss our son's fourth birthday."

"Son? I didn't know she had a son. Works a lot of hours for a mother, doesn't she?"

"Yes, she does. She's been hoping for a promotion." Daniel shook his head at the stupidity of their conversation. The only thing that mattered was finding Katherine. "We have to find her. She could have been hurt in an accident. Maybe the embassy didn't know who to contact." Even as he said it he remembered how he had carefully written his own name and phone number into her passport under "Emergency Contact".

"Well, uh, David was it?"

"Daniel."

"Okay, Daniel. I'm real sorry about this call. I'll get some people on it right away. I'm sure everything's okay. Just a misunderstanding somewhere. Don't worry. I'll call you as soon as I hear something."

Daniel hung up wondering how he was supposed to avoid worrying after a 3:00 AM phone call to tell him his wife was missing. Something must be wrong, he thought. Something has happened to Katherine. His mind raced through the possibilities. Hit by a car, got sick, kidnapped. It never occurred to him that Katherine might have left him.

At four AM he could stand it no longer. He called the agency. The voice mail answered, asking him to call back during regular hours, or transfer to an extension. Of course, Strauss would have been calling from home, he reminded himself. He dialed information and asked for the number. "I'm sorry sir. The number is unlisted."

"It's an emergency," he shouted.

"I'm sorry. I'm not authorized to give out this number. I suggest you contact the police if you have an emergency." She hung up.

Daniel sat holding the receiver in his hand, unsure of what to do next. Eventually he replaced the receiver and picked up the phone book. Who does this sort of thing, he wondered? This isn't the sort of thing people just know how to handle.

He flipped through the phone book frantically until he found the government pages, then dialed one number after another, receiving no answer. Several hours had passed before offices opened and Daniel's call was answered. Quickly he explained his problem. The woman who answered sounded bored, as if people disappeared every day. "We don't handle that here," she said. "You'll need to get in touch with the Crisis Management office." She gave him the number.

Again he dialed, praying someone would be in at this early hour. A woman picked up. Frantically Daniel began pouring out the story to her. "...boss called to say she never showed up for work this morning...haven't been able to reach her all weekend...figured she was just out..."

"Sir!" The woman's loud voice stopped Daniel. "I need you to calm down. I can't possibly help if I can't follow the story. Now, what is your name?"

"Daniel Bayley," he replied.

"And the nature of your emergency?"

"My wife is missing. I can't find my wife. She went to ..."

"Sir! Slow down. Just answer the questions. Now, your wife is missing? When did you last talk to her?"

"Friday, last Friday. I've tried to reach her all weekend." He stopped, took a deep breath, and tried to calm himself.

"Your wife's birthday?"

"October 2, 1955."

"Do you know her passport number?"

"Um, I've got it. I can get it for you." He tried to think where he had put the copy of her passport. "Wait, I'm going to get it okay?" Putting down the phone he hurried to the living room and searched through the file cabinet. Taking the whole folder of important documents out he returned to the bedroom. "Ok, I'm back. Just a minute. I'm looking for it." He opened the file rummaging through a stack of items they had determined were important. Birth certificates, warranties, rental agreement. He threw aside several papers then grabbed up the photocopy. "Here it is. I've got it." His eyes scanned the page looking for the number. "Ok, here, 0788F2698."

She repeated it back to him to verify then went on. "Reason for her trip?"

"Business. She works for the Strauss Brach agency in New York. She was directing a photo shoot in Paris."

"Where was she staying?"

"Um, hold on. I've got it here somewhere." Again he put down the phone and crossed the room searching for the scrap of paper Katherine had left him. He remembered how she had laughed when he insisted he wanted the name of the hotel. Thinking it unimportant she had scribbled it on the back of a receipt and tossed it on her dresser. He picked up a pile of receipts and searched them. Frantically he glanced at the phone as if to ensure himself that the woman on the other end hadn't left. He pushed aside Katherine's makeup and brushes in frustration, not expecting to find the paper.

Abruptly he stopped and took a deep breath. Calm down and think, he told himself. Where did I put it? He started for the living room, then stopped, remembering that he had called from the bedroom the last time. He glanced about the room hoping for inspiration, then crossed to the dirty laundry, grabbed up his pants and reached into the pocket. There he found the missing paper.

Picking up the phone he asked, "Are you still there? I've found it. Okay it's the Hotel Saint Honore. It's...Hmm. She didn't leave me the address. I don't actually know where it is. I've got the phone number. Maybe you could call?"

"What's the number?" the voice asked, still bored.

He gave it to her.

"And you said you last talked to her when?"

"Friday. I talked to her on Friday. And I tried all weekend..."

"Any friends or contacts that you know of in Paris?" she interrupted.

"No friends. She's got some business contacts. You know, people she's working with."

"Names?"

"I don't know. I've never met them. She probably mentioned them before but I don't remember. Maybe her boss would know. He's bound to..."

"His name?"

Daniel gave the name and office phone number.

"And a number where I can reach you?"

He gave his own number, then asked, "When will I hear something?"

"Sir, I really don't know. I'll have to get in touch with the Paris authorities and they will conduct an investigation. We'll let you know if anything comes up."

"But something's got to come up, doesn't it? I mean she can't just disappear!"

The bored voice said, "I'll be in touch sir. Goodbye." She hung up.

Daniel replaced the receiver, then picked it up and called her back. "I want the name of the Paris authorities. The ones you said would investigate."

"Well sir, I have no idea who will investigate. How would you expect me to know that?"

"Well who are you going to tell? You've got to have someone you can contact."

She spoke slowly, as if talking to a child. "I'll contact the American Embassy in Paris. They'll get in touch with the proper authorities and assist in the investigation."

"Then their number. Give me their number." He picked up a notepad that sat by the phone.

"Sir, there's really nothing to be gained by calling the Embassy. I mean you really are just going to have to wait..."

"My wife disappeared," Daniel shouted. "Don't you understand? She's gone! She's missing and no one knows where she went! How do you expect me to just wait?"

"There's really no reason to shout, sir. I'm sure it will all work out fine in the end. This sort of thing really isn't as rare as you'd think. People seem to disappear, but generally they've just moved to another hotel or another city and forgotten to tell you. I'm sure it won't help, but if it makes you feel better, here's the embassy's number." She told him and he scribbled it down.

As soon as they hung up Daniel dialed the embassy and explained the problem. Waiting to be connected to the proper person he thought about the woman's words, hoping she might be right. It was possible. Katherine would never have thought to tell him if she changed hotels.

There was probably something wrong at the first one. Bad service, or the water heater went out. But still, she should have made it to work.

His thoughts were interrupted by a woman coming on the line. "Okay sir? Do you know if your wife registered with the embassy when she entered the country?" This woman also sounded bored, as if she too were used to stories of missing people.

"No, I don't know. I doubt she did. It was just for a short visit."

"Mmmm, Hold on for a minute." The line clicked, then silence. After several minutes she came back on. "Did you file a report in the U.S.? We haven't gotten anything."

"I just called this morning. They couldn't have gotten it to you yet. That's why I wanted to call you right now. So you would be aware of the situation."

"Mmm," she muttered, feeling sympathy for the obviously distraught man. "Well, I really can't do anything until I get the report, but I can tell you it's probably a misunderstanding. You know, people travel overseas, and they're so excited they completely forget that people back home are worried about them. Happens pretty often. Someone changes their plans and they just forget to tell you. They usually show up after a few days. I wouldn't worry."

"But Katherine isn't like that. She wasn't just traveling, she was working. She didn't show up for work this morning."

"Try not to get too concerned sir. She may have had a delay. Gone out of the city for the weekend, and gotten held up on the return. The railway workers are staging a strike today. Highly likely a good number of people aren't where they are expected."

"She wouldn't have done that. She would have told me if she planned to go anywhere. I talked to her Friday. Her plan was to stay in Paris and do some shopping."

"We'll check into it sir, as soon as we get the report, but really, there's probably nothing to worry about. These things happen all the time, and 99% of them resolve themselves in a few days. Now, let me get your number and I'll call you if I can find anything out. The report should be here any minute." She took down his information then hung up.

Daniel picked up the phone and dialed his parent's house next. Quickly, while they were still half asleep, he told them the story. "Can you help me with Andy?" he asked. "I don't know what to tell him. Don't want to tell him anything until I know something. He can go to the day care today, but could you pick him up this afternoon? Maybe keep him overnight if I haven't heard anything?"

"I'm coming over," his mother said. "You're in no shape to even get him ready to go. He'd know right away that something was wrong, and he'll be scared. He's already upset about Katherine being gone."

Normally Daniel would have protested, insisting that he could handle it, but this morning he didn't. "Thanks Mom. That's a big help."

She arrived 20 minutes later, looking as if she had spent hours getting ready. His mother was like that. She got up each morning looking as if she were walking out of the beauty parlor. She wore black slacks and a sweatshirt with tiny embroidered flowers on it. He put his hand out and touched the sweatshirt. "Katherine picked that out. Last Christmas. She said you'd love it."

His mother gave a sad smile, and hugged him. "Think positive thoughts, dear. We don't know anything yet." She entered Andy's room, and a minute later he heard Andy, protesting at first, and then laughing, happy to see his Grandma.

While she was dressing Andy, Daniel made breakfast. He went into his bedroom, calling out "Breakfast is on the table." He sat on the bed in his room, not wanting Andy to see him, afraid that his appearance would scare his son. He felt certain that both he and Andy had good reason to be afraid.

Once Andy and his mother had gone Daniel showered and dressed, then called his office and the ad agency. The receptionist put him straight through to Mr. Strauss. Unfortunately there was no news. His mind began racing through possibilities again. Hurt in an accident or kidnapped, there's no other reason for her to be missing. She's hurt or in danger. Katherine wouldn't have gone to another hotel. She wouldn't have left the city without telling me. He began calling everyone he knew, irrationally thinking that if all their friends knew, they could be looking for Katherine. Then, realizing he was tying up the phone and preventing anyone from reaching him, he hung up and sat staring at the phone, willing it to ring, trying to calm himself. They said it happens all the time he reminded himself. Both of them said it. It usually resolves itself. I'm sure she's fine. Probably has some perfectly logical explanation. He remained there for hours trying to keep the horrible reality at bay, until the phone rang and pulled him back to awareness. It was his brother, alerted by his mother.

"Any news?" his brother asked, by way of greeting.

Daniel shook his head. "No, nothing."

"Listen Bro, I'm going to come over there. Mom's planning to keep Andy overnight. I don't think you should be alone."

"You don't have to do that. I'll be fine," Daniel said.

"I'll just hang out in case you need anything." He didn't add that their mom had begged him to go, terrified that Daniel would receive bad news while home alone.

Daniel, too tired to protest, agreed for Chuck to come over.

The first thing Chuck said when Daniel opened the door was, "Have you eaten?"

Daniel shook his head. "I'm not hungry."

"Well I'm starved. Come on. You can keep me company." Chuck entered the kitchen and began rummaging through the fridge. He pulled out sandwich fixings: lunchmeat, bread, mayonnaise, lettuce, tomato, cheese, and mustard. Taking two plates from the cabinet he made giant sandwiches. "Here." He shoved one in front of Daniel. "You've got to eat. You can't just sit here wasting away." Half-heartedly Daniel picked at the sandwich, comparing it to what Katherine would have made. Will make, he corrected himself. She will be back to make sandwiches again.

After a few bites he gave up eating. "I'm going to call the embassy. Don't want to miss them by calling too late." He rang through and was connected to the same woman he had spoken with before. This time she introduced herself, Mrs. Holt.

"Just a moment, let me pull up the records," she said.

He waited, wondering if Paris really had so many missing Americans that she couldn't remember his earlier call. After a moment she came back on the line.

"Now, Mr. Bayley, here's what's been done. We've checked all the major hospitals in the city. We have no reports of unidentified persons fitting her description. Of course we've also contacted the local police, no record of arrest or anything like that. I also checked with her hotel which confirms that she has not checked out, so I'm sure she'll turn up shortly.

"She hasn't checked out but they haven't seen her either! Just because she hasn't checked out doesn't mean everything is okay."

"Of course not. All I'm saying is these cases usually resolve themselves. Unless of course she doesn't want to be found."

"What? What are you talking about?"

"Well, she may have chosen to disappear. She may not wish to be found. It happens."

Daniel gripped the receiver tightly, turning his knuckles white. "You mean run away? Be hiding from us?" he shook his head incredulously.

Mrs. Holt's voice remained calm and soothing "It does happen," she said.

"She may also have been kidnapped or injured," Daniel shouted. "Why do you assume she ran off?"

"Mr. Bayley. I'm not assuming anything. I realize she may be injured, and we're checking into that. All I'm trying to tell you is that these cases usually resolve themselves. Either it turns out to be a misunderstanding, and the person never knew she was missing, or it turns out to be someone who disappeared because she wanted to. In the second case the missing person often reconsiders and turns up after a few days. Try not to worry too much. I expect you'll be hearing from her shortly."

"But aren't you going to do anything? Is that all you suggest? That I just wait?" He cursed the French in his mind.

"Of course I will do something. I will continue to contact the hospitals in the area to see if they have an unidentified American who was injured or killed, and I will be in touch with the Paris police. Do you have a recent photograph of your wife?"

"Yeah. Yeah, of course I have a photograph."

"Well, why don't you send it to me. That will help with identification. Does she have any identifying marks?"

"Identifying marks? What are those?"

"You know. Scars, birthmarks, that sort of thing."

"No, I don't think so," Daniel paused. "Wait. She does have a scar. She had a cesarean when our son was born. She has a scar from that."

"Very good. Any unusual marks are extremely helpful. Now, why don't you send me the photograph and I'll be back in touch."

The hours dragged by. Daniel refused to leave the apartment, and simply sat by the phone waiting for it to ring. Chuck took over the house, producing boring bachelor meals, usually sandwiches or something out of a can. Daniel ate without comment, mechanically shoving the food in simply because Chuck told him to. He forgot Andy completely, leaving his mother to deal with the boy, while his mind played an endless cycle of worry. Injured, kidnapped, ran off. Injured, kidnapped, ran off. That's ridiculous. Katherine would never run off. She's got to be hurt or kidnapped. Or dead. Please God, not dead, he prayed. He wasn't a religious man, but there didn't seem to be anything else to try.

Chuck did his best to reassure him, reminding him that Mrs. Holt knew her business, and that statistically Katherine was likely to turn up unharmed with a reasonable excuse. Daniel tried to concoct scenarios in which Katherine suddenly called and explained her absence, but couldn't think of anything plausible. In the end he just sat, eating the sandwiches or pizza that Chuck produced, fighting sleep in case someone would call and he wouldn't hear the phone. He called Paris twice a day, with no results, hearing the same unsatisfying news: she hadn't been located. By Wednesday night he was a wreck.

"They've got to do something more," he shouted to no one in particular, then to Chuck, "I've got to go over there. If they aren't going to find her I will."

"Try Mrs. Holt again tomorrow," Chuck replied. "She's been really helpful. Explain it's been long enough for Katherine to resolve problems, long enough to reconsider. Ask her what else can be done."

The next day Daniel once again dialed the now familiar phone number.

"Ah, Mr. Bayley," Mrs. Holt greeted him kindly. "How are you getting along? Still haven't heard anything?"

"No, I haven't heard anything," Daniel snapped. "I thought that was your job."

"Well, that is my job, so to speak. But it's generally the family who will hear something first. What's it been, three days?"

"Four. It's four days, and that doesn't count the weekend. She might have been missing since Friday. That's nearly a week!"

Mrs. Holt spoke kindly. "Don't give up hope. I admit that it's been a long time, but she may still get in touch. We've had cases that went on longer. By the way, has anyone contacted you in New York? About the investigation, I mean?"

"Here? No. The local agency told me they would refer it to Paris and local authorities would investigate."

"Oh, but I mean contacted you about meeting with you?"

"I don't understand. Meeting with me about what?" Daniel frowned, trying to figure out the conversation.

"The New York investigation. They'll want to talk with you of course."

"Investigate what in New York?" Daniel was still puzzled. "She was in Paris when she disappeared."

"Of course we know that, Mr. Bayley, but I'm sure you understand that we have to be very thorough. A woman is missing. We must investigate all options. I'm not saying this to frighten you, but one possible option is foul play by someone the victim knew. Someone should be contacting you for an interview."

"Someone she knew?" Daniel was puzzled, then outraged as he understood the woman's meaning. "Me! Are you saying they think I did something with Katherine? They think I killed her?"

Mrs. Holt remained calm, her voice soothing. "No. Of course I am not saying that. Just that we must investigate every possibility."

"Oh my God," Daniel shouted. "I can't believe this. My wife is missing, and first you tell me she might have run away, then you tell me maybe I killed her? This is crazy!"

"Unfortunately sir, when the missing person doesn't turn up voluntarily, those two options, or suicide, are found to be true far too often. However, I am also investigating less likely options such as abduction. At this time, we really have no information to tell you."

After Daniel hung up Chuck sat passively at the table, waiting for Daniel to finish ranting about the insanity of the investigation. "You know I wouldn't hurt Katherine. You know she wouldn't run away. She sure wouldn't kill herself! Why don't they investigate some real options?"

"That's just it," Chuck replied. "I know you, so I know those things are true. But they don't know you. They have to think of everything. They have to investigate."

"But while they're investigating lame things, the leads are fading away. I'm going over there. I've got to go over there and make them find her." Before Chuck could answer the phone rang again.

"Mr. Bayley? This is Inspector Fitzgibbons. I'm calling regarding the investigation of your wife's disappearance. I'm very sorry to bother you at a time like this, but I need to arrange a time to come over and talk with you."

"Actually I was just getting ready to arrange a flight to Paris," Daniel said. "I thought I should be there. Hopefully after that there won't be any need for us to talk."

"I'm sorry sir, but I have to insist that you remain in the country until the investigation is completed."

"What?" Daniel shook his head sure he had misunderstood.

"I said that you will need to remain in the country until our investigation is completed."

Daniel threw his hand up in disbelief. "You're joking right? Am I actually a suspect in all this?"

"No sir. At this time we have no suspects. Just standard procedure. You're a critical part of the investigation, and therefore you are required to remain available to us for questioning."

"You've got to be kidding. My wife is missing in a country 3000 miles away, and I'm being treated like a prisoner by the only people who can help me?"

"I'm very sorry sir. We just have to follow standard procedures. If we can arrange a time to meet maybe we can clear this up quickly."

"This is insane," Daniel mouthed to Chuck, pointing to the phone. Aloud he said, "Yeah sure. Just tell me where you're located. I can come over now."

"Actually, I'd like to come to your apartment. We'll need to look through things there."

Daniel sighed and sat down. "Right. Come over anytime. It's not like I'm going anywhere."

"I'll come over now if it's convenient. I'd like to get this cleared up as soon as possible."

Chuck answered the door, surprised to see three men all dressed in dark suits standing there. "Mr. Bayley?"

"Uh, yeah, but you're actually looking for my brother." He stepped back, allowing them into the apartment. The men introduced themselves to Daniel and expressed regret at intruding at such a time. Daniel led the way into the kitchen and sat at the table. Inspector Fitzgibbons joined him. The others remained standing.

"If you don't mind, we could speed this up a bit by doing the apartment check while I ask you a few questions."

"What are you looking for?" Daniel looked at the two men who had remained standing.

"Nothing specific. It's strictly routine."

Daniel shook his head, his shoulders sagging in defeat. "Go ahead. Do whatever you want. Just help me find her."

Inspector Fitzgibbons turned back to Daniel. "Now, we just need to gather some facts." He pulled out a notebook, wrote something at the top, and began. They covered everything. How Daniel and Katherine had met, how long they dated, when they were married. Was the marriage good? Any signs of trouble, talk of divorce, depression, suicide attempts? What about the trip? How did he feel about his wife traveling on business? Did she do it often? Did she enjoy going away? Any belief she might have a lover? Did he? Children?

He wrote everything down. Page after page of the details of their life together. He listed family members and friends, all now required to go through similar questioning if the investigators decided to talk to them.

While Daniel endured the questioning, the other two inspectors wandered the apartment. They had brought along a search warrant, so no permission was needed to go through Katherine's closets, her desk, or any other part of the house. Chuck trailed along behind them knowing Daniel would want to hear what they did.

They started in the bedroom, searching through the closets, looking at clothes and making notes. He listened to snatches of their conversation, and assumed this part of the investigation was focused on two things: Had she taken enough clothes to run away, and were there any bloody or torn clothes hidden away somewhere. They searched through the jewelry box, noting what was found there. They spent a long time in Andy's room, searching toy boxes, his closet, and under the bed.

"How many children?" the inspector asked Chuck.

"Uh, one. Just one."

"Boy or girl?"

"Boy."

"Age?"

"Four. He just turned four."

The inspector made some notes on his pad. "Where is he now?"

"With my mother. Our mother."

The man nodded and moved on to the living room. "That desk and computer hers?" He pointed to the corner of the room.

"Well mostly, yeah. She'd work a lot in the evenings."

One man turned on the computer, while the other opened the desk drawers. They worked silently for several minutes, checking computer files, bringing up documents, reading letters found in the desk. "Hey, look at this," the one at the desk said. In his hand he held a letter. The other glanced over his shoulder and read it.

"We'll want to bring that in for copying. Could be significant. Depressed sounding woman. Think she's a suicide?"

The inspector shrugged. "Never know. No one's found a note, but they don't always leave one. Let's see if we can get a number for this lady friend. Might want to talk to her."

Chuck stood off to the side, wondering about the exchange. Finally he broke in, "Mind if I get a look at that?" he asked.

"Oh, sorry sir, it's against procedures. This is private correspondence. We have a policy against sharing it outside the investigation." Chuck retreated to the corner of the room and resumed silently watching.

When they left Chuck debated whether he should tell Daniel about the letter they took. In the end he decided to wait, not wanting Daniel to be more upset.

No sooner had he made the decision than Daniel asked, "Did they say anything? Do anything that seemed unusual?"

Chuck sighed. Not volunteering the information was one thing, but he wasn't going to lie to his brother. "They did take something from Katherine's desk. They wouldn't show it to me, but both of them found it interesting, and one said they should 'try to find this woman'. I'm sure it's nothing really."

"Not nothing. They probably found a letter that was there. I found it myself a couple of days ago when Andy dumped the drawer. It's from Sally, Katherine's old roommate. It was a really weird letter. Sally kept reassuring Katherine that she should be happy and appreciate having Andy and me. She wrote about how awful it can be to be single and how everyone has days they doubt their own lives. It really made me wonder. I don't know what Katherine wrote to prompt such a response. She had to have been griping about us."

"But still, you don't really believe Katherine would do anything, do you? I mean she wouldn't disappear, and I don't see her as suicidal. I can see that Katherine is the kind of independent woman who might decide to divorce you, keep the kid and the job, and do it all herself, but she wouldn't just disappear."

Daniel was stung by his brother's comments about Katherine, but had to admit it was a pretty accurate assessment of her. She didn't need anyone, probably never would. She might choose to share their lives, but she never forgot she could make it on her own. Still, he was sure she wouldn't disappear. "No," he answered Chuck. "I'm sure she wouldn't run off, but that letter may make them think she would, and then this investigation is going to go no where."

Chuck nodded his agreement. "You're right. It'll throw them off the real trail." He sat silently for a minute, his thoughts roaming, then asked, "Have you talked to her? To Sally?"

Daniel shook his head. "I thought about calling her when I found the letter, but I felt like such a snoop. When I found it I read it because Katherine usually shares her letters anyway, but after the first few lines it was obvious this was a private letter. I read it anyway."

"That doesn't matter now. What matters is finding Katherine, and if Sally has any information that might be useful you need to talk to her. You don't have to tell her you read the letter. You can tell her the whole story and that they found the letter."

Daniel nodded. "You're right. I should call her. I'll do it now." He opened the desk and pulled out an address book. Flipping through it he found the number and dialed the phone. Sally answered on the second ring.

"Hi Sally. It's Daniel Bayley." They talked occasionally, but he was never sure how many Daniel's Sally might know.

"Daniel, how are you?"

He wondered if he was imagining the strain in her voice, or if it was really there. "Um, okay," he replied automatically. What am I saying, he thought. I'm not okay, it's just that I don't know how to tell her, don't know what to say.

"Is Katherine back from Paris?" Sally asked. "I've been trying to reach her there, but never found her."

Daniel froze. How did Sally know about Paris. Katherine had said it was a last minute thing. She hadn't called anyone to tell them she was going. "How'd you know she was in Paris?" he asked.

"Oh, she called me. Asked me to call her back."

"When," he screamed. "When did you talk to her?"

"Daniel," Sally replied "Are you all right? What's going on?"

"She's missing, Sally," he blurted out. "Katherine is missing. She's been gone for four days, maybe longer."

"Missing? What are you talking about?"

"Missing! She went to Paris on business, then the company changed her plans and made her stay for the weekend, and all weekend I tried to reach her but I couldn't, then on Monday she never showed up for work. No one's seen her since, and I haven't talked to her since Friday morning." He blurted it all out in a flurry, not sure if he was making sense. "So when did she call you and what did she say?"

"Um, Friday I think. I'm not really sure. I was gone for the weekend. Her message was on the machine when I got back."

"Well what did she say?"

Sally hesitated, not wanting to add worry to Daniel's life. "It was kind of weird, Daniel. She said she really needed someone to talk to and she didn't want it to be you. Then she asked me to call her."

"Didn't want it to be me? She specifically said that?"

Sally nodded vigorously, thinking that was exactly what she'd said. Aloud she simply murmured "Yeah."

"But how could she say that? How could she do that?"

"Daniel," Sally began, obviously trying to calm him, "Sometimes women want to talk to other women. It doesn't necessarily mean anything."

Daniel stood shaking his head, unable to speak. Who was Katherine? Why was she writing mysterious letters about unhappiness and making calls from Paris to talk about things she couldn't tell him? That wasn't the Katherine he knew. Wordlessly he handed the phone to Chuck.

"You want me to talk to her?" Chuck asked, but Daniel was already leaving the room.

"Uh, hello?" he said.

"Daniel?"

"No, this is Chuck, Daniel's brother."

"Oh, is Daniel alright? Maybe I shouldn't have said that." Even as she voiced her concern Sally knew that if Katherine was missing there was no alternative to telling all she knew.

"What did you say anyway? I only heard half the conversation." His brow was furrowed with worry about the news he would hear.

"I told him Katherine called me from Paris and left a message. She asked me to call her in Paris. She specifically said she needed to talk to someone and it couldn't be Daniel."

Chuck's eyes opened wider at Sally's revelation. "Well, what did she have to say?" he asked.

"I don't know. After I got the message I was never able to reach her. I left a couple of messages for her, but when I didn't hear back I figured it didn't matter."

Chuck shook his head. How could she think it didn't matter. But then who would have thought differently. No one would expect a message like that to come just before a person disappears. "Well, what about the letter?" he asked.

"Letter? What letter?"

"There was a letter you wrote to Katherine. It was found here. You wrote a bunch of stuff about being happy with what she has and appreciating her family. What was that all about?"

"I wrote several letters like that to Katherine. She'd write me sometimes, or call, and she'd be unhappy about something, so I'd try to cheer her up. Try to make her recognize the good life she has."

"But was she unhappy with Daniel? Did she say that?" Hearing his name Daniel crept back into the room and stood close, trying to hear the responses.

"No," Sally said. "It wasn't Daniel. I'm sure she loves Daniel. She's just confused about what she wants. You know, she wants to succeed in her job, but that takes time away from her family. When she tries to spend more time with family she feels frustrated at work. It's a struggle that lots of women deal with. But it wasn't specifically Daniel. Katherine's always been complex that way. She seems so sure of herself, but inside she's always doubting. She's been that way ever since I've known her."

Chuck nodded in relief, glancing at his brother to be sure he had heard the conversation. "Well, listen, you're probably going to get a visit, or at least a call, from someone about that letter. If you can tell them what you just told me it might be a big help. They seem to be focusing mostly on the idea that Katherine ran away."

Sally frowned at that news. "Ran away? No, I'm sure she wouldn't have run away. That's not like her." Even as she said it Sally was aware that she didn't really know Katherine all that well any longer. Things had been strange, the letters, the call. Maybe she could have run away.

"I'd better let you go. Daniel will want to hear what you've told me." They said goodbye and hung up. Daniel looked notably relieved that Sally had affirmed the idea Katherine wouldn't run off. He tried right then to reach Inspector Fitzgibbons and tell him, but the inspector was unavailable. His secretary assured him that she would pass along the message and added that it might be in Daniel's best interest to stop contacting people they might want to interview.

Daniel hung up, outraged. "What do they think, that I'm a criminal?" he screamed. "They're screwing up any chance of finding her. She needs my help now!" He spent the rest of the day sitting alone, staring into space, until eventually he fell asleep on the couch and Chuck left him there, stuffing a blanket under his head for a pillow.

CHAPTER
NINE

Chavo hummed to himself, happy to be free for the day. He swayed gently with the motion of the subway as it raced through the tunnels. As the train slowed down, approaching the station, he stood by the door, anxious to be outside, eager for the money he would soon have. As soon as the train stopped he burst through the doors and ran toward the stairs. He dodged around slower people, and jumped nimbly over a subway musician's moneybox. He was half way up the last flight of stairs when an explosion rocked the ground, throwing him off balance. He fell backwards, rolling to the bottom of the stairs. He gasped for breath as much from fear as from the fall, then slowly he got up and crept up the stairs. Poking his head out of the subway entrance he saw mass confusion.

Several people lay on the ground. Some of them were moaning and crying. A few members of the Guardia Civil were trying desperately to restore order, while several others lay on the ground. Creeping out of the entrance Chavo looked at the two women lying nearest him. One of them moaned softly. The other was very still, and blood poured from a wound on her head. He stared at both women for a moment longer then looked away, feeling sick. He'd never seen so much blood before.

On the ground lay a suitcase and two purses. Chavo grabbed them and ducked back into the subway. Inside people milled about, some in shock, others in panic. Two members of the Guardia Civil had entered the subway station and were trying to calm the crowd. Chavo dogged one person after another until he reached the subway platform.

The train stood with its doors closed, and he grabbed them, trying to force them open. An old man took his shoulder and turned him away from the train. "The train isn't running now," he said. "They don't want anyone responsible to escape." Chavo stared in fear and slowly moved the suitcase behind him, not wanting it noticed. He imagined all the Guardia in Madrid looking for the suitcase he had taken.

"ETA," the old man muttered. "The Basques."

It took a moment for Chavo to realize his mistake, then a feeling of relief washed over him. He turned away from the man and ran back up the first flight of stairs. Pausing in the confusion he stuffed the purses into the suitcase and then walked more slowly to avoid attention. The Guardia would be looking for older men, but he still didn't want his suitcase noticed. Near the exit Chavo saw a Guardia standing on the steps, scanning the crowd. He stepped closer to a woman who was holding two small children by the hand. The little girl was crying, taking the woman's attention. He walked beside her son and began a brief conversation with the boy, hoping he looked like he was with the family. In this way he passed by the guard with his suitcase unnoticed.

Once out of the subway Chavo split off from the family and ran through the streets. When he was exhausted he stopped, figuring he was now far enough away to be safe from prying eyes. Ducking into the doorway of a church he sat down and opened the suitcase. He pulled out the purses first. Quickly he examined the contents. A train ticket to Paris, an American passport, some photographs. Chavo's stomach churned again remembering the woman lying there and all the blood. She looked too young to be dead. Making a face he stuffed the items back and opened a small zippered compartment. A broad smile spread across his face. Money, lots of money. More than 15,000 pesetas, and some traveler's checks. He tossed them back into the suitcase and pulled out some clothing. Without much interest he stuffed it back. The second purse yielded more money, and Chavo's mood lightened as he counted over 50,000 pesetas.

On the way home he tried to think of how he would explain the suitcase and its contents to his mother. She was sure to punish him if she thought he'd stolen it. In the end he decided to hide it and work out a plan later. It took nearly an hour to reach the narrow road that lead to his apartment. Too late he remembered that he was going to sneak the suitcase upstairs. By the time he crept to the edge of the buildings his mother, sitting at the window, had seen him. "Octavio! Venga! Come here!" she shouted.

As soon as he walked in the door she grabbed his arm, raising her hand as if to strike him. "What is this? You stealing from someone? Where'd you get the suitcase?" Before he could answer the baby wailed. "Look what you've done. Made me wake the baby. Sit." She pointed to the couch and went into the back room to fetch the baby. A minute later she returned, his little sister held on her hip. She was quieter now, if only so she didn't scare Anita.

"Tell me," she ordered.

"I was at Puerto del Sol. There was a big explosion, a bomb, and lots of people got hurt. This lady was killed, so I took her stuff. I figured taking stuff from dead people isn't really stealing. She doesn't need it any more."

"Octavio," his mother began, "I've told you over and over..."

"But Mama, look!" he interrupted. Opening the suitcase he pulled out the purses and lay the money on the couch beside him.

"How do you know she was dead?" she asked.

"There was blood all over, especially her head. She didn't move at all."

"And the second purse?" she asked, gesturing to it.

"She was dead too," Chavo replied with conviction. He remembered that she had been moving, but she was obviously rich. Someone would take care of her.

"Madre de Dios," his mother muttered, hurriedly crossing herself. She fought her conscience, thinking of the food she could buy for her children. "I guess you're right," she said. "Dead people don't need all this. But promise me no more stealing."

"Sure Mama, I promise," Chavo replied easily.

She took a wallet from him and looked through it. There was a single picture of a young woman with a much older man. Her father maybe, or an older husband. She took the second wallet. Several pictures were in it, and she flipped through them, then pulled a picture from the holder and studied it closer. It showed a young woman holding a little boy. Beside her stood a handsome young man. She showed the pictures to Chavo. "Are these the women?"

He glanced at the pictures, then nodded.

She held up one picture. "Her little boy, was he killed too?"

"I didn't see a little boy."

Christina wavered. If the boy wasn't dead, he should have his Mama's things, she thought. She looked at the picture again. The boy was nicely dressed, and he looked well fed and happy. She looked at her own daughter, just a year or so younger, wearing clothes that were little more than rags. Her hair was lank, her face dirty. Ignoring her conscious she decided to keep everything. The boy had no use for the clothes and though the money was a fortune to her, it really wasn't a lot for a rich person. Besides, there was no way to return the items without risking Octavio's involvement. His dad was a known separatist. She wouldn't risk her son being branded as such just because he was in the Plaza during the bombing.

She took the pictures and crossed to the kitchen. Carefully she placed them on the shelf beside the picture of her missing husband. "Now, we pray for them too," she said to herself. "And their families."

The next morning Cristina left her apartment warily but with determination. It was Octavio's birthday, and she was determined to make it nice.. Ever since Anita was born she hadn't been well, and the thought of venturing out into the city alone intimidated her. It had never occurred to her to see a doctor. In her neighborhood doctors were only for the dying.

But now, thinking of her son, she was sure she could accomplish her tasks and make his birthday special. She had hoped her husband might send a note or even a small gift, but all week she had watched the mail eagerly, only to have nothing arrive. It seemed he had forgotten them entirely. She carried Anita on her hip, hoping the child would be good and not wear her out. As the bus approached she stuck out her free arm and flagged it down. Gratefully she took a seat, putting Anita beside her, then she stared out the window watching for her destination.

When she got off the bus she was directly in front of the Corte Inglés. She had been to the huge department store only twice before, preferring the smaller, more intimate shops, but today she planned to spend some of the money Chavo had brought her and get a few badly needed items. The department store was the logical place to get it all at once. Plucking up her courage she entered the wide doorway and the surging crowds. Momentarily she was lost. The crowd pushing forward, on and off the escalators and around the merchandise frightened her. She stood, staring, and tried to orient herself. Seeing a store guide posted on one wall she moved that way, fighting against the crowd. Supermarket, women's clothes, men's clothes, children's clothes, rebajas. That's the place to start, she told herself. The sale floor. It was on the sixth floor. The very thought of six flights made her weary, but she turned and started for the escalator, determined to see this day through.

As she stepped onto the sale floor chaos greeted her. Large tables filled with goods were surrounded by women, their children playing on the floor or screaming in anger. Her eyes darted about, searching for children's clothes. Eventually she spotted the sign in the back corner. Hoisting Anita higher on her hip she pushed through the people until she reached the tables. Carefully she sat the baby down between her feet so her hands would be free, and stepped on her dress to keep her from crawling away. She sorted through the jeans until she found a pair that would fit Octavio, and quickly selected two shirts. Satisfied, she picked Anita up and once again began pushing her way through the crowds.

Two flights down she found the toys. Normally she wouldn't have spent any money on something so frivolous, but today, for Octavio's birthday, she felt the need. With his dad gone and her sick all the time the boy needed something. She had no idea what her son would like, and couldn't remember ever having bought him a toy, not since he was a baby. Aimlessly she wandered the aisles, wondering what to get. When a sales lady approached her she asked for advice, not telling the woman it was a gift for her own son.

The lady held up a soccer ball. "Does he have one of these? All nine-year-old boys want to play soccer for Royal Madrid."

Cristina took the ball. He certainly didn't have one of his own, and she had seen the neighborhood kids play in the street. "I'll take it," she said.

By now she was worn out, and set her mind to the task of getting home. Octavio would have to go to the market. She had intended to do it herself and surprise her son with a nice dinner, but it was too much for her to manage. She found a cash register and paid for the gifts, then struggling to balance Anita and the packages, she started down the remaining flights. She had only one flight left when a wave of dizziness overcame her. She dropped her package and gripped the handrail, willing herself to not fall. At the bottom of the flight she stumbled to the side scooting the package with her foot. Almost immediately she found herself in a quiet pocket of the store. Everyone else was pushing left, toward the next escalator, while she had gone right. Gratefully she sank to the floor and sat Anita beside her, waiting for the dizziness and nausea to end. When she felt better she cautiously got to her feet. Gathering her baby and her packages she wandered toward the back of the store, still avoiding the crowds and the escalators.

She entered the furniture department and sat down on a couch to rest for a moment. The department was empty and Christina sat Anita beside her. A row of televisions were in front of the couch. Cristina had never owned a television, but she loved to watch it. Every time she saw one she felt the same awe she had known the first time she had seen the magic of a picture coming across the screen to her. Looking around she saw there were no sales girls in the department. Quickly she got up and turned on a TV, then returned to the couch to watch. Within minutes Anita had fallen asleep, so she decided to stay where she was watching the TV. A game show was in progress, and she sat back to enjoy it.

She was interrupted by a sales girl returning from her break, just as the game show was interrupted by a news update. "Can I help you with something?" the girl asked.

Cristina knew she wasn't welcome to sit and watch the TV while Anita slept on the couch, but stalling for time she pointed to the television. "Look, news about the bombing."

The girl turned to watch, and Cristina quietly gathered her packages, her attention only half on the television now. Carefully Cristina picked up Anita, trying not to wake her. She tried to work out how she was going to manage getting on the bus and paying the fare with a sleeping child and the packages. She lay Anita back down and dug into her purse for the bus fare so she would have it ready.

Her attention was riveted back to the screen as she heard the announcer say, "...identified three of the people killed in the blast, while two others remain unidentified." Three pictures came onto the screen, their names printed beneath, and Cristina stared curiously at the faces. The women in the pictures Chavo had found weren't shown. They haven't identified them yet, she thought. With a shock she realized that she should come forward and identify the women. She had their identification and their photographs. She could tell the authorities who the women were. She stared at her packages, purchased with the money stolen from the dead women, and wondered how she could explain having their ID's.

Bored with the news story the sales girl reached out and turned off the TV. "Is there something I can help you with?" she asked again.

"No," Cristina replied. "I'm just leaving now." She was aware of her racing heart as she wondered how to rid herself of the women's items without causing any trouble to her family. Uncomfortable under the girl's unceasing stare, Cristina gathered her packages bought with the stolen money. "I'm going," she said. Quickly she picked up Anita, not caring that she woke the child and carried her, crying, to the escalator and out the door.

Back in the apartment she carefully gathered up everything Chavo had taken and put it in the suitcase. She stored the suitcase beneath her bed until she could figure out what to do with it. That night she confused Chavo by yelling at him for taking the women's things and then giving him the first ever birthday gift he could remember receiving from her. She didn't explain either of her actions.

She awoke the next morning decided on a course of action. She would keep the things and not worry about returning them. The women were dead. Their poor husbands would contact someone and they would be identified. Octavio would never be involved.

CHAPTER

TEN

D r. Montoro entered the room and picked up the chart which hung at the bottom of the bed. The name at the top read *Desconocida, Unknown*. Glancing at the information recorded in the last 24 hours he shook his head and sighed. She had been here for 5 days now, and while her cuts and bruises were improving, she had yet to regain consciousness. His hope was slowly fading. As a specialist trained in traumatic head injury he was used to the idea that many of his patients would never fully recover. But it never got any easier to accept.

He was disturbed by how alone she was. His patients were typically surrounded by family, and he was barraged by their questions. While it was a relief to read a chart in silence, he was bothered by the illusion that no one cared she was here. He glanced through the files again. Young, estimated to be in her early 30's; a cesarean scar from a birth; brought in following the bombing in the plaza with no ID. To date no one had reported her missing. He wondered, not for the first time, if her husband had been killed. But even if he had, he thought, someone should miss her. Someone had to be taking care of the child. His speculation was interrupted by a page calling him to the phone.

"Quién?" he asked the nurse on duty.

"Señor Aznar," she replied. He nodded and took the phone.

Señor Aznar was the chief inspector on the woman's ID case. Dr. Montoro felt confident that he would find the family eventually, but found the inspector's personality clashed with his own a bit. Still, no reason why we can't work together, he told himself. Put aside our personal differences. Greeting the inspector he was cut short. "I think I have the family," the inspector reported. "From Aracena in Andalusia. Say their girl ran off two weeks ago. She was getting married, but she didn't want to. Had always wanted to go to the city. 23 years old, shoulder length hair, had a baby out of wedlock two years ago. They didn't have a picture, but the description fits."

"Good work inspector. They know..."

He was cut short by the inspector again. "They are on the way to Madrid now. Should arrive in about 3 hours. They're coming straight to the hospital."

"Right, do they know..."he began again.

"I told them you'd meet them. Of course I'll be there too," the inspector interrupted.

"Do they know she's seriously injured?" the doctor said forcefully.

"Told them. The mother may be a bit hysterical."

"Right." The doctor checked his watch. "I'll see you here about noon then." They both hung up without further conversation. Dr. Montoro glanced at the nurse. She had been listening in on the conversation, but now she bent her head over her work and began writing furiously. "I'm expecting Inspector Aznar about noon," he told her. "Page me when he arrives."

The three hours passed quickly as Dr. Montoro made his rounds. He saw several patients; felt relief to see several progressing, dismay at two who clearly weren't. Through it all the mystery woman never really left his mind. Since she was brought in she had haunted him. The knowledge that her family was on the way both relieved and troubled him. He wanted her family located, but was bothered by the fact that a woman, in this day and age, had to run away from home to avoid a marriage she didn't want. He shook his head. Madrid was more modern than that, but not all parts of the country were. Still, this accident would change things for the girl. He couldn't tell the family if she would live or die, if she would ever walk or speak again. She might simply remain as she was now, kept alive by machines, unable to respond to any outside stimulus. His reverie was interrupted by a page calling him to his office-the family would be here then.

He entered the room where Inspector Aznar sat with the family. As he was introduced, he surveyed the group. The father was short and stocky, balding on top, with a fringe of gray hair around the sides and back of his head. His clothes were dusty from working in the fields. His shoes were battered. He appeared to have simply left the field, climbed into his car, and driven to the hospital, making no effort to clean up. His hand, which the doctor now shook, was dirty, the nails embedded with years of grime. Still, Dr. Montoro thought, if that were my daughter I would have done the same.

Next was a boy, about 15. Like his father he was covered in dust, his face and hands grimy. In his eyes the doctor could see the difference. There burned the passion of youth. Dr. Montoro studied him briefly. In 20 years he would be like his father, but right now he had the belief that his life would be different, that he could do better and have more than his parents had managed. That must have been the spirit that burned in his sister, to inspire her to run away, looking for a better life. Maybe the boy will find it, he thought.

Moving across the room he came to the mother. She was short and slightly heavy. Her dress was faded from years of washing and working in the sun. Her face was heavily lined, and she wore a defeated look, as though life had been hard, and was getting harder. On her lap she held a little girl, about 2 years old. The child seemed oblivious to the tension in the room. In one hand she held a bottle, in the other a worn out teddy bear that she clutched by the ear. Her clothes were also faded, possibly left over from when her mother had worn them. Only her shoes were new; bright pink sandals that contrasted with the worn garments of the family.

Everyone spoke at once, except the baby. The parents threw out one question after another, never waiting for an answer. The inspector tried to make introductions, and the boy badgered his father with questions as to what would happen to his sister now. Taking control of the room Dr. Montoro spoke loudly "Excuse me. Could you please be quiet so I can speak." The parents and inspector obeyed immediately. The boy kept up his badgering until his father ordered him to stop. He slumped in his chair, sulking, angry at being treated like a child even as his behavior marked him as one. No sooner had they all quieted down than the little girl began to whine. The woman jiggled her on her knee trying to quiet her. When it was obvious that she wasn't going to settle down, Dr. Montoro began to speak to the family, raising his voice so he could be heard clearly. Briefly he explained the state the young woman was in; unconscious, unresponsive, suffering from severe head injuries. He went on to detail the range of problems that could be associated with this type of injury, anything from complete recovery to death. He explained that only time would tell. He stressed to the family that patients in this condition are sometimes aware of things that go on around them, and that the family must be careful about what they said in her presence. He encouraged them to speak to her of love and concern, and not express anger or dismay.

At this point the inspector, who had been standing off in the corner trying to control himself while the doctor went on and on, interrupted. "Doctor, we haven't established a positive ID on the patient."

"Of course," Dr. Montoro replied. "Of course, we need to do that immediately." He had forgotten that they weren't sure this was the family. Turning to the father he said, "You come with me. Why don't the rest of you wait here." He opened the door then glanced back. "Inspector?" he questioned. "Would you join us?"

Inspector Aznar was upset at being an afterthought. He had found the family, so naturally he should get to witness the reunion. Struggling to hide his anger and assume a professional demeanor he headed down the hall with the father and the doctor.

The doctor paused outside the room. He reminded the father that the woman might be aware of all that was said, and warned him that she was still quite battered and bruised, was hooked to a plethora of equipment, and in fact looked quite frightening. The father nodded solemnly. Opening the door the doctor stood aside to let the other men enter first. The father approached the bed gingerly. He gazed at the woman's face for a moment, frowned, and shook his head. "It's not her."

"Are you sure," asked Doctor Montoro and the inspector at once. Continuing alone Dr. Montoro said, "She may look different because of swelling and bandages."

"No," the father replied. "It's not her." His voice was confidant, no room for doubt. "It doesn't look like her at all." He appeared both relieved and saddened that this wasn't his daughter.

Dr. Montoro ushered the group out of the room, quietly closing the door. They returned to his office where the mother waited expectantly, the child now quieted and wandering the room. As soon as they entered the father addressed his wife. "It's not her." Immediately the woman began to cry. It was impossible to tell whether she cried with relief or sorrow. Hearing her grandmother crying the little girl ran across the room, threw herself into her grandmother's lap, and also began to cry. Embarrassed by this display of emotion the boy got up and crossed the room to stare out the window. The father turned apologetically to the doctor and inspector, then approached his wife, at a loss about what he should say or do. He finally settled on a gruff approach, telling her to calm down and come on. The doctor didn't need them here taking up his time. Still crying she picked up the child and they left the room.

The doctor and the inspector faced one another. "Well," the doctor began, "I guess we're back to square one. Any more leads?"

The inspector was embarrassed at his failure to locate the family, and thought the doctor might now be patronizing him. "I'll let you know," he said shortly. "We've just begun our nationwide search." The doctor nodded briefly as the inspector turned to go.

Dr. Montoro entered the room. The woman lay as always, unmoving. Machinery whirred and beeped quietly in the background. He picked up her chart. As expected there was no change noted. Quickly he began going through the routine tests he used to check responsiveness. Laying her left hand flat he drug his finger lightly across the palm, checking for a reaction. Watching closely he saw none. He switched to the other hand. Again he drew his finger lightly across the palm. This time he thought he saw a slight twitch in her fingers. He repeated the test. It was clearly there, a slight twitching that hadn't been present before. Quickly he repeated the testing on her feet. Again he saw the slight twitch, only in the right foot. The left remained unmoving.

He noted the changes in the chart, then stopped by the nurse's station and notified them. "I want her checked twice as often," he instructed Ana, the nurse on duty. "If she comes out of the coma I want to know immediately. I don't care what time it is. Call me!" The nurse was used to this from Dr. Montoro. He was always wrapped up in his cases, especially the most difficult ones. She noted the instructions for the next nurse on duty, and returned to her other work.

Two hours later she got up to make her rounds. Entering the patient's room she checked her pulse and then her blood pressure. As she was tightening the blood pressure cuff the woman's eyes flicked open briefly, then closed again. Ana had worked as a critical care nurse for years, and was immediately aware of the significance of the movement. She leaned over and pressed the emergency call button, not wanting to leave the woman alone. She then spoke," Can you hear me? Can you open your eyes again?" Picking up the woman's limp hand she squeezed it. "Can you feel that? Squeeze my hand." There was the slightest flickering of the woman's fingers, then nothing.

Another nurse hurried through the door. Seeing Ana she stopped. "Oh, you're already here. The alarm's still ringing."

"I rang the alarm. Page Dr. Montoro. Tell him this patient is responsive. Hurry!"

Within minutes Dr. Montoro was in the room. "What happened?" he asked quickly.

"I was checking her blood pressure and she opened her eyes. Just for a second. Then I squeezed her hand and her fingers twitched."

Stepping up to the bed the doctor took her hand. He too squeezed it, waiting for a response. Again her fingers twitched. "Dim the lights," he instructed the nurse. When that was done he spoke directly to the woman. "I'm a doctor. I want to help you. Can you open your eyes?" There was a slight fluttering of her eyes for a moment, and then she half opened them. After a moment she closed them again. "Can you talk? Tell me your name." Her lips moved slightly, but no sound emerged. "I know you can hear me, so just listen. You have suffered a severe head injury. You've been in a coma for several days. You should regain your ability to speak soon. For now I want you to rest, and tomorrow we'll see if you can talk to me." Turning to Ana he gave instructions for administering medication to help her rest.

Returning to his office Dr. Montoro admitted to himself what he hadn't said in front of his patient. This type of injury often didn't recover. He wondered if the woman had lost her ability to speak or to form coherent thoughts. The fact that she had come out of the coma was encouraging, but she was still very much an unknown. Sighing he set aside his thoughts of her and went off to see his next patient.

The next morning, as soon as Dr. Montoro entered the hospital, he stopped at the nurse's station and asked for an update on his unknown patient.

"She slept through the night. Of course we kept up the medicine you prescribed, so that's not surprising. She was awake a bit this morning, but she seemed confused and wasn't speaking." Dr. Montoro nodded his head and entered the room.

She lay on the bed, her eyes closed. He had stopped the medication in the middle of the night in the hopes of finding her more alert and learning her identity. Pulling a chair close to the bed he sat down. "Good morning," he said. No response from her. "Are you awake? Can you hear me?" Trying again he picked up her hand. "Good morning," he repeated. Her eyes flickered briefly, and then shut again. "Can you open your eyes? I'd like to talk to you." Seemingly with great effort her eyes opened partially, and focused on his face. "Can you talk to me?"

Her lips moved, but no sound came out. Closing her eyes in concentration she tried again. "Donde?" she asked.

"Where. Where are you?" Dr. Montoro asked excitedly. The brevity of her speech did not concern him. What mattered was that she had retained the ability to speak, and had chosen an appropriate word, indicating comprehension. "You are in the hospital. You've had a head injury. Can you remember the accident?"

She shook her head.

He wasn't surprised. Most accident victims forgot the details of the injury temporarily, some forever. "Do you know what day it is?" he asked. Of course she wouldn't. It wasn't possible for her to remember how many days she had been in the coma. Most accident victims would simply name the day they were injured, losing all the days in between.

She shook her head.

"You don't know the day?"

She looked about the room, her eyes focusing on the window for a long moment. Again she shook her head.

"Tell me your name," Dr. Montoro directed her.

She hesitated for a moment, then shook her head.

"Never mind," he said softly. "We'll talk about that later." He made several notes on her chart then left the room.

He tried again later in the day, but she was too exhausted and was still slipping in and out of consciousness. He increased her medication for the afternoon, again instructing them to cut the dosage in the early morning, hoping she might wake up again. The next day he tried again to discover her name, but she simply closed her eyes at the question.

For three days she remained the same. She was more responsive to tests and followed simple instructions to squeeze a hand or open her eyes, but her language ability seemed to have dried up. On the third day she surprised him by speaking as soon as he entered the room. "I don't know," she said.

He was unsure what she meant at first, then realized that every day he asked her name. She was telling him she didn't know it. "Your name? You don't know your name?"

She nodded, and he could see tears forming in the corners of her eyes.

"Never mind," he said. "It's not uncommon to forget things following an accident as serious as this one. It will come to you soon enough."

She nodded, but the tears rolled down her face just the same.

He went to his office and called Inspector Aznar. The two men arranged a meeting for the next day, to discuss how to proceed.

Inspector Aznar entered the hospital with the determination that the two men had to work together better. Somehow the woman had to have an identity. They must convince her to tell them who she was. He thought of all the reasons she might withhold her name. Perhaps she was wanted by the police, or she herself had placed the bomb, and didn't get away in time. Of course she would want to withhold her name if she were a known terrorist. Somehow they had to convince her to say who she was.

The inspector conveyed these ideas to the doctor. The next thirty minutes were a heated debate which degenerated into an argument. The doctor attempted to explain head injury and amnesia, while the inspector insisted the woman was simply hiding her identity. Only after producing medical documents discussing amnesia did the inspector finally relent, once again feeling foolish. He was anxious for his retirement next year, and did not want a mystery woman left on his files.

Doctor Montoro recognized that the inspector irritated him. Still, each of them was a professional, and together they had a job to do. He sat back, taking a deep breath to calm himself. Slowly he brought his hands together, fingertips touching, forefingers resting on his lips. After a moment he spoke. "We must try to discover who this woman is. From a medical standpoint this is very important. One of the ways the brain heals and regains memory is through being exposed to familiar things: favorite foods, TV shows, music, perfumes, voices. With any patient in her condition I would recommend the family spend as much time as possible visiting, talking, listening to her favorite music, and they would help the brain to heal. With this woman we can play the music or turn on the TV, but unless we are exposing her to something familiar, we aren't helping her. With exposure to the unfamiliar the brain simply works harder to process the stimulus. There is no assistance in connecting to the past."

The inspector stared slightly past the doctor, as if studying a spot on the wall. "How is she looking? Has the bruising and the swelling improved?"

The doctor nodded.

"I think then that perhaps it is time to make a more public search."

Dr. Montoro looked puzzled. "Isn't that what we've done? The search that brought in the wrong family?"

Inspector Aznar shook his head. "No. That was a police search. We contacted other police stations to see if anyone was reported missing. Now I'm talking about the media. We bring in a news crew, show her on television, and ask anyone who recognizes her to call us."

Dr. Montoro studied the inspector carefully, trying to decide if the inspector just wanted to be on TV, or if it was necessary. "Is that the usual way?" he asked.

The inspector laughed, making a small snorting sound. "There is no usual way. It's not as if I have unknown people, with no ID and no report they're missing, brought in off the streets every day."

"Of course. Of course. Well, I haven't got a better idea. I suppose we'll need her permission."

"That shouldn't be a problem I wouldn't think. Doesn't she want to know who she is?"

"Of course she does. I'm sure she'll agree." In truth he wasn't sure she would even understand the request. While she continued to improve, she still suffered frequent periods of confusion and distress, and slept far more than normal. "Why don't we go and see her now, if she's awake," he said.

They found her staring blankly at a TV program one of the nurses had put on for her. "Hello," Dr. Montoro said. "Do you like the program?"

Slowly, as if it required considerable effort she turned her eyes from the TV to the two men. When she didn't answer he repeated the question. "Do you like the program?"

She shrugged her shoulders slightly.

"Seen it before?"

She wrinkled her forehead in concentration, then shrugged again.

"Mind if I turn it off so we can talk with you?"

Another shrug, this time accompanied by a slight shaking of her head.

"Do you remember me?"

She nodded.

"Do you remember me talking to you before? Explaining about the accident?"

Again she nodded. There seemed to be no damage to her short-term memory. She was able to recall comments the doctor made, and understood that she had been hurt in an accident. He had noted that each day she was becoming increasingly distressed at the fact that she couldn't remember her own name, or any details about her life. He had tried to assure her that this was often the case, and that the memories should come back eventually, but two days ago he had begun medication to calm her distress. The medicine made her groggy and less coherent than usual. Today the effects of the medication were particularly evident.

"Do you remember the inspector?" Dr. Montoro asked.

She hadn't seen him before, though he had been in the room the day the family had been at the hospital. She studied the inspector's face, biting her lower lip in concentration. Her brow wrinkled a bit, and her eyes closed involuntarily. With great effort she opened them again. Finally she shook her head.

"That's okay. He's been here, trying to help us find your family. He has an idea that may help. We want to put your picture on TV, so that anyone who recognizes you will come and help us find your family."

At the mention of the TV she slowly turned her head and looked at the blank screen, then returned her gaze to the doctor. She said nothing.

"Do you understand? Is it okay if we put your picture on TV?"

She continued to stare at the doctor, saying nothing. Her eyes drooped heavily.

"Do you understand me? We want to put you on the TV. We want people to see you so we can learn your name. Is it okay with you?" When she still didn't reply Dr. Montoro turned to the inspector. "I really feel like we need consent before we do this, and I'm not sure she's understanding me right now."

"Well, maybe she isn't capable of giving consent. Maybe we have to do what's best. Doctors are allowed to proceed without consent."

"Only in cases of life threatening emergency. I've never had this sort of thing come up before."

The inspector turned to her and addressed her in a loud voice. "I'm going to put your picture on the TV unless you tell me, right now, that you don't want me to. Okay?"

She continued to stare, saying nothing.

"There," the inspector said. "Apparently she doesn't disagree."

Dr. Montoro frowned at the inspector, but seeing no other option he decided to let the inspector's method pass. "Let's go back to my office and discuss the details then," he said.

After fifteen minutes of arguing it was decided that they would take a photograph and use that on the TV. The inspector had argued for bringing in a news crew, but the doctor had been adamant that the excitement would be too much, and would overexert the woman. The inspector agreed to send around a police photographer that afternoon, and to contact the TV station regarding broadcasting the photo.

CHAPTER

ELEVEN

Alicia was on hands and knees cleaning the bathroom floor, when the buzzer rang. She struggled to her feet, and sighed as it rang again. These days she couldn't seem to move fast enough to please anyone. Without bothering to pick up the phone and talk she pressed the buzzer to release the downstairs door, then opened the door a crack and sank to a chair to wait. She hoped it was someone who would stay a few days. Just that morning she had counted out her money and found it dangerously low. She got to her feet and stepped outside, looking down the stairway. Two girls were on their way up, walking the three flights rather than using the elevator.

With alarm she saw them stop one flight down, by Pensión Gomez. "Aquí," she called out loudly, hoping they would continue climbing. To her relief they did. Americans, she decided, watching them climb the final flight. Arriving, the taller one dropped her backpack to the floor gratefully. A torrent of English flew from her mouth. "Room?" Alicia asked hopefully, using one of the few English words she knew. She pointed inside.

To her surprise, the shorter girl nodded, and asked politely, in good Spanish, for a double room. Eagerly Alicia motioned for them to follow her. She shuffled across the floor, pulled a large set of keys from her pocket, and unlocked the door. She crossed the room and pulled open the blinds, allowing light to flood into the room. "Mira," she said eagerly gesturing to the view outside the window. The girls ignored her and inspected the room, speaking in low voices to each other, as if afraid she might understand something they said.

"Do you like it?" she asked the shorter girl hopefully. She was proud of this room, with its new bedspreads, the view from the window, and the beautiful ivory lamp which had been left behind by the previous owners of the apartment.

"The shower?" the girl asked.

"Sí, sí." Alicia shuffled across the floor and into the hallway. She pushed open the door to reveal the shower, her cleaning supplies still on the floor. The tub was small and square, with a hand held water jet. There was no curtain in evidence. "Mira," Alicia instructed them. She pushed open the next door to reveal the toilet, ancient but spotlessly clean. A rusted chain hung from above for flushing. "1000 pesetas," she said.

Again, the flood of English. She waited for their answer, then fearful that they wouldn't pay the price she dropped it. "Too much?" she asked. "900 pesetas?"

The short one smiled. "Do you have a television we could watch the news on," she asked.

Alicia was puzzled at first. No one ever asked to watch TV. Still, she thought proudly, I have a lovely set. Her face fell a little as she remembered her son sending it for Christmas last year, right after he had cancelled his plans to come visit. She would let the girls watch it because she desperately needed their money. Gesturing for them to follow, she led the way down the hall into her private room. An ancient couch sat in the middle of the floor, a long low table in front of it. Off to one side sat a beautiful buffet, the top covered with pictures neatly framed and arranged by age. On the left were the obviously old photos, moving through middle age and young adults, to a group of babies on the right. Seeing that the girls were looking at the photos, Alicia crossed the room and began to detail them.

"My parents, my sister, my brothers, one of them was killed in the war. My husband, also dead now, my three children, my grandchildren. Lots of family." She sighed sadly.

"It's nice to have a big family," the short girl said quickly.

The old woman shook her head. All she had was a big family that had grown up and moved away. Their children didn't even know who she was. "My son went to America. My daughter," she pointed to a picture "lives in Galicia, and my other daughter" she pointed again, "lives in Jerez. So many grandchildren, but none of them to visit me."

The girls seemed uncomfortable in the private room. Turning away from the photographs, Alicia remembered the purpose of being here. "Look," she said, pointing to her TV sitting in the corner of the room. "It's color." She smiled proudly.

The short girl nodded. "We'll take it. 1000 pesetas."

Alicia was surprised. She had already offered it for less. Perhaps the girl hadn't understood, but she would be happy for the extra pesetas. Impulsively, enjoying the young girl's company, she said, "You can have breakfast too. Café con leche and rolls."

The girl smiled. "Gracias." Turning to her sister she spoke in English and they both left the room, mumbling "adios" as they went.

They were still in their room when the afternoon news began. Alicia knocked lightly on their door and called out to them. Immediately the door opened, and they appeared. "Thanks," the short girl said, following Alicia into her private room.

Alicia nodded, gesturing toward the couch. "Sit, sit."

The taller girl seemed glued to the TV, while the shorter one expressed only a passing interest. Alicia wondered about them. The taller one didn't seem to speak Spanish, or maybe she was just unfriendly. Anyway, the other one was friendly enough for two. She had introduced herself as Kelly and said the other girl her sister, named June. Alicia was happy to sit and talk. She rarely watched the afternoon news, and even more rarely had a visitor to talk to. The tall girl, June, kept interrupting with her flood of English, pointing to the TV and demanding her sister's attention.

"Sorry," Kelly said. "It's just that she's really nervous about being here, because of that bombing and all. She insisted we had to watch the news, and she wants me to tell her what's going on. She doesn't understand any Spanish," she added unnecessarily.

She looked around the room with interest. Through the open doorway she could see the kitchen. It was tiny with a worn looking linoleum floor. A small table, metal with a Formica top, sat in the middle of the floor. Two chairs with yellowish, vinyl seat covers sat beside it. Her inspection was interrupted by Alicia poking her arm gently. "Look," she said. "The bombing."

Kelly turned her attention to the TV. They were showing footage of the bombing. Police ran about the square trying to help the injured. A moment later a woman's picture appeared on the screen. Alicia's mouth dropped open, and she quickly covered it with her hand. She listened carefully. The announcer was saying the woman had not yet been identified. They were asking anyone who might know her to come forward and identify her.

The two girls were both speaking at once, June in English, demanding her sister tell her what was going on, and Kelly in Spanish, asking Alicia what was wrong. "I...that woman... she used to live here. I met her. She told me how she used to live here and play in the front room, and look out the windows."

"Well you've got to call them! Tell them who she is."

Alicia shook her head. "I don't know anything, she didn't stay here. I can't help. I don't know her."

The inspector sat anxiously in his office. He was a bullfighting aficionado, and his walls were covered in framed posters advertising some of the more famous fights. A large photograph that hung just above his desk showed him running through the streets of Pomplona, the traditional red scarf tied around his neck, being chased by bulls. He sighed at the unfairness of age. He was far too old now for anything more strenuous than a desk job. The phone rang, and he jumped slightly, startled from his thoughts. The first news story had aired, and he was anxiously awaiting the barrage of calls he hoped to receive.

He answered the phone, expecting to receive his first lead. It was Dr. Montoro.

"Any leads yet?"

He sat back, disappointed the doctor had called before anyone else. "No, not yet, but soon I'm sure. Very soon."

"Well, let me know as soon as you hear anything," the doctor demanded. "Remember that her best chance for recovery is to expose her to familiar things."

"Of course," the inspector replied. He hung up, angry at the doctor's attitude. Of course he would tell him if they got a lead. He resumed his wait, willing the phone to ring. Five hours after the story had broadcast he was still waiting, and decided it was time to go home.

Alicia was surprised to see the girls come rushing into the apartment and directly to her private room the next day. She had forgotten about the news. Alicia joined them on the couch, more for companionship than to watch.

The lead story was a repeat of yesterday's amnesia victim. "Look," Kelly said, nudging the old woman. "That's the woman who doesn't remember who she is again."

The old woman nodded.

"I think you should call them," Kelly said. "After all, they are good at working with hints. "You have to call and tell them what you know."

The old woman shook her head. "There is nothing to tell. Someone who knows her will see the story and tell."

She watched, amused, as June pulled her sister's arm, like an unsatisfied child, tugging at her mother's skirt. She spoke on and on in English, and Kelly answered her. Suddenly, wide eyed, she leaned past Kelly and directed her flood of English at Alicia.

"She thinks you need to talk to them also," Kelly explained. "Just think, her family could be far away like yours, and she doesn't see them that often. They wouldn't even know she was hurt for ages, because they wouldn't see the story. What if it was your daughter? You'd want everyone to help. So what if it was ages ago that she lived here. There might be records. They might be able to figure it out."

The old woman sat staring at the photographs on her buffet, acknowledging the girl's wisdom. She could be missing a long time without anyone noticing. Slowly she nodded.

"So you're going to call them? You're going to let them know?"
Alicia nodded.

"Well here, I wrote down the number to call when you said you'd seen her." Kelly handed her a piece of paper, torn from a subway map, with the number written across it. "You better do it now. I'll bet they're waiting for the call."

Alicia got up slowly, and shuffled over to the buffet. She opened a drawer, and began riffling through a small cup of coins, searching for duros. She collected a few, and then started toward the door.

"You want us to come with you?" Kelly asked quickly. She thought it was all rather adventurous, and didn't want to miss the excitement.

The old woman smiled at the girls. That one, she likes to feel important, she thought. The other one is timid, I can tell even though I can't talk to her, but this one likes excitement. "Okay," she replied. "Come with me." She didn't need the girls to help her, not after all the years she had lived alone and managed, but she was enjoying them. She waved her hand slightly and the girl got up, said something to her sister, and they both followed her out of the room.

The inspector had sat anxiously by his phone, once again hoping for a call. However, after what seemed a long time and still no calls he leaned back in his chair, propped his feet on the desk, and fell asleep. The ringing of the phone startled him, and he jumped, nearly knocking the chair over backward before answering the phone. Almost immediately he picked up a pen and began making notes. " Señora Alicia Cabanillas, #34 Gran Via, 3o piso."

He paused, pen held above the paper. "She didn't stay? Do you know her name?"

He bit his lip thoughtfully as he listened to the woman. She didn't know much about the victim, but believed the woman had lived in her apartment at one time. He debated whether he should meet with her or not. She sounded like a dead end. He decided to meet her on the off chance she would remember the woman's name. He arranged to meet her at the hospital so she could see the woman in person, and confirm that it was the woman she had met.

After she hung up he sat regarding the phone, debating whether he should call Dr. Montoro. His ego told him not to, but in the end he did, leaving a message with the floor nurse to say they'd be there at 10:00 the next morning.

Alicia woke early, aware of needing to do something, though she didn't immediately remember what it was. She lay in bed thinking, trying to bring it up. The hospital, she remembered. She was supposed to go to the hospital and meet that doctor and that inspector. The Americans were coming with her. It had amused her tremendously when Kelly had asked if they could come along. She wants to feel included, Alicia thought, part of something important. She'll be disappointed. There's nothing for me to tell, really. She got up and dressed, then went to put their breakfast out.

The subway ride was long, and they had to walk several blocks, so they arrived later than expected. They entered the front door, and went straight to a reception area. The attendant on duty showed them to some chairs. A moment later they were approached by a tall, handsome doctor. "Mrs. Cabanillas?" The old woman nodded. "I'm Dr. Montoro. If you'll just come with me we'll meet Inspector Aznar, and go see the woman."

He offered his hand to help her up. The American girls stood too. He looked at them curiously. Addressing June he asked, "And you are...?" She smiled at him.

"She doesn't speak Spanish," Kelly explained. "We came along with Mrs. Cabanillas, to help her with the subway and all."

He nodded. "Why don't you wait here. I'll bring her back to you in a moment."

Kelly's face fell. She had really been looking forward to seeing the woman. "She'd like us to come along," she said hopefully, nodding her head in the direction of the old woman.

"Sí, sí," the woman replied. "I want the girls to stay with me." She didn't care one way or the other, but she enjoyed their company and thought perhaps this intrigue would keep the girls in town a little longer.

The doctor nodded. "Vale. Come on." The four of them left the room and walked slowly to an office. A man sat in a large leather chair, impatiently thumping a pencil against the desk. As soon as the group entered he stood up and introduced himself. "Mrs. Cabanillas. I'm Inspector Aznar. We spoke on the phone."

"Buenas días."

Addressing the doctor he asked, "Who are they?" He jerked his head toward Kelly and June.

The doctor shook his head. "They're all together," he said. Then, speaking to the group as a whole he indicated where they could sit, and left to confirm that the patient was awake and alert.

He returned a few minutes later. "Come with me. She's awake and prepared to see you all." They entered the room, and her eyes turned toward the door, regarding them slowly. Dr. Montoro took Mrs. Cabanillas gently by the elbow and led her forward, leaving Kelly and June standing in the doorway. He indicated a chair by the bed, and she sat down. He turned to the patient. "Do you recognize this woman?" She stared intently at the old woman. Her lips moved, but no sound came out. Slowly she shook her head.

"Is she the same woman who was at your pensión?" he asked Alicia.

She nodded.

"Can you identify her? Is there some record of her name in your books?"

Alicia shook her head. "No. She didn't stay at the pensión. She came to visit and to see the rooms. I think she said she used to live there."

"When did she live there? Did she say?"

Alicia shook her head. "I've been there 18 years. She would have been a child. The building used to be very grand. I think that's what she didn't like. All of the nice things are gone-except a few dishes and a couple pieces of furniture. Those were left behind. I've kept them ever since. I should have showed them to her." Mrs. Cabanillas looked sad, as if it was somehow her fault the woman had left and been injured.

"Let's go back to my office," Dr. Montoro suggested. Once there he explained briefly to Mrs. Cabanillas what he hoped to do. "I need to find some connection to her past. If I can find people or things she can remember, maybe she can begin to recover her memory. So far you're the only link we have. Can I stay in touch with you?"

Alicia nodded. The doctor pulled a paper from his desk. "What is your phone number?"

"I don't have a phone."

"Your address then."

She nodded and took the paper. Carefully she wrote down the address and handed it back to him. "When she's a little better someone might bring her by. Maybe being in the old apartment would jog her memory. In the meantime, if you think of anything else she might have said, any clue at all, give us a call."

At this Inspector Aznar stood up. "Give *me* a call," he said forcefully. "I am the inspector on the case. I will let the doctor know any information that he needs."

Dr. Montoro gave him a disgusted look but spoke pleasantly, "Of course you should call the inspector. However, if he is unavailable, you may call me."

Alicia nodded and stood up. The girls joined her, and together they went back to the apartment.

The next day the two girls left, after a considerable argument, for southern Spain. Kelly apologized, explaining she wanted to stay in Madrid and see if any further intrigue developed regarding the woman with amnesia, but that her sister insisted they stick to their original travel plans. She took Mrs. Cabanillas' address and left her own, asking to be updated on the woman.

The inspector tried valiantly to put Alicia's information to good use, working long hours, searching records, interviewing older people who might remember who had lived in the apartment. He uncovered very little, only a woman who lived one floor up, who remembered a child named Maria. She couldn't remember the last name she said, but the father had worked in government. The child sometimes snuck up to visit her while her nanny was resting. They would sit together and have cookies before the lonely little girl would creep back to her own apartment. It wasn't much to go on, but he called Dr. Montoro, and the doctor added the name Maria to the woman's chart. A first name was preferable to no name at all.

Dr. Montoro consulted with other experts in the medical field and finally developed a plan to stop the medications and place Maria in an intensive counseling program. Though he had not yet told her, she had passed the point in recovery where he hoped her memory would return.

Two days after stopping her medications he entered her room accompanied by Dr. Fernandez, the psychiatrist who would be working with Maria. She was considerably more alert now that she was off medication, but was constantly distressed by her lack of memory. As soon as he entered the room Maria greeted him and looked at Dr. Fernandez expectantly. Dr. Montoro introduced them, then sat on the chair beside the bed.

"How are you doing today, Maria?"

She smiled slightly. "I feel okay, except for a headache. I've been trying to remember something from the past, and it makes my head hurt."

Dr. Montoro nodded his understanding. "You're working too hard. You can't force the memories," he told her. "They will come back when your brain has healed enough."

She frowned. "But I hate waiting. What about my family, just wondering what has happened to me?"

"Yes, I know it's very distressing. That's why I've brought Dr. Fernandez. He is going to see you every day so you can talk about these concerns."

She turned and looked at Dr. Fernandez, then back at Dr. Montoro. "Why not you? You're my doctor, aren't you?"

"I am. I'm your medical doctor. Dr. Fernandez is a psychiatrist. He will be able to help you with your concerns better than I. In addition, his schedule will permit him to visit for longer periods of time than I can stay with you."

Maria nodded.

"Well then, I'll leave you two alone for a bit. I'll be by this afternoon to check in again." He left the room, and Dr. Fernandez moved into the chair.

"Well Maria, why don't we start. Tell me a little bit about yourself."

Maria sat silently for a moment, watching the doctor, wondering what he thought she might know about herself. Quietly she asked, "What do you want to know?"

He smiled at her. "Anything. Just whatever comes to mind."

Anger surged through her. "Nothing," she shouted. "Nothing comes to mind. I don't know anything about myself that I can tell you."

Ignoring her anger he prompted her, "I'm sure you can tell me something. It doesn't have to be from before the accident. We just need to get to know one another a little better."

Still angry she said, "There's nothing to tell. There's nothing about me that is me!"

"Maria, that's not true," he said patiently. "Even if you can't remember things from the past, there are new things about you being formed every day. That's true of all people, not just amnesia victims. Everyone forms new likes and dislikes every day. Tell me something about the new you. What's your favorite food now?" Without voicing it he was moving her in the direction of forming and accepting a new identity, a process he knew would be long and painful, but might be necessary.

"Food? I like the tortilla española. And the spaghetti."

"Good. Very good. And what about TV? Anything you particularly like?"

Maria shrugged. "I don't know. The game shows, I guess."

"What about the nurses? Do you like any one better than another?"

"Ana is really nice. She always stops by to talk to me even when she isn't assigned to this floor."

They talked on, Maria hesitant and angry, Dr. Fernandez encouraging, until nearly an hour had passed. After that Dr. Fernandez excused himself and left, promising to return the next day. He went immediately to Dr. Montoro's office, and waited for the doctor to join him.

Dr. Montoro rushed in, apologizing for being late. "So, how did it go with Maria?"

"Not bad. She's very angry, but that's to be expected." He explained his intention to help her discover a new identity prior to actually telling her she might never recover her old one. "It would be very helpful if she could be exposed to new things. Is her health strong enough that she could go out occasionally if someone were to accompany her?"

Dr. Montoro frowned, thinking about the question. "Where would you propose taking her?"

"Anywhere really. The park, the grocery, the movies. The idea is to expose her to a variety of things so she can begin to form new likes and dislikes. Over time the loss of her old identity will hurt less because she will have a new one."

"Yes, I see. She is physically healthy. There's really no reason why she needs to stay here. It's mostly a case of not having anywhere for her to go."

"Then I think we should move in that direction. We need to find her a place and begin exposing her to as many new things as we can. In the meantime, while we're looking why don't we provide a companion who can take her out occasionally. I will suggest my daughter who is studying psychiatry. At the moment she is in her second year of college. I think she would be happy to spend several hours a week with Maria. It would give her valuable experience. Of course I will completely oversee the treatment. She would not be doing any actual clinical work."

Dr. Montoro hesitated. He felt very protective of Maria, as if in the absence of real family he had become her family. But seeing no flaw in the plan he had to admit that Maria should get out of the hospital. She had been there for weeks, and the beautiful weather outside would do her good. "Okay," he agreed, "I think we can try that. Of course I would like to meet your daughter and be involved. Maria has been hospitalized for some time, and her strength will need to be built up."

The two men agreed to meet the next day with Dr. Fernandez's daughter.

"Maria." Dr. Fernandez greeted her warmly as he entered the room. "How are you today?"

Maria smiled but did not look happy. "I'm okay. How are you?"

"Fine thanks. I want you to meet my daughter, Carmen."

Carmen stepped up to the bed and smiled warmly. "Maria, how nice to meet you. I wanted to invite you to come for a walk with me." Seeing Maria's surprised look she added, "Dr. Montoro has already said it's okay."

Maria raised her eyebrows in surprise. "Do you mean a walk outside of the hospital?" she asked.

"Yes, of course. We can go down the street and look in the shop windows or something. It's a lovely day, and the doctor says there's no reason for you to remain in bed as long as we don't wear you out."

"Oh, I'd love that," Maria said. "I'd love to be in the sun. When are you going?"

Carmen was pleased at her eagerness. "Why don't we go now?" she said. "I brought you some clothes in case you needed them. I'll just wait outside while you change."

"And I'll stop in this afternoon to see how you enjoyed the walk," Dr. Fernandez added.

They walked arm in arm, typical Spanish fashion for two ladies out for a stroll. Maria was hesitant at first, drawing back from the noise and the crowds. But after a few minutes she relaxed and began to enjoy herself. They walked down the street to a row of shops, not going in but gazing through the windows, commenting on the clothes. Skin tight, black stirrup pants worn with huge oversized shirts were the fashion. They stopped outside a shop displaying the look, the shirts striped in florescent orange or lime green with white. "Do you like that look?" Carmen guided the conversation.

Maria hesitated. "I'm not sure. I can't imagine how it would look on me." Her happy spirits sagged. Quietly she said, "You can't imagine what it's like not knowing anything about yourself, not even which styles look good."

"It's got to be awful," Carmen agreed sympathetically. Then hoping to restore some of Maria's joy at being out she suggested, "Why don't we try on the outfit. That way you'll know how it looks."

"Oh, I don't know."

"Come on! It will be fun. I'll try one too. You're going to need some clothes if we're going to go out together."

"But I haven't got any money," Maria protested. "Until we figure out who I am I can't buy any clothes."

"Actually," Carmen said, "You do have a little money, enough for a couple of outfits. It's come from a collection they took up at the hospital to help you get reestablished until you're found."

Maria protested. "I can't take their money."

"They'll be very hurt if you don't. All the nurses and doctors have contributed and they're looking forward to seeing you in something other than a hospital gown. So what do you say? Come on." She took

Maria's arm and opened the shop door before she could protest further. "Now, which do you like, the orange or the green?"

Maria reached out and touched each, looking at the colors closely. "The green I think."

"Good, and I'll try the orange." Carmen took the two shirts. "Now, pants. Mine seem to fit you fine, so we must wear the same size." She selected two pair of black stirrups and steered Maria in the direction of the dressing room. "Come out and show me. I want to see how it looks!"

Maria quickly changed, excited at the prospect of owning her own clothes again. In the new outfit she twirled around admiring herself in the mirror. "Carmen, I like it," she called excitedly. "What do you think?" She opened the door and waited for Carmen to appear.

Carmen poked her head out. "Oooh. Very stylish. It's what all the young people are wearing now days." She retreated back into her dressing room.

Maria frowned. "Do you think I'm too old to be a young person?" she asked.

"You don't look old. How old are you anyway?" Carmen asked.

"How old am I?" Maria shouted, the anger instantly coursing through her again. "You know I haven't any idea how old I am!" She stormed back into her dressing room banging the door behind her.

Carmen's door popped open. "Maria, I'm sorry. I just wasn't thinking. I'm so sorry. Please forgive me." Behind the closed door she could hear Maria crying. "Maria." She tried to open the door. "Maria, please open the door." The other women in the shop stood staring openly at the drama being played out before their eyes. "Maria, come on. Open the door. I'm sorry I said that. It was foolish."

Reluctantly Maria opened the door, once again wearing her borrowed clothes. Her eyes were red from crying. "I'm tired. I want to go back to the hospital," she said softly.

"Oh Maria, I'm sorry. Please don't let it ruin our day. We were just getting started." Remembering the doctor's warning to take things slowly she stopped. "If you really are tired we'll go back, but please don't be angry at me."

"I'm not angry at you," Maria snapped. "I'm angry at the situation. You can't imagine what it's like."

"You're right," Carmen agreed. "I can't, and because I can't I made that remark without thinking how you would feel. I wish I could do more than just be a friend, I wish I could fix your memory, but the doctor says only time will do more. Why don't we go across the street for a coffee, and after that if you still want to go back we will." She didn't mention the outfit Maria had loved for fear of setting off another episode.

While they were having coffee Maria began to calm down and enjoyed watching people passing by. They were sitting at an outdoor table drinking large cups of café con leche. "What you told me about the outfits, is that true? They really took up a collection and are anxious to see what I choose?"

Carmen took a huge swallow of coffee. "Absolutely. They all hoped you'd find something today, but if you're not up to it it's okay. I'd like to go out with you again, maybe in a day or two."

"I really liked the one I tried. I'd like to get it, unless you think it didn't look right," she added uncertainly.

"No, I thought it was great. It's so stylish. I mean, look." She pointed out several girls passing by in similar styles. "Everyone is wearing it this year."

Back at the hospital everyone was eager to see what Maria had chosen. In familiar surroundings she enjoyed showing off the outfit, parading up and down the hallway in it. The nurses clapped their hands as if she were in a fashion show, but after a few minutes Dr. Montoro suggested she should rest. Reluctantly she agreed but once in her bed she realized how worn out she was, and quickly fell asleep. She was still sleeping when Dr. Fernandez showed up, so he left her and went in search of Dr. Montoro instead. The two men discussed the day's activities, in particular Carmen's blunder in asking Maria's age, and Maria's reaction. Dr. Montoro expressed concern that Carmen would make such an insensitive comment, but Dr. Fernandez reminded him that the goal of the outings was to expose Maria to everyday situations.

"I'm not just defending my daughter here, the comment was very insensitive, but Maria will have to learn to deal with people asking her age. She'll have to find a response she's comfortable with that doesn't involve collapsing in tears. This was an important first step."

Dr. Montoro nodded. "You're right. It is important. I just feel very protective of her and I hate to see her suffer more."

His colleague nodded in agreement. "I hate to see her suffer too, but I'm afraid there isn't any other alternative for her. She is bound to suffer as she comes to terms with this."

CHAPTER

TWELVE

After ten days Daniel was a wreck. Chuck continued living in the apartment with him, sleeping on the couch, producing food at regular intervals, and generally trying to keep his spirits up. Andy remained with their parents. He had settled in to his new routine happily, and seemed to accept the explanation that "Mommy will be home later. We're not sure when." Because he seemed to do better away from the apartment, Daniel left him where he was. In the apartment everything was a reminder of Katherine; cosmetics in the bathroom, her clothes in the bedroom, her work and her hobbies scattered around the house. He was grateful to his parents for getting Andy away from the memories he couldn't escape.

Daniel refused to go out. He had become obsessed with the idea that Katherine might call, and he had to be there to take the call. Three days after his interview a woman had called and politely told Daniel he was now free to travel. He was not a suspect. But he had already formed the belief he couldn't leave. Mrs. Holt at the Paris consulate had encouraged him to stay home, stressing that there was nothing to be accomplished by racing off to Paris. And so he stayed. He wouldn't leave to shop, work, take a walk. He didn't visit Andy, and he refused to let his parents bring Andy to the apartment, convinced that the sight of Katherine's things would upset the boy. Day after day Chuck watched Daniel slip further into depression, and further away from reality.

One afternoon Inspector Fitzgibbons stopped by, bringing with him information about the letter Katherine had sent to Sally. He was polite, but clearly uncomfortable with Daniel's obvious depression. "Mr. Bayley, I just need to ask you a few questions," he said.

Daniel was sitting on the couch. He nodded without looking up.

"You're aware we removed a letter from the apartment several days ago when we did the initial investigation?"

Again Daniel nodded.

"Are you aware of the contents of the letter?"

Another nod.

"I'd like you to comment on the letter."

Daniel looked up as if he had suddenly been asked to fly to the moon. "Comment. What's to comment on?"

"Did your wife discuss the letter with you?"

"No."

"How did you become aware of the letter before we located it?"

"I found it when my son took some stuff out of the drawer. I read it because Sally is a good friend of us both. I figured Katherine got the letter just before she left, and didn't have a chance to show it to me, so I read it."

"And what did you think?"

Daniel exploded. "What did I think? Hell, what am I supposed to think. I find a letter that says my wife is unhappy with me and with her son, and that she questions her life with us. What am I supposed to think? I feel like I don't even know that person. That's not Katherine."

"Not the Katherine you knew."

"Not the Katherine anyone knew," Daniel shouted. "Sure she had doubts about her life. She struggled to balance work with family. Everyone does, but she wasn't miserable with us. It wasn't like that."

"I'm sorry sir, but once again I must say it's not the Katherine you knew. Her friend, your friend too from what you say, wasn't surprised by the letter. She said she's received several in the last few years. She didn't keep them so we only have her word, but she indicated that your wife regularly had moments of doubt, both about this marriage and about her role as a mother.

"But we weren't unhappy! Didn't Sally also tell you that Katherine would never run away? That Katherine loved me? Why can't you understand that? Katherine wasn't unhappy, and she isn't a child who would run away."

"I realize that's how you see your wife, sir. However, as an impartial party looking at the situation from the outside, I have to tell you that your wife seems to exhibit the personality of one who might voluntarily disappear, and she does seem to have a motive."

"What motive?" Daniel threw his hands up in frustration.

"She was unhappy, had been for quite some time, and was no longer able to see hope that the situation would change."

He glared at the inspector. "That's not true! It wasn't like that. You don't know her."

"That's my point sir. I don't know her. I'm just looking at the facts we've discovered, and numerous people have commented on her obvious dissatisfaction with her life."

"Who? Who said anything like that?"

"I'm not at liberty to disclose names. Friends, co-workers, employees at the daycare your son attends. Apparently your wife was a very unhappy lady."

"She wasn't. Just before this trip she told me she wanted to spend more time at home with Andy. She was planning to cut back on traveling and work."

"Maybe the pressure of that decision was too much for her." He paused. "Are you aware your wife placed a call from Paris to this friend Sally shortly before she disappeared?

Daniel hung his head in defeat. The call said so much. A message that she didn't want to talk to him. He didn't know his own wife.

"You were aware of that call?" the inspector asked again.

Daniel nodded. "Sally told me when I talked to her a few days ago." He got up and began pacing the room. Suddenly he turned to the inspector and shouted, "This is bullshit. This whole conversation is bullshit. You don't know my wife, you never met her, and you come in here telling me she was a very unhappy woman and she chose to run away because she couldn't deal with us anymore? She wouldn't do that! It's not her." He stopped pacing, and stood, facing the inspector. Speaking more calmly he asked, "Didn't anyone tell you she's not the type to run away? Didn't anyone say anything good?"

"Oh, yes sir. A number of people expressed shock that she is missing, and felt she would not voluntarily run away from her life here. She was spoken of very highly by a number of people. Still, our experience tells us that friends and family usually do overlook the personality traits that allow someone to abandon a family. It's not a pleasant thing to consider, and often an abandonment is completely unexpected by the family left behind."

"I can't believe it. You're convinced that she choose to leave."

"The facts do seem to indicate that."

"Well, not to me they don't. I'm convinced Katherine is in trouble and needs my help, so what do I do next?"

"Well sir, that's really up to you. Given the facts that we've uncovered we're considering this a voluntary disappearance. We are closing the file. Any action you choose to take, provided it's legal, is fine with us. We're not involved at this point."

"That's it? You talk to a few people, decide she ran off, and that's it?"

"Well, of course we would re-open the investigation if any further evidence came to light, but I don't anticipate that."

"Get out!" Daniel shouted, pointing to the door. "Get out of my home! You're no help to me or to Katherine. Just get out."

"I'm very sorry sir," the inspector said, getting to his feet. Pausing at the door he spoke to Chuck. "You better have your brother see a doctor. He's not going to handle this alone."

Chuck nodded, holding the door open for the inspector. As he left Daniel crossed the room and slammed the door. He slumped against it, then sank to the floor.

For two weeks Chuck tried to get Daniel to see a doctor, hoping to pull him out of his depression. Daniel refused, and continued to stay at home, insisting he could not go out. Chuck got the doctor to provide a prescription for anti-depressants, but he couldn't make Daniel take the pills. When the private detective Daniel had hired asked to meet with him Chuck went instead. He couldn't make Daniel leave home.

After the meeting Chuck entered the apartment and found Daniel sitting on the couch, staring at nothing. At the sound of the door closing Daniel looked up. "Any luck?" he asked.

Chuck shook his head. "Nothing. Everything comes up blank, and he says he's out of leads."

"Then we'll find someone else. The guy's no good or he would have found something!"

"Daniel, you have to listen to me. The guy is good. He's one of the best private detectives in New York, and he's investigating leads we never even dreamed existed. He's interviewed dozens of people in Paris, visited all the shops and cafes near the hotel, talked to the hotel clerks. He's checked credit card records. He's traced the traveler's checks. Everything is a blank. It's like she just disappeared. The last traveler's check she used was cashed the Friday before she disappeared, in Paris. He hasn't talked to the bank yet, but he didn't expect to find anything." Chuck hesitated, reluctant to say anything more, but knowing he had to. "There was one thing that seemed odd. The Friday before she disappeared there were a couple of phone calls made from the hotel to airlines." He stopped, not wanting to voice his concern that Katherine had been looking for a place to disappear to.

Daniel shook his head. "I knew about that. She checked into flying home for Andy's party. We talked about it and she had already checked the prices."

"Then everything's a blank. She hasn't spent any money from the traveler's checks, her credit cards or her checkbook. I don't know what she's living on!"

"What do you mean what she's living on," Daniel exploded. "You think she took off too? Maybe she isn't living on anything because she isn't living."

Chuck let his brother continue yelling, expressing his frustrations until he was spent. Then he tried to reason with Daniel yet again. "Daniel, listen. We really have to talk about what happens next. I know it matters whether she's dead or ran away, and you want that answer, but either way it appears she isn't coming back."

"I haven't given up hope yet."

"Well, what are you going to do about Andy?" Chuck asked. "He's been living with Mom and Dad for awhile now, and it's not getting any easier on him. He's not only lost his mother, he also seems to have lost his dad. Did you ever think of how much he might need you?"

Daniel felt a momentary pang of guilt. He hadn't actually thought about Andy much in the last few weeks. "Mom says he's doing fine. She said she doesn't mind keeping him until this is straightened out."

"Daniel, that was weeks ago when she said that. Don't you see that the longer you leave Andy there the harder it will be for him to come home?"

"Andy's fine. I talk to Mom every day. She says he doing fine. I'm not ready to have him back here. I know I should, but I can't. I just sit here all day doing nothing. I can't make myself get up, I cry over nothing. How would Andy deal with that?"

Chuck didn't reply. He hadn't realized Daniel's depression was so bad. He left for work early each day, usually before Daniel was out of bed. When he returned to the apartment in the evening he often found

124

Daniel staring at nothing, but he hadn't thought the whole day was spent that way. "Daniel, I've still got those pills the doctor prescribed," he said. "I think you should start taking them."

"No! I won't take pills for depression. Those are for lunatics. I've got a perfectly good reason to be depressed."

"You've got a perfectly good son who needs his dad back."

"I don't need your help Chuck. I didn't ask you to move in here and baby-sit me."

"Just think about it Daniel. You've got to think about Andy."

Two days later Chuck was still trying to convince Daniel he should try the medication and should bring Andy home. He was in the kitchen putting a frozen pizza in the oven when the phone rang. Quickly Chuck picked up. "Chuck Bayley here. What can I do for you?"

"Mr. Bayley, this is Kevin Scott, the detective your brother hired."

"Mr. Scott! Yeah, I just talked to you a couple of days ago. Do you have new information?"

"Well, possibly, though I wasn't able to verify anything. I talked to the bank employees where that last traveler's check was cashed. The guard at the bank thinks he remembers Katherine."

"Yeah, how's that help us out?"

"Well," he paused. "I tried to talk to your brother about this earlier today, but he's not willing to hear it. The guard says she wasn't alone. She was with some guy and they both had suitcases."

Chuck didn't answer for a minute. "No, It's... it's... well it's hard for me to believe too. I can see why Daniel doubts it. Anyway, how credible is a bank guard on a memory that happened a month ago?"

"That's a point, and like I said his story is not verifiable. Unfortunately the security tapes are overwritten fairly quickly. But you've got to remember, the guy is a guard, and it's his job to remember people. He said one thing he's always wary of are people carrying suitcases. He tends to remember them. He seemed pretty definite that she was with someone."

"Well if she's left Paris we can figure out where she went then, right? I mean there'd be records or something. We can still find her."

"Two thoughts on that Mr. Bayley. First of all, I'd say she doesn't want to be found, so even if you find her what's it going to accomplish. You can't make her come back. Second thought: We might not find her anyway. If she left by plane there's a record, if she drove out, took a bus or a train there most likely isn't. Passport control in Western Europe is pretty lax. It's not unusual for people to be waved across the border without the custom's agent even opening the passport, especially for Americans or Europeans. We're talking about a huge investment of time and money to trace all those records, and in the end what do you get? Maybe nothing, maybe a chance to ask her why. Either way your brother doesn't have a wife. My recommendation is don't waste the money. She's gone and she isn't coming back. Now of course like I said before, I can't verify that guard's story, but he sure convinced me he remembered her. Let me know what you want to do."

CHAPTER

THIRTEEN

D r. Montoro entered his office and pulled Maria's file from the drawer. His brow was furrowed as he thought about her. Her body had healed, but her amnesia continued. He knew that Maria still held onto a strong belief that time would restore her memory, and didn't realize that the doctors had given up hope. Doctors Montoro and Fernandez had agreed she needed to be told soon that she would most likely not regain her memory, but Dr. Montoro had one more plan he hoped might work. Leafing through Maria's file he pulled out a slip of paper and stuck it in his pocket, then left the building.

Alicia was taking a break, having just scrubbed the toilet and the shower, when she heard the bell. Her rooms were all full, so she didn't buzz the door. Instead she spoke through the speaker mounted by the front door. "Diga".

"Mrs. Cabanillas, please. This is Dr. Montoro."

She hesitated, trying to place the name, then frowned as it registered. She had nearly forgotten the whole thing. What does he want after all this time, she wondered. She pressed the buzzer to release the door. A minute later she opened the outer door and looked into the stairway to see the doctor. He was walking up. She stood outside the door, watching him. When he reached the top she stepped back into the doorway, but didn't invite him in. He greeted her, then stood for an awkward moment before asking if he could come in. Reluctantly she stepped inside and led the way to her sitting room. She was hesitant to get involved in the life of the woman. Just now, for summer, her rooms were always full, she was busy, and she no longer missed the two young Americans who had been so eager to be involved. Occasionally she came across Kelly's address, tucked away in a drawer, but there was really nothing to write, so she just put it back, vaguely wishing she had some scrap of news to pass along. It was still several weeks before the universities would start, and business would drop off. Until then she was busy, and didn't want her free time taken up with talk of an unknown woman.

Dr. Montoro sat on the couch facing her. "It's about the woman in the hospital," he began. Alicia watched him silently, not really wanting to know how the woman was. "She's doing much better, but she's never regained her memory," he continued. "She's quite ready to come out of the hospital and live on her own, it's just that she really doesn't have anywhere to go." He hesitated. The old woman was looking at him steadily, saying nothing. He had hoped she might be eager to help, but that didn't seem to be the case. "I thought maybe she could stay here for a bit." He spoke quickly to avoid any possible rejection of the idea. However none was forthcoming. The woman just continued to regard him silently. "I thought if she could stay in familiar surroundings maybe something would jog her memory. If she could just remember something. Once she starts to she's likely to have a flood of memories. One will lead to another, and so on." He broke off, aware that he was rambling.

For a moment they sat quietly watching each other. Alicia shut her eyes and turned away slightly. She didn't want the woman coming to her, really couldn't afford to have her taking up one of her rooms. She needed every room and every peseta to get through the fall and winter months when she wouldn't have as many tourists.

As if he could read her mind Dr. Montoro spoke. "We could pay you well. There's a group, they help victims of the terrorism. They've agreed to pay for a place for a couple of months. If there's still no improvement, no memories, they'll help her get established again. Of course we're hoping she'll remember or be found. She's bound to have a relative somewhere, or friends."

Even as he said it Dr. Montoro thought how untrue the statement seemed. Inspector Aznar had worked tirelessly on the case. He had notified police stations across the country, sending out her photograph and investigating replies. Every single one had led to nothing. Mostly just sad stories of families that didn't stay in touch. An aunt calling to say the girl looked like her niece, and she hadn't heard from her niece in the past several months. Inspector Aznar had rushed to investigate, only to find that the girl was living happily in the next town, refusing to speak to her aunt over some petty jealousy. A mother who insisted the girl was her daughter, until her husband explained that the woman hadn't been able to accept their daughter's death. A young man calling to say perhaps it was his girlfriend who had been missing for two months. But the girlfriend's family said she was happily living in Barcelona, and please don't tell the boy who was rather obsessed with her and thought to be unstable. The list went on and on, filling a file that was now nearly two inches thick, and they still had no clue to the woman's identity.

While Dr. Montoro was reminiscing about the variety of calls, Alicia sat thinking. If they could pay her, rent the room like a tourist, there was really no reason not to take the woman. Of course there was food to consider. She couldn't be expected to eat out every day. She cleared her throat and muttered softly to herself until she had the doctor's attention. "Food?" she asked. "Would she be needing to eat here?" As she said it she thought of the lovely plates, left behind by the former residents. Of course the woman would need to eat off the lovely plates.

"We would be prepared to pay for food also. We can offer you 1000 pesetas a day, for two months."

The old woman pursed her lips and wrinkled her forehead. On a good day a room rented, without providing food for 1000 pesetas. Of course there were plenty of days that a room sat empty. Guaranteed income for two months would be a rare luxury, Alicia thought. If she used the small single room and left the doubles for tourists it might work. The single only rented for 800 pesetas, and it was often empty. She relaxed a little, realizing that having the woman might not be such a bad idea, wondering if with the regular income she could save enough to go see one of her daughters. She nodded her head. "Okay, she can come here."

The doctor looked relieved. "Thank you so much. I really think this is her last hope, the only place we can hope to jog her memory."

The old woman nodded. She stood up, signaling to the doctor that the conversation was done as far as she was concerned. He followed her into the hallway. "She's ready to discharge any time. We've really just been waiting on a place for her to go. Can she come tomorrow?"

The old woman nodded. "Sí, tomorrow. Come tomorrow in the morning." She held open the door for the doctor, and stood watching him walk down the stairs.

Dr. Montoro, Maria and Inspector Aznar arrived the next morning at 11:00. Alicia had done her best with the room, getting a young French boy who was staying with her to help her move some furniture around and make the room more attractive. She had gone into the other rooms and removed the antiques that had been left behind. The new room now held all the articles she could locate that might jog a memory.

In one corner stood the bed, covered in a green spread. Next to it was a small table with a marble top. On the table was an iron lamp with a pink shade. She had it lit to make the room more inviting. A small cabinet stood by the window. It had sat in the pantry for years, and now finally she had cleaned it up and moved it to this room. It was surprisingly pretty. In one of the drawers she had found two old photographs. She had bought cheap frames, and placed them on the cabinet. There was no way to know if the woman was in the photos, but surely they couldn't hurt.

Alicia led the group consisting of the doctor, the inspector and Maria into the bedroom. She hovered in the corner, unsure whether she was a landlady or a caretaker. Maria looked about the room in a daze, then moved slowly about, looking out the window, touching things. Slowly she approached the old woman. "Hello," she said softly. "What's your name?"

The old woman hesitated a moment. Never in all of her years running the pensión had anyone asked her name, until this woman entered her life. Now in the space of two months she'd had the American girls wanting her name and address, and this strange, unknown woman. Slowly she put her hand out to the younger woman. "Alicia," she said. "My name is Alicia." She offered only her first name. Somehow that was all that seemed appropriate in greeting a woman who could offer no more.

Maria took her hand, not shaking it, but simply holding it, gently squeezing. "Alicia," she repeated. "I am Maria. I've forgotten my last name." Alicia nodded, not answering, just holding the woman's hand. After a moment Maria turned and resumed her wandering around the room.

The doctor spoke. "Maria, we're going to go now. I'll be back to see you soon." Alicia turned to him, alarmed. Seeing her look of concern, Dr. Montoro gently took her by the arm. "Mrs. Cabanillas, why don't we talk out here." He led her into the hallway and the inspector followed, shutting Maria's door behind him.

"There's nothing to be concerned about. She's quite healthy now, and new memories are retained normally," he said. "She won't wander off and forget where you live, or forget your name, or anything else. She simply can't remember anything from before the bomb."

The old woman nodded without feeling reassured. "Okay, we'll see you in a few days." She walked the two men to the door and watched them start down the stairs. She was hesitant to go back inside, unsure of what she had taken on. Maria seemed normal enough, and yet everyone knew she wasn't. It wasn't normal to forget everything, to have no family who missed you enough to look for you. The old woman sighed, hoping she hadn't taken on too much.

As soon as she re-entered the apartment Maria's door popped open. "Alicia," she began, "I was wondering if you'd like some help fixing lunch?"

Alicia stopped. It was odd to hear her name called out like that in the apartment. No one had done it for years, not since Carlos had died. She smiled at Maria and thought that perhaps having her would be good for both of them.

Over lunch they talked about all sorts of things, as if they were two old friends rather than two strangers, or landlady and tenant. Alicia asked about the memories, what it was like to not know who you were, and Maria poured out her feelings. The anger and frustration of it all. The wondering if she would ever regain the lost years. The pain of not knowing who or where her family was. Alicia spoke of her loneliness since her husband died. Her sorrow that the children had all moved so far away and didn't visit. The frustration of running the pensión on her own, always haggling with tourists over a few pesetas, afraid if she didn't give in they would go off somewhere else and she wouldn't have the money to eat, always earning just enough to scrape by, never any extra for a luxury or a day off. Both women realized they were lonely, and could be good company for each other.

That afternoon when Alicia went shopping she invited Maria along. Together they walked the street, stopping at the panadería, the frutaría, and the mercado near the Plaza Mayor. Alicia was pleased to have someone help with packages, and found that she and Maria liked many of the same things. They bought enough for two days, planning the menus as they went. Gambas for dinner tonight, with salad, fruit and wine to go along. A big dinner because they both felt like celebrating their new friendship and the hope that this move represented for Maria. Besides, Alicia had a pocketful of money, the first week's rent paid in advance. They chose a sack full of small, green plums for dessert, and stopped in the bakery for two palmeras de chocolate as an added treat. They planned gazpacho for lunch the next day, and tiny wedges of cheese to serve as dessert. For supper they planned paella, which Alicia claimed was her specialty, though she hadn't had reason to make one for years. Several small, hard rolls, strong coffee and a carton of milk for breakfast rounded out the purchases.

When the doctor returned the next week, the two women were fast friends. The 30-year gap in their ages was insignificant, and neither felt like they had just met. They prepared all the meals together, shopped together, and spent hours in Alicia's living room, talking or watching the TV companionably. Together they studied all the antiques Alicia had, hoping something would trigger a memory, and Alicia dug into the back of her mind, telling all the stories she could remember about the time when her children were young. Maria had been a child at the same time, and both hoped something would sound familiar. Happily Alicia recounted memories of taking her children to school or the park, and less happily recalled all she could of the political upheaval Spain had gone through. Maria listened to it all as if she were in a history lesson. She could recall the carefully told details, but could add nothing of her own. There was no hint of a memory to indicate she had lived in this time they discussed.

Nearly a month had passed when Maria began to lose hope. She woke up one Saturday morning with the realization that this attempt to help her had done nothing. They had a Saturday routine, she and Alicia-- clean the kitchen and living room and their own rooms, then do the shopping for the weekend-- but today Maria didn't participate. Instead she lay in her bed feeling exhausted. It's useless, she told herself I'm never going to remember anything. She looked around the room, her eyes resting on the objects Alicia had placed there. The table, the lamp, the photographs. If she had ever seen them before she didn't know it. Silent tears slid down her face as she stared about her. For the first time since the accident she felt fear rather than anger. Who am I to be, she asked herself. How am I to live?

An hour after their usual breakfast time Alicia tapped on the door. "Maria?" she called. "Maria, are you alright?"

Maria didn't answer. Instead she wiped her face with the edge of the sheet and turned her back to the door, pulling the covers half way over her face. After a moment Alicia opened the door and peeked in. "Maria," she said again, "What's wrong? Are you sick?"

Vaguely Maria nodded and mumbled something about not feeling well. She didn't want to admit to Alicia that she had given up hope. Instead she feigned illness and apologized for leaving the work all to Alicia.

For three days she remained in her bed, unable to force herself to do anything. She picked at the food Alicia brought her and was vague about her symptoms. On the third day Alicia appeared with Dr. Montoro. She had called him, worried about Maria.

When the doctor entered the room Maria sat up angrily, feeling energy for the first time in days. "This isn't working," she shouted. "You've got to do something else. I can't go on like this forever."

Dr. Montoro wanted to tell her the truth, that she might well have to go on like this forever, but he remembered Dr. Fernandez's suggestion that they let Maria establish a new identity prior to telling her anything. He stood in the middle of the room trying to calm her while Alicia hovered in the doorway, wanting to support her new friend, but unable to help. "Maria," Dr. Montoro said, speaking softly, "We need to give it a little more time."

"Well, how long?" She lowered her voice, but was still quite agitated.

"No one can say for sure," he replied. "Of course in cases of amnesia we hope for a quick recovery, but no one can say for sure how long it might take."

"Well, what's normal? How long do most people take to recover memories?" She stared intently at the doctor.

Dr. Montoro stared back, unsure of what to say without revealing the whole truth. Speaking carefully he said, "Every case is different, Maria. In truth it is very unusual to see such total amnesia in someone who appears to have recovered normally in all other respects. We might see it in someone with severe brain damage, but complete amnesia is quite rare. I haven't got a time line to judge normal because there aren't enough cases." He shrugged his shoulders helplessly.

"But what else can I do?" Maria yelled. When Dr. Montoro said nothing, just shook his head, she leaned forward, curling herself into a ball, and began to sob. Alicia came forward, sat beside her, and attempted to comfort her, but nothing she said helped. Instead Maria grew increasingly agitated, her sobs punctuated with angry shouts. "This isn't fair! Why me? What about my child?"

Helplessly Alicia looked up at the doctor, not speaking, but pleading for him to help Maria. Wordlessly he opened the small medical bag he carried with him and produced two pills. Crossing the room he lay his hand on Maria's shoulder and gently pushed her into an upright position. "I want you to take these," he said. "They will help you feel better."

Relieved for any sort of solution Alicia fetched Maria a glass of water and held it to her lips while she drank. The two remained with her until she began to calm down, then slipped out and shut the door.

"She'll sleep for several hours," the doctor said.

Alicia nodded, thankful the doctor had given her something.

"Here." He reached into the bag and pulled out a bottle of pills. "You may need to give her another when she wakes up, but only one. After that she can take one every eight hours if needed. I'll see about getting Dr. Fernandez over to see her as soon as possible."

Back in his office he called Dr. Fernandez and explained how he had found Maria. "I think we have to tell her that she might never recover any memories. We have to help her accept and get on with her life."

"It's better to wait," Dr. Fernandez argued. "It's better for the patient to have hope."

Dr. Montoro shook his head. "I'm convinced she needs to be told," he said. "She's giving up hope anyway, and she isn't making any effort to establish a new identity. She isn't meeting people, she isn't working. We have to move her forward."

"No," Dr. Fernandez insisted. "She will just lose all hope. You are suggesting, in effect, that we tell her there is no hope. How can you expect her to go on after that?"

"I expect her to go on because there is no other choice. Hiding the truth from her won't make it go away, and every day it is more obvious to everyone, including her, that she isn't recovering her memory. It's time to move on."

"We were going to put her there for two months and see what happened. It's only been one month. Why don't we wait a little longer?" Dr. Fernandez suggested.

Dr. Montoro gripped the phone, frustrated by the other doctor's disagreement. "This is what I will agree to," Dr. Montoro said. "We will meet with her in one month, as you suggested, to discuss her future. However, in the meantime I want her to meet with you regularly, several times a week, to talk about the future and introduce the idea that she might not recover. We will meet with her in one month," he repeated, "and you must prepare her."

The month passed quickly. Dr. Montoro thought of Maria often, but didn't check up on her. He saw her only once, when she sought him out, at the hospital, and asked him about giving her a different medication, one that would help calm her without making her so tired. The meeting seemed to him a sign of positive progress. She was getting out, doing things, and was concerned about the drugged feeling the stronger medicine had created. At the end of the month he arranged a meeting to discuss future plans, inviting Alicia, the inspector, and Dr. Fernandez to join him and Maria.

They gathered in Alicia's living room, bringing the two chairs from the kitchen so there was space for everyone. Dr. Montoro opened the meeting with a businesslike air. "Unfortunately," he began, "the group who has been paying for the rent and food won't be able to help after this month. We were hoping for some recovery of memories shortly after you moved in here, but we have seen no progress."

Maria felt she had somehow failed them all, and wondered what was in store for her next. More tests? Another hospital? "So," she asked, "What else can be done to help me? What do we do now?" She looked from Dr. Montoro to Dr. Fernandez, not sure who held the answers.

Dr. Montoro was alarmed, knowing she wouldn't ask that question if Dr. Fernandez had prepared her. She would have come to the conclusion herself that there was nothing else to be done. He looked at Dr. Fernandez, eyebrows raised in question, but the other man looked away, unwilling to meet his gaze. He searched for the kindest way to tell her, wanting to leave her some hope though he himself had none. "Maria," he said slowly, "What we do next is find a way to help you start a new life. We can help you find work, find a place to live, move on in your life."

Maria's heart began to pound wildly. The answer had stunned her, and she shivered in fear as she realized what they were saying. There was no more hope of returning her to her former life. They were giving up.

Dr. Montoro read her face and told her they were not really giving up. There was always hope that she would remember something, and in the meantime the files would remain open, and any possible leads would be investigated. But there was no reason she couldn't get a job, find a place to live and, he suggested gently, begin to move forward with her life.

The inspector explained how they could create a persona for her. She would become a legal creation, able to work and live in society, but unable to state her birthday, birthplace or family name. She would live under a created name, and all records would simply state that no one knew who she truly was.

Maria shook her head fiercely. "You can't mean this!" she shouted. "There has to be something we can do. There has to be some way I can know who I am! What about my child? My husband? There has to be a way to find them!"

Dr. Montoro spoke patiently, "We can't know why they haven't come forward or reported you missing. Of course there has to be a reason." He stopped, hoping to avoid saying more.

"What reason?" she shouted. "How is it possible no one misses me?"

Dr. Montoro shook his head slowly. "Maria," he said, hoping to calm her. "It is very strange. Really the only explanation is that you must have no family." Or friends he said to himself. It almost seemed impossible, but of course there were people, living in the midst of the city, that no one really knew and that no one would miss.

"But the baby," Maria insisted. "There's bound to be someone who was taking care of my child."

The doctor shook his head. "It's possible there wasn't. The baby may have died, or you may have given it up." Ignoring Maria's blank stare he went on. The memories might return in time, but they might not, he told her. Long-term amnesia was very rare, but it did happened. Occasionally people simply learned to get on with life, building new memories, and always feeling a little left out when people talked about the past. Some even created fantasy lives for their childhood, inventing parents, brothers and sisters, vacations taken, hobbies enjoyed. But he didn't recommend that. If there were memories, far better to know for sure they were real. After several years time a person could begin to forget that the stories they told were just stories.

Without speaking, Maria got up and left the room. They could hear her in her own room down the hall, sobbing. Alicia spoke softly, but with authority, to the men. "She will need a little time to get used to this. Give us a few days, then we will call you." She stood up, indicating the meeting was over for now. After showing the men out she went to her friend's room, entered without knocking, and sat beside her, trying to offer comfort, but Maria turned away from her and refused to speak or look at her. Sadly Alicia left the room, closing the door behind her.

For two days Maria barely spoke, and refused to leave her room. She alternated between sitting silently and weeping inconsolably, and she refused to take the medication or eat the food that Alicia brought her. On the third morning she appeared for breakfast, setting the table while Alicia prepared the coffee. "Forgive me for the last couple of days," she said formally. "I haven't been a very good boarder, leaving all the work to you."

Alicia put down the coffeepot and turned to face Maria. "I don't consider you a boarder. I've thought of you as a friend," she said angrily. The anger caught Maria off guard. Her formality crumbled and she began to cry. Alicia crossed the room and put her arms around her friend, leading her into the living room and seating her on the couch. "I think this will all go much better if we talk it out as friends rather than you hiding in your room and pushing me away," she said.

"But you can't imagine what it's like," Maria sobbed. "No one can imagine. All this time I thought if I just waited patiently I would recover and discover who my family was, but now they tell me it's not true. You can't imagine! I've got a child somewhere. I can't remember it, and I don't know where that child is or if it needs me. Most of all I can't imagine why that child, or the father of that child, or someone hasn't come forward and admitted to knowing me. Am I such a horrible person, was I such a horrible person, that no one wants to claim me? Are they all better off for having me gone, relieved I can't find them? I mean Alicia, think of it. If you were in my place wouldn't someone know you? Your neighbors, the shopkeepers, people would know you. For me it's like I never existed. You are the only person who remembers me from before the bombing, and you don't know anything about me."

Alicia sat quietly, letting her friend pour out her sorrows. Eventually Maria stopped, and the two of them sat, not speaking for a few minutes. Then Maria added quietly, "and I don't know where to go. I don't know what sort of work I'm able to do."

Alicia looked at her. "I've been thinking about that," she said. "We're happy together and we get along well. I don't see any reason why you can't stay on here if you want. You could find a job to help with the expenses, and keep the single room. I enjoy your company."

Maria thought over the proposal. "Are you sure you're not just feeling obligated?" she asked. Reassured that Alicia did indeed want her to stay, the two began to make plans. So it was all settled when they called Dr. Montoro, and he arranged for the inspector to bring the paperwork that would prove Maria was a legal resident of Spain, birthplace listed as Madrid, age set at 34. He told her to pick a birth date, because she had to continue to get older, and a name, because she had to be someone. She chose to keep the hospital's name for her: Maria Desconocida. She chose July 3rd, the date of the paperwork, for her birthday.

The next morning she was up early, and forced herself to get out of bed. After a quick cup of coffee she left the apartment and went in search of a job. She wandered down to the Plaza Mayor, trying to decide what sort of work she used to do, wondering what she was qualified for. If she had ever had a university education she could no longer remember it, so for all practical purposes she was looking for something that required no special skills. She had been wandering aimlessly for an hour when she saw a sign in a shop window advertising for help. It was a touristy place, selling goods from all over Spain, for the benefit of tourists who didn't visit the rest of the country.

She paused outside the window looking at the wooden trays and tables from Granada, the jewelry from Toledo, the lace from Salamanca. A shop like that would benefit from hiring her, someone who spoke English and could help foreign customers. She wondered again about her education, for she had realized gradually that she understood both English and French, and in the last month had taken over dealing with the guests at the pension who didn't speak Spanish. I suppose I could be a benefit to a tourist shop, she thought. She entered and greeted the woman behind the counter. "Buenas días. I'm interested in the job you have posted in the window."

Before the woman could answer the shop door opened again, and two customers entered. "Just a moment," she said to Maria, and turned to greet the customers. As the woman showed them one item after another Maria studied the shopkeeper. She was in her early fifties. Her hair was short and graying at the temples. She was average height, and wore a plain black dress. She's probably widowed, Maria thought, and resigned to black for the rest of her life. Her shoes were sensible lace ups, and her ankles swollen. She was obviously struggling to understand the English couple and to answer their questions.

Maria stepped closer to the trio and said softly, in Spanish, "I could translate for you."

The woman looked at her with new interest, and nodded her head eagerly.

Smoothly, as if she had been selling lace tablecloths all her life Maria began to explain about how and where they were made. The shop woman held one out, spreading it across the counter to show off the pattern. Maria translated, word for word the description she gave, and threw in a sales pitch encouraging them to consider a gift for someone who hadn't been able to come on holiday with them.

To her delight the couple began discussing who might appreciate the tablecloths, and in the end bought three, one for themselves, one for the lady's sister who was getting married next month, and the third for his mother who was watching over the house and the dogs. By the time they left the shop Maria was hired.

The shop owner thanked her for her assistance, and introduced herself. Her name was Consuela Arasa. Maria offered her hand. "Maria Desconocida," she said, introducing herself and accepting her new name all at once.

Consuela gave her an odd look. "Desconocida. That's an unusual name."

Maria nodded. "Yes, not too many around." she replied. She felt strangely calm about the situation. The successful sale of the tablecloths had given her confidence. This was something she could do. Perhaps she had even done it before, but if she hadn't she would now. If she couldn't go back to who she was she would go forward to who she could be: Maria, who works in the tourist shop and lives in a pensión on the Gran Via. She decided she would save her money carefully, for someday she might have an opportunity to know more about herself, and it would come in handy to have the money. If people felt she didn't give enough information about herself she wouldn't worry about it. Perhaps someday she would have a group of people who knew the truth about her, but for now she would keep it to herself, and the small group who knew her story. No one else needed to know.

FOURTEEN

Nearly two months had passed, and Daniel still lived in limbo. Regardless of the detective's findings, he didn't fully accept that Katherine had run away. He agonized daily, alternating between believing she had, and the conviction that she had been kidnapped or killed. He was functioning better now, mostly thanks to Chuck's refusal to leave him alone. Chuck had hounded him constantly about taking the medicine the doctor had prescribed until finally Daniel had agreed just to appease Chuck. To his surprise, after a couple of weeks he had begun to feel differently. He began managing life again, slowly at first, and then one day he realized that he no longer slept the day away, or sat staring for hours on end. But neither had he returned to work or brought Andy home. Now it was time. He picked up the phone and dialed his parents.

"Andy, come here please."
Andy ran into the kitchen, smiling up at his grandma.
"Sit down for a minute. I want to talk to you." She pulled out one of the big, wooden chairs for him and sat on another, turning to face the boy.
Andy climbed onto the chair, and sat swinging his legs. She looked at her little grandson, hesitant to disrupt his life yet again. He had settled into her home beautifully, and it almost seemed as if he'd forgotten Katherine ever existed. She reached out and smoothed his hair.
"Would you like a cookie?" she asked.

Andy nodded enthusiastically. He took a huge bite of the cookie she offered, still smiling at her.

Taking a deep breath she began, "Do you remember how we've been waiting for your Mommy to come back?"

"Is she here?" he asked eagerly, looking around the room as if she might be hidden somewhere.

"No, honey. No, she isn't here."

"Oh." His face was solemn now, the cookie lying forgotten on the table in front of him.

"Actually, she's...well, it's just that...Well, Andy, your Mommy isn't going to be coming back we don't think."

His eyes filled with tears which threatened to spill over. "Why won't she come back? Is she mad at me?"

"No honey. It's not that. When your Mommy went to Paris something happened to her. We're not sure what happened, but she died and she can't come back." That was the official story the family had agreed on. Andy would be told she had died. Each of them had their own personal opinions on the disappearance, but all agreed that Andy should not be told that she had chosen to abandon the family.

"So when is she coming back?"

"Andy, when a person dies they don't come back. They go to heaven and live with God."

"Can I go there and see her?" he asked. Tears were running freely down his face.

"Not now you can't. People who are alive can't visit people who are dead. When we die we can go to heaven and see her again."

"But I want to see her now." He began to sob. Reaching over she picked him up and pulled him onto her lap. Rocking him gently she wiped his tears with the hem of her blouse.

"We all want to see her now, but God didn't work it out that way."

"Well you said God was nice and he's not nice if he won't let me see Mommy," Andy shouted.

She hugged him to her tighter, fighting back her own tears. "Oh, honey. God is nice. That's just how life is. People die, and those of us who don't die have to wait to see them. But I've got some happy news too. You're going to go back and live with your Daddy."

"No!" Andy screamed. "I want to stay here. This is where I live."

"Not actually. Remember how you used to live in the apartment with Daddy?"

"I did not! I did not live there with Daddy," Andy shouted. "I lived there with Mommy!" He stared up at his Grandma, a defiant look on his face. "And Daddy," he added, so softly she almost couldn't hear him.

"Well now you're going to go back and live there with Daddy."

"I don't want to. Daddy said I was staying here until Mommy came home, and you said she isn't coming home, and I don't want to." He broke into racking sobs. For a long time Margie sat and held him, saying nothing, just letting him cry it all out. She held him tightly until eventually he sat silently, occasionally wiping his eyes with the back of his hand. Then she stood, carried him across to the sink and sat him on the counter top. Taking a damp washcloth she gently wiped his face.

"Daddy is coming to get you tomorrow," she said softly. Andy didn't reply. He remained on the counter top refusing to speak to her or look at her until she lifted him down. Then he ran out of the room and she could hear him pounding up the stairs to his room.

Monday evening Daniel drove to his parents' house to collect Andy. They had arranged for him to move back on a weekday so the biggest part of his day, spent at the daycare center, would remain unchanged. Daniel was apprehensive, realizing suddenly how much he had ignored Andy and lived in his own world. He had hardly seen him in the last few weeks, and hadn't done anything to care for him.

When Daniel entered the house Andy was withdrawn and quiet, refusing to speak, and clinging to his Grandma. Daniel realized then how much his own problems had effected his son. The little boy who two months ago had happily gone everywhere with him now wasn't speaking to him. He was afraid to return to the only place he had ever called home. Daniel realized that Andy must have felt abandoned by him as well as by Katherine. When it was time to leave Andy cried and clung to his Grandma, refusing to be consoled. In the end she came with them, bringing enough clothing to stay for several days, hoping to help Andy adjust.

When they arrived at the apartment he wandered about warily, looking at things, running his hands over the couch and chairs as if to reassure himself they were still there. Daniel had carefully put away all reminders of Katherine, though he had disposed of nothing. In his heart he still believed she would be back, so he had carefully boxed her things and rented a storage unit to hold it all. When Andy reached his own room he brightened a bit at the sight of his things, still laying where he had left them except for some minor straightening up that Daniel had done.

He picked up a toy airplane and began to spin around, a hint of a smile on his lips, a faint airplane buzz emerging from them. A moment later he threw the plane across the room into the wall. "Everybody's dead," he announced to no one in particular. "When you go on an airplane, everybody's dead." He picked up his favorite teddy bear next. "Where's your Mommy?" he asked.

"I don't have a Mommy. She's dead," he made the bear reply.

"I don't have a Mommy either. She's dead too," Andy told the bear. Suddenly he collapsed on the floor, sobbing. Daniel went to him, but the more Daniel tried to comfort Andy the louder he screamed until eventually Margie went to him and took him. He clung to her, weeping. For nearly 20 minutes he cried, then quieted and quickly fell asleep. She tucked him into his bed carefully, not bothering to remove his clothes for fear she would wake him.

Over the next several days Andy slowly adjusted. On the third night Margie decided to go home after Andy was sleeping. When he woke the next morning to find her gone he fell to the floor, screaming. Daniel first attempted to comfort him, then finally carried him, still screaming to the kitchen for breakfast. There Andy ate three bites of cereal and threw the rest to the floor. Daniel patiently cleaned it up, then spent 30 minutes trying to dress his son. Eventually he gave up and took him, in jeans and his pajama top, shoes in hand, to the daycare.

After that first morning without Margie Andy settled into having her gone, allowing Daniel to dress him and get his breakfast, but refusing to have anything to do with him in the evenings when Margie was there. When this had gone on for a week they decided that she should stop coming over. She packed her final few items and left, reminding Daniel she was just a phone call away if he needed her.

That evening, as soon as Daniel returned with Andy, Andy began running through the apartment yelling for his Grandma. Daniel dreaded the evening, anticipating more tears and fearing he wouldn't be able to console Andy. He had never been uncomfortable with Andy, until recently. Now he felt helpless, living with a feeling of dread over the next fit of weeping. It wasn't that he was angry with Andy, just that he felt helpless. He was aware that his withdrawal during the last two months had changed their relationship. Eventually he stopped Andy's roaming search for his Grandma. "She's not here right now," Daniel said, his voice calmer than he felt.

Andy didn't reply, but continued to roam the apartment, convinced she would be somewhere. Eventually he settled in his room, sitting on the floor, not playing, but just staring. Daniel let nearly an hour pass before he approached his son and invited him to McDonalds for dinner. For the first time since Andy had come home he smiled at Daniel, and Daniel felt a tiny bit of the dread melting away. Maybe Andy will be all right, he told himself. We'll get back to how it used to be, and he'll forget that I left him. Maybe someday we'll be happy again.

Over the next several weeks Andy continued to improve and Daniel began to feel more comfortable. But Andy never mentioned Katherine, not since that first night back in the apartment, and Daniel didn't mention her for fear of causing more harm. He thought about putting some pictures out so Andy wouldn't forget Katherine entirely, but decided it was too painful, so the pictures remained stored away, and no one ever mentioned her name.

In private Daniel still kept in touch with Mrs. Holt at the Paris embassy, calling at least once a week to see if anything had been discovered. She was polite and consoling, but could offer no encouragement other than to say some people disappear, then later decide to come home, realizing that the people in their life were not the cause of their problems. Daniel wondered if he would ever forgive Katherine if she did return. Slowly he and Andy settled into a new routine, and Daniel found himself looking forward to a new school year in the fall. He wasn't yet happy, but he could imagine that someday he might be. He hoped Andy was feeling the same.

PART TWO
1991

CHAPTER

ONE

Daniel lay on the bed, reluctant to start his day. It was the same every anniversary. He'd wake up wondering why she'd left, and if she'd ever get in touch with him. Years ago, after the first anniversary of Katherine's disappearance he had devised a plan to get through the day. He would get up, take a few minutes to think about Katherine and her disappearance, then contact the detective to check for new leads. After that he and Andy would go out and do something special. The plan had worked well the past couple of years, helping him through the awful anniversary, but this year, *four years,* somehow seemed more significant. He sighed heavily. It's time to move on, he told himself. Forget about her and what she did to us. Forget about ever getting to ask her why.

The first year he had convinced himself that sometime in the future he would know what happened to her. Know for sure, not just speculate. Know why she had left and where she had gone. Have the opportunity to ask her how she could have left them. That first, awful, year he had called the detective every week, hounding him for information. Then, on the first anniversary of her disappearance he had sunk into a depression of such magnitude he had forgotten Andy and had lain in his bed all day. It had been late afternoon when Andy, bored with his toys and hungry had suddenly become aware of Daniel's absence and broken into hysterical screams, running about the apartment, searching for him. That was when he had realized for the second time that his own ability to deal with Katherine's disappearance would effect their son. He had resolved to move on with life, no matter how difficult.

The second year he had called the detective once a month, then every other month, and finally, at the end of the year, had admitted to himself that there was no real hope, and once a year was probably more than enough. That was the year he had decided to leave New York.

They had gone to Vermont where so many of Daniel's happy memories were. He had spent school breaks there with his grandparents, skiing, skating and sledding in the winter, camping and hiking in the summer. Andy had taken to the move wonderfully, and loved the rural atmosphere. Daniel taught now at a small liberal arts college. Not as prestigious as Columbia, but where he wanted to be. He had kept his mouth shut about Katherine, so there were no whispered comments, pitying looks, or prying questions. The staff and few friends he had made believed Katherine had died in an accident while traveling overseas, the same story Andy believed. He had instructed the staff at Columbia to notify Detective Scott immediately if anyone came looking for him, but to give his address to no one.

He pushed himself up off the bed and walked toward the bathroom. Their house was simple, just a cottage really, but they liked it. The upstairs, built to look out over the living room, was small, just two bedrooms with sloping ceilings, and a tiny bathroom at the end of the hall. Downstairs they had a large living room, the kitchen and another bathroom. Daniel had wanted the place as soon as he saw it, all wooden floors and exposed beams, with a huge stone fireplace in the living room. Andy had been thrilled with the yard, surrounded by trees, with a little creek running along the back of the property.

Passing Andy's room he pushed open the door and looked in. The bed was empty, covers thrown back and sliding to the floor. Toys were strewn about, the clutter of a seven-year-old. Eight-year-old, he reminded himself. Andy's birthday was forever linked to the awful day Katherine had disappeared. He crossed to the window and looked out. Andy was there, throwing a ball to Boogie, the lovable mutt they had rescued together from a shelter as their second anniversary outing.

Pushing open the window he called out to Andy, "Happy Birthday, Sport."

Andy looked up, ball still in his hand, while Boogie danced wildly around him trying to snatch it. "Hi Dad."

"Did you have breakfast yet?"

"Yeah. Me and Boogie had breakfast together. I made him toast. With peanut butter," he added.

Daniel grimaced at this news. "I'll be ready in about an hour, okay?"

"Yeah." Andy had gone back to his game.

Their plan was to head south to a state park for a couple of days of hiking and camping, and to watch the Ball Mountain Dam release. Andy was ecstatic about the event. The only thing that would make it more perfect for him would be if the two of them were to kayak the river, but Daniel thought Andy was too young for that.

Quickly Daniel showered and dressed. Carrying a cup of coffee he sat at the desk in the living room which made up his entire office. A file cabinet of bills was on the right side. Opening the bottom drawer he reached into the back and pulled out a thick file. He scanned the contents, reviewing the facts he would never forget. *She called on Friday to say she had to stay over for the weekend. Her boss called Monday to scream at me because she wasn't at the photo shoot. The embassy investigated and found nothing. The detective found a guard at a bank who insists he saw Katherine with another man and a suitcase. Further investigation turned up nothing.* He picked up the phone and dialed.

"Detective Scott."

For a moment Daniel was unable to speak, his breath frozen within him, wondering what he would do if the detective ever heard from her. Clearing his throat he said, "Mr. Scott, it's Daniel Bayley."

"Oh, hello Mr. Bayley. How are you?"

"Fine, doing fine."

"Boy doing okay?"

"Oh yeah. Eight-years-old today. He's getting big."

"Yeah, they have a way of doing that, don't they?"

Their conversation was light, both of them knowing that there would be no information. If there were Daniel would have been notified immediately.

"So, uh, I guess there's nothing new?" Daniel ran his hand through his hair nervously.

"No sir. You know I'd call you if anything came up."

"Yeah, yeah of course. It's just kind of my little routine. Call once a year and make sure. I always think she might remember Andy's birthday and try to contact him."

"Makes sense. You'd hear from me right away if we found her."

"Yeah. Okay. Good-bye and thanks." He hung up and slumped back in his chair, wondering why he couldn't let go. After a moment he sat up straighter, a determined look on his face. I won't call him again, he vowed. Hearing Andy enter the house he put the file away and turned toward his desk.

"Come on Dad. We're going to be late." Andy stood, impatiently shifting from foot to foot, the dog beside him.

"We've got plenty of time. Just let me finish my coffee."

Andy looked behind him at the clock on the kitchen wall. "It's almost 8:00. We need to get going."

"Well, tell you what, you start hauling our stuff out and get Boogie in the truck, and I'll be ready in five minutes." He looked over at the mountain of gear they were taking; tent, sleeping bags, cooler, suitcases, portable cook stove, pots, pans, the pile seemed endless. As Andy began lugging their gear, Daniel got up and loaded the food into the cooler. He had prepared everything the night before so they could get an early start. Heaving the cooler up he took it out and loaded it into the truck.

"Boogie gets to ride in front with us, right?" Andy asked him.

"Oh Andy. That dog smells."

"It's not his fault. He's a dog. He's supposed to smell." Andy knelt and put his arms around Boogie, rubbing his face in the dog's fur.

Daniel looked at the truck bed, loaded haphazardly. It was an extended cab, late model Ford that he had bought just after they moved to Vermont. He hopped into the bed and rearranged a few items, making them more secure. "Ok, put him in front, but the back of the front!"

"Come on Boogie," Andy yelled, jumping to his feet. He pulled the door open, encouraging the dog, but Boogie needed no encouragement. Andy scrambled into the back with the dog. Opening the small window to the back he hollered, "I'm riding in the back seat too, okay?" Daniel nodded his acknowledgement.

By mid-morning they had arrived. They checked in to claim their campsite, but left the set-up for later. Daniel had brought sandwiches, and they ate the first of them as they hiked through the woods, Boogie now confined to a long leash. The water release had begun early, but would continue until mid-afternoon. Daniel figured they could hike there from the campsite and arrive by lunchtime as long as they kept moving. Andy and Boogie made it difficult though, ducking down every side path, running up the hills and repeatedly tangling the leash around trees. He gave up trying to hurry them, not really caring what time they got there.

Eventually they reached the river. Staking out a good spot Daniel sat down to watch while Andy and Boogie continued to explore. Looking up the river he saw several colorful kayaks bobbing about. "Andy, come here," he called. Andy arrived with Boogie, Boogie's nose to the ground. "Here they come," he said, pointing up the river.

Andy looked up river eagerly, then switched his attention to Daniel. "Can I have another sandwich?"

Daniel nodded. "Why don't you sit down here to watch?" he asked. He was nervous about Andy being out of reach so close to the rushing water.

"We want to walk around," Andy replied, then added "Can Boogie have a sandwich?"

Daniel shook his head. "No sandwiches for Boogie, but you can walk around if you stay on the path."

"But Dad," Andy protested, "Boogie likes to get near the water."

Daniel shook his head again. "Stay on the path. The river is dangerous when it's rushing so fast."

"Dad," Andy gave him an exasperated look. "I'm eight-years-old. I know how to swim."

"That's not the point. The water is very cold and very rough. Stay away!" When Andy didn't answer he added, "If you don't you'll have to come sit with me."

"Okay," Andy said. "We'll stay away." Taking his sandwich he ran down the path.

Daniel sat, lost in thought, remembering his own youthful kayaking adventures. Before Andy, before Katherine. He was startled when he heard someone say, "Daniel? Is that you?"

Turning around he saw Ellen, a woman who had taught with him at Columbia. They had been friends at the university, talking in the halls and sharing an occasional cup of coffee, but when he had moved they hadn't kept in touch. "Ellen." He got to his feet, brushing his pants off.

"How are..."

"What are you..." They spoke at the same time, both laughed, and started again.

"How are you?" he asked.

"I'm fine. What are you doing here?"

"Andy and I are camping for a few days. What about you?"

She laughed and looked longingly at the river. "I was planning to kayak, but I hurt my arm two days ago so now I'm watching." She held up her left arm, wrapped in an ace bandage.

"Oh, too bad. I hope it's not serious."

"No, it'll mend soon, but I'm out of the river until fall." The dam release only occurred one weekend in spring and one in the fall.

"Have you done it before? Andy's wild to try it, but I think he's too young."

"I went last year. Great fun. He's probably okay if he's not afraid and has the basic skills."

"Yeah, well I don't know. Maybe someday. I haven't been kayaking for years. I'm out of practice." They stood for a moment, each out of things to say. Then Daniel asked, "Do you want to join us?" He indicated the ground.

"Yeah, sure. I'd love to. I'm here on my own." They sat side by side catching up on the last few years.

"I want to leave Columbia," Ellen confided. "I'm so sick of the city. I've gotten to where I drive up here at least once a month just to get some fresh air and exercise. This summer I'm really thinking about looking for something different, Maine or Vermont I think. I want somewhere rural, out of the way. I used to think I wanted all that powerful, prove myself stuff, but lately I've started to realize I don't."

Daniel nodded. "We've really enjoyed the move. Andy loves it here." As if on queue Andy appeared, dragging along behind Boogie. He flopped down beside Daniel.

"Hi Dad. We went way up the hill." He turned around, pointing to the large incline behind them.
"You should try it. It was cool."

Daniel smiled. "Hey Andy, this is Ellen. She was at Columbia when I taught there. Do you remember her?"

Andy glanced at her. "I don't even remember Columbia," he replied. They all laughed.

"Well I remember you, though you were a lot smaller."

Andy nodded, bored with the whole exchange. Daniel nudged him. "You know, Ellen was planning to kayak today, but she hurt her arm so she can't."

Immediately Andy was interested again. He turned toward her, eyes wide. "You kayak?" he asked with amazement. "I've been wanting to go but Dad won't take me until I'm older. I'm eight," he added as an afterthought.

Ellen smiled at him. "Maybe soon you'll be old enough." She reached out her hand to Boogie. "Who's your friend?"

"That's Boogie. He's our dog," he added unnecessarily.

"He's a good looking dog. I'd love to have one but can't until I move out of the city."

"Why don't you move by us?" Andy asked. "Then I could go kayaking with you."

Ellen laughed again. "I'll have to move wherever I find a job, unfortunately." They fell silent, watching, until the water began to slow and it appeared to be over. Andy got up and began running along the bank again, stopping back frequently to ask when it was time to go. "We still have to set up the tent," he reminded Daniel.

Reluctantly Daniel stood up. "Well, I guess we better get moving. We hiked down so we've got a ways to go."

Ellen nodded. "It was nice running into you."

"Aren't you coming with us?" Andy asked. "You can convince Dad that we should go kayaking in the fall." He looked hopefully from one to the other.

"Oh no," she said. "I couldn't impose on your dad like that."

"I'd like it," Daniel replied quickly. "We've got plenty to eat. We'd be glad to have you, talk about old times."

That night Daniel lay awake in the tent. Beside him Andy slept peacefully, Boogie restlessly. He was thinking of the evening and the unexpected pleasure of Ellen's company. He had missed that since Katherine had left, missed having a grown-up to talk to and to share the day with. Ellen had provided companionship that Andy couldn't, and for the first time in four years Daniel wondered if he would ever marry again. I'd have to get divorced first, he reminded himself. Maybe I should do that, just in case I ever meet someone. Eventually he slept, looking forward to the next day when Ellen planned to join them for a hike.

It was still dark when he was awakened by Boogie walking over him. Groaning at the dog his son answered from outside the tent. "Oh, sorry Dad. I told him to be careful so he didn't wake you."

Looking through the tent flap into the pitch-black night Daniel asked, "Where are you two going?"

"Just for a walk."

Daniel considered it for a moment. "No, not yet. It's too early. I don't want you in the woods alone this early."

"Come on Dad," Andy pleaded. "Nothing's going to happen to me. I've got a flash light and Boogie'll take care of me."

Daniel looked at his watch, squinting in the darkness. "What time is it?"

"I don't know."

"Well shine your light in here so I can see." A moment later the light blinded him as Andy pointed it at his face. "Not my face, my watch."

"Oh, sorry." He redirected the light.

"Andy, it's 4:30. "Stay here for another hour and then you can go. It'll be getting light by then."

"But Dad!" he protested. "That's the whole point. We want to go while it's dark."

"It'll be dark enough in an hour. Now back in the tent."

Huffily Andy crawled through the opening and flopped on his sleeping bag. Boogie followed, laying himself across Daniel's legs, his head by Andy's hand. Daniel shifted to free his legs. Andy lay beside him grumbling. Under his breath he muttered, "I'm not even tired. I don't see why we have to sleep, just because he's tired." Daniel ignored the comments, turning his back to the pair.

When he woke again it was light out. Beside him Andy and Boogie slept soundly. Glancing at his watch he saw it was already 8:00. He crept out of the tent, wondering if Andy had had his walk and fallen back asleep, or slept right through it. In the cool morning he built a fire, then boiled water for coffee. He dug a blanket out of the Ford and sat on a log, wrapped up. He was still sitting there when Ellen appeared, 30 minutes later, ready for the hike.

"You look like you had a long night," she said.

"Yeah, a little. First I couldn't get to sleep, then Andy woke me up, sneaking out with Boogie."

She laughed. "Where were they going?"

"Out for a walk. At 4:30."

"Well hey. I was out at 5:30. That's the best time. No one else around. It's beautiful."

"I told Andy he could go at 5:30, but I have a feeling he slept right through it. At least I didn't get woken up by a dog crawling across me." The tent flap opened and Andy's head appeared.

"Dad," he said angrily, "You made us miss our walk."

Hiding his amusement Daniel replied, "I didn't make you go to sleep. I just told you to wait."

"Well, you knew we'd go to sleep and miss it. It's your fault." He was shoved onto his side by Boogie frantically wriggling to get out of the tent. Once freed Boogie ran a wild circle around the fire, stopping at Daniel and Ellen only long enough to sniff, then dashing off again. Suddenly he turned and ran into the woods. Andy sprang to his feet to chase the dog. "Boogie, come back here."

"Andy," Daniel yelled. "Your shoes."

"I have to get Boogie."

"No, you have to get your shoes. He'll come back." Andy turned back toward the tent. "You haven't said good morning to Ellen yet."

Andy glanced at her. "Hi Ellen." Bringing his shoes over he sat beside her. "I was going to go on this really cool walk while it was still dark out, but Dad woke up and wouldn't let us." His face was mutinous as he looked at Daniel.

"I don't blame him," Ellen said. "It's not a good idea for someone your age to go out by yourself too early."

"I wasn't by myself. Boogie was going too."

She nodded her head, smiling. "I was thinking of a grown-up. Maybe you could find someone to take you out on an early walk tomorrow." She glanced at Daniel, eyebrows raised in question. He nodded imperceptibly.

"Dad doesn't get up early enough to go on an early walk. It'll be light before he gets up."

"Maybe you could find someone else," she suggested.

Andy shook his head, looking dejected. "Only kids like to get up that early. Grown-ups are boring and want to sleep."

She laughed and he looked angrily at her. "I get up early. Does that make me a kid?" she asked.

He looked suspicious. "How early?"

"I was hiking down at the river at 5:30 this morning."

Andy's eyes opened wide. "Really? Would you take me? That'd be cool!"

She smiled and inclined her head toward Daniel. "I'd take you if your Dad agrees."

"Can I Dad? And can Boogie go too?" Turning back to Ellen he added, "He'd hate getting left here sleeping with Dad."

"Maybe I'd like to come along," Daniel said.

"You wouldn't be able to wake up early enough Dad. We'd have to get up really early."

"Well, you can go, but what do you say that if I wake up early I can go too."

"Sure," Andy nodded agreeably, his good spirits restored. Hearing a commotion they all looked up and saw Boogie tearing down the hill toward them. "Boogie," Andy yelled. Immediately the dog turned and ran to him. Andy wrapped his arms around the dog, burying his face in the furry neck. "Boogie, Ellen's going to take us tomorrow morning, and we get to go by the river." The dog wagged the entire back half of his body, his tail smacking Ellen's arm.

Daniel got up and crossed to the truck, pulling the cooler out of the back. "I'm going to start some breakfast," he said. Boogie joined him, sticking his furry head into the cooler. Daniel pushed him away. "Get out of here, Boogie. Andy, get this dog or I'm going to tie him up." Andy ran over and grabbed Boogie's collar, pulling with all his might. Boogie continued straining toward the cooler.

Andy tried reasoning with the dog. "Boogie, come on. You're going to get tied up. You won't get to play in the woods." Boogie broke away, sticking his head back in the cooler, sniffing frantically for the bacon. Daniel shoved him again, lay down the meat, and took him by the collar.

"That's enough out of you." He pulled Boogie over to a nearby tree where his leash was already secured. Reaching down he snapped the leash to the collar and let go. Immediately Boogie ran for the cooler, jerking to a stop as he reached the end of the leash. He continued to strain, whining while Daniel returned to his work.

"Andy, get him some dog food and a bowl of water," Daniel suggested.

"He wants bacon, Dad. It's better than dog food." Turning to Ellen he said, "I know because last year I ate some of his food, and it's not very good."

"You better give him some anyway. I bet he likes it better than you do." She got to her feet. "What can I do to help?"

"No, sit," Daniel said. "You're a guest. I'll cook." She didn't protest, but settled herself back onto the log and sat watching. "You want coffee?" he asked.

"That sounds good."

"It'll be a minute. I only brought two mugs. I'll wash mine out."

"She can have mine Dad. I don't mind," Andy said.

Ellen looked at him. "You don't drink coffee do you?"

"No, hot chocolate. But I don't mind if you use my mug."

"Well thank you, Andy." He smiled at her.

"I do believe the boy's smitten with you," Daniel said, as he handed over the coffee.

She smiled. "He's a nice boy. Friendly."

Within minutes the air was filled with the smell of frying bacon. Boogie sat down and barked furiously. Daniel looked at the dog, then at Andy. "See if you can make him be quiet."

Andy went to Boogie, talking to him softly. "You can have some bacon when it's done," he promised. "We can't eat it raw. It'll make you sick." He turned toward Daniel. "Hey Dad, will raw bacon make dogs sick too?"

"I don't know, probably." He turned back to the fire. "Alright grab your plates, it's ready." Looking at Ellen he added, "There are plenty of plates. We bring paper."

"I already ate over at the restaurant, but thanks anyway."

"There's plenty here. It's better than the restaurant."

"It does smell good. Maybe I'll try just a little." She spooned scrambled eggs onto a plate and added two strips of bacon. Andy had taken his plate over by Boogie, sitting just out of reach. Occasionally he would stretch out his hand to share a bit of bacon or eggs.

"Andy, are you eating with the same hand as the dog?" Daniel asked.

Andy looked at his dad, then at his hand. He frowned. "Yeah."

"Stop it. That's gross. Come over here with us."

"Can I just give him one whole piece?" Boogie was once again straining at his leash, threatening to choke himself.

"I'll take care of Boogie, you eat." He pulled a piece of bacon from the pan and crumbled it. Pushing the dog back he sprinkled the bacon over the dog food. "That should keep him busy so we can eat in peace," he said.

CHAPTER

TWO

Maria lay in the bed, listening carefully. Beside her Luis slept deeply, unaware of any sounds. There it was, a chuckle and the rattling of toys. Smiling to herself she got up quietly and walked down the hall. Entering the baby's room she greeted Marta happily. "Good morning. How's my baby girl? Are you wide awake and ready for the day?" At the sound of her mother's voice Marta screeched happily and waved her arms. Maria picked her up and crossed to the window. "Look at the sunshine. Maybe we'll go to the park today. Would you like that? We'll stop and get Alicia and take her with us. She'd like that, wouldn't she? Yes, she would."

She changed the baby's diaper, and carried her into the kitchen. As Maria fed the baby it occurred to her how content she was. A few years ago she never would have believed this was possible. Whatever I had before, I'm sure I never had this happiness, she thought. Meeting Luis, and then marrying him last year had made her feel more complete. The birth of Marta, eleven months later had been the pinnacle of her happiness. Of course she had never thought she would marry, considering her background. She had assumed no one would want her, but Luis had taken it all in stride.

She sat now spooning the food into the baby's mouth, remembering the last few years. The awful day when they had told her she had to accept that all memories were gone, making the arrangements with Alicia to stay with her, finding the job. And then the first awful year, always wondering, looking at people on the street, hoping for a glimmer of recognition, and thinking she would never again feel truly comfortable with her place in life.

It had come as a shock to Maria when she had entered the shop one day and Consuela had mentioned that she had been there a year. She had realized that slowly the feeling of being lost, of wondering who she had been, had faded, and she felt happy more often than not. I created a person really, she thought. A woman named Maria who worked in a tourist shop and lived on the Gran Via in an old pensión. She had met Luis that same day, in the market where she stopped to buy fruit.

She smiled, remembering. As soon as she walked in he had been there, attentive, wanting to help her. She hadn't even considered dating anyone, so when he asked he out for coffee it came as a surprise, and she had immediately said no. And then when she had told Alicia about the whole thing Alicia was adamant that she return to the market and accept. Of course she hadn't, but after thinking about it a bit she had started shopping there more regularly.

Luis had never asked again, but was always attentive and friendly when Maria stopped in. Finally, after two months of waiting for a repeat invitation she had been forced to ask him. Not wanting to appear too bold, she had asked simply if his invitation was still open. When he had finished work at 8:00 she had met him and they had joined the crowds in the evening paseo. He had made a dinner reservation, and offered to cancel it if she wasn't interested. But she was interested. Walking with Luis, Maria had realized how restricted her life was. She never spoke to anyone but Alicia and Consuela, and to Carmen on the phone. Ever since Carmen had moved to Barcelona she had been lonely for someone her own age, and Luis was perfect. Eighteen months later they had married.

The ceremony had been small, though Luis had a huge family. The family were all in Andalusia, and he had used the distance as an excuse not to invite them. Maria knew the real reason was because she had no one to ask. Of course Alicia was there, and Consuela. Dr. Montoro had come too, and Carmen had flown in for the weekend. Luis had asked two friends, and his mother had traveled from Andalusia with his youngest sister, Alana, to inspect the new wife. She had cried all through the wedding, convinced her son had made a terrible mistake to marry a woman who claimed to have forgotten her past. As soon as the wedding was over she had returned to Andalusia and had refused to speak to Maria until Marta was born. Then, as if the relationship had always been friendly, she had returned to Madrid, staying in their apartment for three weeks, suddenly best friends. Maria had been unsure at first, not trusting the sudden change, but in the end had forgiven and accepted the overwhelming love and friendship of her mother-in-law.

She was startled out of her reverie by the baby grabbing the breakfast plate and throwing it to the floor. "Oh Marta, look at the mess!" She was annoyed but not angry. Picking up the cloth she wiped up the baby and set her on the floor away from the spill. Then she cleaned up the mess. Turning back she saw that Marta had disappeared. "Marta! Where'd you go, sweetie." She started down the hallway and nearly fell over the baby who was busy investigating some dust she'd found in the corner. Maria scooped her up, wiped the dust off her hand, and re-entered the baby's bedroom. She opened the closet door, still holding the baby on her hip. "What should we put you in today?" She surveyed the closet full of clothes. Her favorites were the lacy white dresses, which hung on the right, but if they were to go to the park she would need something more practical.

She settled on bright red sweat pants and a white T-shirt covered in red flowers. Marta squirmed and fought, laughing at her mother's efforts to dress her. She was an unusually good-natured child, rarely crying and completely at ease with strangers. Luis and Maria took her everywhere they went and she was the center of their lives. For her first seven months she had alternated between staying at the shop while Maria worked, or staying with Alicia. Once she had begun to crawl she had been too active for either venue and so Maria had recently begun to work only two days a week, leaving Marta with another woman in their building on those days. Having succeeded in tying Marta's tiny white tennis shoes, Maria picked her up and carried her to the other bedroom. She deposited her on the bed with Luis.

"Wake up Daddy," she whispered.

The baby crawled over and plopped herself onto her father, squealing with delight at finding him there. He opened his eyes slowly, peeking at Marta. Suddenly he grabbed her and swung her into the air. She screamed with joy as he hung her above him. Lowering her he hugged her generously. "How's my baby today?" He placed her on her back next to him and tickled her gently. Smiling up at Maria he commented, "You're up early."

She nodded. "She was up early. Watch her for a few minutes and I'll get breakfast on the table." She returned to the kitchen where she fixed strong black coffee and a pot of hot milk. She filled a basket with rolls and set it out, adding a bowl of butter. "Ready Luis," she called.

She could hear him down the hall, still playing with Marta. She glanced at the clock, and decided she'd better hurry him along. Entering the bedroom she said, "It's getting late."

He smiled at her. "You haven't had a good morning kiss yet." She crossed to the bed and bent to kiss him. Suddenly he grabbed her and tossed her onto the bed, careful not to hit the baby. Pinning her shoulders he kissed her passionately. Marta crawled over, kneeling beside them, thumping Luis on the back. "I think she's jealous," he said. Maria hugged him, enjoying the happy time with her family.

In the kitchen Maria held Marta on her lap and fed her bits of a roll while Luis poured the coffee. Breaking her own roll into pieces she ate it without butter, dipping the crusts into the coffee. Occasionally she handed Marta a crust dipped in coffee too. The child ate it happily. Luis buttered his rolls and ate them quickly. "You're not working today. What are you two going to do?"

"I thought we might go to the park," she replied. "Do you want to meet us for lunch?"

"Mmmm, yeah. I could meet you about 2:30."

Maria nodded. "That sounds good. Can you bring some fruit along from the shop?"

"Yeah, I'll get something." Noticing the time he added, "I've got to go."

Maria sat Marta on the floor, placing some toys in front of her while she cleaned the kitchen. She made a list for groceries and then picked Marta up and left for the market. The Portero greeted her, gently pinched Marta's cheek, and then held open the door for them. She started down the street, pushing Marta in her stroller. They stopped for bread first, and Maria bought several rolls for tomorrow's breakfast, and two long, crusty loaves for lunch.

Her next stop was at the butchers for ham, then the fish market for a half-kilo of shrimp for dinner. By the time they arrived home Marta had fallen asleep, so she lifted her into her crib, and went to prepare the picnic while Marta slept. She sliced one loaf of bread into smaller pieces and buttered it, then filled it with ham. She wrapped the sandwiches in a plastic bag, then removed half a tortilla from the refrigerator. She sliced it and packed it into the cooler. Next she added a bottle of beer for Luis and a bottle of mineral water. Luis would bring some sort of fruit, and they could buy ice cream at the park. Satisfied with the meal she began to clean the living room. At 1:00 she woke Marta and they left for Alicia's house.

It was a fair distance to walk, but the day was so nice that Maria decided not to get the bus. It was hard to manage the stroller and the cooler on the bus anyway. She had, with some effort managed to tuck the cooler in under the stroller, but it threatened to spill onto the ground at any moment. Rather than going up to Alicia's apartment she left the stroller at the foot of the stairs and used the intercom. Alicia was quite some time in answering. She was getting old, and moved slowly. When she did answer Maria invited her to the park. Alicia was happy with the invitation, and Maria returned to the bottom step and sat next to Marta waiting for her to come down.

When Alicia arrived, they walked toward the subway, moving at a slower pace to accommodate the older woman. The two women saw each other frequently, but still they talked non-stop, never short of things to say. Maria reported on every cute thing Marta had done, and Alicia reported on all the tourists who had stayed at the pensión in the last week. Maria was grateful that the subway was not crowded. They both found a seat near the door, and the stroller was placed in front of them. When they reached the park Maria spread a blanket for Marta. Alicia was tired, and sat gratefully on a bench nearby and watched the baby play.

It was 2:45 before Luis arrived, bringing with him plums and grapes. Maria laid out their picnic on the blanket and they ate sitting on the ground, except for Alicia who remained on the bench. When they had finished Luis proposed a walk.

"I'll wait here," Alicia said. "I'm tired and I'll find someone to talk to shortly."

Maria nodded her acknowledgement and placed Marta in the stroller. "No, give her to me," Luis said. He took the child and placed her on his shoulders. Marta laughed with joy at her lofty spot. Leaving the stroller and cooler with Alicia they strolled through the park, talking about their day.

It was 4:00 before Maria and Luis started back to meet Alicia. They stopped along the way to buy ice cream, selecting a vanilla for Alicia, and sharing their own with Marta. Once reunited Luis left for work while Maria gathered the picnic. The trip home took nearly an hour, and when Maria entered her own apartment Marta was sleeping again. She turned on the television and sat watching it, waiting for Luis to come home.

Two weeks passed before Maria saw Alicia again. They sat in Alicia's little living room visiting. "Watch this," Maria said. "She's starting to walk." She sat Marta on the floor. The little girl used her mother's leg to pull herself up. She stood looking around, wobbling slightly.

"Come here." Alicia clapped her hands to attract Marta's attention. The baby turned toward Alicia. Unsteadily she took three steps before falling down. She blinked in surprise, but didn't cry. After a moment she struggled to her feet and tried again. Alicia reached out for her and the baby fell into her arms.

"I think I'm pregnant again," Maria confided to her friend.

Alicia smiled. "Good. That's good. She needs a brother or a sister."

Maria nodded. "We're happy too. I'm seeing the doctor next week to make sure."

"Luis wants a boy this time I bet."

Maria shook her head. "I really don't think he cares. He's so thrilled with Marta I think he'd be just as pleased with another girl." She turned to watch Marta's progress across the floor, then got up as the baby reached the doorway. "Back in here honey. You can't go down the hallway." She turned Marta back toward the room and put her down, standing to block the doorway. The baby attempted to pass her for a minute, then headed another direction. Maria returned to the couch. "I think I'd like another girl. Somehow it seems easier to have what you're used to."

Alicia nodded. Unexpectedly she asked, "Do you ever think about the first one?"

The two women rarely spoke about Maria's missing past, and at the unexpected comment Maria's eyes clouded. It was the one part of her past she never stopped wondering about. To Alicia she said, "Sometimes I think about it. A lot really. I've accepted that there's nothing I can do, but I never stop wondering."

"It is odd that no one ever found you. I always thought they would, eventually." Maria felt a tear at the corner of her eye. She wiped it away. Alicia said, "I'm sorry. I shouldn't have brought it up. Now I've made you sad."

"No, it's alright. You're the only person I talk to about it. It's good to mention sometimes." She paused. "I wonder if the baby died, or maybe I put it for adoption. I can't imagine that I raised it. If I were the mother someone should have missed me."

The two women sat in silence for a few minutes. Eventually Alicia said, "At least you've got another chance. I hope you're happy with Luis and Marta."

"Oh, I am," Maria assured her. "Four years ago when I came to live with you I never would have thought I could be this happy again. They are my whole world now. I know how lucky I am." She noticed the time. "Oh, I'd better get going. I still have to do the shopping, and I want to be home before Luis. He's insistent I get extra rest now." She got up and gathered Marta's things. Picking up the baby she carried her close to Alicia. "Kiss, kiss," she instructed Marta. The little girl laughed and put her hands out to Alicia. Sitting her on a hip Maria pushed the stroller out of the room. "We'll see you in a couple of days, okay?"

Alicia struggled to her feet. "Okay. Bye-bye Marta." She waved. At the door Maria stopped and bundled Marta into her stroller against the child's protests.

"She gotten so independent since she started walking. It's a fight everywhere we go."

Alicia nodded. "I remember those days. Don't mind them too much. They pass by so fast."

THREE

"O ctavio! Octavio, wake up." Chavo rubbed his eyes then opened them. His mother stood beside the couch. Slowly he sat up. "You need to wake up. It's time for school. I've got to leave now."

Chavo groaned. Ever since his mom had gotten the job it was school this and school that. He was glad she was no longer sick, but her increased energy had sorely limited his freedom. I used to be late for school all the time, he thought, and no one cared. I don't see why I have to get up now. He didn't speak, but got to his feet and stretched. His mother was dressed in her uniform, Anita beside her. Seeing Anita he smiled. At least he wasn't like her, stuck in a room all day while Mama cleaned. He crossed over to Anita and kissed her goodbye. "Be good and I'll bring you some candy," he whispered. She smiled up at him and nodded.

Cristina reached down and took Anita's hand. "Come on Anita. I'm going to be late." She was very proud of her job, the first she had ever had. She worked in a home for the handicapped, cleaning floors and bathrooms. Every day Anita went with her and sat in the cleaning closet until her mother was done. At first she had cried with fear at being there alone and complained of boredom, but now she accepted her fate and went quietly. Chavo tried to make it better for her by bringing her candy or gum he would steal on his way home from school. He crossed to the window now and watched the two of them walking to meet the bus. Then he noticed the clock and hurried to get ready.

Cristina walked quickly, encouraging Anita to hurry. Beside her the child struggled to keep up. In her hand she carried a small bag of toys to play with while she waited. Cristina knew it wasn't ideal, leaving her daughter in a cleaning closet while she worked, but there was no other option. She couldn't afford to pay someone to watch her, and Anita was too young for school or to be left alone.

Anita was quiet on the bus ride. She was planning her day. Mama always left her in the closet, but lately she had discovered better places to play. Some of the people who lived in the home let her play in their rooms. She smiled thinking about them. She would go see Lucia today. Lucia was pretty, like Mama, and she always had chocolates. Happily she swung her feet back and forth, kicking the seat in front of her.

Cristina reached out and stopped her legs. "Don't do that. You'll bother people."

When they reached the home Cristina and Anita walked around back. Her mother opened the door and looked in. No one was there. Taking Anita by the hand she quickly led her to the cleaning closet. It wasn't actually forbidden for Anita to accompany her. She had asked about it before taking the job, but she still tried to keep it quiet. The man who hired her had shrugged and said, 'It's okay to bring her once in a while, as long as she's no trouble.' Jobs were hard to come by, and it wasn't just once in a while, so she had to be careful.

The storage closet was large, and she had fixed up one corner for Anita. On the floor were a blanket and a pillow where she could rest or play. A straight-backed chair sat nearby. She put Anita's toys on the blanket. Leaning over she kissed her. "Be good," she whispered. "I'll see you in a little while." Picking up her mop and bucket she left the room. When she first started the job she had checked on Anita all the time, terrified something would happen to her. But time had made her confident. Anita was a good child, very quiet. She seemed perfectly content to sit with her toys all morning. Now she rarely went back to check on her, and was able to finish her work quicker. Humming to herself she began to mop the floors.

Anita waited quietly in the corner until her mother had been gone several minutes. Then she got up, crept to the door and peeked out. She looked both ways. Quietly she stepped into the empty hallway and shut the door behind her. She turned to the right and ran on tiptoe past several doors. Stopping outside Lucia's door she knocked, then opened the door and entered without waiting for an answer.

Inside Lucia sat on her bed staring at the TV in the corner. Looking around she smiled at Anita. "Anita," she called, clapping her hands. Anita smiled. She liked Lucia. She was a grown up, but she acted like a little girl. She loved to play with the same things Anita did.

Anita held up her bag of toys. "Look what I've got," she said. Lucia got up and crossed the room. Together they dumped the toys on the center of the bed.

Lucia looked at them carefully, then picked up a doll and began moving the arms and legs. "What's her name?"

"Lucia. I named her after you." Anita rummaged through the pile on the bed and held up a small dress. "Look, she's got different clothes."

Lucia reached out and grabbed the dress. Anita knew if Mama was there she'd say 'Don't grab things away from people. It's not nice', but Anita didn't say anything. Playing with Lucia was the best part of the day. Anyway, Mama had told her that the people who lived there were different. She said they lived there because they couldn't take care of themselves and they acted like children even though they weren't. Mama said that was how God made them, and that Anita should always be nice to them.

Chavo looked around the room in despair. The job would take all day. He stared longingly out the window where the other kids were playing in the street. It was sunny and a noisy game of soccer was in progress. After a minute he sighed and turned away from the window. He went down the short hallway to the bedroom and looked in on Anita. Now that summer was here she no longer went with Mama to work. Instead she stayed with Chavo, and he had to stay near home so he could watch her. Today they were supposed to be packing things to prepare to move. He had sent Anita to the bedroom to pack the clothes. He had told her to do it neatly, but she mostly just threw them in the box, shoving on the pile as it got bigger.

He returned to the kitchen and carefully began removing dishes from the cabinet, wrapping them in paper like his mother had shown him, and placing them in a box. He hurried, hoping to be finished in time to join his friends. The cabinet took a long time, and before he was finished Anita appeared.

He looked up at her. "Did you finish all the clothes?"

She shook her head. "I'm tired of doing the clothes. I want to go outside."

"Well Mama said we had to stay here until we packed this stuff."

Anita began to pout. "Well, I'm tired of the clothes. Let me do the dishes," she whined.

Chavo shook his head. "Go finish the clothes. If you get done I'll let you help me with the pictures."

Anita's face broke into a smile. "Okay," she agreed. She loved Mama's pictures that sat on the kitchen shelf.

When the cabinet was finished he went to check on Anita. She was sitting on the floor with clothes all around. The box was full, but she had simply continued to pile things on top, allowing them to slide to the floor. "Anita," he shouted. "You're supposed to put it in the box so we can close it and carry it."

She looked up startled, then burst into tears. Chavo stood staring at her, unsure what to do with his crying sister. Eventually he crossed the floor and knelt down beside her. "Here," he said. "I'll help you get it done."

She sat watching him work for a minute, then stopped sobbing and picked up the nearest items. She wiped her eyes with a shirt, then put it in the box. When they had finished the clothes he took her back down the hallway. He started on the shelf above the stove, handing the pictures to Anita to examine before he wrapped them. "That's Grandma, and that's her house," Chavo explained. He was glad he didn't live in a little house like that, way out in the country. Taking the picture back from Anita he carefully wrapped it and placed it in the box.

He took down the next one. "That's Grandpa."

Anita took the picture. "He looks mad," she said.

Chavo nodded.

"Is he mean?" she asked.

He shrugged. "I don't know. He's dead." Chavo had never known his grandparents.

He took down the next one and handed it to her, wrapping the stern looking Grandfather carefully. "That's Mama's brother. He died when he was little."

Anita took the picture and studied it intently. "How little was he?" she asked.

"I don't know. I think he was little like you." He started to take the picture from her, then reconsidered. While she was engrossed in it he took down the next one. He stood for a minute looking at his father's face, then he thrust the picture into the box without showing it to Anita. I don't know why Mama keeps it, he thought. He never sent for us, he never came to visit, he never even wrote us a letter. Still frowning he reached for the next picture. The dead woman. Carefully he laid the picture with the others and took down the other dead woman.

"I want to see that one too," Anita demanded, handing back the little boy.

He traded her, wrapping the picture carefully. "Who's this one?" she asked.

"It's just some woman Mama wanted to pray for. She's dead too." He started to take the picture back.

"Wait," Anita said. "Who's that little boy?"

"That's her little boy, I guess."

She reached out a finger and touched his face. "Is he dead too?"

"I don't know," he replied impatiently. "Now give me the picture." He wrapped it quickly and turned to the drawer where they kept the silverware.

FOUR

For two months Daniel pondered his choices. Thoughts would crop up at odd times, late at night, or on a quiet afternoon, and he always had the same argument: it's so final. It would wipe out any possibility that Katherine didn't choose to leave. He sat staring out the window, avoiding the final admission. Finally he shook his head and muttered to himself, "just face it. She left you. She left you and she left Andy. It wasn't the happy marriage you pretend it was." He picked up the phone and called his lawyer. After speaking to the lawyer he dialed Ellen's number. Her machine picked up. He left a message telling her that the university had an opening in her field. He hung up thinking he should have told her he'd like her to live closer. They had talked on the phone several times since the weekend at the park, and had renewed their friendship. But now Daniel was wanting more.

"I don't see why we have to clean the house so much," Andy said angrily. He was sweeping the floor in the kitchen half-heartedly.

"Ellen's coming to visit, and I want our place to look nice. You want her to think we're a couple of slobs?"

Andy stopped sweeping and stared at Daniel. "Dad, we've been cleaning for days."

Daniel looked at his watch. "Two hours actually. Not exactly slave labor." Andy continued to glare. "Tell you what," Daniel said, "You finish sweeping, and then you can go play with Boogie. I'll mop."

"Okay," Andy said. He attacked the floor with renewed vigor. Ten minutes later he was finished. He stuffed the broom in the closet and ran for the door.

"Andy," Daniel called.

Andy stopped, one hand still on the doorknob. He turned toward his dad, a look of dread on his face. "What?"

"Don't let that dog in the house today, okay?"

"Yeah, sure." Andy didn't stop to argue, afraid some other chore would be discovered if he didn't escape immediately. He ran out the door, slamming it behind him.

Inside, Daniel inspected the house. The floors were clean, the tabletops cleared. He had always been a neat person and forced Andy to keep the shared areas of the house neat too. Satisfied with the downstairs he went up. The hallway was vacuumed and the bathroom scrubbed. He'd done those himself. He pushed open Andy's bedroom door. Not bad. Satisfied at the condition of the house, he went downstairs.

In the kitchen he opened the refrigerator and began removing items. Tomatoes, onion, green pepper, ground beef, mushrooms. He was planning a spaghetti dinner. He began chopping ingredients for the sauce, adding garlic, oregano and pepper from the spice cabinet. When the sauce was simmering and he was pleased with the flavor he began browning the beef. Then he picked up a long loaf of French bread and sliced it. He spread it with butter, sprinkled on some garlic, and sat it beside the oven.

The back door flew open and Andy burst in, Boogie right behind him. "She's here Dad, she's here," he yelled.

Boogie danced around the kitchen in excitement, sniffing madly for the source of the smells. "Andy, get that dog out of here," he said. His voice was calmer than he felt. This was the first time he had seen Ellen since the weekend at the park, and he wanted everything to be perfect.

Before Andy could catch Boogie Ellen's head poked in the back door. "Hi," she said. "Mind if I just come in the back?" Boogie ran to greet the new arrival. Daniel followed, and grabbing Boogie by the collar shoved him outside.

"Come on in. Sorry about the confusion. I told Andy to keep that dog outside, but ..." He threw up his hands and shrugged.

For a moment they all stood about awkwardly. Then Ellen broke the silence. "It smells great in here. What are we having?"

"Spaghetti, salad and garlic bread." He frowned. "Except I forgot to make the salad, so I guess it's spaghetti and garlic bread. I'm almost finished."

"Let me help. I can whip together a salad in no time. Andy'll help me, won't you Andy?"

Daniel laughed. "Andy hates helping in the kitchen."

"Uh, uh, Dad. That's not true," Andy protested. "I like making salad." He crossed to the refrigerator and began removing ingredients. Daniel smiled but kept his mouth shut. He placed the pasta into a pot of boiling water, then put the garlic bread in the oven. While he finished the spaghetti Ellen guided Andy through chopping ingredients for a salad. Within a few minutes they were all seated around the table enjoying the dinner.

"So, how'd the interview go?" Daniel asked. Ellen was in town interviewing for a position at the university.

"Pretty good I think. They've got three candidates, but I should know something next month."

"Are you going to move here?" Andy asked.

"I'm not sure. If I get the job I'd like to."

"Is it because of us?" he asked bluntly. Both Daniel and Ellen blushed at his frank question.

Ellen hesitated before answering. "It's not exactly because of you. I've been wanting to leave New York and move up this way for a while. Of course it's always nice to have friends near you, so you two would be a bonus."

Andy nodded. "And it's nice to have people who have the same interests, right? I mean like kayaking for example."

She smiled. "Of course. It's always nice if friends like the same activities. That's part of what makes them friends."

When dinner was done they took the obligatory tour of the house. Ellen declared it perfect. "It's so rustic. Not a bit fussy like things tend to be in New York. It feels like country." They wandered around the yard as well, Boogie dancing around them, begging for attention. Finally, while Andy took his bath Daniel and Ellen sat out in the yard drinking coffee and talking.

She brought up the subject of kayaking. "Andy's so anxious to try it, I wondered if you'd want to try some easy trips this summer. Then if he's enjoying it you could consider taking him back to the park this fall."

"I just hate the thought of him in that rough water. What if something happened to him? I'd never forgive myself."

Ellen didn't answer. She sat staring out into the darkness. Eventually she spoke. "If I'm out of line here just tell me, and I'll shut up, but is part of the reason you're afraid because of Katherine's disappearance?"

Daniel was caught off guard. No one except family had mentioned Katherine's disappearance since he'd moved up here. He had forgotten Ellen was from Columbia and knew the whole awful story.

She mistook his silence for anger. "I'm sorry. That was out of line I guess. He's your son and you have the right to decide what he does."

"No, I'm not upset. I was just thinking, considering your question. I think you're right, partially. I know all the evidence shows that Katherine ran off, but sometimes I still think she just couldn't have. She wasn't that kind of person." He paused. "Sometimes I still wonder if something else happened. and I'm just never going to know. I think I am a little overprotective sometimes, but actually I was before she disappeared too." He sat quietly, embarrassed at having spilled his soul to Ellen when really he barely knew her.

"Well," she said, "it's something to think about. I'd be willing to help teach him if you wanted."

"Yeah? Well thanks, I will think about it."

Ellen looked at her watch. "I'd really better get going. It's late." She stood up and stretched. Boogie had been lying quietly by her chair. Now he stood up and stretched too. "Do you think Andy's finished? I'd like to say goodnight."

"I'll check," Daniel said. He opened the back door and listened for running water. Not hearing any he went part way up the stairs. "Andy?" he called. "Are you finished?"

Andy appeared at his doorway. He was in his pajamas and his hair was plastered against his head. "Yeah."

"Ellen's going. She wanted to say good night."

Andy came down the stairs. His eyes were already heavy with sleep. He opened the back door and stepped out. "Good night, Ellen," he said. He stepped forward and hugged her. She wrapped her arms around him and bent to whisper in his ear. "Good night, Andy. Thanks for helping with dinner."

"Good night," he murmured again.

When Daniel woke up the next day he was surprised to find Andy still sleeping. Normally Andy woke very early. He was already in the kitchen making breakfast when Andy appeared, tousle-headed and still in his pajamas. He sat at the table, uncharacteristically quiet.

"Morning Andy," Daniel greeted him.

He muttered his reply. "Morning."

"You're late getting up today."

"Yeah."

Daniel turned from the stove where he was making pancakes and studied his son. Andy sat slumped on his chair, elbows resting on the table, still half asleep. "Andy? Are you feeling okay?"

Andy didn't answer, but nodded. He remained silent and slumped until Daniel set a large plate of pancakes in front of him. Only after he had buttered them and eaten several large mouthfuls did he speak again. "Dad, was Mom anything like Ellen?"

The question caught Daniel off guard. Andy rarely mentioned his mother. He looked closely at his son. The boy sat, still eating, as if he had just asked whether it was going to rain, or if they had any orange juice. Daniel suspected the question was more important than Andy pretended. Finally he answered. "No, not really. Your mother didn't care for the outdoors much. She was an indoor person. And busy. She was always working on a project of some sort."

"She didn't like being outside?" Andy sounded shocked at the thought of it.

"It wasn't that she didn't like being outdoors, she loved the summer. But she wasn't a hiker or a camper, and she hated the snow."

"You mean she never went skiing with us?"

"No, never." He frowned, thinking back. "Actually, she did go once with me. It was before you were born, but she hated it. She ended up spending most of the day in the lodge, sitting by the fire."

Andy nodded thoughtfully. "Do you like Ellen?" he asked, looking up at Daniel.

Daniel didn't answer immediately, wondering where his son was going with this conversation. Eventually he replied, "Yeah, I like Ellen."

"Well what do you like about her?"

Daniel thought about the question. "She's nice to you, and that's important to me. She's interesting and she enjoys a lot of the same things we do. And it's nice to have a grown-up to talk to sometimes."

Andy nodded. He shoveled in several more bites of pancake, his brow furrowed in thought, before he asked his next question. "So what did you like about Mom if she didn't like the stuff we do."

Daniel thought back to Katherine and what he had admired about her. At first he had liked her boldness, and the way she was so sure she'd get what she wanted. Later, he admitted to himself he had just wanted things to work out so Andy would have a good life. Admitting this to himself was a shock. He had insisted for so long that they had had a perfect marriage. Now he recognized that it hadn't been perfect. It hadn't even been particularly great.

"Dad!" Andy's voice drew him out of his reverie.

"What?" He looked at Andy. Andy had put down his fork and sat staring at Daniel.

"You didn't answer my question."

"Oh, yeah. What I liked about Mom? Well, she was smart. Really smart. She was great at her job. She designed advertisements, and she was really good." He struggled for something more to say. She didn't take much interest in you, or in me for that matter, he thought. We were more the finishing touches to her idea of a perfect life. "She loved you a lot," he finally said, knowing that Katherine had, in her own way.

Andy didn't answer. He silently finished his pancakes and milk. When he was done he took the dishes to the sink and rinsed them. Finally he said, "Do you think it's bad if I like Ellen?"

"No, of course not. Why would it be bad?"

"I mean would Mom be mad because I like Ellen?"

Daniel reached out and pulled Andy close to him, wrapping his arms around Andy's thin shoulders. "Since your Mom can't be here with you, I think she'd be happy you like Ellen." He stroked Andy's hair for a minute, then released his grip. Transferring his hands to Andy's shoulders he pushed him away slightly so he could see Andy's face. "Listen though. I want you to realize that Ellen isn't like a Mom to you. She's a friend."

"But if you married her she'd be like a Mom, right?"

Daniel nodded. "That's right, but it's way too soon to be talking about marrying her. When two people want to get married they should know each other for a long time, and spend lots of time together."

Andy screwed up his nose, looking puzzled. "Why? You know you like her and she likes the same stuff as you."

"People can't tell that when they first meet. It's kind of like the first day of school. Everyone tries to act their best, hoping the teacher

175

will like them, but after a few months some kids don't do their work, some throw spit balls, and some are still good. That's when you can tell what people are really like."

Andy nodded. "Can I go out and play now?"

"Get dressed first." He nodded his head toward the steps. Andy ran up the stairs two at a time, much more like his usual self.

The summer passed lazily. One thing Daniel loved about teaching was the long summers he could spend with Andy. They developed a ritual together, going down to the creek to swim each evening before dinner. Though Daniel didn't tell Andy, he was testing to see how well Andy could swim in the moving water. Of course it was nothing like swimming in the dam release, but it was harder than a swimming pool. He challenged Andy to races, and intentionally took him downstream to the narrower part of the creek where the water flowed faster. Andy's skill at swimming improved steadily.

Late one Friday night Ellen called to announce she had gotten the job at the university. She was excited, bubbling over with enthusiasm. "I'm already planning to come up next weekend to look for a place to live, so keep your ears open and let me know if you hear about anything."

Daniel was smiling. The news had lifted a weight from his shoulders that he hadn't known was there. Only once it was gone did he realize he had been waiting to hear, hoping she would get the position. "I'd be glad to help you look around," he offered. "I could contact the real estate agent who helped me with this place."

"That would be great. Since I'm teaching a summer course I'm going to have to squeeze moving into the weekends. The quicker things go the better."

"Well, tell me what you want so we don't waste time..."

She detailed what she was looking for. A rental. "I don't want to buy until I'm sure I'm staying." To herself she admitted that staying depended a lot on how their relationship went. "I'd like a small house, but I'll look at apartments. Something with a yard would be nice." Daniel wrote it all down and promised to call in a couple of days.

The next morning he was up early. He rushed Andy through breakfast and getting dressed. "I've got somewhere special for us to go today."

"Where? Where is it?" Andy hopped eagerly from one foot to the next.

Daniel was washing the breakfast dishes. Half turning he said, "If I tell you it's not a surprise. Just get ready."

"Come on, Dad." Andy continued jumping up and down, spinning in a circle at the same time.

"No. Just get ready."

Andy started for the stairs. Jumping onto the first step he turned. "Can Boogie come?"

Daniel smiled. "No, not today."

"Why not? He'll be lonely."

Daniel shook his head. "No dogs allowed. Now come on. I want to leave in 15 minutes."

They drove to a nearby town. As they reached the outskirts Daniel instructed Andy to close his eyes. "You're not allowed to know where we're going," he said.

"Dad!" Andy sounded exasperated. "That game is for babies."

Slowing down Daniel said, "We can just go back home if you don't want to play." They had created the game together just after they moved to Vermont. Daniel would make Andy close his eyes and guess where they were going.

"I'll play," Andy said good-naturedly.

Daniel glanced over as he drove. "Now no peeking. You'll spoil the surprise."

"I'm not peeking," Andy insisted.

Daniel parked the truck and came around to Andy's door. He took his arm and led him carefully through the parking lot. "Step up," he instructed as they reached the curb. Andy slowed, his foot reaching in front of him, searching for the curb. "Now, watch the door." Daniel opened it and led his son inside. "Can you guess where we are?"

Andy stood still and sniffed deeply. "It's not a restaurant," he announced.

"No, it's not a restaurant."

Andy listened carefully. "It's a store of some kind."

Daniel laughed. "That's a given. Keep your eyes closed." He led Andy through the store to the back.

"It's big. Is it K-mart?"

"No, not K-mart." He stopped at the back of the store. "Any more guesses?"

"I give up. I don't think we've been here before."

"That's right. We haven't. You can open your eyes."

Andy opened his eyes. They were standing at a large window, and just beyond was a pond and several brightly colored kayaks. People filled the dock, inspecting kayaks, trying them in the water, and talking to sales people. Andy stared wide-eyed for a minute. "Oh cool," he shouted. He broke away from Daniel and moved closer to the window. "Are we getting one?" He looked at Daniel wide-eyed.

Daniel nodded. "Yep, we're getting one."

Spontaneously Andy ran to Daniel and hugged him. "Thanks Dad. This is going to be great."

With the help of a sales person they tried three different models. In the end they picked a bright red Eskimo duo, and Daniel added life jackets and helmets to the purchase. Andy protested he didn't need a life jacket because he could swim so well, but Daniel was firm "No life jacket, no kayaking." Together they loaded it into the back of the Ford and drove home. As soon as they arrived Andy wanted to try it.

"We'll get a quick lunch first," Daniel said, opening the cabinets.

"Dad, you can't fix a quick lunch. Can't we eat peanut butter?"

Daniel smiled at Andy's eagerness. "Ok, we'll eat peanut butter."

When Ellen arrived the following weekend Andy ran to show her the kayak. "We've been out on the river every day. Yesterday Dad even let me ride in front! I think he's going to take me to the dam release this fall." The words tumbled out in one breath, causing Ellen to laugh.

Daniel found them in the shed laughing together. "Andy, you could at least let Ellen say hello before running off with her," he reproached gently.

"Sorry Dad. I just wanted to show her what we got." He smiled broadly.

"What do you think?" Daniel asked Ellen.

"It's great. If I'd known I'd have brought mine along."

They all climbed into Ellen's rented Honda and went to meet the real estate agent. True to his word Daniel had already done some preliminary work, and the agent had four places ready to show. By mid-afternoon Ellen was satisfied. She selected a small one-story house with a neat yard full of flowers. It had just one bedroom, one bathroom, a living room and a kitchen. The kitchen window looked out over the river about a half-mile downstream from Daniel and Andy's place.

Ellen was pleased, but it was Andy who was ecstatic. "You'll practically be our neighbor," he exclaimed. "I'll be able to just get in the kayak and float right to your house."

Daniel and Ellen exchanged smiles. "Andy, you'll have to be invited first. No dropping in unannounced," Daniel said.

Andy rolled his eyes. "Ellen wouldn't mind, Dad." Turning to Ellen he added, "Would you?"

She avoided the question by answering, "I think you'd best do what your Dad says."

They spent the rest of the day wandering the town, Andy acting as tour guide. Happily he pointed out the library, the school and the ice cream parlor. For dinner they went to Jack's for pizza. The little restaurant had a long wooden counter where you placed your order, and ten booths lining the walls. A jukebox sat in the back corner. They ordered double pepperoni and Cokes. While they were waiting Daniel found some quarters and sent Andy off to the jukebox. "That should buy us five minutes of peace," he joked.

Ellen smiled. "It may be the last bit of peace, depending on what he picks."

"It shouldn't be too bad. He likes oldies right now. The Beatles, Joni Mitchell, Meatloaf. He always plays 'I want to hold your hand.'" He paused. "I was thinking, next time you come up maybe I could get a sitter and we could go out alone."

"I'd like that," Ellen said. "Not that I mind Andy, but I would like that."

"I'm glad you don't mind having him around. That's important to me."

Her reply was cut short by Andy's arrival. On queue the jukebox began to play The Beatles. Both Ellen and Daniel laughed.

"What's so funny," Andy demanded.

"Nothing," they replied together.

In August Ellen moved, bringing all her things up in a rented U-Haul. Daniel and Andy helped carry the boxes in stacking them in whatever room was written on top. "Do you want us to unpack them?" Andy asked.

"No, honey. Just put them in the corner. I'll have to decide where everything goes." If anyone noticed that she had called him honey they didn't comment. Since the weekend she found the house Ellen had been back for two long weekends, and she and Daniel talked on the phone several times a week. Every time she was coming up Andy was thrilled, even if he was getting left with a babysitter. He had looked forward to the final move for weeks, talking about how he could visit Ellen or they could kayak together when Daniel was busy.

When the last of the things had been moved they went to drop off the U-Haul, Andy riding in front with Ellen, Daniel following in the Ford to provide a ride home. Ellen hadn't even owned a car in New York, but now she had bought an old beat up Subaru. It was parked in the driveway. "It makes the place look homey," she said.

Privately Daniel agreed, but he couldn't resist teasing her about the age. "I guess the college isn't paying you this first year, huh? Tough to afford a reliable vehicle."

"It's a Subaru. They run forever," she replied. She winked at Andy and whispered, "Remember that Andy. Subaru's run forever."

He smiled, thinking they shared a secret.

CHAPTER

FIVE

Maria looked at the suitcases standing by the door. She felt surprisingly nervous. In the two years she had been married to Luis they had never gone to Andalusia to visit his family. When Luis had told his mother of the second pregnancy she had insisted they come down to meet everyone. Luis had a huge family. His mother and youngest sister lived together. Nearby were two more sisters and four brothers, all married with children of their own. In addition there were countless cousins and children of cousins, and old aunts and uncles. Only Luis had left Andalusia. All the others lived within a few blocks of each other in Cordoba. "Luis, we're going to miss the train," she called.

He appeared, carrying Marta, and put her in the stroller, where she immediately began to struggle to free herself. Maria opened the door and pushed the stroller out. Once they were moving Marta's cries quieted. Luis gathered the luggage and followed. On the street he deposited the luggage and flagged a taxi. Maria removed Marta from the stroller and struggled to close it while holding the squirming child. The driver took the stroller and collapsed it, storing it in the trunk. He smiled at Marta, rubbing her chin with his rough fingers. "Where are you going, sweetie?" he asked.

The baby quit struggling and watched the old man intently. "We're going to Cordoba to visit my husband's family," Maria answered.

He nodded his head, his brow furrowed in thought. "That's a long trip."

Maria nodded but didn't answer. Instead she climbed into the taxi hoping to spur the driver into action. The move seemed to work. He began helping Luis load the luggage, then climbed in. "Atocha?" he asked.

Luis nodded. They sped off through traffic, the old man driving with a ferocity that contrasted with his relaxed personality. They reached the station in good time, found a cart, and loaded the luggage. By the time they reached the platform the train was waiting. They had opted for the fast day train even though it was more expensive. Both had agreed that Marta would have a hard time traveling through the night, and they wanted her to meet her relatives in good spirits. They boarded, settling into their seats with books and toys nearby. Just after the train pulled out Marta fell asleep and continued to sleep until they were close to their final destination.

As the train pulled into the station Luis pointed to the platform, then opened the window and called out a greeting. Maria's eyes widened in surprise. Nearly twenty people were gathered in a group, apparently to greet them. "I'm glad Marta slept. This could be a little overwhelming," she said.

Luis smiled. "A big change for you I know. We haven't had much family around before, but I'm glad we came. Marta needs to know her family." The train stopped and suddenly three men were on board, grabbing Luis and kissing him, then turning to her to kiss her and exclaim over Marta. She was introduced to Enrique, Jose Maria and Pablo. The men gathered the luggage and the stroller, leaving Marta to Maria. As she stepped off the train the others swept forward. Names were called out, and arms wrapped her in hugs. Catarina, Luisa, Rafael, Arturo, Gabriela. She gave up trying to sort out who was who.

Everyone squeezed into the waiting cars for the drive to Luis' mother's house. They would stay there, with plenty of opportunity to visit the other relatives. Maria was separated from Luis by his exuberant family, and she and Marta were stuffed into the front seat of a sister's car. When they arrived at the house the street was crowded with more cars, parked haphazardly, and people spilling out of them. As she stepped out of the car she was again overwhelmed with hugs, kisses and names, as the newest group of relatives surged forward.

The house was located in the old Moorish quarter, the street nothing more than a narrow cobblestone lane. The houses were blindingly white in the hot afternoon sun. Inside was also chaotic, being filled with some 30 relatives. The table was filled with food, and several people had already begun to eat. Maria looked about, hoping to locate Luis. Instead she saw Ana, Luis' mother. Relieved she went over to greet the old woman, but even this respite was short lived, for the relatives all wanted to greet Ana as well, and Maria was bumped and shoved good-naturedly. Overwhelmed by all the people, Marta began to cry. In desperation Maria stepped outside again, hoping to find some space and her husband. She looked around for a bit of yard for Marta to play in, and finding none eventually put her down on the cobblestones, listening carefully for cars.

"Hola." Maria looked up to see Alana, Luis' youngest sister standing there.

"Hola." She smiled broadly and embraced the younger woman. "It's nice to see a familiar face."

Alana nodded. "There are a lot here today." Nodding her head toward Marta she asked, "Why don't you take her into the garden?"

Maria glanced around. "I didn't see one."

Alana laughed. "I forgot you don't know Andalusia do you? The garden is on the roof."

Maria looked up. From the ground she could see nothing. "Will you show me?" She was reluctant to return to the house full of family.

"Sure," Alana replied. "We'll go around the back way. It's not so crowded." She reached down and picked Marta up. The child immediately began to cry. Alana tried unsuccessfully to quiet her, then handed her to Maria. "I guess she doesn't like her Aunt Alana."

Maria shook her head. "No, it's not you. Since she started walking she can't bear to be carried." She sat Marta back on the ground. "Take her hand. She'll walk with you."

Alana reached down and took Marta's hand. She started toward the back of the house, her steps slow to match the baby's. Maria followed. In back of the house was a small stone courtyard. A set of narrow stone steps led up the side of the house. "I'd better carry her on the steps," Maria said. "She's not used to them." She picked Marta up and began climbing.

At the top she found Luis relaxing in the garden, an Águila in hand. A group of male relatives surrounded him. As Maria approached he held out his hands. "Let me have her," he said. Gratefully Maria handed Marta over, irritated that Luis had disappeared in the first place. She went to the corner where a cooler of drinks sat and looked in. There was nothing but beer. She closed the cooler again and sat on a nearby bench.

"Tell me what you want. I'll get you something," Alana said. "Lemonade?"

Maria nodded gratefully. She sat back and surveyed the garden. It was really a rooftop patio, still no grass for Marta, but it was nice. The floor was stone, and a narrow wall which surrounded the roof protected people from falling. Stone benches were built into the wall, and several other chairs were scattered about. Plants and flowers in pots were everywhere. The sun was scorching, but Maria had gotten a bench on the shady side.

Alana returned, carrying two lemonades. She sat next to Maria and handed her a glass. Maria took a long drink. "Thanks. That tastes great. It's so hot here." Alana nodded but didn't speak. Maria looked at her closely. Her face was carefully composed, as if she bore some horrible secret and was trying to make the best of it. Maria had always liked Alana. She felt sorry for the girl being stuck in the role of youngest daughter. In Luis' family, tradition was for the youngest daughter to stay at home caring for her parents. As such, Alana did not expect to marry or have a family, at least not while her mother was alive. She reached out her hand and covered Alana's. "What's the matter. You look strained."

Alana didn't answer, but looked away. When she looked back her eyes were troubled. "I've been told to tell you something. It isn't very pleasant."

Maria sat up straighter. "What. What is it?"

Alana looked down. "It's about your family. Mama couldn't bear to tell everyone about the amnesia. She said they would never accept you or believe such a story. So she's made one up and told it to them." She looked away.

Maria frowned. "What do you mean she's made one up?"

"She made up a family for you. She's told everyone all about your past, but it's not a real past. She wrote it all down." The girl reached into her pocket and withdrew a folded paper. "I'm sorry. I asked her not to, but lately she's been a little..." she paused. "I don't know. A little crazy, I guess. I can't reason with her."

Maria took the paper and unfolded it. It was cleverly done, a collection of notes without too many details to remember. Three sisters and two brothers. Everyone lives in the north, near Zaragoza. Parents are dead. Family is from Zaragoza. "I've never even been to Zaragoza," Maria said angrily.

Alana shrugged. "It doesn't matter. Neither have any of us. You can say anything you want about it. No one will know the difference." The girl looked distraught.

Maria reached out and placed her hand on Alana's arm. "It's not your fault," she said. "You didn't do it."

Alana looked relieved. "You're angry, though."

"I am. I'm furious, but not at you. You didn't do it." She sat fuming at Ana, first for the awful lie she would now have to live, and second for forcing Alana to tell her the news. The old woman must be crazy, she thought. She could have just said there is no family, or let me answer for myself.

"Does Luis know?" she asked.

Alana shook her head. "I'm supposed to tell him too, but I haven't gotten him alone."

"Never mind, I'll take care of it." She got up and crossed the patio, muttering to herself, "I ought to just let him blunder and expose the old woman as a liar." Marta was playing happily on the ground surrounded by a circle of men. Maria scooped her up and spoke sharply to Luis. "Can I talk to you for a minute?" Without waiting for an answer she headed for the stairs. Behind her she could hear the good-natured jibes of the men ribbing Luis for his wife's boldness, but she knew he would follow.

She waited at the bottom of the stairs. Luis could see the fury in her face even before he reached the ground. Maria was rarely angry, and he wondered what his sister had said to set her off. Reaching the ground he placed his arm around her shoulder. "What is it? What's wrong?"

She twisted away from him. "Not here. I want to go for a walk." She set off firmly, leaving him to catch up.

He pointed to a road winding off to the left. "Here, this one leads to a park." The walk calmed Maria a bit. Over and over she reminded herself it wasn't Luis' fault. Only Ana was to blame. As soon as they reached the park she deposited Marta in a sandbox and sat on a bench. Luis sat beside her. "Tell me," he said.

Silently she handed him the note. He read it and looked at her puzzled. "What is it?"

"My family," she said angrily. "Your mother created a family for me because she was ashamed. She said the others would never accept me. She expects me to lie to everyone."

The shock on his face made it clear he knew nothing about the lie. "I will tell her she can't do this," he said. "She doesn't have the right."

Maria shook her head. "No, Luis. I don't want that. If we tell the truth now everyone will side with her. You will lose your whole family."

"You are my family," he said loyally. "I don't need all of them."

"Nonsense," she replied. "I saw how you suffered when we were first married and your mother wouldn't speak to us. I see now how much your family means to you. You're thrilled to be here, showing off your daughter. I won't take it all away from you."

"It wouldn't be you taking it. I want to tell them the truth."

"No," Maria spoke firmly. "I won't let you. I hate what she did, but I'll stand by the lie. I've got no family to offer our children. I won't lose yours as well."

That night Maria slept fitfully. In her dreams she was in a strange city surrounded by people she didn't know. Everyone called out to her, waving and laughing. She turned, looking for a familiar face. In the corner of the room a child played, its back turned to her. It was impossible to tell if it was a boy or a girl, yet she knew it was hers. She started toward the child, but the crowd closed around her and the child disappeared. She whirled about, searching. The child's voice pierced the darkness. "Mama, where are you? Mama!" She sat up, suddenly awake, shaking all over. Beside her Luis slept. Marta lay on a mattress in the corner of the room. She slipped out of bed and stood at the window, staring out. Tears slipped silently down her face.

"Maria," Luis spoke softly. "What's wrong?"

She shook her head. "Nothing. Just a dream." He came and stood beside her.

"You're crying." He wiped her face with his hand. "Tell me. What was it?" He led her to the edge of the bed and sat, drawing her down beside him.

"It was just a stupid dream. I don't know. It just upset me."

"What was it? Tell me the dream." He wrapped his arms around her.

"It was a child, my child, calling for me. I was surrounded by people I didn't know, and I couldn't get to the child."

"Marta?"

"No, not Marta. A different child. The first child."

He hugged her closely. "The first child is gone," he said. "Let it go. You can't remember, and the child probably can't remember you. If that child is alive someone else is taking care of it. It was just a dream."

Maria shook her head. "You don't understand. I know there was a first child. I'll never forget that, even if I can't remember the child. Imagine if Marta disappeared. Would you ever stop thinking about her?"

Luis shook his head sadly. "I can't imagine it," he said. They were still sitting there an hour later when the first rays of sun lightened the sky.

After a few days in Cordoba they settled into a routine. The relatives returned to their own lives, dropping in alone or in pairs to visit occasionally, and leaving Maria and Luis alone to relax and enjoy their vacation. In the hot afternoons when the city retired for siesta Marta refused to sleep, so Maria endured the heat, walking through the narrow streets, exploring the city where her husband had grown up.

One day, wandering aimlessly through the sleeping city, Maria came upon the park where she and Luis had gone before. Marta squealed happily at the site of the toys, and Maria deposited her in the sandbox, gratefully sitting on a shady bench. At this hour the park was nearly deserted. Only an old woman dressed in the colorful clothes of a gypsy sat nearby. Instinctively Maria pulled her belongings closer, keeping her arm over them. She was startled when a moment later the woman sat on her bench. She hadn't seen her move.

The old woman spoke first. "Your little girl?" she asked, indicating Marta.

Maria nodded, wary of the gypsy woman. Madrid had a fair share of gypsies, but Andalusia had far more, and Maria found them unnerving. "You're very happy with her," the woman said. It was a statement, not a question.

Again Maria nodded. "And your husband. He is a good man." Maria turned to face the woman.

"What do you want?" she asked.

"I want to help you. You are very sad even though you have a beautiful family."

Maria was surprised. While she had felt somewhat unsettled here she thought she had hidden it well. Looking the woman directly in the eye she said, "I do have a beautiful family, and I don't need your help." The old woman shrugged and turned away, but did not leave. For several minutes Maria sat in uncomfortable silence. Finally, unable to bear it any longer she began gathering Marta's things.

As she stood up the old woman muttered, "Of course you must miss the other one."

Maria whirled about, eyes wide. "What did you say?"

A triumphant look flickered across the woman's face. "I said you must miss the other child."

"What child? What are you talking about?"

"You have another child, don't you?" The woman stared at Maria as if seeing into her soul.

"I'm pregnant," Maria said. "The baby will be born this winter."

"But you have another. An older child. He is not with you."

"What do you know about that? Who are you?" Maria felt panicked. She glanced at Marta in the sandbox, then back at the gypsy woman. "How do you know who I am?"

"I have the sight. When I see you, I know." She shrugged as if this were an everyday occurrence.

"Who am I? Tell me who I am?" Maria was practically shouting.

The old woman shook her head, clicking her tongue several times. She held out her right hand, rubbing the thumb and index finger together.

"Money," Maria said. "How much do you want?"

"5000 pts."

"I haven't got it."

The woman shrugged. Without speaking she stood up and began to walk away.

"Wait," Maria shouted. "Wait, come back." The woman turned and came to stand before her. "I don't have the money. I'll have to go home for it. Wait here for me. I'll be back."

The old woman turned and sat on the bench. Quickly Maria got up, grabbing Marta's things. She scooped the child out of the sand box and began walking toward Ana's house. Marta screamed and kicked her feet, wanting to be let down, but Maria ignored the cries, practically running to the house. Inside she hurried to their room and rummaged through her things, finding the needed money. She wondered if Luis knew how much was there. Before coming to Andalusia he had told her over and over again about the gypsies who swarmed everywhere in his hometown. She knew he would be angry that she had fallen under the old woman's spell, but she had to find out what the woman knew. Still rushing she deposited Marta on the floor of the living room where Ana sat resting. "Can you watch her for a few minutes? I need to get out," she said to Ana. Without waiting for an answer she left.

When she reached the park the bench was empty. She whirled about looking for the woman, then sat down, hoping she would return. After nearly an hour the park was still empty. Maria sat slumped on the bench. It's all a hoax anyway, she told herself. She couldn't know anything about me. She heard us talking or something. Maria tried to remember if she and Luis had discussed the first child here, in the park. We must have. That's all it was. A hoax. She just wanted to get my money. Slowly she stood up and returned home. That night Luis did not mention the missing money, and she did not return it.

Every day after that she returned to the park, hoping to see the woman. She tried daily to convince herself it wasn't real, but the possibility still intrigued her. One night, four days after the meeting she brought up the topic at dinner. Ana, Alana, Luis and herself were seated at the table. For once no other family members had joined them. "I see a lot of gypsies down at the park when I take Marta," she said casually.

Ana and Alana nodded. "I hope you're careful down there," Luis said.

She nodded. "I am. They seem to tell fortunes for the tourists."

"That's a scam," Luis said. "They take their money and make up lies. Everything they say is happy. According to the gypsies everyone has a wonderful life."

Maria raised her eyebrows slightly, watching him carefully. Luis was enjoying the dinner and didn't notice that she was agitated. Ana spoke. "That's not always true Luis. You know some of them have the gift."

"Gift." He spoke contemptuously. "Some gift. They have the gift of taking your money."

His mother shook her head. "Not all. Some of them really do have the sight." Alana nodded.

Maria looked at the two women curiously. "What do you mean, the gift, the sight?"

Alana answered. "Some of them seem to be able to see things that aren't obvious. They know things about people."

Without intending to Maria blurted out, "I met an old woman at the park. She was like that. I want to talk to her. I want to know what she can tell me."

"No!" Luis' voice startled them all. "I forbid you to see her. You are not to talk to gypsies."

Maria was startled. It wasn't like Luis to order her around. "But why, Luis? What harm is there in it?"

At first he didn't answer, then he muttered, "I don't want our money wasted that way."

"But Luis, she knew something. She came up to me and asked me about my first child. I could find out something about my past."

"No! I said no!" He sat back in his chair glaring at Maria. They ate in silence for the remainder of the meal.

That night Maria brought up the subject again. "Why are you so opposed? You know it's important to me."

Luis sat on the bed, glaring at her. Finally he exploded. "Do you think that first child was a miracle? That child has a father somewhere. If you find that child what will happen to us?" He gestured angrily toward the corner where Marta slept.

"I don't know," Maria replied, trying to remain calm. "That doesn't mean I don't want to know that child."

He stood up and crossed to the window. For a moment he stood looking out, hands on the windowsill. When he spoke again his voice was soft, "Maria, if you found that other child what would you do? Would you go back to your old life and leave us?" He turned toward her. His face was no longer angry, but anguished. He waved his hand toward Marta again. "Would you leave her?" he asked.

She crossed the room to him, put her arms around him. "I would never leave you," she assured him. "If I had another husband it's obvious he didn't want me. If he did he would have claimed me. You know as well as I do how exhaustive a search they did. But just because the child's father didn't want me doesn't mean the child doesn't want me. I would never leave you, but I would like to know that child. I would like to know who I was before."

Luis turned away, looking out the window, digesting the information. Eventually he said, "Very well. I will take you myself."

The next day they left Marta with Ana and set off. Instead of going toward the park they turned the other direction, heading further into the Moorish quarter. The further they walked the more convoluted and narrow the streets became.

After twenty minutes they stopped in front of an old, rundown house. It was two stories tall and badly in need of new whitewash. The front door was painted dark green. Old flower boxes at the windows held straggly plants in need of water. Luis knocked on the front door and waited. After some time it was opened by a little girl. She looked up at them quizzically, but didn't speak.

"We've come to see Zurina," Luis said.

"She's with someone now. You'll have to wait." The child's voice and manner were confident. She stepped aside to allow them to enter the house.

The front room was dimly lit. An old couch and a battered table were the only furniture. The girl indicated the couch and left the room without speaking again. They sat together, not touching, silent.

After several minutes Maria broke the silence. "How did you know about this place?" she whispered.

Luis shrugged. "Everyone knows Zurina. She's the best." They sat silently again. Eventually the girl reappeared and beckoned them. They followed her through the doorway covered with a curtain of filmy material into the kitchen. Maria was shocked to see that the woman seated there was the same she had met in the park.

"That's her," she whispered. "That's the woman from the park."

The woman looked up. "I knew you would find me," she said. "I have been waiting to see you. Please." She indicated the single straight-backed chair, which sat opposite her at the kitchen table. Maria sat, and Luis stepped back into the dark corner of the room. The old woman reached out and took Maria's hand. She laid it on the table, palm down, and covered it with her own. "You are very unhappy," she said.

"No," Maria protested.

The woman held up her hand, cutting short any further protests. "You are very unhappy about the first child. You wonder where this child is and why you cannot find him." This time Maria only nodded, holding her breath for fear of breaking the spell. "But the child is happy. You should not worry anymore. He is very happy."

"But where is he? How can I find him?"

The old woman shook her head. "He is not yours anymore."

"But where is he," Maria shouted. "You've got to tell me where he is!"

The old woman closed her eyes and sat silently. After a moment she said, "Enjoy the family you have found here. Sometimes one gets the thing most desired, then finds out she didn't want it at all." She sat silently, eyes closed, for several minutes. "I'm sorry. There is no more." She withdrew her hand.

"But you've got to help me," Maria cried. "That was no help at all. I still don't know who I am."

The woman raised her chin slightly in Luis' direction. "There. Your husband will help you to know who you are." Abruptly she stood up and left the room. The child appeared silently and stood by Luis, hand outstretched to receive his money. He laid 5000 pesetas in her hand, and she withdrew.

Luis crossed the room and laid his hand on Maria's shoulder. "Come on. We must go now."

Maria looked up. Her face was streaked with tears. "We can't go. There has to be more. How could she know about the child and not know more?"

Luis shrugged his shoulders. "Sometimes it's that way." He took Maria's hand and pulled her to her feet. Together they left the house and walked home in silence.

They did not discuss the visit with family or each other. Maria played it over and over in her mind, searching for clues. Was it coincidence? Had Luis already met with her and paid her to say those things, thinking she would lose hope? Could the woman know more? Three days passed before Maria discussed the woman with Luis. She awoke in the night with the woman's voice ringing in her ear. '*Your husband will help you to know who you are*.' She lay awake until morning thinking about the words. At sun-up she woke Luis. "What do you think she meant?" she asked him.

He rubbed his eyes sleepily. "I think she meant you must be content to live with what you have. Stop trying to live in the past."

Despite being awake most of the night Maria was not tired. She sat up, eager to convince Luis of what she believed. "I think there was more to it. You're supposed to help me find the child."

Luis sighed and turned toward Maria. Reaching out he covered her hand with his own. "She said the child is no longer yours. She told you to be happy with the family you have found. She warned you that what you think you want will not make you happy. She warned you to be careful Maria." His tone was solemn, serious.

Ignoring his voice she smiled and said, "She didn't warn me. That wasn't a warning at all. It was some silly comment."

Luis sat up and took her face in his hands. Turning her toward him he stared directly into her eyes. "Maria, you are not familiar with the gypsy ways," he said. "I tell you that she warned you, and she meant what she said. You and I will both be happier if you listen to the warning."

Maria stared back, shaken by the intensity of Luis' words, and did not reply.

The next day they returned to Madrid. Maria planned to tell Alicia about the gypsy woman, but at the last minute changed her mind.

She wanted to ignore Luis' words, and was afraid Alicia might only reinforce them. Instead she held the encounter in her heart, hoping and praying that some day she would learn more.

As the months passed Maria's ever-growing belly made her work more tiring, but she was determined to continue at the shop for several more months, to help with the Christmas sales. The main tourist season was winding down, but their shop, prominently located, still brought in a large crowd every day, and would continue to be busy until after Three King's Day in January. Maria was working on a display of lace tablecloths from Salamanca. They were beautiful pieces, and she draped one over a wooden table to show off its stitching. She stacked several others on the shelf, pinning tiny notes onto each showing the size. The tablecloths were always a popular item, though tourists who had been to Salamanca were a harder sale. The gypsies there regularly sold the tablecloths as 'handmade by my grandmother' when in truth they were all factory made. Maria had explained that scam dozens of times to unsuspecting tourists who wanted to know why the handmade versions in Salamanca were the same price as these 'lesser quality' machine made ones. Some believed her when she explained and some ignored her, insisting they would return to Salamanca and buy the hand-made ones.

She looked up as the doorbell tinkled. Two women were entering the shop. "Hello," the taller one said. "I saw the sign that you speak English."

Maria nodded. "Yes, what can I help you with?"

The woman smiled at Maria. "We just want to look around a bit. It's just so nice to find someone who speaks English. We've been here nearly a month, our husbands are stationed at the air base, and we just find it so hard to get around. We don't understand the money, don't understand the language. I mean once we leave the base it's like being in a foreign country."

Her friend nudged her. "It is a foreign country," she whispered.

"Oh," the first woman rushed on, "how silly of me. Of course it is a foreign country. I just meant, well, I meant it's all so different. I didn't expect it to be so difficult to get around. I was just thrilled when I heard Jimmy was getting stationed in Madrid, but now that I'm here, with three kids no less, it's a different story."

Maria listened to the woman's onslaught of complaints silently. During her time in the shop she had gotten used to the Americans and their odd ways, always smiling at everyone, telling her all sorts of things she don't want or need to know, and asking all sorts of personal questions that were really none of their business. Now she said to the woman, "Perhaps you would like to take some language classes. If you could understand the language you might feel more comfortable."

"That's not a bad idea," the woman replied. She turned to her friend. "What do you think? We could learn to speak Spanish then we'd really be set, go anywhere we wanted, and the guys would be dependent on us. Plus," she added with a broad smile, "They'd never know what we pay for stuff!" She laughed at her own joke. Turning back to Maria she said, "You speak pretty good English. Is that where you learned it? In a language class?"

Maria shrugged. "Mostly practice I guess. We get a lot of Americans in here."

"Oh yeah?" the woman was interested in hearing more. "Have you ever been to America?"

Maria shook her head but didn't reply. Over the years she had learned to avoid vague answers like 'I'm not sure' or 'I don't remember,' and just reply in the way least likely to generate questions.

"You ever want to go?" she asked. She was absentmindedly looking over some necklaces from Toledo as she spoke.

"I would like to go, someday," Maria replied. "I think it would be nice to see America."

The woman moved away from the necklaces to some jewelry boxes on display. "It's a great country," she said proudly. "I'm sure you'd like it." Looking up at Maria again she pointed to her swollen belly. "So, is this your first?"

"Child?" Maria asked. She lay her hand on her belly and gently rubbed it.

"Yeah, is this your first kid?"

"No," she replied, "I have a little girl at home. She's a year and a half." Immediately she thought of her other child, still lost to her, still unknown, but she said nothing.

The woman nodded. "Like I said, I've got three, all boys. What I wouldn't give for a little girl, but I don't want to go through all that again." She shook her head. "Ten, seven, and five. They're a real handful."

The woman's friend had come to the counter and was waiting patiently for a break in conversation. Maria turned to her and asked, "Can I help you with something?"

"Yes," she said. She pointed toward the back of the store. "I was interested in those swords. Are you able to package them for shipment?"

"Yes, of course." Maria started toward the back of the shop.

The more talkative friend stopped her. "It was nice talking to you. I'll think about those language classes. That might be a nice thing. We're going to be here for a couple of years, at least."

Maria nodded and continued to the back.

CHAPTER
SIX

Cristina and Anita hurried down the street to the subway stop. Anita liked living in the new apartment and being near the subway. Sometimes they still took the bus, but the subway was more fun. She loved to ride the escalators and stop to watch the musicians who played in the tunnels, but today there was no time. Mama was in a hurry. Chavo had started back to school last week, and every day since then Anita had gone back to work with her mother. Today she drug her feet, reluctant to go. The new apartment was pretty, and she liked being there. Sometimes Chavo had left her alone, then he brought her candy so she wouldn't tell Mama. She missed staying home with Chavo.

Today she was especially reluctant to accompany her mother because Lucia, the resident she normally visited, was gone for a week. Yesterday she had spent all day in the closet, waiting for her mother to get finished. Today, she decided, she would find another friend to play with.

They hurried down the stairway and Mama bought the tickets. The train was already waiting, and Mama made her run, holding her hand, and yanking her arm when Anita stopped to watch a man playing guitar. Once they were in the train Mama sat down and left Anita alone. She stood by the open door watching the man. A young woman tossed money into his open guitar case, but she didn't stop to listen. Suddenly a whistle blew, and Mama pulled her back from the doorway. A moment later the doors slammed shut and the train began to move.

When they reached the home, Cristina opened the back door and peeked in. Quickly she took Anita by the hand and led her to the storage closet. She was looking forward to next year when Anita would start school, and she would no longer have to worry about bringing her to work. She gathered up her cleaning supplies, kissed Anita on both cheeks, and left. Anita waited for what seemed a long time, then she opened the door and peeked out. No one was in sight. She picked up her bag of toys and crept into the hallway. She passed by Lucia's room and stopped at the next door. Quietly she turned the knob and pushed the door open a crack. She tried to peek in, but couldn't see anyone. In the distance she could hear someone walking down the hallway. She glanced around, wondering if she had been seen, but seeing no one she pushed the door open and stepped inside.

An old woman was seated by the window, looking out. She turned when Anita entered the room. Her wrinkled face looked scary, and Anita considered running out, but then the woman smiled. "Buenas días," she said. The scary wrinkles turned to friendly wrinkles.

"Hello," Anita replied. She stood there not sure what to say next.

The old woman continued to smile at her, not speaking either. Finally Anita spoke, "My name's Anita. What's yours?"

"Rosa," the old woman replied.

"Oh. Can I stay here with you for a little while?" Anita asked.

Rosa nodded.

"I've got some toys, if you like toys," she said uncertainly. She held the bag up for Rosa to see.

Rosa looked at the bag without much interest. "Can I play on your bed?" Anita asked. Lucia always let her play on the bed. Rosa nodded. At first Anita sat alone on the bed playing with her dolls while Rosa continued to look out the window. She talked to the dolls, pretending they were rich and were going out to a party. After a few minutes Rosa came over and sat beside her. She watched Anita playing, but didn't join in. Anita looked up at her. She had never seen anyone with such wrinkly skin before. She stared, fascinated, wondering what it would feel like to touch Rosa. Eventually she became aware that Rosa was staring back at her. She turned her head aside, suddenly embarrassed.

Rosa had a little shelf beside her bed, and Anita fixed her gaze on the things that were displayed there. She had a vase of flowers, a pretty wooden box, and three pictures. Eager to see the pictures better Anita stood on the bed. Looking closer at them her eyes opened wide with surprise. "Mama has that picture," she said. She reached out and picked up the picture. Happily she sat down on the bed again, bouncing in her seat. "Look," she said, pointing. "We have this picture too. Mama keeps it in the kitchen." She spoke earnestly, as if trying to convince Rosa it was true. Rosa sat, not answering, watching the child closely. "Do you know if that little boy is dead?" she asked suddenly.

"Katherine's baby," Rosa said. She reached out and snatched the picture back. "Katherine's baby isn't dead." She seemed angry, and Anita was suddenly afraid of the old woman. She wasn't fun like Lucia. She didn't talk to Anita and she didn't like the toys.

Anita slid off the bed on the side nearest the door, leaving Rosa seated on the far side. Quickly she grabbed up her toys and stuffed them in the bag. "I have to go now," she said. "Mama's probably waiting for me." She hurried back to the cleaning closet and sat on the blanket in the far corner. She dumped her toys out and half-heartedly played with them, but the old lady stayed in her mind. She was scary, and Anita wondered why she had a picture of the dead lady too.

Cristina hummed to herself as she mopped the floors. Today Anita was safely at home with Chavo, not stuck away in the closet, and she worked more easily. Ever since she had discovered Anita was leaving the closet and roaming the building she had been anxious about bringing her. Surely she would lose her job if Anita were discovered bothering the residents. She had found out about the transgression easily enough. One morning while she was getting breakfast ready Anita had come into the kitchen and announced, "This lady at work has the same picture you have, Mama." She had pointed out the picture of the woman Chavo had robbed following the bombing. Of course she had been wrong, no one at the home could have a picture of the poor American woman and her family, but Cristina had demanded an explanation of how Anita knew what the residents had, and Anita had admitted to visiting their rooms. She shook her head at the memory. Anita was rarely punished, but for that admission Cristina had gotten out Octavio's old belt, bent her over the chair, and spanked her thoroughly. Since then she had needed to keep a closer watch on Anita, and was relieved that Chavo was now home on fall vacation to watch Anita. The poor child had been so shocked at the spanking Cristina had a feeling she wouldn't break the rules again soon.

In the apartment Anita wandered about, bored. It had been a long time since Mama left, and Chavo had left just after Mama. She was hungry, but Chavo had told her not to fix lunch, but to wait for him. He had promised to bring her some candy so she wouldn't tell their mother. I wouldn't anyway, Anita thought. I might get in trouble. Ever since she had gotten spanked Anita was careful about what she told Cristina. She wasn't sure what tales might produce the belt again. She had thought her mother would be happy to know someone else was praying for that woman. Instead she had been mad. I guess she wants to pray for her all by herself, Anita decided.

She went into the living room and looked out the window, hoping to see Chavo coming home. Instead she saw just an empty street, with no one about. She wandered into the kitchen and pulled open the refrigerator. Inside was a box of milk, a dozen eggs, and some sausage. She didn't like milk, and she knew she wasn't allowed to turn on the stove and cook the eggs or the sausage. Closing the door she turned to the countertop. A long loaf of crusty bread sat on the counter along with a half dozen plums. She took two plums and ate them. Still bored she wandered into the bedroom she and her mother shared. Mama's bed was by the window and hers was in the corner farthest from the door. She sat on her bed kicking her feet against the side. Being home was as bad as being at work with Mama. She wondered briefly about visiting the neighbors while Chavo was gone, but thinking about the belt she decided she'd better stay home.

She got up and went back into the kitchen. She looked at the food on the counter again, and picked up the loaf of bread. She tried to break off a piece, but only succeeded in getting crumbs all over the place. Shrugging to herself she took the entire loaf and began eating. Standing in the kitchen she looked around until her eyes came to rest on Mama's pictures. She took a chair and dragged it across the floor to the shelf. Climbing onto it she eyed the picture of the dead woman carefully. "Mama's wrong," she said aloud. "This is the same picture. I know it is." She slipped the picture into her pocket and climbed down from the chair. She sat down and resumed eating the bread. By the time Chavo returned she had finished half the loaf.

Seeing her sitting there, eating her way through the bread he yelled, "Anita, what are you doing! I told you not to start lunch until I came back." He crossed the room and yanked the bread away from her. "Look what you did. You practically ate all of it."

"I did not," Anita protested. "I only ate half, and I was hungry. You were gone a long time."

"So what," he yelled. "Now Mama's going to know I left you here, because you ate the bread she got for supper. She'll spank us both for that."

Anita turned toward him, her eyes huge and full of tears. "Don't tell her," she pleaded, then burst into tears.

Chavo turned away, smiling. He knew they wouldn't get in trouble for eating the bread, but Anita's sudden and unexpected fear of their mother was proving to be a great way to gain his freedom. He ignored her sobbing for a couple of minutes, then turned back to her. "Ok," he said, "I won't let her spank you. I'll go and get another bread, and you can eat this whole piece for lunch. That way she won't know what you did."

Anita looked at him warily. "Are you sure?" she asked.

He nodded. "As long as you eat it all. You can't leave any."

"Ok," she agreed. She wiped her eyes with her sleeve, sniffled, then wiped her nose on the other sleeve.

"You'll have to stay here," he pointed out. "I haven't got any money, so I'll have to steal the bread. You can't come with me."

"I'm tired of staying here. There's nothing to do," she protested.

Chavo shrugged. "I can't help it. You can't run fast enough. If we got caught stealing Mama would kill us. So you stay here, ok?"

Anita wiped her eyes again and nodded. "But will you hurry?" she asked.

He shrugged again. "I'll be back when I can. I have to wait for the right chance." He opened the refrigerator and took out a large sausage. Without bothering to heat it he bit into it.

"I want some sausage, too," Anita said. She held out her hand.

He shook his head. "You'll get too full. You've got to finish all the bread. I'll eat this so Mama thinks we shared it. That way she won't find out."

"I won't get too full," Anita insisted. "I want some sausage too."

He broke off a small piece and handed it to her. "Here, just make sure you eat all the bread." He checked the clock then left the apartment humming to himself. He hated being stuck taking care of Anita, and was pleased with how he had handled things. Now he had the whole afternoon free and nearly the whole sausage to himself, and Anita wouldn't dare to complain.

Happily he ran down the street finishing the sausage as he went. Two blocks away he passed a group of friends who were playing soccer.

"Hey, Chavo," one of them yelled, "Where's your sister? Aren't you babysitting today?"

Chavo ignored the taunt. "I don't have to anymore," he said. "Can I play?"

A week passed before Chavo returned to school and Anita returned to work with her mother. She sat on the chair in the closet, swinging her legs. Mama had been gone a long time, and she was bored. She slipped off the chair and picked up the bag of toys. She dug through it until she found, at the very bottom, the picture she had taken from the kitchen. She took it out and studied it. It was wrinkled from being in her pocket and then in her toy bag. The woman's face had a big crease across it, and somehow the corner had gotten torn off. She had meant to return it to the shelf as soon as she made sure it was the same, but she hadn't had the chance to check it yet. Now it was nearly ruined, and Mama would notice. Anita frowned, trying to work out her dilemma. Eventually she decided there was only one thing she could do. She would switch it with the picture in the old lady's room.

She stood up and crept to the door. Slowly she opened it and peeked out. No one was around. She went down the hallway past Lucia's room and stood, staring at the doors, trying to remember which one she had gone into. Eventually she opened one a crack and peeked in. A young woman turned to see who was there, and Anita quickly shut the door and moved on. She tried another door and then a third before her fear drove her back to the closet. She rushed inside and sank to the floor, pulling the blanket up around her, trying to figure out where the room had been. Frustrated, she kicked her feet as she lay on the floor weighing her options. If she didn't switch the pictures Mama would notice and she would be in trouble.

She pulled the picture out again and smoothed her hand across it as if to remove the wrinkles. She pressed hard, then looked again at the picture in her hand, thinking what trouble it had caused her. She heard the door open, and quickly she stuffed the picture under the folds of the blanket and buried her face. By the time her mother came across the room Anita appeared to be sleeping. She could hear her mother humming softly, and heard her whisper, "Good, she's sleeping. I'll finish the upstairs without having to come back and check on her." She moved about the closet gathering supplies, then left, closing the door softly.

Anita wasted no time. She sat for as long as she thought it would take her mother to reach the stairs, and then jumping up she crossed the room and opened the door. Once again the hallway was empty. She hurried past the rooms she had already tried and began opening doors again.

On her second try she found the room she wanted. The old woman was seated by the window as she had been last time. "Hi Rosa," Anita said, trying to ignore the fear the old woman inspired in her. The woman looked at her, but didn't greet her. "Remember me? I'm Anita. I brought my dolls here and we played with them." She crossed over to the old woman and dumped the toys on the windowsill. "See what I've brought?" Rosa looked at the pile without any particular interest. Anita picked up a doll and handed it to Rosa. "You can play with her," she said. "I'm going to play on the bed." When Rosa still didn't answer Anita climbed onto the bed. Quickly she stood up, grabbed the woman's picture off the shelf and replaced it with her own. She looked at the picture in her hand. It was in a nice gold frame, and the one she was leaving behind was unframed and torn. She shrugged and stuffed the picture into her pocket. Chavo would know what to do about the frame.

Hopping off the bed she began to gather her toys. Rosa was holding the doll like a baby on her shoulder. Anita reached up and grabbed it away. "I have to go now," she said. "Maybe I'll come back later." She ran back to the closet feeling light hearted. All that was left was to get the picture out of the frame and back on the shelf.

CHAPTER

SEVEN

When Andy woke up on Saturday morning it was snowing. He crossed to the window and let out a whoop of joy at the sight of the ground. It was the first day of Christmas break, and several inches of fresh snow blanketed everything. He imagined sledding, skiing and snowball fights with his friends filling the next two weeks. First though there was the Christmas tree to get. Every year for as long as he could remember it had been the same. They would go into the woods and find a tree they both liked, then Daniel would cut it down and they would both carry it to the truck. When they got home they would get out the Christmas ornaments and Daniel would tell Andy all about each one as they hung them. 'That one your Grandpa McCarter gave you on your first Christmas and that one you made when you were three, in day care in New York,' and on and on until they were all hung.

He ran down the hallway to Daniel's room. "Hey Dad, wake up. It snowed!" He pounded on the door until Daniel responded.

Opening the door, still half asleep, Daniel said, "I bet that news would have kept for another hour."

Andy bounced from one foot to the other. "Come on Dad, wake up. We're getting the Christmas tree today!"

Daniel rubbed his eyes. "I remember," he said. "Just let me get a shower and a cup of coffee." He picked up his towel and started for the bathroom.

"Want me to make the coffee?" Andy asked. "That way it'll be ready."

"Don't touch the coffee maker," Daniel replied. "Just eat your breakfast and I'll be quick."

An hour later they were ready to leave. Andy climbed in the back seat with Boogie, leaving the front seat empty. As they drove down the highway past Ellen's house Andy asked, "Isn't Ellen coming with us?"

Daniel glanced back at Andy. "Not today. I thought this was our tradition for Christmas and we'd just keep it that way." Actually, he reminded himself, Ellen thought this was our tradition for Christmas and maybe I should just keep it that way. He had initially been afraid that her comments indicated a desire to put more distance in the relationship, but she had assured him that wasn't the case. 'You need to spend some time alone with Andy, just like you spend time alone with me,' she had pointed out, and he had to admit she was right. Lately every single thing they did included Ellen.

"But I wanted her to hear the story of the ornaments when I hang them up. That way she'll know about them too."

Daniel was pleased to hear Andy wanted her included in the tradition, but determined to honor her suggestion that they do this alone. "I guess we'll just have to invite her over and you can tell her the stories yourself."

"But Dad," Andy protested, "I might not remember them all."

"I'll be there if you have questions. We can invite her over for cookies and eggnog when the tree's up. What do you say?"

"Okay," he agreed, "but you have to help me with the stories. I don't want to tell her the wrong stuff."

The tree they found was declared perfect by both of them. It was a spruce, nearly nine feet tall and fairly thin. Daniel cut it down and took the trunk while Andy struggled along with the top. The minute they were home Andy wanted to decorate it. Eagerly he pulled the decorations from the closet while Daniel secured the tree in the stand. As the decorations were hung he listened extra carefully to the stories, repeating some of them back to Daniel. When the last one was hung he asked eagerly, "Can we invite Ellen over now?"

Daniel laughed. "Why don't we wait until tonight? You can call her up and invite her to dinner if you want."

Andy ran to the phone. "Can I call her right now?" he asked, the receiver already in his hand.

"Sure, go ahead. Tell her we're having chicken and rice." He began gathering the decoration boxes and restacking them in the closet while Andy made the call.

When Ellen arrived that night Andy took her by the hand and led her to the tree. He began pointing out the different ornaments and telling her where they came from. He proudly showed her a photograph of himself at age three, pasted to a cardboard frame, which had been decorated with red and green macaroni. "I made that when we lived in New York. I was three then. That's why it doesn't look so good."

"I think it looks great," Ellen said. "You were a real cutie at three."

Andy ignored her comment, hurrying on to the next one. "Look at this one," he insisted. "See, it's made in Spain. My Grandpa McCarter bought it when he lived there and then when I was born he gave it to me." He pointed to a small, hand carved wooden star. Without waiting for her to comment he selected the next one. It was a picture of Daniel and Katherine in a small frame, which read 'Our First Christmas'. "This one's my Mom and Dad when they first got married. I wasn't born yet, then." He pointed out the picture.

Ellen wasn't sure what to say, wondering why he had chosen that ornament out of the dozens he could show her. Eventually she said, "That's nice. Your mother was very pretty."

"Not as pretty as you," Andy replied loyally, smiling up at Ellen. Without further comment he moved on to the next ornament, then the next until Daniel finally called them to dinner.

Nurse Patricia knocked on a door, then opened it. "Pilar, ready to go?" she asked. An older woman appeared at the doorway, coat on and purse in hand. The nurse crossed the hall to collect a second person, and then a third. All were older women. She gathered them together and spoke kindly, as if speaking to children. "Now remember, it's important you stay with me. We're going to be in a busy part of the city and I don't want anyone to get hurt or lost." The women nodded.

She dug into her pocket and pulled out three pins. "I've got a pretty pin for everyone to wear too. If anything would happen and you would get separated from me just show someone your pin." The pins were designed to look decorative so the women enjoyed them, but their purpose was strictly practical. Neatly lettered on each was the name of the home "Casa Santa Luisa."

"Do you have your lists?" the nurse asked. Pilar dug into her purse and produced a piece of paper. "Clara? Rosa? Do you have your lists?" They nodded. "Okay, let's go then." She led them off down the hallway like a mother hen.

They were just passing the back door when Cristina opened it and stepped inside, holding tightly to Anita's hand. "Oh," she exclaimed, surprised to see anyone there.

Seeing the women Anita shrank back behind her mother, afraid Rosa might mention the picture. She had thought that drama was behind her. Chavo had figured out how to remove the picture from its frame and had taken the frame as payment for his troubles. He had even sneaked the picture back into place one night after she and Mama had gone to bed. Now, seeing Rosa, her fears poured back over her. Rosa might have reported the damaged picture and known Anita did it.

But Rosa appeared not to have noticed her, and her mother hadn't noticed her nerves. She was busy explaining to the nurse about how she had gotten permission to bring Anita to work on occasion. "I didn't have anyone to leave her with today," she explained. "But she's no trouble at all. When she has to come with me she just waits in the closet. I've brought her a bag of toys to keep her busy."

The nurse was unconcerned about the little girl, thinking ahead to the planned shopping trip. All three women accompanying her were in high spirits. The home arranged only a few outside trips each year for residents, and the annual Christmas shopping trip had been the topic of discussion for weeks. Now she waved Cristina and Anita aside. "I'm not worried about her as long as she doesn't make trouble."

She continued on her way with the women. Out of necessity they kept the groups small and this was Nurse Patricia's third day in a row to take a group shopping. She had gotten quite good at negotiating the trip. She walked the women to a nearby bus stop. Once on the bus they were seated together. They chattered excitedly. The trip included not only shopping but also lunch out in a restaurant. Nurse Patricia sat back and relaxed. The day should go smoothly.

The bus stopped near Sol, and she ushered the women to the back door and down the steps. At the sight of the crowds Clara became frightened. Patricia linked arms with her, talking softly, and encouraged Pilar and Rosa to do the same. They moved slowly through the crowds, the women staring at the people and the shop windows. Patricia led them down Calle de Preciados toward the Corte Inglés. Each of the women needed to buy a gift for the gift exchange, and the home encouraged practical items such as soaps, shampoos or basic clothing.

As they entered the store Clara pulled Patricia in the direction of the fancy soaps on display. All of the women picked them up, smelling them and admiring the colors. "I want to buy this," Clara said.

Patricia smiled. Clara always wanted the first thing she saw. "Do you want to look around a bit? There are lots of things to see."

Clara shook her head. "No, this."

"Okay," Patricia agreed. She helped the woman select several different soaps, then counted out the money to pay for it. Turning to the other two she asked, "What do you want to look at?"

They both stared back without answering. The choices were overwhelming after the peaceful day-to-day life they led. "Let's look around a bit," she suggested. She led the women through the store stopping at perfumes, shampoos and candy to let them look.

Eventually Rosa said, "I want to get perfume."

They returned to the perfume counter and tested several before settling on a nice large bottle of something cheap.

Patricia turned to Pilar. "Have you seen anything you liked yet?"

Pilar shook her head. Patricia had expected this, for Pilar was always undecided on what she wanted. Patricia looked at her watch. She had planned to have a late lunch so the crowds would be small. Now would be a good time. She said, "Why don't we go to lunch and then we'll look afterward." The women nodded eagerly. They were hungry after the excitement of the day.

Patricia took them back out on the street. She knew a nice café not far away that was quiet and would be good for the women.

Maria struggled to her feet. Eight months pregnant now, she had gotten huge and found it hard to get up. Luis watched her struggle, then took her hands and helped her. "I don't think you ought to be working at the shop any more. You've gotten too big," he said.

She laughed and ran her hands over her belly. "I am huge, aren't I? I can't quit now though, right before Christmas. Consuela would never make it. As is she's run off her feet the days I'm not there."

"It's too hard on you. You'll get exhausted."

She shook her head. "I'm fine, really. I'll take a break if I need to. Anyway it's only for a couple more weeks. I told her I can only stay until after Christmas."

"Well, don't wear yourself out. You need to take care of our baby." He laid his hand possessively on her stomach.

"I'll be careful. I've got to get going though. Siesta's nearly over. Will you take Marta down?" He nodded and she waddled off through the door. She was working three afternoons a week rather than the two full days because Consuela was so busy in the afternoons. She allowed an extra ten minutes to reach the shop because she moved so slowly, and sometimes she was still late. Consuela was so glad to see her that she never complained. Today she arrived on time.

"Buenas días." She greeted Consuela.

Consuela looked up. "Hola." She returned to stocking the shelves with sweatshirts. "It's been really busy all morning," she said.

Maria smiled sympathetically. "What do you need me to do?"

Consuela pointed toward the back. "There are three new boxes from Sabariego's in back. Unpack as much as you can and put them here on the table."

Maria found the boxes and cut the first one open. Inside were numerous handcrafted trays. She lifted them out one by one, unwrapping each and wiping it with a soft cloth. When she had finished six she picked them up and carried them to the table. She lay some flat and placed others on stands. Consuela always left the tables for her because she had a talent for making them attractive.

Setting the remaining trays aside she opened the second box. This one also held wooden products, but a greater variety. She unpacked jewelry boxes in several sizes and several sets of coasters. She wiped these also, and arranged them on the table beside the trays. Glancing at her watch she saw it was time to open the shop. "Want me to unlock?" she asked.

Consuela looked up. "Oh, is it time? Yes, we'd better."

Maria unlocked the front door and placed the sign in the window. It read "Abierto". Under that was hand lettered "We speak English. Nous parlons francais." She went behind the counter and sat gratefully on the stool. She preferred the stool over the chair because it was higher off the ground and easier to get up from. No sooner had she sat down than the door opened and a couple walked in. The woman greeted her in French. Maria replied and got up to help them. They were interested in jewelry from Toledo. The woman did the buying while the man stood back, looking bored. In the end she bought four pair of earrings, two bracelets and a necklace. Consuela congratulated her on the sale as she always did. Maria's language ability was a big boost to sales.

A few minutes later two American women entered the shop. One was noticeably pregnant. She smiled at Maria's big belly, sharing the joy of expecting a new baby. Maria hoisted herself off the stool and went to help them. They were interested in the wooden jewelry boxes she had just unpacked. The pregnant woman quickly picked two to buy, but her companion was difficult to please. She asked for bigger sizes, smaller sizes, different color combinations. Maria hurried back and forth from the back room to the showroom bringing different choices. Finally, exhausted, she told the woman to come to the back of the store. Consuela had a strict rule against customers in the storeroom, but Maria figured she could save some steps by moving her closer. She pulled the partially emptied box out for the woman to look through, then went back for the third box which she hadn't opened yet.

When the bell jangled on the door she glanced up to see four women entering the shop. She was relieved to hear that they were speaking Spanish. Consuela would handle them. She cut open the third box and began lifting out boxes, trying to please the American woman. From the front of the store she heard one of the women yelling in a loud voice, and looked up to see an old woman struggling with a younger woman. "I want to see her," the woman shouted. Watching the scene Maria noticed the younger woman was wearing a nurse's uniform. She was trying to calm the older woman.

The other two who had come in with them stood to the side, clutching their hands, staring. Abruptly one of them began to cry and stepped forward, trying to pull the nurse's hands off the old woman. The nurse spoke sharply, "Clara, stop that. Move back, out of the way. Everything is okay." Consuela took her arm and tried to move her back, but she pulled away and cried harder.

"Excuse me," Maria said to the American ladies. "I'd better go help out here for a minute."

She walked to the front of the store intending to help Consuela calm the women while the nurse dealt with getting them out of the shop. However, her presence only worsened the situation. As soon as she approached the front, the woman who was fighting with the nurse grew more agitated. "I want to see her," the woman screamed. She broke away from the nurse and lunged at Maria. "Where is your baby?"

Consuela shoved her away. "Maria," she yelled, "Get in the back. Don't let her hurt the baby." Maria hesitated. This was her job and her shop too, and she felt an obligation to help out.

"The baby," the old woman screamed again, reaching for Maria. "Where is your baby?" Suddenly fearful Maria turned and ran into the back shutting the storeroom door.

Nearly ten minutes passed before Consuela knocked and Maria left the storeroom. The shop was empty. The nurse had finally gotten the old women out of the store, and the Americans had fled. Consuela had locked the door for the time being. "Are you alright?" she asked Maria.

Maria nodded. "Are you?"

"Shaken up, but I'm not hurt." Together they crossed the shop floor, moving carefully as if they might encounter the woman hidden behind a display. Going behind the counter Maria sat on the stool and Consuela took the chair.

"I wonder what got her so worked up?" Consuela asked.

Maria shook her head. "Something about the baby. She wanted to see the baby." She sat silently for a minute. "She was retarded," she said. "She must not realize you can't see the baby until it's born."

"Well, thank heavens she didn't reach you. No telling what she might have done."

Maria nodded her agreement. They sat for half an hour, ignoring the people who came to the locked door, before feeling calm enough to reopen the shop. Consuela offered to take Maria home and work alone, but Maria insisted on staying. Mercifully the afternoon was quiet. They made several sales, but all were easy customers, anxious to finish their Christmas shopping, and Maria spent most of the afternoon sitting down, relaxing.

CHAPTER

EIGHT

When Maria reached home she recounted the incident to Luis. He listened silently, frowning at her story. Before she had even finished he interrupted. "She didn't hurt you, did she?" he asked.

"No," Maria assured him. "She didn't even touch me. Consuela got her away and I locked myself in the store room."

"Even so," he said, "I don't want you working there. She might come back."

"No, it's fine." Maria replied. "The nurse assured Consuela that those women never go out alone, and she promised that this one won't come near the store again." She hesitated, not sure how Luis would take her next statement. He sat, still frowning, and seemed to hardly be listening to her. "I really want to continue," she said eventually. "I can't leave it all to Consuela."

Luis didn't respond, but continued frowning into the distance. He must be very angry, Maria thought. He's angry and he doesn't want to overreact. She sat quietly too, waiting for him to speak. When he did she was caught off guard. "Maria," he said quietly, "Do you think she knew you?"

"No, of course not," she answered.

"Not you now, who you used to be. Did she know who you were?"

Maria shivered suddenly. "I never thought of that. I was so upset by the whole thing it never even occurred to me. All I could think was that she was going to hurt the baby." She rested her hands protectively on her stomach. Eventually she shook her head. "I don't think so, Luis," she said reassuringly, but in her mind she wondered if she was wrong.

The next day Maria went to visit Alicia and recounted what had happened. "...she was yelling for someone, and kept saying she wanted to see the baby. When I went to the front to help out she lunged at me and Consuela had to push her away." She paused, then continued, "Luis wondered if she knew me."

Alicia raised her eyebrows in interest. "Do you think she might?"

Maria shook her head. "I don't know what to think. I mean she was acting crazy, and she lives in some sort of a home for retarded women, but still I can't help wondering. She shivered violently. "Every time I think of it I get chills."

Alicia leaned forward in her seat. "What harm is there in looking into it?" she asked.

Maria shivered again. "I don't know. It might be hard to find her. I suppose there are a lot of those type homes."

Alicia studied her intently for a moment. "You sound almost reluctant."

Maria attempted a smile, but failed. "I am. I'm afraid. I didn't tell you this before, but last summer, when we went to see Luis' family, I went to see an old gypsy woman. She warned me not to look for my past. At least that's what Luis said she meant. He said I was being warned against looking for my past and told to appreciate what I have now."

Alicia's eyes opened wide. "Who was she? Was she someone good?"

Maria shrugged, sorry she had brought up the gypsy. "I don't know. Luis said she was good. She talked to me in the park, and she knew about the first baby. I was just sitting there, watching Marta, and she came up and said, 'you must miss the first one.'"

Alicia answered immediately. "I think you'd better listen to her. They know, the gypsies, they know things we can't see. If she told you to avoid your past you should listen."

Maria folded her arms over her chest, rubbing them. She suddenly felt cold. "I don't know," she said. "I just don't know."

The next day she arrived early for work. Consuela was there, straightening the shelves and sweeping the floor. Maria had scarcely slept, too bothered by the thoughts that swirled through her head. Now she went directly to Consuela. "Can I talk to you for a minute?" she asked.

Consuela stopped what she was doing, alerted by the tone in Maria's voice. "What is it?"

"I want to tell you something and ask your advice." She sat on the high stool, leaving the chair for Consuela. She was hesitant to tell Consuela the whole story. Quite possibly she would be angry that Maria had never told her before. After all they had known each other for several years, and Maria knew Consuela considered her a good friend. Sitting forward she began, "There's something about me that you've never known. It's pretty important and I'd like to tell you now. I hope you won't be angry that I've kept it a secret all this time." She bit her lip, waiting for a response.

Consuela didn't answer, but looked intently at Maria as if she could see into her and find the secret for herself. Eventually she said, "Go on. I won't be angry."

Maria looked at the wall behind Consuela, unable to meet her gaze. "A long time ago, I was in an accident. It was before I met you. There was a bombing at the Plaza del Sol." Consuela nodded, remembering the bombing, but didn't speak. "I was hurt pretty badly, and I suffered from amnesia." She paused, not sure how to continue. Eventually she said, "I never recovered my memory."

Consuela didn't answer, and Maria realized she didn't fully understand what she had been told. She continued, "I never recovered my memory. They did everything they could to help me, but nothing ever came back, no one ever came forward to claim me. What I'm trying to say is I don't really know who I am. All they ever found was a woman who said I used to live in her apartment, and her neighbor who said my name was Maria. Everything else about me is made up. They made me up because they couldn't figure out who I was."

Consuela was staring at Maria, open mouthed and wide eyed, unable to hide the look of horror on her face. "What do you mean they made you up? How can they do that?"

Maria took a deep breath before continuing, "They created my last name, my birthday, everything about me, and they gave me papers to make me legal, but no one knows who I was before."

Still staring in shock Consuela came to Maria and put her arms around her. "To imagine I'd be mad. No, I'm not mad, just shocked. What a thing to go through alone. What a terrible secret."

"It's not a total secret," Maria said. "Luis knows of course, and my friend Alicia. I went to live with Alicia when I came out of the hospital. She's the one who said I used to live in her apartment. She took me in hoping the location would spark some memories, but it never did."

Consuela returned to her seat. She shook her head slightly. "I can't imagine what that must be like for you."

Maria nodded. "There's more." She paused, hesitant to reveal the worst secret of all. "Before the bombing I had a child. Before Marta I had another child."

Consuela covered her mouth in horror. "The child was killed?"

"No, no," Maria shook her head. "Not killed, lost. I can't remember the child. I don't know if it's a girl or a boy. I don't know the age, I don't know anything. They just knew I'd had one because it was a cesarean."

Consuela still sat with her hands covering her mouth. "How can you bear it?"

Maria shrugged. "I bear it because there's no other choice. But there's a reason I wanted to tell you this now." She bit her lip again, struggling to go on. "The woman who was in here the other day, the retarded woman, I keep wondering if she knew me."

Consuela looked puzzled. "Well, did you know any retarded ladies before?"

Maria shook her head, laughing slightly, though it wasn't a funny situation. "Consuela, you don't understand. I have no idea who I knew before. If I'd been your best friend I wouldn't know it unless you told me. There's no way to know if I knew her. The question is did she know me, or was her interest random?"

Consuela nodded, her brow furrowed in thought. "I see. If she knew you she might help discover who you were before."

"Right. She kept yelling about seeing the baby. The more I think about it the more I wonder. Does she just like babies in general, or did she know me before, when I had the other baby."

Consuela didn't answer, but sat rubbing her arms as if she were chilled. After a long pause she said, "I do think it was you she wanted. I'm not saying she knows you," she added quickly, "but I do think she was after you. As soon as she saw you she got excited, and she didn't attempt to touch me or those American women who were in here, and one of them was pregnant too."

Maria frowned, trying to remember. Eventually she said, "You're right. She was pregnant, but the old woman didn't even notice her. And there's more."

Consuela looked shocked, then amused. "I'm sorry," she said covering her smiling mouth with her hand. "It's the stress. I can only take so much, then I start to laugh. Very inappropriately, I might add."

Maria waved away her concerns. "I do the same thing myself. I know you've got to be thinking how can there be more after all this, but there is. Last summer when Luis and I went to see his family, I was in the park with Marta. This old gypsy woman came up to me out of the blue and started talking to me. She talked to me about the first child, and no one knows about that child. She said she could tell I missed him. It was like she could see right into me."

Consuela was shaking her head emphatically. "It's a fake. Don't fall for that Maria. They're just after your money. No one has that kind of ability."

"Luis believes in it, and I wanted to, at first. But then she told me I shouldn't go looking for my past. She said it will make me unhappy, and that I need to be happy with what I have. After that I didn't want to believe her, because I can't help thinking that I'd feel more complete if I knew my past."

"It's nonsense," Consuela repeated. "If I were you I'd ignore everything she said. Act like you never met her."

"I don't know," Maria said. "Luis was really upset by the whole thing, and Alicia thinks I ought to heed the warning."

Consuela shook her head. "Well, I think it's ridiculous. I think those gypsies are just full of lies and after your money. I think if you want to know about your past you should find the woman who was in here and see if she knows you. That's nonsense to warn you off your own past." She stood up from her chair. "We'd better open up. It's past time." As she was walking to the door she added, "Of course I can see why Luis is worried. If you had a child that child has a father, and there's a good chance that father is your husband. Of course Luis is worried. You have to think about how you would handle that situation."

Maria lay her hand on her forehead. "I know," she said. "I have thought about it, but I don't have any answers. Sometimes I wonder if the baby died or if I gave it up, because if I had been married my husband would have found me. They really did search. They tried for a long time." More quietly she said, "But I just want to see my other child. I just want to know what happened."

Equally softly, as if she weren't sure she should offer the information, Consuela said, "Well, if you decide to look for her, they were from a home called Casa Santa Luisa. They were all wearing pins with the name."

Maria didn't answer, but went to her purse, took out a piece of paper and wrote it down.

That night she waited until Marta was sleeping, then brought up the subject with Luis. "I want to find that woman," she told him. "I know it's a long shot, but I want to talk to her, find out what she knows. If she knows anything."

Luis was furious at the suggestion. "She acted like a crazy woman," he yelled. "I won't have you going near her." Then he voiced his true concern, "You can't do this to our family!"

"Luis!" she said, speaking more sharply than she usually did, "Quiet down. The baby is sleeping." She got up from the couch and paced across the room. Turning to face him she said, "I'm not doing anything to our family. I just want to know, that's all. It's been four years, and no one anywhere in this city has ever even hinted they might know me. No one! You knew when you married me that someday I might remember. I told you. I took you to Dr. Montoro so you could talk with him and he could explain it. You have to help me." Tears were streaming down her face and she wiped them away impatiently with the back of her hand.

Luis sat on the couch, elbows resting on his knees, his head in his hands. Eventually he looked up. His eyes were sad, his face tired. "Maria," he said, "What will you do when you find out? Will you try to bring the other child here to live with us? Will you go back to his father? What will you do?" He stared at her, his face a mixture of anger and sorrow. "If you find the child you may find you have another husband. What will you do when you have two husbands and three children? What will you do?"

She crossed the floor and sat beside him, taking his hand in hers. Softly she said, "I don't know what I'll do, but I need to know. I'm not going to do anything to hurt you or Marta. You are my family now, no matter what I had before. But I need to know. I need to know why they didn't come forward when the hospital was searching." She looked in his eyes, pleading with him to understand. "I don't know how I'll handle it, I just know I've got to try."

Luis stared at her angrily. "No," he said. "I forbid you to talk with that woman."

His words angered her. Normally Maria was content to let Luis have his way and run the household, but never before had he forbidden something to her. Softly she said, "You have no right to forbid me. I am not your property."

"You are my wife," he said angrily, "and I forbid you to speak to the woman." Abruptly he stood and left the room.

Maria sat, refusing to follow him. She stayed on the couch until she heard him get in bed, then she crept down the hallway, used the bathroom and returned to the couch. Taking a small blanket from the back she lay down and covered herself. The couch was lumpy and she shifted her weight trying to find a comfortable position. Eventually she gave up and lay staring at the ceiling.

She was awakened at 5:00 AM by a searing pain. The couch was soaked, and she realized immediately that she was in labor. She struggled to sit up, fighting against the pain. Marta's birth had been a fairly easy one, and the baby had come quickly. Now Maria calculated the pains. They were close together and strong. Possibly the baby would be born soon. Gripping the back of the couch she waited for the pain to ebb, then pulled herself up. "Luis," she screamed, "Luis, help me." Marta woke and began to cry.

A moment later Luis appeared, his hair tousled from sleep. "What is it..." he began, then seeing her on the couch he realized. "The baby," he said. "It's the baby?"

She nodded, unable to speak.

"It's too early. The baby's not due until the end of January."

She pointed to the door. "Get Angela. Get a taxi, now."

He stood frozen for a moment. Maria groaned, and the sound spurred him into action. Quickly he ran into the hall and pounded on their neighbor's door. As soon as Angela answered he grabbed her, pulling her toward his open door. Gratefully he left her with Maria while he went to find a taxi. Marta's birth had terrified him, but this was far worse. The baby was too early.

When the taxi was secured he ran back up the stairs. Angela sat calmly beside Maria encouraging her to breath. Marta was on her knee. Maria seemed far calmer as well and no longer fought to get up. He pointed to the front door. "The taxi is waiting," he said.

Angela took Maria's hand. "Do you think you can get up?" she asked.

Maria nodded. "Just wait until after the next one." Together they waited for the labor pain to finish, then Angela helped Maria to her feet. Luis supported her under her arms and got her to the elevator.

Mariana was born at 7:00 AM. She was small but healthy, and Luis stood by the nursery window watching her proudly. He hadn't told Maria, but he had been hoping for a boy this time. Seeing his new daughter he no longer cared. She was beautiful and he was grateful that she seemed to be healthy despite her early arrival.

Maria lay resting in her room. It had been an easy birth and she was thankful. The baby was healthy, just very tiny. She closed her eyes, dreading the moment Luis would enter the room. Now that the crisis was passed he was bound to be angry again, even angrier because she had slept on the couch. She closed her eyes thinking she would pretend to sleep. Within moments she was asleep.

She woke when Luis entered the room in early afternoon. Reluctantly she opened her eyes. He stood beside the bed, a large bouquet of roses in his hand. "She's a beautiful baby," he said.

She didn't return his smile. "Thanks for the flowers," she said. "You can put them there in the window."

He crossed the floor and sat the flowers on the windowsill, then returned to the bed to sit beside her. "How are you feeling?" he asked.

"Mmmm, okay. Sleepy I guess." She looked at him warily. He didn't seem to be angry. In fact he acted like the earlier fight had never happened.

"You'd better rest then. I'll come back and see you tonight." He stood up and opened the door.

"Luis," she said, stopping him. He turned to look at her. "About the fight earlier..."

He shook his head. "Never mind the fight. That was all nonsense. We have a new daughter to take care of." He smiled at her then walked out into the hall closing the door behind him. Maria understood that he hadn't changed his mind about anything. He just didn't want to discuss the subject. Sleepily she lay back on the pillows, and vowed to do what she thought was best.

The next morning Maria was awakened early by a nurse bringing Mariana into the room. She handed the baby to Maria to feed, then left. Maria gazed down at the little girl in her arms. Already she was filled with love for this tiny, unknown person, but she was not content. Thoughts of her first baby kept hounding her. Where was he? Who was he? Was the gypsy woman right that he was a boy? Silent tears ran down Maria's face and dripped onto Mariana's forehead. Maria hadn't suffered this agony after the birth of Marta, but the knowledge that a woman may have recognized her had opened a flood of emotions. She understood Luis' fear of her past. Indeed she feared it herself. What would she do if she found she had another husband? Was her marriage to Luis legal? Who would she pick? The thought of it all boggled her, and she could see that Luis was right. It was far better to let the past be. Listen to the gypsy woman.

The baby's hunger was satisfied, and Maria lay her gently in the bassinet which stood beside her bed. For a long time she sat, looking at the sleeping baby, then she got up and crept down the hallway to the public phones. When she returned 15 minutes later the baby was still sleeping. She climbed into her bed and stared at the paper in her hand. *Rosa Mirandas*. Maria had spoken to the woman's nurse. The nurse had apologized profusely. She insisted Rosa had never acted that way before.

"You look quite a bit like a relative of hers," the nurse had said. "I think she might have been confused."

"Oh," Maria had said. "Does she see the relative often?"

"Oh no," the nurse had replied, "Not for years, but she has some pictures she enjoys."

Maria shivered and pulled the covers up over her shoulders. Of course it doesn't mean a thing, she told herself. Lots of people look like me. Lots of people in homes don't see their relatives. Her head began to ache and she rubbed her temples with her hand. Once again tears slid down her cheeks.

Her door opened and she hastily stuffed the paper under her pillow and wiped at her eyes. Luis looked alarmed and crossed to sit on the edge of the bed. "What's the matter? Why are you crying?" he asked.

She smiled through the tears. "It's nothing, just the baby blues I guess."

He frowned at her answer. "Baby blues, what are baby blues? You don't like our baby?"

"No, it's not that. It's hormones. Sometimes women get depressed after having a baby. It's fairly common."

He looked at her suspiciously. "You weren't like that with Marta. Why now?"

She shrugged and lay back on the pillow, wiping her eyes again. "I don't know. Sometimes it's like that. Ask the nurse. She'll explain."

He ignored the comment. "My mother is coming tomorrow. She'll be staying for a couple of weeks to help out."

Maria nodded. She had expected Ana to come up when the baby was born, and in fact looked forward to the help. Now she realized that with Ana in the apartment she would be able to get out, go see this woman Rosa, if she wanted to.

Maria went home the next morning. Luis had been hard at work arranging the apartment, and Marta's room had been transformed. A borrowed crib had been added, and the cribs now stood one on each side of the window. A regular bed, what would be Marta's bed when she was old enough, stood in the corner. For now Ana would sleep there, Luis explained.

"Oh Luis, you can't put your mother in with the babies. She'll be up all night. Put her in our room and I'll sleep here. You can go on the couch."

"She wants it this way. She said she'll take care of them at night so you can rest properly. I told her about the baby blues, and she's very worried."

Maria started to protest, then stopped. If she were to investigate her past she would need to do so without Luis' knowledge. Having Ana take over caring for the babies would be a big help. "Okay," she said, "If you're sure she doesn't mind I won't protest. I'm going to lay down for a few minutes."

For two days Maria stayed in the apartment visiting with Ana, caring for the children, and resting. It was a huge help having someone else there during the day, and Maria gratefully let Ana do a fair amount of the work. Her emotions seesawed up and down, and while she knew the true reason, she accepted Ana's sympathy and listened to her stories about her own baby blues.

"It was so bad after Luis that I couldn't even get out of bed," she related. "Nothing could make me get up. He'd cry and cry and I couldn't make myself go to him. Finally we got a nice day and my mother took the baby and me to the park and made me take a long walk while she kept the baby. It helped. After that I started to feel happier and I took care of him."

Maria seized the opportunity. "Maybe that would help me," she said. "I haven't gotten out since she was born. Maybe tomorrow I could get out for a couple of hours if you didn't mind keeping them."

Ana nodded. "Of course I'll keep them. That's what I've come here for, to help you out."

The next morning Maria waited until Mariana was sleeping, then suggested she get out, just for a few minutes to test her strength. "I'll just walk down to the corner store for some bread. You said we were about out." She wanted to go alone, but Marta clung to her, crying, so she gave in and took her.

As soon as they reached the corner she entered a phone booth and dug the crumpled paper from her pocket. She dropped her coins in the phone and dialed. "Can you tell me when visiting hours are?" she asked the woman who answered. "I'm a friend of Rosa Mirandas', and I was planning to stop by tomorrow."

The aide entered Rosa's room just as her nurse was getting ready to help her bathe. "Well, Rosa," she said cheerily, "It looks like you're getting a visitor tomorrow."

The nurse looked up expectantly. "Who's that? Rosa never has any visitors."

The aide shrugged. "She didn't say. Some woman called to ask about visiting hours. Said she was coming to see Rosa."

The nurse waited until Rosa was in the bath, then took the aide aside. "I don't like that call that came in. I've been here for five years and Rosa has never had a visitor. Never. Then last week I got a call from a young woman asking about Rosa. She worked in the shop where we went Christmas shopping, the one where Rosa got upset. She asked a lot of questions about Rosa. Tomorrow you stay with Rosa and don't let that woman in to see her. Send her to me."

The following morning Maria waited until Luis had left and Ana sat happily holding Mariana while Marta napped. Getting up she said, "Well, I think I'll get out for a bit again. See if it helps. Are you sure you're comfortable being alone with the two of them?"

Ana nodded, smiling broadly. "I had eight of my own. You don't need to worry." She smoothed the baby's fine hair and kissed her forehead. "Take your time and enjoy the day. We'll be fine here."

"Thanks Ana. I really do think this might help me." She picked up her purse and left quietly so Marta didn't wake up. Once on the street she walked toward the subway. However, as soon as she was out of sight of the apartment she flagged a taxi and got in. Giving the address she sat back breathing deeply and trying to relax. Her palms were sweaty and her heart was pounding at the thought of meeting the woman.

When the taxi stopped she paid the driver and got out. The building was a fairly small one, two stories tall and made of stone, with nicely landscaped grounds. She walked down the street a bit looking, hesitant to go in, not sure she wanted to explore her past. She thought of Marta and Mariana, and then of a faceless, motherless baby, a child now, who was hers. Slowly she walked up the steps and into the lobby.

A young woman sat behind the reception desk. She looked up as Maria came in. "Buenas días. May I help you?"

Maria wiped her palms on her pants. "I'm here to see Rosa Mirandas, please."

"Just a moment." The girl picked up her phone and called someone. "Visitor for Rosa Mirandas here," she said. Hanging up she indicated some chairs nearby. "Someone will be right out if you'd like to have a seat."

A minute later a woman came down the hall. "Hello," she said, "I'm Patricia."

Maria nodded her greeting. "I'm Maria Desconocida," she said. "I'm here to see Rosa Mirandas."

The woman nodded. "Come with me." She walked briskly down the hall and Maria followed. They entered an office and the nurse shut the door. "Please sit down," she said, indicating a chair. Maria did as she was told. The whole procedure for visiting was more complex than she had anticipated. She had expected to be given a room number and sent on her way.

The nurse took a seat behind the desk and smiled pleasantly at Maria. "Now," she said, "Can you tell me why you're here?"

"I've come to see Rosa Mirandas," Maria said. Again she wiped her palms on her pants.

The nurse nodded, then shuffled some papers on her desk. When she looked up she stared at Maria intently. "Do you know Rosa?" she asked.

Maria hesitated, not sure how to answer. "I...I'm not actually sure. I think I might," she finally said.

The nurse continued to stare at her. "You work in the shop near Gran Via, correct?"

Maria nodded. She didn't recognize the nurse, but this must be the woman who had come into the shop.

"Rosa was substantially upset by seeing you there. What relationship do you think you have with her?"

Maria sighed, her eyes clouding over. She hadn't intended to reveal the whole story to anyone. She simply wanted to see Rosa and talk to her. "I just think I might have known her a long time ago. I'd like to find out if she's the same person."

"I'm afraid I can't allow that," the nurse said. "My job is to protect the women who live here. Seeing you in the shop upset Rosa greatly and she didn't calm down for several days. I can't have that again. I've been here for five years and Rosa has never had a visitor or a phone call. Her only correspondence has come from her family in America, and even that has dropped off to just a Christmas card with a photograph each year."

"On the phone you said I looked like her relative. You said she had photos. I've really got to talk to her."

Patricia shook her head. "Sorry, but looking like a relative isn't going to get you in. Obviously you aren't related or you'd know Rosa."

Maria wrestled with her thoughts and emotions. She wondered if she should just walk away, heed the gypsy's warning. Instead she said, "Have you got a few minutes? I can tell you the whole thing, and you can verify it with a doctor if you want to."

The nurse nodded. Maria leaned forward in her chair and began.

When she had finished the nurse was looking at her differently. Her eyes were sympathetic and all brusqueness had gone. "That's an awful story," she said. "A true horror for you. Of course I can understand why you question whether she knows you. I question it myself considering how she reacted. Still, I would wonder how she could recognize you. As I said she's never had visitors." The nurse stared intently at Maria, studying her face and her features. "But you do look a bit like that relative of hers. I suppose it is possible you're related somehow."

"I don't know," Maria said. "I truly don't know. But you see why I have to try to find out? In all these years she's the only person I've come across who might have known me."

The nurse nodded. "Why don't you wait here a minute," she said kindly.

She went directly to Rosa's room and ask for Rosa's photographs. Taking them off the shelf she noticed the unframed and ruined photo of Katherine and her family. "Rosa," she said, "What happened to your picture?" She held it up for the old woman to see.

Rosa looked at the picture then turned away, not answering.

"Rosa," the nurse repeated, "What happened to this picture? Where's the picture frame?" She crossed to where the old woman sat by the window, and was surprised to see tears running down her cheeks. "What is it?" she asked. "Did you break the picture frame?"

Rosa shook her head. "She took it," she said, turning further away from the picture.

"Who? Who took it?" Patricia asked. When she received no answer she spoke more sharply, as if to a naughty child. "Rosa, look at me! Who took the picture frame?"

Rosa looked at her, but merely shrugged her shoulders.

Patricia clenched her teeth in exasperation. Something was going on. A strange woman and her strange stories in the office, and now Rosa's pictures destroyed by a mysterious 'she'. "Never mind then," she said. "We'll find out later. I need to take these for a few minutes, okay?'"

Again Rosa shrugged her shoulders and turned away, and Patricia left the room taking all the photos with her. Returning to her office she sat at her desk, intentionally not allowing Maria to see the pictures. For a minute she studied them, also looking closely at Maria. Eventually she said, "There is definitely a resemblance. I can see why she was convinced it was you."

Maria wanted to reach out and grab the photographs, to study them for herself. She clasped her hands together to control them. Forcing herself to speak evenly she asked, "May I see the photographs?"

Slowly the nurse leaned over and handed her one. She could have been looking at her sister. The hair was shorter, just shoulder length, and worn loose about her face, but the eyes, the face, the mouth, all of them were the same. Next to her was a man. He was tall with sandy colored hair. He wore glasses and a tweed jacket. On his lap sat a little boy, maybe two or three years old. Like the father he had sandy-colored hair. He smiled openly at the camera, his eyes bright and happy. Maria reached out and touched the photograph, running her hand over the boy's face.

"May I see the others," she whispered.

"These are just the boy," the nurse replied. She handed them over.

Maria looked. The boy grew up before her eyes. In one picture he was about five, his hair tousled as if it hadn't been combed. In the next he was about seven, his front teeth missing from his huge grin. Again she ran her finger over the photos as if she were smoothing his hair. Her eyes filled with tears and she wiped them away with the back of her hand. "They've got to be relatives," she said, ignoring her suspicion that she was looking at a picture of herself. She looked at the nurse through her tears. "Will you help me?" she whispered.

"What can I do?" the nurse asked kindly. "I'll try to help, but I don't know how."

"Her name," Maria said. "Can you tell me this woman's name?"

The nurse hesitated for a moment, then said, "I can check the records." She got up and went to a file cabinet that stood nearby. She pulled a large file out and opened it on her desk. Maria leaned forward, anxious to see what the file contained. The nurse flipped through several pages of documents before stopping. "Here it is," she said. She smiled encouragingly at Maria. "Katherine Bayley, niece." She read a bit more. Apparently Rosa is Katherine's aunt, and her care is being paid for by a trust fund. I've got an address in New Jersey and phone number for Katherine Bayley. That's all I've got. No notes on any other relatives."

Maria leaned forward. "Oh, please..." Her eyes pleaded for the information. "The little boy, do you have his name?"

The nurse flipped through a few more pages, searching, then shook her head. "Neither the boy or the father, but the phone number may help."

"Can I talk to Rosa? Maybe she can tell me."

The nurse looked warily at Maria. "I can't have her upset like last time. It isn't good for her."

"Please," Maria pleaded. "You've got to help me."

The nurse closed the file and put it away. She sat back down at the desk and looked at Maria closely. "If I agree to help you further, you must agree to do things my way."

Maria nodded eagerly. "I will, I'll do whatever you say."

The nurse thought for a minute, then said, "You can't see her today. Go home and I'll talk to her. I'll tell her Katherine is coming to visit. That way she's prepared and you won't excite her. You can come back next week."

"Next week!" Maria was distressed. "I can't wait a week! Do you know what this means to me? I've been looking for years."

The nurse sat silently for a minute. "I don't want to upset her. You can't just walk in on her."

"Can't you just tell her now that I'm here? She'll be excited, but not like at the store. There she thought I didn't want to see her."

"Can you act like Katherine? Rosa loves children and she'll ask about the boy. What are you going to tell her?"

"I'll say he couldn't come with me. I'll tell her he's in school,"
Maria answered quickly.

"Can you say that without crying?" the nurse asked. "I don't
want you crying in front of her."

"I won't. I promise I won't. I just want to see if she can tell me
their names." She pointed to the photographs lying on the desk.

The nurse stood up. "Alright, let me see how she responds to the
news. Perhaps you can see her today." She picked up the photographs
and left the room.

Maria sat back in her chair and breathed deeply. Her heart was
racing again and she felt exhausted. She looked at her watch. She had
been gone two hours already. She wondered how Ana was managing
with the babies. They hadn't discussed how long she would be gone.

Suddenly she was overwhelmed with fear. What if the woman
wasn't a relative? What if it was her? The picture showed a happy
family. A mother, a child and a husband. A happy family all together.
She thought about Luis and the girls, and wondered what she was doing.

She didn't have time to ponder her own question, because the
nurse returned. "You can come with me," she said. "Rosa is very
excited." She led the way down the hall and into a nearby room.

As soon as they entered the room Rosa got up. "Katherine," she
said excitedly. "Katherine came to visit me." She came forward and
embraced Maria.

"Hello Rosa," Maria said evenly. "How are you?"

Rosa smiled broadly. "Look," she said. She picked up her
photograph which showed the three people sitting together. Pointing to
the little boy she said, "Katherine's baby. Where is Katherine's baby?"

"He couldn't come," Maria replied. Then seizing the opportunity
she asked, "Do you know the baby's name?"

"Anita," Rosa said. "Anita took my picture. She tore up
Katherine's baby."

"What?" Maria said impatiently. Turning to the nurse she asked,
"What's she talking about?"

Patricia shook her head. "I'm not sure," she admitted. "Rosa's
conversation tends to be disjointed, and something's happened to her
picture. Last time I saw it it was in a nice frame. Now it's torn up and I
don't know how it happened.

"Anita," Rosa said.

Again Patricia shook her head. "We don't have anyone named
Anita here. She's not making sense."

"Rosa," Maria said, trying again, "Do you know the little boy's name?" She pointed eagerly to the picture, trying to cajole an answer from the woman.

"Andy," Rosa replied quickly.

Maria fought to swallow the lump in her throat. "Andy. Very good. Andy. And this one?" she pointed to the man.

"Daniel," Rosa replied without hesitation.

"Andy and Daniel," Maria whispered.   "Andy and Daniel". Louder she said, "Rosa, I've got to go, but I'm going to come back and visit you again. I promise I'll be back soon."

Again the old woman got up and embraced her, not protesting the short visit. Quickly Maria turned and left the room. As she reached the hallway tears began to pour down her face. She walked until she reached the nurse's office. There, she sat in a chair sobbing, waiting for the nurse to catch up to her. When she had composed herself she stood up. "Thank you so much," she said to the nurse. "You don't know what this means to me."

The nurse nodded. "Good luck," she said softly. As Maria left the room she whispered, "You may need it."

CHAPTER

NINE

Maria returned home to find Ana and the babies all sleeping. She crept quietly about the apartment, trying to be cheerful. Wanting Ana to think that the time alone had helped cheer her. She reached into her purse and pulled out the paper where she had written the names, *Katherine, Daniel, Andy*, and she wondered if she should throw it out.

For several days she did nothing but try to convince herself that that there would be no connection between those people and herself. If there was a connection the woman would be a relative, she told herself. There was no way she was American. Americans were loud and talkative. They rarely learned foreign languages, but she spoke Spanish perfectly. There was no way she was American.

She slipped into tears at all hours of the day and night, and Ana decided she'd better stay indefinitely. She'd never seen such a bad case of baby blues, she declared.

Maria tried hard to be more cheerful for her children, but the best she could manage was to sit quietly while Marta played, and not cry. Every minute of the day the boy's face danced before her. He looked so happy. He couldn't be mine, she assured herself, because he'd miss his mother, be sad. She had no idea when the photographs were taken, so therefore no idea of his age. She desperately wanted to know.

One week to the day after she had met Rosa she suggested to Ana that she try getting out again.

"Whatever you think will help, dear," Ana replied. "Just try to be more cheerful for your babies."

Maria returned to the home to visit Rosa, hoping to gain more information. This time she was admitted directly to Rosa's room, though Nurse Patricia joined them. Maria talked with Rosa for several minutes, and was disappointed to find that Rosa knew nothing about Katherine, Daniel or Andy. Apparently the only contact had been through photographs. On her way home she stopped at a pay phone. She had carefully checked the time differences, and she figured it was now 7:30 in New Jersey. Before she could change her mind she picked up the phone and dialed.

The ringing seemed to go on forever, then a man's voice, "Hello? Hello?" Her breath came in gasps and her mouth went dry. "Hello? Who is this?" The voice sounded angry, then the receiver was slammed down. Carefully she replaced the receiver and stood leaning against the phone booth until someone stopped outside, waiting to use the phone. She returned to the apartment and went to bed, claiming she didn't feel well.

The next morning Luis demanded she see a doctor. "You can't go on like this forever," he said. "Every day you cry, you sleep the day away, you cry some more. They have to be able to do something for you."

She tried to brush off his concerns. "It happens to some women. You just have to wait it out."

"No, I'm taking you to a doctor. Even you admit you've never seen anyone act like this after a baby. You don't even take care of Mariana. You just leave her to my mother. You never even hold her."

Maria had to admit he was right. The events of the last few weeks had drained her, and though she wouldn't admit it to herself she was wary of bonding with Mariana.

"I'll take myself," she said. "There's no reason for you to be off work as long as your mother doesn't mind keeping the girls." She didn't want Luis to take her to their family doctor.

That afternoon she went to see Dr. Montoro. She told him the whole story only after he promised not to tell the inspector. Dr. Montoro agreed with Maria that after so much time, and considering Luis and the children, Maria should be left to handle the situation on her own. He prescribed an anti-depressant, warning her that it might not help much given the nature of the situation. Maria shrugged off his concerns. She could tell Luis she had seen the doctor, and as long as she took the pills she would buy herself a couple more weeks of time. After that she would have to tell him.

On the way home from the doctor's she once again dialed the New Jersey number. This time it was answered on the first ring.

"Hello?" It was a child's voice.

Maria gulped in her breath. "Hello," she said. "Is this Andy?"

"Who?" the child asked.

"Andy. Is this Andy?" She chewed nervously on her lower lip.

"No."

"Is Andy there?"

"Who's Andy?" the child asked.

An older woman's voice came on the line. "May I help you?"

"Ah, I was, I was calling for the Bayley's. Is this their number?"

"Bayley? No, I'm afraid you've got the wrong number."

"Oh, but I, just a minute...." She pulled the paper from her pocket and read the number to the woman.

"Well, yes, that is our number, but this is not the Bayley's. It must have been changed."

"I'm sorry," Maria stammered. "I must have written it down wrong." She hung up and called Nurse Patricia to check the number.

Anita sat ramrod straight in her chair, not even daring to swing her legs. Her worst nightmare had happened. As soon as she and her mother had opened the door that morning and she had seen Rosa in the hallway the fear had started. Anita was relieved when they passed by Rosa and nothing was said. Safely in her closet she had sat playing with her dolls, reminding herself that she had seen Rosa before, and nothing had been said. Then, about an hour ago the tragedy had happened. She had heard someone open the door and looked up to see Rosa with a nurse.

"Are you Anita?" the nurse asked her.

Mute with fear Anita had nodded.

"Well, I need to talk to you about something, Anita," the nurse said. She came into the closet with Rosa following her.

Anita shrank back toward the corner of the room, looking for an escape, but there was nowhere to go. Her heart did a somersault as the nurse held up the picture.

"What do you know about this?" she asked. Her voice was kind but Anita wasn't fooled. Her eyes were mad.

Mutely Anita shook her head.

"What's the matter? Don't you talk? I want to hear about this picture."

Still Anita didn't answer, and without further questioning the nurse had left, taking Rosa with her. Anita's reprieve was short lived. Moments later they had returned with her mother, and Anita had seen that she was furious. She had crossed the room and grabbed Anita roughly by the arm, pulling her onto her feet then shoving her into the chair. "Did you do this to her picture?" Mama asked.

Again her heart somersaulted and Anita bit her lip. She shook her head. Mama took her shoulders and shook her roughly, and tears sprang to her eyes. "Anita!" Mama demanded, "Tell me the truth."

And fearful of making Mama madder she had told the whole story beginning with seeing the picture in Rosa's room and ending with the return of the stolen picture to Mama's shelf. Now she sat on a chair outside Nurse Patricia's office awaiting her fate. In her mind she could already imagine the spanking she would get at home.

Inside the office Cristina's anger was hidden away by the fear she felt. She would lose her job, of course, and Octavio's theft would be exposed, he might be arrested. Cristina had already explained how she had come to have a picture identical to the one in Rosa's room. There had been no time to make up a story. She had simply told the truth. Now, with time to consider the consequences, she thought of stories that would have protected Octavio. She could have said he found the things, or blamed the theft on her missing husband.

Cristina was startled from her reverie by the nurse addressing her. "You know, this woman is not dead. She's been here to see me, to try to find out who she is. Your son has committed a terrible crime against her. By taking her things he removed her identity and prevented her family from being notified about the accident."

"But he didn't know," Cristina protested. "He thought she was dead. He was sure of it. He was just a little boy when he took those things. And anyway, if she didn't die," Cristina said, "then she was able to notify them herself. That was years ago."

The nurse shook her head firmly. "The woman suffered a head injury which left her with amnesia. She has been unable to remember her name or any details of her life since the bombing." Raising her voice she said loudly, "For years! Do you understand what your son has done? For years she's lived without knowing! She has another husband and two more children. This is a disaster for her!" More softly she added, "She came here after Rosa identified her, by chance, in a shop where she works. We thought she might be a relative. Your story confirms that she isn't. This is a picture of her." She waved the picture in the air.

Cristina sat mutely, unable to think of a suitable reply. If only she had insisted on returning the things, but it was too late to correct it now. It was a mistake. We thought she was dead, she reminded herself.

Patricia stood up and leaned over her desk. "Don't you have anything to say?" she shouted. "Your son commits a horrible crime against this woman and you just sit there, refusing to speak?"

Cristina shook her head. "There's nothing to say. I'm sorry doesn't begin to correct the damage."

"I'm calling the police," the nurse said. "It's obvious they have to be involved in this." She picked up the phone and began dialing.

"No, wait. Please." Cristina stood up and leaned her hands on the desk close to the nurse. "Please listen to me. You should talk to the woman first, tell her what you have found out, and see if she wants to go to the police. Perhaps, from what you have told me of her life, she would prefer to keep this quiet."

Patricia stared at Cristina intently. "You don't care a thing about what she wants," she said. "All you care about is trying to save your no-good little brats from trouble."

Cristina sat back in her chair and spoke carefully. "You're right, I don't care about what she wants and I do want to protect my children. But that doesn't change the fact that it might be kinder for the woman to discuss this with her before going to the police. You tell me she has another husband and two more children. Perhaps she would prefer they not know the full story."

They were interrupted by the phone ringing. "I'm sorry to bother you," the receptionist said, "but I've got Rosa's visitor on the phone and she sounds very distressed."

"I'll take it," Patricia replied. To Cristina she said, "This is the woman now. I'll ask her to come here and discuss what has happened." She picked up the phone.

Immediately she heard Maria's voice on the line, distressed or even panicked sounding. "I'm so sorry to bother you," Maria said, "But I've tried to call the number and it's wrong. Can you check it for me?"

Patricia spoke calmly, hoping her voice would calm the panicked woman on the other end. "Maria, listen, I can check the number, but I also need to speak to you in person. Can you come here to see me?"

Maria looked at her watch. She had already been gone longer than expected, and couldn't possibly return to the home today. "I can't come now," she said. "Maybe tomorrow. I'll come tomorrow."

"Okay, tomorrow. Can you come about 10:00?"

"10:00, okay, I can do that." She made a mental note to herself, then hung up the phone. On her way home she stopped in a nearby bar and ordered a Fanta, then pulled the new bottle of pills from her purse and took one, hoping it would help. She felt like she was losing her mind.

At the home Patricia spoke firmly to Cristina. "Tomorrow you come here at 10:00, and bring your children with you. Your son should see the pain he has caused." Without speaking further she jerked her face in the direction of the door, indicating the discussion was over.

Cristina stood up and left silently. Outside the door she roughly grabbed Anita's forearm and pulled her along, still not speaking. Anita struggled to keep up, not daring to ask her mother to slow down. Cristina hurried from the building leaving the floors only half polished. She flagged the bus and shoved Anita into a seat, then sat furiously reviewing the day. How could it have happened? There were a dozen times it could have worked out differently. If only Octavio hadn't taken the things, or if she had made him return them. If only she hadn't put the woman's picture up on the shelf for Anita to see. If only Anita had stayed in the closet like she was told to. She glared at her daughter, her anger mounting. If only Octavio hadn't left, leaving her in such desperate need. Since he wasn't there to hate she further glared at Anita, and a shiver ran up the child's spine. Seeing her fear Cristina sat back, trying to calm herself. It wasn't the child's fault really. She must stop thinking of how it could have been different and decide what to do. She leaned her head against the seat and sighed. Just when I almost had everything in order, she thought. A nice apartment, a steady job, enough money for food and even a little left over at the end of the month, sometimes. And next year Anita in school, so work would be easier. She felt tears of frustration welling in her eyes and wiped them away, hoping Anita didn't notice. She would have to get them away from Madrid. That was the only thing to do. Take them somewhere safe. Let Octavio and Anita grow up in peace, not like their father. Not always in trouble.

She looked over at Anita. The child stared back at her mother, eyes huge. I've got her scared to death, Cristina thought. My poor baby. No father at all and a mother she's scared of. Unexpectedly she leaned over and kissed Anita on top of the head. "Don't worry," she whispered. "It'll be all right. Mama will take care of everything."

When the bus stopped she hurried Anita along, nearly running to the apartment. She had thought of a plan and didn't want to waste a moment. Rushing in she began pulling suitcases from the closet. She opened one and instructed Anita to put as many clothes in the suitcase as possible.

"Why Mama? Where are we going?" Anita asked. She was bewildered by her mother's strange behavior. Not only did it seem she wouldn't get spanked, but Mama had kissed her head, and now was packing the suitcases.

"Never mind where we're going. I'll tell you later. Just get the clothes packed." She turned to her own things and began stuffing them into a suitcase. When Chavo came in from school he found his mother in his room sifting through his things.

She hadn't heard him come in, and he stood watching her for a moment, angry at finding her in his things. He stepped into the room, intent on confronting her, then stopped as he saw the suitcase.

"Mama," he said hesitantly. His voice was unexpectedly small.

She turned and relief swept over her at the site of him. "Octavio, thank God you're here." She crossed the room toward him.

"Mama," he said again, "What's going on?"

She shook her head, looking defeated. "Oh, Octavio." She pointed to the bed. "Sit down. Sit down and I'll tell you."

Fearfully he crossed to the bed and perched on the edge. She sat beside him and told him the whole story, beginning with the old lady at the home accusing Anita of damaging her picture, and ending with the admission that the nurse knew the whole story and was meeting the woman tomorrow morning to discuss going to the police.

Chavo's normal bravado wavered as he imagined himself led away by the police, Anita crying and begging him to come back or to take her along. He saw himself in jail, surrounded by frightening criminals, never allowed to see his mother. Tears threatened to spill from his eyes and he fought them back, swiping at his face with the back of his hand.

"I know it's not great, but it's the best I can think of. Maybe someday, when this is resolved we can come back here."

Chavo realized he hadn't been listening. "What?" he asked. "Where did you say we're going?"

"My sister's house. I'm sure she'll take us in."

"Where is it?" he asked.

"In Extremadura. She lives in a small village. No one will look for us there."

"We're leaving Madrid?" Chavo asked.

His mother nodded. "We have to. There's no one here I can ask for help. My sister is all I've got."

"I don't want to," he said defiantly. "What about Papa. How will he find us?"

She shrugged. "He's not coming back Octavio. I don't want to leave here either, but what choice do I have? You could be in a lot of trouble. I don't know what they'll do to you. We can't stay around here to find out. We have to go tonight."

"But we don't even know your sister," he protested. "And we've never lived in a little town. Anita and I don't know how."

"You'll get used to it," she assured him. "We've got to Octavio." She stood up and began packing again, then turned to him. Placing her hands on his shoulders she stared intently at him. "You've got to help, Octavio. You can't be upset and argue with me. You've got to help me with Anita." Without waiting for a reply she left the room, leaving him to pack his own things.

Carefully she pulled the woman's suitcase from the back of the closet. She handled it gingerly, as if the trouble it had brought was on the case itself, ready to burn her hands. She opened it and looked at the woman's clothes. She had taken two blouses for herself, years ago, but the rest remained intact. A pair of pants, shoes, a jacket, some personal items. Leaving the suitcase open she went into the kitchen and took down the woman's picture. Returning to the bedroom she laid it on top of the clothes. She took a piece of paper from the drawer. Sitting at the table she carefully wrote a note.

I'm sorry cannot begin to make up for the troubles my son caused you when he took your things. The nurse at the hospital has explained it all to me, and I know he has caused you much pain. You are the same woman that was in Rosa's photograph. Your passport had the name Katherine Bayley. I do not ask for your forgiveness or your understanding, but I will offer you an explanation in case it might help you. My son was very young, and his father had just abandoned us. I was sick and had a new baby to care for, and the money he took from you was too much to pass by. He believed you were dead and never imagined he would cause you any trouble. I am sorry that I can't repay the money, nor can I replace the two blouses I

took to wear.   Other than that, here are the rest of your things,
including a picture of you with your husband and your son.   If it's any
consolation, I have been praying for you since the day he took your
things, and I am forever sorry for what he did.

She didn't sign her name, but took the letter to the bedroom and
laid it on the top of the items in the suitcase, then closed it. Quickly she
returned to the kitchen and gathered her own photographs from the
shelf. She stuffed them into her suitcase and shut it, then set the case by
the front door. She gathered Anita and her suitcase and called out to
Chavo to hurry. He appeared, lugging his suitcase with him.

"I didn't have time to get everything, Mama," he said.

She shook her head. "It doesn't matter. We have to go. I
haven't gotten everything either."

Chavo looked back into his room. "When will we get the rest?"
he asked.

"We won't Octavio. We have to go, and sometimes we have to
leave things behind. You and Anita and I going, that's what's important."

"But my soccer ball," Chavo said. Roughly he sat his suitcase
down and ran back to his room. He returned with the ball tucked under
his arm. "Okay, he said. "I'm ready."

She waited until the children had left, then turned and stared back
at the apartment. Tears filled her eyes at the thought of leaving. It was
the first really nice place she had ever had. She reached out and ran her
hand over the nearest chair as if she were caressing a child, then turned
and followed her children.

Maria lay awake watching the early morning light. It had been a
sleepless night, and her stomach flopped as she thought of the situation.
Hearing Luis stir she turned on her side and pretended to sleep. She was
still laying there pretending an hour later when she heard Ana get up to
tend the baby. She waited until Luis was dressed and gone to work
before she got out of bed. Then she dressed and went into the kitchen
where she found Ana feeding Marta while Mariana lay on the floor.

She picked up the baby, then stooped to kiss Marta. "Good
morning," she greeted Ana. "Thanks for doing all this. You know you
can wake me if you need to."

Her mother-in-law frowned. "No need to wake you. I can
handle them. Maybe the rest will do you good."

Maria nodded. "I am feeling a little better," she said. She poured herself a large mug of coffee and added a generous amount of milk from the steaming pitcher. "Actually, I was thinking of getting out for a walk this morning. If you could keep the girls I could get out for a bit and do the shopping while I was out." She looked at Ana, waiting for an answer.

"Don't you think she could go with you?" she asked, nodding her head toward Marta. "She misses you an awful lot."

"Oh, I know she does. I've been awful these last few weeks. I don't know what I would do without you." She crossed the room and sat at the table. Taking a roll she broke off a piece and dipped it in her coffee. "She's an awful handful at the market these days. Could you keep her and I'll try to take her to the park later in the day."

Ana nodded, but her lips were set in a tight line, showing her disapproval.

Maria left after breakfast, ignoring Ana's disapproving stares. Quickly she flagged a taxi and directed the driver to the Casa Santa Luisa. She hurried to Patricia's office, anxious to hear the information the woman had. Patricia greeted her uncomfortably, avoiding eye contact, but motioning Maria into a chair.

Still staring at her desk Patricia began speaking. "Like I told you on the phone, I have some information for you."

Maria sat forward on the edge of her chair. "What is it?" she asked eagerly. "Tell me." She was eager, knowing that no information could be bad when compared to the shambles her life was becoming.

"It is you in the picture, and I've discovered how it all happened," Patricia said. "You remember the picture? Rosa's picture that was out of its frame and torn up?"

Maria nodded, frowning at Patricia, realizing that she had known since the moment she saw the picture that it was her.

"It was torn up by a little girl whose mother cleans for us. She stole the picture from Rosa's room because she believed it was the same as one in her home."

Maria's eyebrows shot up, her mind whirling. "You've found more family?" she asked eagerly.

Patricia shook her head. "No, not family. I mean not relatives of yours. This family did have your picture in their house. The mother has a group of photographs she keeps, people she's praying for. She put your photograph there after her son brought it home. Apparently he stole your purse and suitcase immediately after the bombing. The mother claims they believed you were killed in the bombing and therefore they kept everything her son took."

Maria sat back, stunned. The whole nightmare was created by a thief. She could picture him; a thin ragged teenager ranging through the crowded plaza after the bombing, gathering people's possessions. Anger flowed through her. "Who is he? He'll pay for this!"

"I'm afraid it's too late," Patricia said. "I should have called the police yesterday, but his mother convinced me that you might not want the police involved, given your situation..." She held her hands up helplessly. "Your second family."

Maria nodded. "I do have to think about it. Try to decide what's best."

"Well, it may be too late to prosecute. A taxi dropped off that suitcase this morning, along with this note." She gestured to a suitcase that Maria hadn't noticed earlier, and handed Maria the note Cristina had written. "I'm guessing they've fled, and that sort of family might succeed in disappearing."

Maria took the note and read it through. Despite the news that the boy had fled she felt excitement flowing through her blood. "This is mine?" she asked, pointing to the suitcase.

Patricia nodded.

Eagerly Maria took the case and opened it, looking at the items inside. Carefully she picked through the clothing, examining the fabrics and styles. The clothes were nice, obviously expensive, though no longer stylish. She picked up the traveler's checks and flipped through them. $800-A lot of money. Carefully she tucked them back away, thinking.

Patricia waited while Maria searched her suitcase, but eventually grew impatient. "So shall I notify the police? I've got the woman's name since she was an employee. Might be they could find her. Of course they might not do much. The boy was pretty young."

Maria shut the suitcase and looked up. "How old was he?"

Patricia frowned trying to remember exactly what the mother had said. "I think she said he was eight. Eight when he took the case. He'd be older now."

"Thirteen," Maria said quickly. "He'd be thirteen." She was always aware of exactly how long it had been since the bombing. She sat back, sighing. Eight-years-old. Her life had been destroyed by an eight-year-old, a child who might be the same age as her own son "No police," she said. "I don't want to call the police." Wearily she stood up and took the suitcase. Thanking Patricia she left the building. Outside she sat the suitcase on the steps and jammed her hands into her pockets, trying to think what to do. The day was cold, and an icy wind whipped around the corner of the building. Think, Maria prompted herself. What are you going to do with this? She glanced at the suitcase sitting beside her. Nothing in it was worth having, except the money. It was all out of style. She would just leave it behind, she thought. But she was unable to walk away from her only link to her past.

Another blast of cold air hit her and she shivered. Picking up the case she walked quickly toward the subway stop, still undecided on what she would do. She couldn't take it home. She stood, waiting for the train, grateful to be out of the wind, but still cold. The platform was nearly empty, but the cars, when the train arrived were full. No one was getting off and Maria wandered the platform looking for a spot. People with suitcases filled every car, coming from the railway station, and she decided to wait for the next train. She stepped back, then turned suddenly and walked up the stairs and onto another platform. The train station would be perfect, she thought. She could store the suitcase at the station until she decided what to do. Within minutes she had reached the station and tucked her suitcase into a locker and was on her way home.

The next several days Maria tried to behave normally. She got up with Mariana in the night, and during the day she played with Marta, but at every moment Andy's face danced before her eyes. Luis was pleased because she seemed to be feeling better, and Ana made plans to return home. Maria counted the days until Ana planned to go, still undecided on what to do. Finally on the day before she left Maria once again asked her to keep the children.

She flagged a taxi as soon as she left the building. She knew exactly where she was going. She stopped at her bank, having the taxi wait while she hurried in, then continued on her way, satisfied that the pesetas from her personal account combined with the traveler's checks in the locker would see her through her search, even if Luis tried to stop her.

When the taxi arrived at her destination she stood, looking up at the building. At the front door was a row of buttons to call the offices, but at this hour of the day the building was open. She stepped inside and took the elevator to the fifth floor. The building was modern and very quiet. It felt formal and professional. She walked down the hallway and stopped outside a door. A small brass plaque beside the door read "Juan Alavardo, investigaciones".

The man behind the desk was small and dark. His eyes were jet black, as was his hair. He was dressed in an expensive suit and a starched white shirt. Her initial thought was that if he wore dark glasses he'd look like a Mafioso. However, he stood up and greeted her warmly, smiling and shaking her hand, and the thought fled from her mind. She didn't tell him the story, just who she wanted him to find. He was leaning forward, elbows on the desk, as if excited by the challenge she brought. "Of course you will need an American detective," he said. He pulled out a stack of papers and began leafing through them.

Maria was dismayed. "I came here because you advertise world wide investigations," she said.

He nodded. "World wide with the help of the other agencies. I will contact a detective living in the area, and he will do the actual research."

Maria nodded her understanding. "How long will it take?" she asked.

He shook his head. "No way to say really. Sometimes it's fast, sometimes it takes a long time. Of course we'll work as fast as possible." When she didn't answer he went on, "Now, let me make sure I've got all the facts straight." He looked at a sheet of paper on which he had been making notes. "Okay, Katherine and Daniel Bayley and son Andy..." He paused and looked up at her. "How old did you say the boy is?" he asked.

"I didn't say. I don't know."

"Okay, well anyway, they lived in New Jersey. Now the father and son have moved, and you want to find out where..." he stopped, checking his notes. "Where they moved to, and where Katherine is. You don't think she's with the family anymore."

Maria nodded. "That's right." She appreciated that he hadn't asked how she knew these people or why she wanted them found. Very professional.

"Okay. Why don't you check back with me in about a week, and we'll see if anything has turned up." He stood, stretching out his hand. The meeting was over.

Three weeks passed before he had any information. She arrived at his office with Mariana held close in a chest carrier, pushing a sleeping Marta in the stroller. If the detective was surprised to see the children he gave no indication. She sat down rocking the stroller back and forth, hoping Marta would sleep a few minutes longer. As before he was all business, wasting no time on small talk.

"Here's what I've got," he said.   He checked his notes, then continued.   "Daniel and Andy Bayley moved from New Jersey to Vermont in 1989. Daniel is 39 years old and Andy is eight. We weren't able to find Katherine Bayley. She abandoned the husband and son in 1987 and hasn't contacted them since. Daniel Bayley filed for divorce last year," he added.

"Did you find anything about Katherine?" she asked.

He flipped through a few more pages, glancing at his notes. "History. Nothing from after 1987."

"Well, what did you find?" she asked.

He rattled off the facts of her life and she struggled to commit them to memory. "Born in Madrid, American father, Spanish mother, moved to New York at age 16. Attended Columbia University majoring in advertising. Got married, had the kid, took off. Apparently she ran off with some guy while on a business trip in Paris."

Maria fought back tears. How could they say she abandoned them. She hadn't done that. She had been injured. And run off with some other man! She hadn't even known Luis. Even as she considered the injustice of the claim she realized they couldn't have known any different. They weren't talking about Luis. They were talking about some other man. "You couldn't find anything on Katherine Bayley after 1987?" She asked.

The detective shook his head. "Not after she took off. She really succeeded in disappearing."

Katherine nodded. They still didn't know where she was then.

She glanced down at the stroller. Marta still slept peacefully. In her arms Mariana was beginning to stir. She looked directly into the detective's eyes for a moment, then she said, "I have reason to believe that I am Katherine Bayley." Then, while Marta slept and she jiggled Mariana in her arms to quiet her, she told him the rest of the story. Now only Luis was left to tell.

She waited until the children were in bed and they were seated on the couch together, talking companionably about the day.

"Luis," she said, "I have something serious to discuss with you." She bit her lip, waiting for a response.

He was looking at her, frowning slightly when a moment ago he had been smiling. "What is it?" he asked warily.

"I've got some information about my past. I know you didn't want me to," she continued rapidly, "but I had to know. I had to." She saw that he wasn't angry as much as he was afraid.

"What is it?" he asked. "What did you find?"

She leaned forward and took his hand in hers. "My name was Katherine Bayley, and I lived in New Jersey. I had a husband and a son. His name is Andy. He's eight years old now." She stopped. Luis had pulled his hand away, and was sitting with his head in his hands, face hidden. "I don't know yet how everything happened, but apparently Daniel told people that I ran off with a man, abandoning the family."

Luis looked up at her, surprised.

"That isn't true, Luis. You know I wouldn't do something like that. Somewhere there was a mistake. But anyway, after the accident they never found me, Daniel filed for divorce and I'm here." She paused. "Here living as someone else."

Luis' face was tortured. "Maria, why did you do it? Why? And now that you know, what are you planning to do? The girls..." he gestured helpless toward the bedroom where they slept.

"I know," she said. "I know it's a nightmare. What do you think I feel? But I had to. I've got another child, a son, and I need to see him."

He leaned forward, gripping her arms. "No, you can't mean that. You're going to go to him? What about us?"

She pulled back, out of his grasp. "I'm not going to leave you. I promise I'm not going to leave you, but I've got to see him. I need to know if he's happy."

"How are you going to do that without ruining our lives?" he asked angrily.

"Luis," she replied, "I don't know how I'm going to handle it, but I have to go. Your mother can come stay with the girls. She won't mind helping."

She left that same week, despite Luis' protests. Never in their relationship had he seen her so determined about anything. Surprisingly he felt no anger, only fear that she wouldn't return. Remembering his mother's early dislike of Maria because of her past, he told her little of what was going on. Instead, late at night, while everyone slept he would creep into the girls' room and watch them sleeping, and quietly pray that Maria would return.

CHAPTER

TEN

A s soon as the plane landed in New York Maria caught a taxi to
the detective's office. As they raced through traffic she stared at
the huge buildings and crowded sidewalks, finding it hard to
believe she had ever lived there. When the taxi deposited her on a corner
she stood staring, unsure of where to go. Eventually she approached a
doorman working nearby and obtained directions. She entered the office
building with trepidation. The detective had spent the last several days
finding all the information he could about Katherine Bayley. Today
Maria would learn what he had found.

The office was on the 27th floor. A receptionist greeted her and
told her to take a seat. While she waited she studied the room. It was
nicely decorated with floral wallpaper and a pale green carpet. A wooden
chair rail ran around one side of the room. The chairs were dark green,
luxuriously large, upholstered in an expensive fabric. The receptionist
was a young blond woman wearing too much eye make-up. A large
bouquet of roses sat on the corner of her desk.

Maria was about to comment on the roses when a door opened
from a side office, and her name was called. She stood and went to greet
the man. He introduced himself as James Smith, shaking her hand
warmly. He was non-descript, neither tall nor short, not heavy or thin,
very average. It occurred to Maria that looking average was probably a
good thing for a detective. She sat across from him at his desk. The
desk was messy, cluttered with folders and mail. He began shuffling
through the piles, searching for something. Eventually he pulled out a

folder and sat down. He opened it, then looked at her expectantly. "Do you prefer that I call you Maria, or Katherine," he asked.

"Maria, please," she said. "I'm Maria."

He didn't dispute that, simply said, "Very well Maria, what exactly do you want to know?" He was already aware of the full story, having been filled in by the detective in Madrid.

"Everything," she said, leaning forward eagerly. "I want to know everything you found."

"Well," he said, "Why don't we start at the disappearance and work our way backwards." She nodded. He checked his notes then began, "Katherine worked for an advertising agency. She took a last minute assignment to Paris in..." he glanced at the notes again, "in April of 1987. In Paris she claimed that an unexpected problem would delay her return. She spoke to her husband on Friday, and Monday she never showed up for work. That Friday is the last time anyone had heard from her. Until you showed up in Madrid, of course."

"The other man, did you find out about the other man?"

He nodded, glancing at the notes again. "The husband conducted a very thorough search. Used a good agency too. The only clue they found was a bank guard in Paris who swore she'd been in his bank the Friday she disappeared. Said she was traveling with a man. They both had suitcases. " He shrugged. "You never know about witnesses. Some of them make it up, but this convinces me. The guy provided a lot of details. Good memory."

Maria felt a chill throughout her body. Surely she couldn't have abandoned her husband and son. Surely she wouldn't have run away with another man. She tried not to think of the three men who had died in the bombing.

"What else," she whispered, slumping back in her chair.

"Well, let's see, I've got educational information, former jobs, what do you want to know?"

"Did you find Andy?" she asked. At his nod she sat up straight, leaning toward him. "What did you find? I want to know everything."

"I got a couple of snapshots of him. He goes to public school up in Middlebury. Your husband, or excuse me, your ex-husband, teaches at the college there." He flipped through the folder and produced the pictures. Maria took them and stared at the boy. In these most recent photos he had grown up a bit. His front teeth were in and his hair was slightly longer. One picture showed him with a backpack, apparently going to or returning from school, the other showed him playing with a big shaggy dog with dirty white fur.

"Where were these taken?" she asked. She held them tightly, unwilling to return them to the file.

"One just outside the school, the other in his backyard." Seeing her concerned look he added, "Don't worry, I was discrete. No one has any suspicion I took these. I was very far away." He sat waiting for her to continue the meeting.

Eventually she asked, "So, what do we do next?"

He shook his head. "It's not what we do next, it's what you do next. As I explained on the phone, you have to make the decisions. I just gather information." When she didn't reply he stood up. Offering her the folder he said, "Perhaps you'd like to look through the information before making a decision. You can sit in our conference room."

Hesitantly she took the folder. He pointed to a door next to his office. "Go in there and look it over. I'll check on you in a bit."

Maria entered the room and looked about. There was a large wooden table, polished to a shine, surrounded by ten comfortable chairs upholstered in black leather. At the far end of the room a window looked out over the city. She went to the window and looked out at the view. There was nothing but tall buildings for as far as she could see. She took the seat nearest the window, and opened the file. For nearly an hour she read, marveling at all the information one individual could gather on another. Copies of interviews done with Daniel just after the disappearance, notes from the investigator who had searched for her in Paris, job notes, tax returns. When she had finished she had a better picture of Katherine.

She had been, apparently, a very hard-working, successful businesswoman. The salary from the tax return stunned her. How could any one person make that kind of money? The personal side was less flattering. Interviews with Daniel as well as with friends painted a picture of a woman without much time for her husband or her son. Over and over again the subject came up in the notes. Her husband admitting they had fought about her going to Paris, friends saying they thought the couple disagreed on Katherine's work hours. She was ashamed to have been this woman. She thought of Marta and Mariana, and again she was sure she could never have left her son. Yet the evidence was there. The bank guard had given a good description of her and of the man who was with her. She looked at the notes again, reading what he had said, '...both had suitcases, and they were speaking first English, then Spanish together. They seemed happy and they laughed a lot." Maria stared at her hands resting on the table in front of her. How could this be me, she thought. How could I be so different now? She remembered Dr. Montoro telling her how brain injury worked, how she might have a totally different personality.

She flipped through the folder again, pulling out the most definitive piece of evidence against her. It was a letter from a woman named Sally. The attached notes described Sally as Katherine's college roommate and good friend. The information from Sally told the whole story as far as Maria was concerned. Obviously Sally had been the intimate confidante of Katherine. She had told of Katherine's dissatisfaction with Daniel and his lack of ambition. She had told of Katherine's frustrations of motherhood, and her arguments with Daniel over having another child. But she had also said she didn't believe Katherine would ever leave her husband and son. And yet it seemed she had. Maria blinked back tears, determined not to cry. I don't know who I was before, she thought, but somehow I've got to make this right.

Carefully she formulated a plan. She would go to Daniel and ask him to talk to her. She was sure that even if she had been having an affair she had intended to go back. It was the accident that had stopped her. She couldn't see how Daniel would fit into the plan, but maybe he wouldn't even want to. They would work out something about Andy. She couldn't be kept from her son over an affair. It would be a shock to the boy, but the accident would explain that she hadn't run off because she didn't love him. Andy could come to Spain with her, to visit, or even to live if he wanted to. Luis would accept him. She would go to Vermont, figure out the best way to approach Daniel, and meet them.

She was still thinking it all through when the door opened and James appeared. She kept the plan to herself, telling him only that she wanted him to travel to Vermont with her and help her identify Daniel and Andy. They set the travel date for three days away. She left his office both exhilarated and devastated. Finally knowing something of her past made her feel more complete. She had a history now. On the other hand it wasn't much to be proud of. She had neglected her son and husband in favor of her job, and she had engaged in an affair with the disastrous consequences that she had been injured in a foreign country and never found. She thought carefully about what she would tell Luis before calling him. In the end she decided to tell him only that she was going to Vermont and would work things out there.

She waited a full day before calling, and in that time she carefully rewrote her history to show what she wanted it to. She decided to tell Luis that Daniel thought she had left without mentioning the affair. He would never trust her if he heard she had been unfaithful. And she could never tell him how she had neglected her own son and her husband. Already he was concerned about her job in the shop. She didn't want him thinking a job could be more important than family. Of course in America jobs were different. Lots of women worked, and lots of children went to day care. Really she felt proud of the job. James had shown her some of the work attributed to her, and she knew it was good. She had won awards, and doing a job well wasn't something she should be ashamed of. But she could never let him know the marriage may have been in trouble. She would tell him it was a happy marriage but they had decided...well, the decision wasn't made yet.

Luis sat at the table in front of the huge dinner his mother had produced. She was an excellent cook, but tonight nothing tempted him. Instead, thoughts of Maria ran through his mind. Where was she now? Had she met up with the boy and suddenly decide she would stay? She had been so vague about her plans. Did seeing them bring back all the lost memories? And if so, had she now forgotten him, forgotten the girls? He jumped as the phone rang. Before he could get up his mother had answered it.

"Maria," she said, distaste in her voice as she handed him the phone.

Relief flooded through him. She hadn't forgotten them. She was calling to say when she'd be home. He took the phone. "Could you please take Marta into the other room?" he asked his mother, then waited until they had left before speaking. "Maria, where are you? When are you coming back?"

She ignored his question. "I've found a lot of information," she said.

His stomach knotted at the sound of her voice, aware that she sounded happier than she had in a long time. "When are you coming home?" he asked again.

As if she hadn't heard him she went on talking. "I found out what kind of work I used to do. I was in advertising. And Luis, I worked for a really big company. I traveled all over the place. And I found out where they live now. They moved to Vermont. I'm going up there to see Andy and talk to Daniel about what happened. There's a lot of confusion about the case. He never knew I got hurt. He thought I left him.

He sat down, fighting nausea. She sounds so happy, he thought. This is what she wants. Has she forgotten all about us? He looked at Mariana, sleeping nearby on her blanket. How could she leave her baby? "Maria," he said loudly, hoping to get her attention, "when are you coming home?"

"I don't know yet. I've got to get to Vermont and meet them, see what we can work out. I mean Luis, they think I left them. They don't expect me to just show up on their doorstep. I've got to work things out, figure out how to do this without giving Andy a shock. I'm going there in two days. I'll call you after I know something else. Can I talk to Marta?" she asked.

"No, Marta's sleeping," he lied. For days Marta had cried for her mother. Now that she had calmed down he wasn't about to let her hear Maria's voice.

Luis had barely hung up when his mother appeared. "Is she coming back?" she asked. It angered him that she asked 'is' not 'when'.

"She'll be back when it's all arranged. It's a complicated situation." He got up and left the apartment. Outside the streets were filling up as people finished their dinner. He walked aimlessly, the conversation rattling in his head. *I worked for a big company. I was traveling all the time. I was on a business trip when I got hurt.* That's how she can leave the babies, he thought. She left them before. That's who she is. All she needed was a little jog to the memory, and she's the person she used to be. She used to leave her baby behind. 'I was traveling all the time,' she said. Even her voice was different now.

CHAPTER

ELEVEN

Maria shivered in the cold and laid her unread newspaper on the bench beside her. Sitting back she studied the school. It was a small building, long and low and made of bricks, with a row of windows that ran the full length. Even with everything covered in snow she could tell that the grounds would be well cared for. The sidewalks were neatly cleaned, the snow covered bushes trimmed. A nice school, she thought. Children of the elite. Probably rich. But what's that mean? Rich doesn't mean he's been happy. It doesn't mean he's adjusted. She heard the bell ring and looked up expectantly. Children began to come out of the school, slowly at first, then in a flood. They called out to friends, ran to parents. She watched until the flow had slowed to a trickle, then turned to the man who sat beside her, wanting an explanation. Before she could ask he spoke, "There he is, in the middle, denim jacket, green backpack."

She spotted the boy, walking between two friends. From this distance she could see only that he was slightly shorter than his companions, sandy-haired and handsome. As he came closer, she studied his face, looking for her eyes, her mouth, any features that would show he was hers, but he was still far away and at this distance she couldn't tell. She startled slightly as he broke away from his friends and began to run directly toward her. He's recognized me, she thought! Even after all these years and with this awful hair. He's running right to me! She was just ready to get up, hug him and welcome him back into her life when the man beside her gently laid his hand on her arm, reminding her that she must act rationally. Ridiculous to think he could know who I am. He was a baby, and I look completely different now. Still, she wanted to reach out, to call his name and tell him who she was. She gripped the hand of her companion and bit her lip, reminding herself that she mustn't.

The boy crossed the street, passing not ten feet from where she sat. Her mind screamed out. Honey! I'm here. Do you remember me? She squeezed her companion's hand to keep from reaching out to him, pressed her lips together to avoid calling his name aloud. He ran to a tall blond woman and smiled up at her. As Maria watched the woman smoothed his hair, then kissed his cheek. In her mind she screamed. You have no right. He's mine, my son. I am the one who should fix his hair, kiss his cheeks, pick him up at school. As she watched the boy slipped his hand into the woman's and they walked away.

Maria slumped forward on the bench, covering her face with her hands. Her shoulders shook with her sobs, and the man beside her leaned forward. Laying his hand on her shoulder he said softly, "We should go. You don't want to attract any attention here until you've make a decision."

Blindly she stood up and allowed him to take her arm and lead her to the car. As he opened the door she looked back, wanting one more glance of her son, but the boy and the woman had gone, and the sidewalk was empty.

Maria dug through her purse, searching for a tissue, as the car pulled away from the curb. She wiped at her streaming eyes and blew her nose. Beside her James spoke. "I'll take you by the college and the house quickly. We've just got time before my flight." He glanced over at her, then added, "I'm sure you understand the importance of keeping a low profile here. You've made it clear that you haven't decided what to do yet. Don't let your heart start running the show."

Maria didn't answer. She sat staring out the window, lost in thought. Every building she passed was one he had seen dozens of times. That little girl could be a friend. That dog could be his.

"Maria." She turned, suddenly aware that James had been speaking to her. "Did you hear what I said?"

She shook her head. "I'm sorry. I guess I was lost in thought."

"I was warning you to be careful up here. As long as no one realizes who you are you are in control of your life. If you let them discover you before you're ready you may lose that control. Think before you act."

She nodded, realizing she had nearly screwed up at the school. He won't come to me, she reminded herself. I've got to remember it won't happen like that.

They had left the town and were driving along a tree-lined highway. "Daniel's place is up here on the right. I'm not going to pull in of course because someone might be home. I'll just slow down a bit." He glanced in the rear view mirror, and seeing no cars behind him dropped his speed considerably. "This is it here, the little cottage." Maria saw the house, set back a bit from the road and surrounded by trees. The lawn was neatly landscaped in front, and a stone walkway led up to the front door. For a moment she imagined getting out of the car and going up the walk. She would knock on the door and introduce herself. She would meet her son. She sat back suddenly as she saw the blond woman and Andy come around the corner of the house. Realizing they couldn't have seen her she turned and looked for them out the back window. The trees blocked the view, and she imagined that was why someone had planted them there.

James was pulling into a driveway to turn the car around. "We'll go by the college now. That way you know where everything is. It won't take long. This is a little town. Nice place for a kid to grow up," he added.

"No place is nice without your mother," Maria snapped, angry that James seemed to think she was disposable.

"I wasn't trying to imply anything. All I'm saying is this is a nice town. The kid's got a good dad and the girlfriend seems pretty nice too."

"She's not his mother," Maria said angrily. "I'm his mother."

Unexpectedly James pulled the car to the side of the road. He turned to face Maria. "Look," he said, "I'm not trying to give you a hard time. I know this has been bad for you, but I hope you're thinking about the boy. If you care about him, and you say you do, you need to make sure you've got a clear picture of what's realistic. You're not going to come in here, tell a story about amnesia to the judge, and walk away with custody of that boy. Visitation maybe, but not custody. And how's it all going to work? Are you going to move up here to be near him or are you going to bring him to you in Spain once a year? You've got to think it all through." He smiled a bit sheepishly. "Sorry to lecture you. It's just that I used to be a lawyer, and I've seen kids go through hell when a parent who has been absent decides to re-enter a life. You know, a kid loses a parent, eventually adjusts, and then the parent reappears and throws life into chaos. I just hope you'll think about what's best for Andy before you act."

"That's exactly what I've been thinking about since I discovered him," Maria replied. "It's all I've thought about. I'm sure it's best for him to know the true story. No kid can live a happy life thinking he's been abandoned."

"You may be right there. Abandonment definitely leaves a kid feeling guilty, wondering if he's at fault." James restarted the car and pulled onto the highway. A moment later they were at the college. It was small and very exclusive looking. The students were well dressed and well groomed, the sidewalks neatly cleared of snow. James turned down a side street and slowed in front of a two story stone building. "Your hus..., I mean Daniel teaches here, in this building. He's usually coming from the parking lot over there into the building at 8:15 or so, just in case you want to see him." He didn't stop the car, well aware how much attention two strangers could attract on a small campus. Turning the car around slowly he drove to the airport and left her with the car.

Maria had made arrangements to stay in town near the school, avoiding the university area. She didn't want to take any chances on Daniel recognizing her. She parked the car and walked up the street to the bed and breakfast where she was staying. It was a 19th century Victorian house, set back from the road, and surrounded by a decorative wrought iron fence. The house was painted a creamy white with blue green trim that just matched the spruce trees in the front yard. A wide porch wrapped around three sides, and wicker chairs waited patiently for nicer weather when guests would move outside. Maria barely noticed the elegance, and forced herself not to think about the price. It was the only place she had found that was close to the school, so she had taken it.

Inside she greeted the owner, Mrs. Brown, then went to her room. Sitting on the bed she tried to work out the details of her future life with Andy. He could live with me, she thought. When Daniel hears the true story he'll have to share the boy. It's best for him, much better than thinking I abandoned him. Still, she wasn't sure how it would work. Spain was too far away to visit on weekends or short breaks.

The next morning Maria waited until she thought Luis would be home for lunch, then she left the house and walked to a nearby gas station. She was taking no chances by leaving a record of calls to Spain. Using a pay phone she dialed her number and waited for the call to connect. Luis answered, his voice brusque. "Diga".

"Luis, it's me," she said.

"Maria." His voice softened as he recognized her. "Where are you?"

"Vermont. Remember? I told you I was going to Vermont."

"You know that's not what I mean," he said. "What's going on? When are you coming home?"

She switched the phone to her other ear, irritated by the slight delay in their conversation, a constant reminder of the distance between them. "I saw Andy," she said hesitantly.

He didn't answer her, afraid of what she might have decided now that she had met her son. When the silence became awkward he finally asked, "Well, what happened? What did he say?"

"Nothing. I mean I didn't talk to him, just saw him. And I saw his house and his school, and Daniel's new girlfriend." She stopped talking, remembering how another woman had reached up and smoothed Andy's hair, kissed him on the cheek. She wished she could tell Luis how it had broken her heart, but somehow they weren't that close anymore. She remembered the gypsy woman's warning to leave the boy alone and accept the happiness she had found.

Luis gripped the phone as the silence again grew awkward. "The girls miss you," he said finally. "Well, Marta misses you anyway. Mariana is very content, but you're missing her. You've been gone a week. When are you coming home?"

"I don't know," she said simply. "I don't know how long it's going to take to straighten all this out."

"Well, tell me where you're staying. How can I reach you?"

She shook her head fiercely, as if he could see her. "No, Luis. You can't reach me. I don't want any trail between Spain and me. No calls, no letters, nothing. I'm calling you now from a pay phone in a gas station. If you called me at the hotel there would be a record and they could link it to me. She realized she sounded like a criminal, trying to hide herself from discovery.

Luis gritted his teeth in frustration and fear She hasn't decided if she's coming back, he thought. She doesn't want me to know where she is in case she decides to disappear from my life. He stifled a sob, aware of his mother lurking in the next room. "When will you call me then?" he asked. "When will I get some answers?"

"I'll call tomorrow," she promised, "But I don't know if I'll have any answers." She waited for a reply, but when none came she added, "I'd better go now. I love you, Luis."

"I love you too," he replied. As soon as he hung up his mother entered the room.

"When is she coming back?" she asked.

He shrugged. "I don't know."

"You see," she said. "You remember how I warned you before you married her? I told you to keep away from a woman who didn't know her own past. Now you're in trouble. She left her husband and her child before. Now she's gone back to them and left you with two babies. I warned you."

"Mother," he shouted, "Stop it. You know Maria didn't leave her first husband. She was injured and couldn't identify who she was."

Ana stared at him, not backing down. "So she says, but the proof is in her actions. Where is she, and where are her babies?" She gestured to the room next door where Mariana slept and Marta played.

He turned away from her. "I'm going back to work. Don't expect me for supper." Without further comment he left slamming the door behind him.

He walked aimlessly, wandering up one street and down the next not caring if he was late for work. He stopped outside a neighborhood bar and stood staring down the street. Then he opened the door and went in. Ordering an Águila he sat at a corner table smoking a cigarette and drinking the beer. When he was finished he hollered to the waiter and held up the empty glass. Stubbing out his cigarette he sat back in the chair waiting for his beer. Maria is a perfect mother, he told himself. She always spent so much time with Marta, and she was so happy. She never complained about the work, the baby not sleeping, nothing. She was just happy, perfect. I can't see her as the person she says she used to be, traveling, leaving her baby at home, working in an office building. He sat forward, putting his head in his hands, eyes closed. I don't know her at all, he decided. She seemed so content, when all the time something was missing. Now that she's found it she may not be back. He lit another cigarette and sat back, smoking until the waiter brought his beer. He took the beer, raising it in a toast, and drank half in one gulp. "I want a rum," he told the waiter. "And another beer."

It was early morning when he stumbled noisily through his front door. Slamming it behind him he fell into the wall and cursed loudly. Mariana began to cry, and he heard his mother get up and go to her, speaking softly. He crossed to the doorway. Outside the dawn was beginning to break, and in the faint light from the window he could see his mother leaning over the crib speaking softly. The baby continued to cry. He crossed the room, misjudging the distance and slammed into the edge of the crib. His mother turned to him, her eyes hard and angry. "Get out of here," she said. "You're drunk and you've already woken one of them."

"Give her to me," Luis said. "She wants to be held." He reached past his mother, attempting to pick up the baby. She stepped between him and the crib, her sudden motion setting him off balance.

"Get out of here. You're too drunk to hold her. She'll sleep in a minute." She turned back to the baby, reaching over the crib and shaking her gently, speaking softly. Luis watched the pair for a minute, then went to the kitchen and took a bottle of wine from the rack. He opened it and drinking directly from the bottle he went to his own room.

It was late afternoon before he appeared again, hung over and unshaven. His mother sat in the living room, Mariana in her arms. Marta was playing on the floor. Ana glanced up as he entered the room, then returned her attention to the baby. "Lunch is still on the stove," she said. "Get your own if you're hungry."

He entered the kitchen and opened the medicine cabinet, searching for something for his headache. The small cabinet was crammed with old bottles of pills, vitamins, things the girls had needed, but never finished. He searched through a dozen items before deciding none were what he wanted. Angrily he shoved the bottles back, not caring that several fell and rolled onto the counter. He slammed the door and stalked to the living room. "I'm going out," he said. "Don't bother about supper for me."

"Luis, wait," Ana said. She got up and laid Mariana on the couch. Crossing the room she stepped into the hallway, gently pushing him away from the door. When they were out of site of Marta she whispered furiously to him. "You can't just storm out and get drunk again. That won't solve your problems. You need to stop this, take care of your children."

Her hand was resting on his arm. He pulled away from her angrily. "Don't tell me what to do in my own house," he shouted. "It's my concern, not yours." In the living room Marta began to cry.

"Those children should be your concern," Ana whispered loudly. "They've already lost their mother. A father would be nice." Without waiting for a reply she turned and went to Marta. Luis walked out, slamming the door behind him.

~

Maria woke early the next day, planning to visit the university. As she dressed she thought out the plans for the day. She wouldn't actually speak to Daniel, just see him, watch him from a distance. She wasn't sure what that would accomplish, but hoped that seeing him might jog her memory. It would be nice to know something about him before she met with him. She stopped what she was doing and shook her head. How very odd to have been married to someone and yet know nothing about him. Would he even give her a chance to explain?

She sat down at the desk and stared out the window. Maybe she should send him a letter instead. He'd surely be intrigued enough to read it, whereas the sight of her might set him off. She decided to skip breakfast and write the letter. She could decide later whether she wanted to deliver it.

She opened the drawer and took out a piece of stationary. 'Asenbaugh's Bed and Breakfast' was engraved on the front. She stared at it for a moment, then tore off the name and threw it in the trash. Using the remainder of the sheet she began.

'Dear Daniel,'

Dear Daniel? Do I call him dear, she wondered. He was my husband, someone I loved, and he loved me. But so much has happened. She took out another sheet of stationary, tore off the heading and began again.

Daniel,
I have tried for years to find you.'

That will get his attention, she thought.

'My story will sound unbelievable to you, but please, read this through before deciding whether you will throw it away or respond. Several years ago I was involved in an accident which caused a severe head injury. The injury caused me to have amnesia, and prevented me from contacting you. As you have probably guessed by now, I am your wife, Katherine. I have learned through the private investigator I hired that you believe I abandoned you and our son. Please believe me when I say nothing could be further from the truth. I spent years trying to regain my lost memories so I could find you, and to this day I question why you didn't find me. It is

only through an odd coincidence that I have found you now. I was recognized by someone who knew me when I was married to you.'

She stopped writing and read over what she had written. The letter was impersonal, a difficult letter to a stranger. But really, she told herself, that's what he is. A stranger. She thought about telling him more, giving the details, then decided against it. The less he knew the more she could control the situation.

I would like the opportunity to meet with you and discuss the situation we are in. I greatly desire to see our son, and I believe it would be best for him to know that I didn't intentionally abandon him. I will contact you by phone so that we may arrange to meet.

Again she read over what she had written, then added 'Sincerely, Katherine Bayley'. She folded the letter and put it in her purse. Picking up her jacket she went down the stairs and out the door. She got into the car, but instead of driving to the college as she had planned, she went toward the elementary school. She stopped two blocks away and got out, then walked toward the school. Children walked along the sidewalks in groups of two or three, or occasionally alone. She passed by the school and continued walking in the direction she had seen Andy leave the day before. She was a block past the school when she saw him round the corner of a building. He was walking with two friends, one on each side. Playfully they pushed and shoved, laughing as they went. She glanced around looking for somewhere to hide. She hadn't meant to be this close to him. Seeing no place to go she tried to calm herself. He couldn't possibly recognize her. She continued on toward the boys. When they were fairly close, she spoke loudly. "Excuse me."

All three stopped and looked up at her. Momentarily she was unable to speak, overwhelmed at being so close to her son, at speaking to him. Involuntarily she reached out and pushed his hair to the side. He stepped back, frowning, and brushed her hand away.

Realizing her mistake she spoke quickly. "I'm sorry. I shouldn't have done that." She smiled and shrugged her shoulders. "I'm a mother. When I see messy hair I fix it."

They were all three staring at her, and she realized suddenly that they wondered why she had stopped them. "Umm, I'm visiting around here," she said. "I was wondering if you can tell me someplace nearby to get breakfast?"

The three looked at each other, turning back and forth. She listened to their quiet banter, not caring what they said, just trying to pick out her own son's voice.

"McDonald's?"

"It's not really nearby."

"There's Jack's."

"Yeah, but they don't have breakfast. It's just for supper."

"The college?"

"Yeah, that's good."

"I guess so." They looked up at her, not needing to repeat the agreed upon choice since she had heard the whole discussion.

"The college?" she said. "They got good food?"

The boys shrugged, shuffling their feet, anxious to go.

"Is that where you all go?" she asked.

The tallest boy spoke quickly. "No way. The college is expensive."

"Well, where do you go for snacks?"

They answered in unison, "Brutus'. It's cheap, but they don't have breakfast."

"They have root beer floats and banana splits."

"We gotta go now," his friend added. "We're going to be late." They skirted around her as if afraid she might once again try to fix someone's hair.

"Ok, thanks. I'll try the college now, and Brutus' later." She watched them go, running now to beat the bell, backpacks flopping on their skinny shoulders. She waited until they had entered the building, then shook her head and blinked as if coming out of a trance. The whole town would think she was crazy, staring after three little boys, fixing their hair. She had to remember what she was doing, not screw up.

Returning to her car she drove to the McDonalds and had a cup of coffee, then contemplated her options. Once she sent the letter Daniel would be on the lookout for her, suspecting she had come to see Andy. She figured he might try to stop her from seeing him, so better not to send it yet. She would see her son a bit first. She was surprised how easy it had been to talk to Andy. He was friendly and open, and his friends seemed nice.

She passed the day in her room, mostly lost in thought, trying to work out how it could all end. At three o'clock she left her room and went to Brutus'. The ice cream shop was small and cramped. Along one wall was a counter filled with flavors, the toppings lined up on top. A young blond boy was behind the counter. She took a table and ordered a hot fudge sundae. The tables were metal, painted white, with small metal chairs. She thought briefly that she shouldn't have come. It was too dangerous to try to see him without being discovered. Still she sat, eating her sundae and watching the door. At three-thirty an older man appeared from the back, and a moment later a few kids came in.

"Hi Brutus," they called, and he answered them, calling them by name, asking about their schoolwork, calming the rowdier ones without them realizing they had been reprimanded. She looked about anxiously, hoping Andy would appear, but he didn't. She sighed. Of course he wouldn't come every day. She finished her ice cream and left.

On the third day he appeared, flanked by the same two friends. They were the first to arrive, running hard to beat the crowd. "Hi Brutus," they called in unison, and he answered, calling each by name, Andy, Dan and Kevin.

"The usual?" Brutus asked, already reaching for the stack of cones. They nodded eagerly. He handed over the first cone and Dan took it. Moving on to Andy he asked, "How was that math test? You passed it?"

Andy shrugged his shoulders, but grinned up at Brutus. "I think so. We didn't get it back yet." He took his cone and quickly licked the edges, waiting for Kevin to be served.

Maria sat in the back corner, trying to shrink into the chair, suddenly not wanting to be seen. It hurt to hear that the ice cream man knew her son better than she did. Knew all about the math test and that he wanted the bubble gum ice cream with sprinkles. She picked up her napkin and wiped her eyes. They immediately filled again, tears threatening to run down her cheeks. She realized that spying on Andy was a very bad idea, and hoped the boys would take their ice-cream and leave.

Instead they took their cones and turned toward her. They took a table and she thought they hadn't noticed her, but as soon as they were seated Kevin pointed to her. "Hey look," he whispered loudly, "that's the woman from the other day. The one who fixed your hair." They all three laughed and turned toward her.

Seeing her dab her eyes they stopped laughing. "Are you okay?" Dan asked her.

She nodded. "Allergies," she said. "I think I'm allergic to ice cream."

The trio frowned doubtfully at her. "Then why do you eat it?" Andy asked.

She smiled. "Just found out. It must just be this flavor."

They shrugged and turned back to their table. Katherine knew she should leave, yet she was glued to her seat, stuck by the site of her son eating an ice cream cone. She sat listening in on their conversation for several minutes until Dan jumped up. "I've got to go," he yelled. "My mom is going to kill me."

"Piano lessons," Kevin taunted, speaking in falsetto.

"Oh shut up," Dan replied. "You know I don't want to, but she makes me."

"Mama's boy," Kevin sang out. "Gotta do what Mama says," but Dan was gone, already running down the sidewalk.

"Doesn't your mother ever make you do anything you don't like?" Maria asked, unable to resist getting into a conversation with the remaining boys.

Both Kevin and Andy turned to stare at her.

"Well, doesn't she? I mean he said he doesn't like the piano but she makes him. Not that there's anything wrong with piano," she added.

Kevin shrugged. "I guess so," he said. "She makes me wash dishes."

Maria nodded, not really interested. "What about you?" she asked, looking directly at her son.

"My dad does," he said. "I live with my dad."

"Oh," she frowned, wanting to show concern. "Are your parents divorced?"

Andy shook his head. "No, my mom died when I was little."

Maria leaned forward, shock rendering her speechless. He thought she was dead? Eventually she forced herself to continue. "I'm so sorry," she said. "That must have been awful."

He shrugged. "I guess so. I can't remember her, really."

Her mind raced. Can't remember her. Dead. Why would they tell you I'm dead? It's kinder than being abandoned I guess. "Well, I'd better get going," she said. "Thanks for telling me about the ice cream place the other day."

The boys nodded, returning to their ice cream and their talk. Maria climbed in her car, then sat, thankful for the darkened windows so no one would see the tears streaming down her face. Dead, what do I do now, she wondered. Oh hi, I'm your supposedly dead mother, returned from the grave. Your dad's a liar, see? Sorry to screw up your life. She remembered the detective's words. *I've seen kids go through hell when one parent decides to re-enter a life. I just hope you'll think about what's best for Andy before you act.* How was she supposed to know what was best for Andy. No mother because she was dead or a part-time mother because she lived a continent away with little babies to take care of. She thought of the blond woman kissing Andy's cheek, holding his hand. A substitute mother. It was obvious he liked her, and vice versa. But he's mine she reminded herself. My son, and I'm not responsible for the lies his father told him. It's not my fault he said that. Why should I pay the price?

Luis sat on the couch, the crumpled note in his hand. His eyes were bloodshot from lack of sleep and too many nights of drinking. The apartment was unnaturally quiet. He rubbed his eyes as if to clear them, then looked at the note again.

> *Luis,*
> *I've taken the girls and gone home. With no mother and a father who's becoming a drunk, it seemed the best thing to do. At least at home I'll have Alana to help me, and they won't have you crashing into the bedroom at all hours.*

Crashing into the bedroom at all hours. She was right, he had. Woke them up, then stumbled around tripping over furniture and running into walls. But still, she couldn't take his girls. Why didn't Maria call? It had been four days, and still no calls. Now with his mother gone Luis wanted to sit by the phone night and day, fearful he might miss her if she did call. Anger at Maria raged through his veins, mixing with fear that she would never come back. He sat on the couch, note in hand all morning, then got up and roamed the apartment like a caged bull.

The phone jangling on the cabinet startled him and he grabbed it, dropped the receiver, then retrieved it. "Diga," he demanded, then felt his heart drop when he realized it was only his boss. How long had it been since he'd gone to work, he wondered. He had completely lost track of time. He apologized to his boss, told him he needed a few more days to straighten something out, and hung up. Angrily he reached out, picked up a glass sitting on the counter, and threw it into the wall. It shattered, sending glass everywhere. He stared briefly at the mess he'd made, then picked up the phone and dialed his mother's house.

Alana answered and he demanded to speak with his mother.

"She's not here," Alana said. "She told me she was coming, but the train isn't in yet."

"What time does it arrive?" he asked her.

"Five o'clock," she told him. "I'm meeting her at the station."

"Tell her she has no right to take the girls. Those are my children and I want them brought home."

"Luis," Alana said, trying to reason with him, "She's doing what she thinks is best. She needs help to care for them. She's gotten old you know, and an infant is a lot of work."

"I'm here to help her, and Maria is coming back. They belong here."

Alana hesitated. She liked her brother and didn't want to damage her relationship with him. On the other hand she knew her mother was tired and needed help with the children. She said, "Luis, it isn't as if you've been helping. She told me you've been no help at all."

He ignored her comments. "You could have come here to help her. There was no reason for her to take them." When Alana didn't answer he added, "Tell her to call me when she arrives."

When he finally called back at seven o'clock no one answered. He tried again at eight and at nine, but there was still no answer.

It took two days to reach her. When he demanded she return the children she refused, insisting they were better off where they were. "Marta is adjusting now. It would just be more difficult for her to come back. You were scaring her, always drunk or sleeping, and she doesn't understand what happened to Maria."

Luis was gripping the phone tightly. "Those are my children," he shouted. "You have no right to them. I admit I was wrong to drink so much and to frighten you all, but I'll stop. I want them back."

"I'm not bringing them," she replied calmly. "If you want to come and get them that's fine, but I'm staying here."

Angrily he slammed the phone down, wondering what he was supposed to do? Maria was gone, the girls were gone. He couldn't go for the girls because he had to wait for Maria's call. Anyway, two little girls were too much for him to handle alone. He slumped to the floor and sat staring into space.

A crumpled tissue brushing her face woke Maria and she sat up quickly, startled at the sunlight already streaming through the windows. She glanced at her watch trying to figure out what day it was. She stood up and stretched, no answers for herself. She had lost all track of time, laying in the bed crying and trying to work out her problems. She sifted through her clothing feeling too tired to bother with selecting anything. Luis. When was the last time she had spoken to him? She tried to figure out what day it was and count backwards. Four days, maybe five days. He would be frantic. She picked up the clothes on top of the pile and put them on, not caring if they were clean or dirty. Silently she crept down the stairs, hoping to avoid her landlady.

She went directly to the gas station and dialed Luis' number. When he answered she barely greeted him, and began to pour out her story with relief. "...and he thinks I'm dead. I don't know what to do. I mean it's not my fault Daniel lied to him and said I was dead, so why should I give up my son, but on the other hand he seems so happy and easygoing, and it's bound to be a shock. It's bound to mess up his life. I can't figure it all out anyway. Would he visit us? Would I visit over here? How would it all work?"

"Maria, shut up about that boy and these problems for a minute." Luis' angry shout startled her into silence. "Your daughters are gone. Do you hear me? Gone! Mother took them to Andalusia because I couldn't care for them, and she needed help."

Maria was startled. How could he have let them go? "How could you just let her take them?" she asked. "Marta must be terrified. She's never been away from us before."

"I didn't let her take them. She just did it. Left while I was sleeping."

"Well, get them back," she insisted. "You can't just let her take them. I have no idea how much longer I'll be gone, and you can't just leave them there."

He ignored her concern for the girls, hearing only that she didn't yet know when she would be back. She isn't coming back, he thought. She isn't coming back and she wants the girls here because she'll have better access. "Maria," he said, "you've got to come back. We need you here. You said yourself the boy is happy. He's well adjusted and he thinks you're dead. You have children here who know you and need you. You've got to come and help me get them back."

"Luis," she cried, "I can't come back. Not yet. Don't you understand that I've got to finish this? I've got to decide what to do."

"What are you deciding Maria? Which family to choose? Choose the one that knows you and wants you. Leave the past alone."

She started to protest, but he had already hung up. She stood, leaning against the phone booth wall, unable to decide what came next.

Eventually a young girl, visibly pregnant banged on the side. "Hey, you done in there?" she asked.

"Oh, sorry," Maria replied leaving the booth.

"That's alright. Sorry to rush you, but I gotta call my boyfriend, and I only get 10 minutes for break."

Maria returned to her hotel and sat in the room trying to solve her problems. There was no way to work it all out. She had lost not one, but three children, and knew she might not get any of them back if she didn't act quickly. Andy is happy, she told herself. He's a friendly, happy little boy with a father who loves him, and a future stepmother he adores. She imagined leaving him alone, maybe coming each year to spy on him. She'd become the town eccentric, that funny, foreign lady who loved this small town and had made friends with the school children. She closed her eyes, picturing a lifetime of spying on her son. But I couldn't live that way, she told herself, knowing him but never really connecting.

She opened her purse and pulled out the note she had written to Daniel. Quickly she reread it, and satisfied she put it in an envelope and addressed it to him in care of the university. She stopped downstairs to buy a stamp and walked toward the main road. It was 3:30 and school was letting out. She scanned the children, looking for his green backpack, his denim jacket. He was coming down the road, running furiously, trying to be the first to Brutus'.

For a moment she stood still, watching him as he came closer. She looked at the envelope in her hand. The letter that would give him back to her. She heard Kevin call out, and Andy stopped, waiting for his friend. She looked again at the envelope, then stuffed it in her pocket and turned away. At the corner she stopped and pulled the envelope out again. Quickly, not giving herself time to reconsider, she tore it into pieces and threw it into the trash can, then turned to look back. Groups of children still filled the sidewalk, but Andy and his friends were gone, and through her tears the sidewalk looked empty.

www.ingramcontent.com/pod-product-compliance
Lightning Source LLC
Chambersburg PA
CBHW022005010726
47494CB00003B/894